ellen c. maze

Book Two of the Rabbit Trilogy

Rabbit Legacy
By Ellen C. Maze
Fifth Edition
©2017 by Ellen C. Maze

*This Fifth Edition is released in tandem with the long-awaited Book Three in
the Rabbit Trilogy —Rabbit Redemption—freshened for old and new readers.*

ISBN-13: 978-0615747828
Also available in eBook

Little Roni Publishers
Byhalia, MS
www.littleronipublishers.com

Cover Design: Hyliian Graphics, http://hyliian.deviantart.com

Mild Language, Sexual Situations, Vampire Violence

The following is a work of fiction. Names, characters, places, and
incidents are fictitious or used fictitiously. Any resemblance to real
persons, living or dead, to factual events or to businesses is coincidental
and unintentional.

PUBLISHED IN THE UNITED STATES OF AMERICA

BOOKS BY ELLEN C. MAZE

NOVELS

Rabbit: Chasing Beth Rider (Book One)
Rabbit Legacy (Book Two)
Rabbit Redemption (Book Three)
Anomaly: Beyond the Rabbit (Fall 2018)
Conundrum: The Lost Rabbit (Projected for Summer 2019)
The Vestige (Projected for Fall 2019)

The Judging: The Corescu Chronicles Book One
Damascus Road: The Corescu Chronicles Book Two
Tree of Life: The Corescu Chronicles Book Three
Anathema: The Corescu Chronicles Book Four

PARANORMAL SHORT STORY COLLECTIONS

22 Sideways: Twenty-Two Bloodthirsty Tales
Loose Rabbits of the Rabbit Trilogy
Feckless Tales of Supernatural, Paranormal, and Downright Presumptuous Ilk

ELLEN'S LINKS:

www.ellencmaze.com
Email the author at ellenmaze@aol.com
Ellen writes and illustrates children's books and nonfiction under the pen name Ellen Sallas.

This book is dedicated to my Muse.
He has many names; here are a few of my favorites:
Lover of my soul, *El Gibbor, Aviad, Pele Yo-aytz, Sar Shalom,*
Yeshua Hamashiach, Elohim, God.

Vampires are fiction;
The Rakum are real...

Rakum (RAH'-kum) – a.k.a **Wraith**, from Heb. *raca*; vain thing. Def: From Semitic mythology; a race of vampire-like beings thought to be descended from fallen angels.

♦♦♦

"I live under the shadow of the Almighty. Whom shall I fear?" ~ *David ben Yishai*

♦♦♦

"Not everyone suffers on a cross, Hope. You'll get your chance to prove yourself to God..." ~Tony Agricola in *The Judging*

CAST OF CHARACTERS
(In Order of Appearance)

Canaan *(Kay'-nen)*– b.1652, apparent age ~30; Rakum Elder, mate of Marcy Haddle since 1971. Currently resides in Nashville, TN

Javier *(Hah'-vee-ay)* – b.1877, apparent age ~35; former Rakum, now human, resides with David in Tuscaloosa, AL

Roman – b.1633, apparent age ~50; former Rakum Elder, now human, currently resides in Los Angeles, CA

Beth Rider-Stone – 30, apparent age ~23 (because of the Rabbit mark); human, (daughter, Grace Louise, age 6), currently resides in Montgomery, AL

Michael Stone – b.1879, apparent age ~40; former Rakum Lieutenant, now human, married to Beth Rider.

Damien – b.12AD, apparent age ~70; former Rakum Father, has been human one week, currently resides in Nashville, TN

Marcy Haddle – 56; human mate to Canaan, currently resides in Nashville, TN

Meryl & Beryl – b.1901, apparent age 18; infamous Rakum twins, currently Rufus's lieutenants, residing with him in Jackson, MS

Isaac – b.1965, apparent age 13; the last Rakum born, blood-son of the High Father, currently resides in Raleigh, NC

David Walker – b.1935, apparent age ~21; former Rakum grunt, now human, resides with Javier in Tuscaloosa, AL

Chloe Mina Bushman – 18, human, freshman student at the University of Alabama, dating David, currently resides in Tuscaloosa, AL

Rufus Delouve – b.1262, apparent age undetermined; Rakum Elder, self-proclaimed leader, based in Jackson, MS

Selene Cherrie – 30; human, former mate of Rakum Elder Yosef, married Jesse 12 months after Last Assembly (they have a daughter, Dae Lee age 5), currently resides in Birmingham, AL

Jesse Cherrie – b.1881, apparent age ~35; former Rakum, now human, Michael Stone's long-time associate, resides with his wife and daughter in Birmingham, AL

Book Two of the Rabbit Trilogy

A Novel by
ellen c. maze

PROLOGUE

1897 New York City

The blood of a brother was not particularly tasty, so why was Javier compelled to honor a stranger in such a way? Tonight, Roman was moving them to New York City to live on the grounds of a hospital secretly owned and operated by Rakum. Javier was excited at the prospect of having an endless supply of human victims, helpless and without recourse. But now that the Rakum who picked them up at the train station was slated to drink his blood, he wished Roman had not so cavalierly volunteered him.

Javier surreptitiously looked the guy over. He was tall, broad, and bound with muscle; much different from the slender figure of his Elder. His every glance exuded confidence and a cool laissez faire that Javier only dreamed of one day developing.

Just before he asked his name, the brawny Rakum beat him to the punch.

"Call me Canaan," he said in a British accent and then turned to remove the sweat-stained harness from the carriage horse. "Can you clean tack, little brother?"

"Yes, of course," Javier said as he watched his Elder disappear through the door of the attached dwelling to meet their host. Feeling abandoned and awkward, Javier received the traces from Canaan. When both had their arms full, the older Rakum gestured to the barn and Javier led the way.

He was uncomfortable with the stranger for several reasons. Since coming to stay with Roman at age eight, he'd lived a sheltered life. Now he was twenty, but he could count on one hand how many Rakum he'd met in the last decade. More than that, Canaan was too quiet. Elder Roman explained to him long ago the tendency of their people to keep to themselves; saying that it was appropriate and even desirable that a Rakum remain aloof. Knowing this did not make it easier for Javier to accept. His propensity for chattiness remained a bane to his Elder. For the moment, if Canaan would speak a little more, Javier was certain his nerves would settle.

"I will attempt to be more communicative," Canaan offered as he pulled open the barn door.

Realizing that the older Rakum was a telepath, Javier made an effort to think happy thoughts. Canaan chuckled then and tossed Javier a cleaning rag from a bucket on the floor.

"Ask me a question," Canaan said as he rubbed moisture from the bridle in his hand.

Javier ran the traces through the cloth and tried to think of something to say. He didn't want to give his blood, but he couldn't very well say that. Canaan made a soft noise of amusement a few feet away and Javier grimaced. The guy was a *superior* telepath and none of Javier's thoughts were getting past him.

"Do not fret, little brother. I'm not your enemy." Canaan threw him a wink and hung the cleaned tack on the wall peg. He made a grab for what Javier had cleaned and hung it up as well. "Pretty good job."

Javier said nothing and watched him push closed the door on the tired gelding's stall. Canaan collected his oil lamp and checked the animal's water trough before heading for the door.

"What now?" Javier asked dreading the inevitable.

Canaan grinned and winked. "Shortly, I will begin the tour of the hospital."

Javier nodded his head and stood from the low stool as if perhaps they would put off the bloodletting, but Canaan gave him a smile. His blue eyes flashed as he leaned against the closed barn door and crossed his arms at his chest, the lamp dangling from one forefinger.

"I like your master, Javier. He has a soft spot for you; thinks of you very tenderly. You've lived with him alone for how long?"

"Almost thirteen years. Since I was eight."

Canaan whistled and shook his head. "I knew you were young, but not that young." Maintaining eye contact, he lowered his chin and licked his lips. "And Roman is your main buzz all this time?"

Javier nodded. Canaan was referring to the blood Javier consumed, and since he lived alone with Roman isolated in a forest miles from town, his was the most available. His infrequent jaunts to visit Roman's brothel Cow barely counted.

Canaan made a noise of surprise and Javier was curious.

"What? Is that strange?"

"You have no idea," Canaan laughed and tucked the oil lamp on a set-in wooden shelf. "Rakum are raised in group-lairs for a reason. One of those is so they have a variety of blood donors available to them. You were raised in isolation. Why, only the Fathers know."

Canaan lifted his eyes to the dark rafters above and paused. Javier remained silent; the guy might be communicating with the Fathers as far as he knew. They were known to spy on their children, and with Canaan's promotion to Elder on the horizon, they probably had him under close surveillance.

The Rakum lowered his gaze.

"Indeed," he said, answering Javier's unspoken observation. "I am 245 years young, Javier, and I have never met a Rakum like you. You are a rarity…"

Canaan sounded wistful and finally Javier's mouth curved into a smile. Of course he had a notion that he was special, that his situation with Roman was quite singular.

"This is why Roman consented. As a favor to me." Canaan took a deep breath and stepped off the door, remaining across the floor for now. "Who is your father? Theophilus? Johann?"

Javier shook his head. "Father Damien."

"Ahh…" Canaan nodded and approached, stopping a few feet away. "I can see that." He then closed the distance between them and touched Javier's wavy black hair, looking thoughtful. "Your mother was very dark, then? A Gypsy perhaps?"

"Yes," Javier answered, unnerved at the close quarters. Rakum were not permitted to meet their mothers, but he'd accidentally met his during an excursion with Roman a few years back. Javier furrowed his brow and met the other Rakum's gaze. "What happens now?"

"So impatient," Canaan chastised. "Have you met Father Damien?"

Javier shook his head and Canaan reached for the collar of his plain white cotton shirt. Unlike Canaan and Roman who dressed in the upper-class fashion of the day, Javier wore plain brown canvas trousers and a roomy white farm-boy shirt. He looked down at Canaan's fingers under his chin.

"Father Damien is an extraordinary Rakum. He sees the future. He can levitate objects. Utterly amazing." Canaan successfully opened Javier's shirt a few inches and stepped closer. "Can you, Javier? Move things with your mind?"

Javier inhaled sharply and shook his head. Normally he'd be extremely interested in learning anything about his true Rakum father, but with Canaan close enough to embrace him, he finally began to resist the prospect of volunteering his blood.

"I don't like this..." Javier breathed.

"Matters not, little brother. This is for training purposes, nothing more." Canaan lowered his voice to a soft whisper, only inches from Javier's chin. "An Elder needs experiences, as many as he can gather. I may never meet another brother like you, with your circumstances. Buzzing from one source—that could cause you to take on the attributes of your donor. It might make you very powerful."

Javier didn't care for the man's reasons, and he was wounded that Roman would give permission so hastily. He pressed his palms into Canaan's chest.

"Be still," Canaan commanded and put a long thumbnail to Javier's throat.

When he had pressed through the skin, Javier ground his teeth, but made no sound. He'd endured several years of bone-crunching torture already in First Ritual, so a little puncture wound barely registered. Still, he had not buzzed Roman but a handful of times, and the sensation was unpleasant to say the least. Maybe that was it. Perhaps Roman was testing him.

Javier sighed, wondering if he'd ever complete the Ritual. The average Rakum graduated at seventeen and Javier passed that mark three years ago. Even as Canaan held him tighter, Javier wondered how much longer he'd be forced to linger in his current status. Roman promised he'd meet Father Damien while in New York. Meeting one of the ten Fathers was one of the last things a Rakum did before graduation.

Javier pushed against Canaan forcefully, but was held fast with one hand behind his neck and the other gripping his shoulder. The stranger showed no sign of stopping and Javier didn't want to lose too much blood. After another few long seconds, the older Rakum still hadn't let up and Javier returned to his thoughts.

Perhaps he would soon be on his own. If he graduated, Roman would put him out, set him up somewhere, and let him start his adult life. He'd have his own Cows, his own interests, and his own choice of brethren with which to carouse.

Lightheaded now, Javier grunted and pushed Canaan with real

zeal. The larger Rakum's mouth slipped from his skin and he stood back, rolling his eyes.

"Javier," Canaan grinned and took his time with the last swallow, his handsome face shining with something akin to revelation. "Buzzing only from an Elder…it makes a difference."

"Fine and well for you, brother," Javier began, putting his fingers to his healing throat wound. Canaan wagged his pointer finger in Javier's face.

"Don't be cross, little brother. I have dinner waiting for you." Still grinning like a drunken Cheshire cat, Canaan stepped to the door and picked up the oil lamp. He touched his temple. "Elder Roman says begin the tour. I will show you my favorite floor—the lunatic ward. I will introduce you to my Isabella."

Opening the narrow service entrance, Canaan led Javier down an empty hallway to a door that opened into a large circular room with stark and filthy walls. The floor was without furniture, but snoring bodies slumped on every surface. Canaan gestured to the padlocked doors that surrounded the ward. They were approximately twelve feet apart, with a small barred window at the top of each.

"The rooms are for the violent ones. But over here," he led Javier to a door on their right, "I stashed a little treat for myself."

Inside the smelly ten-by-ten cell, sat a soiled cot and a full toilet basin. On the rough stone floor beside the cot was a woman, short, but pretty, if he could imagine her without the grime that clung as if a second skin. Her black hair had been shorn off and because of the dank condition of her cell, dozens of angry red welts puckered and glistened on her extremities. Canaan quietly approached the woman and stood over her.

"With these people, you can be yourself," Canaan said and grinned, showing white teeth. "They can report vampires all day long, and no one will give them a listen. I take my fill, sew her up, and come back the next week. She never runs dry."

Javier nodded with understanding.

"So, you're hungry, right?" Canaan bent, grasped the woman by her upper arms, and lifted her to her feet. She came awake slowly, but as soon as her eyes focused, she prepared to scream. Canaan covered her mouth and trained his eyes on Javier. "Taste this one. She came in for a broken arm and a concussion two months ago. I found her on my rounds the night they casted her."

Javier stepped close to the girl and looked into her terrified pale-

5

green eyes. Canaan removed his hand from her mouth and she pressed her lips together tightly, her initial startle response quieted. She shook and perspired, but didn't struggle as Canaan continued his story and Javier considered her throat. He put his hands on her shoulders and stepped forward. When he took blood from the Cows and prostitutes Roman provided, they were seasoned donors. Plus, Roman always took from their arm or wrist; Canaan was a throat guy. Hoping to impress the older Rakum, Javier put his hand to her cheek and moved her chin aside.

"I intended to heal her arm and send her on her way," Canaan continued, "but look at her, Javier. She is exquisite. And innocent, barely sixteen."

Javier blinked at her age as he pressed his thumbnail to the taut skin just below her jaw. He usually used a knife, but a fingernail was handy too; he was learning new things in New York.

"I had her transferred down here. She cemented her fate by telling them she was frightened of vampires. Beautiful, eh?"

Javier's nail broke through, but it took much more pressure than he expected and the girl recoiled, gagging at the sensation. When he pressed his mouth to her and began to draw of the trickle that leaked from the insufficient laceration, he almost choked with surprise. Canaan was right; the girl was different. Her blood caused his head to rush and his gut to tingle with pleasure, and he no longer noticed the awful smell of the basement ward.

"That is her consent you taste, little brother. Her consent," Canaan emphasized. "She wrestles with herself, not us."

Javier grunted a reply, the rules of drawing blood from females not on his mind at present.

"I'm leaving her to you, Javier," Canaan whispered, the girl's back held against his chest. "Isabella," he spoke into her ear softly, "this is your new master. Treat him well."

The girl squirmed half-heartedly until Javier reluctantly stopped himself. It wasn't easy to quit her, but she was small and Roman taught him to be aware of how much he drew out. Drinking them to death caused a Dying Buzz; a crime worthy of severe punishment.

Overhearing his thoughts, Canaan laughed. "Indeed, little brother. In a hospital, with little threat of interruption, it's easy to drink too long. Be very careful."

Javier nodded and covered Isabella's wound with his palm until it healed.

"Visit her once a week and she'll last several months. Visit her once a month and she'll last several years. Keep her locked up, innocent and untouched by the others, and her blood will always be this smooth, understand?"

Javier nodded, his head still fuzzy from the pleasure of the meal. He watched Isabella's face as Canaan lowered her onto the rumpled cot. She didn't make a sound, but watched him with sorrowful eyes.

"I'll keep her as long as I can." Javier gave the girl a grin, which she ignored, and he nodded to his brother. "I'll make her last. And Roman has to have her. I'd like to know what he thinks."

"Fine, but this hospital is full of Isabellas. On the second floor, there's a charity orphanage filled with children and infants. Whatever you're in the mood for. Take a tiny bit from each one. Heal them up. You're in paradise."

Javier tried to imagine what Canaan was describing, but it was unfathomable.

His host abruptly moved to the door and motioned for him to follow. "Come, Elder Roman is waiting for us in the lobby."

Javier trailed Canaan up the stairs, his thoughts dancing on the future. For one year at least, he would have all the blood he wanted from any number of hapless donors.

And a locked up princess named Isabella.

Javier laughed aloud and self-consciously glanced at Canaan. He was smiling, too.

ONE

Present Day
Jackson, MS

"BOW, you idiot, BOW!" the crazed Elder barked, although his malformed palate squeezed the pronunciation of every word into a new language of its own. "Elder Yu! I command you to BOW! DON'T YOU KNOW I HOLD YOUR LIFE IN MY HANDS?!"

Beryl's eyes flicked to his twin Meryl, who held his expression static although neither of them approved of the scene before them. Rufus was killing off the brethren who refused to pay him allegiance; his current focus, one of their oldest Elders.

Rufus surged into Elder Yu in a blur and with a mighty swipe of one grotesquely-clawed hand, he slashed the imposing Chinese Rakum across the face and neck. Near-black blood oozed down his shirtfront and Rufus slashed again with the opposite hand, inflicting criss-cross patterns to the powerful Elder's cheeks. The wounds closed even as Rufus circled the man who stood erect, his eyes set straight ahead, his expression stoic. This Elder would never bow and every man in the room knew it.

"Mind your thoughts, brother," his twin sent silently, blocking their brethren from the transmission.

Beryl appreciated the reminder and he turned his mind to studying Rufus's monstrous look. Before he succumbed to the Dying Buzz, he'd been a shining example of their race—strong, fearless, and stunningly attractive. Now? His lustrous brown locks had fallen out during the first year until eventually, even his eyebrows refused to grow. The Elder's fingers had elongated into claws and his teeth into fangs. His skin had taken on a bluish hue, draping over prominent musculature no longer layered with body fat and purple veins snaked across his forehead and cheeks. He resembled a mythical being—a vampire straight out of the movies.

8

"BOW, YOU SHIT!" Rufus shouted again, shoving the taller Elder with all of his might. Yu stood 6'10", with broad shoulders, shimmering ebony hair to his waist, and the formidable stance of a proud Chinese warrior; as such, he was barely affected by Rufus's physical assault. Still, he did not resist or retaliate. Their insane new leader had taken the throne by force years earlier and with the acquiescence of the Rakum minions that filled his stolen Mississippi mansion, he had indeed become the Rakum's king.

"He could crush Rufus so easily..." Beryl thought and his brother picked it up.

"He's too much of a true Rakum Elder to subvert his master," Meryl returned, his tone wistful and confounded altogether. *"Even when his master is insane."*

"MERYL!" Rufus screamed.

Beryl's twin came to attention and jogged to the far wall to return with a container of diesel fuel. Without a spoken command, his brother approached Elder Yu and doused the brave brother until the can was empty. Meryl lobbed the jug aside and stepped back, his face to Rufus. One emotion flowed from his brother's mind and only Beryl would be able to discern it: *melancholy.* A longing for the days before Last Assembly, before their High Father deserted them, before Elder Dawn ruined everything by bringing the Rabbit into their midst.

With the flick of Rufus's chin to his subordinate, Meryl palmed a box of matches, lit the first one that fell free, and tossed it to Elder Yu's near shoulder.

Every Rakum in the room watched the Elder gallantly represent his station; no screams, no flailing, no reaction whatsoever as the carnivorous flames ate away layer after layer of skin and tissue. Yu did not inhale the smoke, which would have lessened his suffering and quickened his death. Instead, he endured every second of the hell lashing his nerve endings, standing tall, shoulders back, black eyes set and brow furrowed, until his life slipped away and his corpse collapsed to the cement floor.

"LET it BURN!" Rufus screeched when one of the brethren stepped close with a blanket to smother the flames. "Watch! Remember! This is the consequence for anyone who crosses me!"

Only when the smoke filled every corner of the space did Elder Rufus release them to cover the smoldering effluence of their oldest Elder and exit for the fresh air up top.

Beryl and his brother held their thoughts close and headed out for their nightly mission. There were more Elders to collect and they needed to get to it; neither of them were prepared to die, no matter how insane their master had become.

"It is better to be breathing and serve a lunatic than to wink out forever in a roar of flames," Meryl mused as they headed out for the night. Beryl agreed and looked away. It took some doing, but the two-in-one-brain twins put away the sight of the magnificent Chinese Elder melting before their eyes and got to business.

◆◆◆

Beverly Hills, CA
October 30th, 6:00 p.m.

"You can't hide forever…we will find you…"

Roman blinked at the telepathic message that had been looping in his subconscious for the better part of a year. For the first few weeks, he puzzled at who might be sending it and who might be capable of such a feat. He was human now and telepathy with humans was never easy—even before the Rakum race disbanded. Why was he still plugged in? After a month of similar warnings, Roman finally accepted that some of the Rakum were still transmitting, some of them were still viable, and some of them were searching specifically for him and literally hunting him down.

Roman shook his head and pulled into the garage of his newly-purchased home on Cherokee Boulevard. It wasn't the view of the Hollywood sign that clinched the sale, but rather the needs of the homeowner, another former Rakum. A friend from way back, Emil needed money quickly and Roman needed a place to hang his boots. Although his new home was situated in a large, established neighborhood, he enjoyed quite a bit of privacy from his affluent and standoffish neighbors.

Roman exited the car and entered the house. The small entryway led to a study where he left his briefcase on the desktop and jostled his computer awake.

"We found your little Javier. Gonna grab him real soon. Then you'll come out of hiding, won't you?"

Roman pursed his lips and closed his eyes. He'd heard that threat already. It was old news that the one they put in charge was assembling allies and eliminating enemies in an effort to rebuild their race. Most alarming was whomever had taken the throne had already assassinated dozens of transformed Elders and all but two of the Fathers. Who was it? Did they know Javier's location? He wasn't hiding; using his real name, he worked from home in north Alabama. Would they abduct him to hurt Roman? Almost certainly.

Roman pulled up his account and typed in Javier's email address. The kid was grown now, over a hundred, but in Roman's mind, he'd always be that eight-year-old boy who stumbled into his life in the Fall of 1885. Roman chuckled, a sad smile on his face.

...He was barely a proselyte, really.

Roman was not accustomed to such young ones; nonetheless, as his appointed Elder, Roman was expected to prepare him for an eternity of life at the top of the food chain. The boy was brilliant, knew several languages, and was plenty bloodthirsty. In the beginning, wasn't that his most redeeming quality?

But Javier was also congenial and friendly; neither of which were positive Rakum traits. Fortunately, the little guy was mad about the blood, and Roman did all he could to help the youth squash his empathetic tendencies and instead, embrace those that would eventually mature him into a leader. It was well known that Father Damien sired Javier and expected great things from his blood-son. But now, like Roman, Javier was human; his Rakum life ended by a confession of faith. How would the old Father react if he knew? Did he know already?

Clearing his mind of the past with a soft grunt, Roman began typing a message to Javier. What should he say? Warn him that their former brethren were coming to get him? That may not be entirely accurate and Roman was not given to histrionics. How would the boy take the news? How well was he adjusting to his mortal existence? As a Rakum, he'd never been especially fearful, even with his naturally sensitive nature. When it came to self-preservation, Javier scored as well as any proselyte Roman had ever trained. His reaction to meeting his mother was a good peek into his psyche, and Roman recounted the circumstances behind closed lids.

Javier's mother was a Gypsy, purchased with gold by the Fathers for the sole intention of impregnating her. As far as Roman knew, after the live birth, she had been moved to America to serve as a Cow to another Elder. As a result, she was the farthest thing from his mind as he brought seventeen-year-old Javier into the small Canadian village one blustery October evening.

The plan was to visit a familiar brothel where Roman could procure a willing blood donor for himself and the boy, but tonight, his regular girl was out sick and he settled for a replacement. Her name was Esmeralda and when she sauntered into their rented room a little past eleven, everything proceeded as expected.

She seemed to know the drill, which didn't surprise him—after all, Agatha might have shown her the ropes. But when she pulled out a small dagger she kept strapped to her thigh in a leather sheath, Roman suspected she was more than familiar with his people.

"Who would be first, master?"

She spoke in a rare East European dialect and although versed in dozens of languages, Roman strained to understand her. When she repeated herself more slowly, Roman gestured to Javier and the woman turned to face him in the dimly-lit room.

"Like this, then."

She mumbled this time in broken English and sliced deep her forearm as she approached the youth. Javier lurched forward and brought her arm to his lips, dropping clumsily to his knees.

Roman shook his head in chagrin and watched as the woman bent at the waist and scrutinized the nape of the boy's neck. After a few moments, she transferred the knife to her donating arm and touched his hair with her now-free hand.

"Szív és a rózsa," she mumbled, returning to her mother tongue.

Hearts and roses? Roman understood enough. He stepped to her side and snatched her fingers from Javier's head. Her only response was to look at him with huge, black eyes that filled with water.

"Hearts and roses!"

She cried now and Javier ceased his meal to look at the adults standing over him. Roman reached for her lacerated arm and covered it with his palm.

"What are you babbling about, woman?" Roman asked, and removed his hand, her wound completely healed. He was irked that she touched a Rakum uninvited and if she didn't appear to be insane, he would have chastised her physically. She mumbled the same three words a few more times in English and fell silent, her eyes glued to the boy. Shoving Javier's head forward, Roman spied what she referred to: right at the boy's hairline was a birthmark in the shape of a heart. It was a very deep red. *Rose* red.

Javier wiped his mouth with the heel of his palm. He looked as if he were about to ask a question when Roman held up his hand to silence him. Burying his fingers in Esmeralda's thick black hair, Roman pulled her head backward forcefully. She whimpered and angled her eyes to keep the boy in sight.

"Hearts and roses. Mine," she whispered, her larynx compressed by Roman's rough treatment.

Roman froze, finally understanding what was happening; a hearts-and-roses birthmark, something she might have seen when the infant was pulled from her body seventeen years ago. The woman was claiming to be Javier's mother. It was bad news and Roman's mind raced over possible scenarios. A Rakum was never to meet his birth mother. Ever. Without exception. An unavoidable weakening occurred when a Rakum looked into the eyes of his mother and Javier was weak enough already.

Decided on a course of action, Roman placed his free hand over the prostitute's face.

"Javier! Stand outside." He gave the boy a stern look and watched him exit. When the door was closed, he released the woman.

"Szív és —" she began and Roman cut her off.

"I'll cut out your tongue if you say one more word," Roman hissed. Esmeralda crossed herself and mumbled a prayer under her breath in her dialect.

"Én baba," she whispered, barely audible.

Baba—*baby.*

Roman's jaw tightened and he shoved her to the floor where she landed hard on her hip and elbows. She yelped, but stayed put, her eyes wide with fear. Exhaling, Roman worked to calm himself. Why was she here, so close to where he lived and hunted and raised her son? Was it a trick of the Fathers? A terrific prank devised for their amusement? Were they even now watching him telepathically as they'd been known to do?

Roman regarded the prostitute coolly and took a deep breath.

"Woman, if you leave this town in the morning and never return, I will allow you to live." He took another cleansing breath and hardened his gaze. "But if I return and find you here, I am an Elder and I will mark you. Do you know what that means? Are you familiar with this term?"

Esmeralda shook her head back and forth. "No. No *Nyúl.* No Rabbit, master. Please, no."

"No, if you leave town." Roman switched to Hungarian and she

13

understood him plainly. "Yes, if you remain. I'll mark you as a Rabbit and then you'll know hell like you've never imagined."

The woman cowered and covered her mouth with both hands as she sat on the dirty floor. Satisfied, Roman replaced his wide-brimmed hat and left the room.

Outside of the building, sitting on a bench covered with snow, Javier looked up to see him approach.

"She's leaving town then?" he asked without emotion.

Roman paused thoughtfully, but then allowed a small smile. "What do you mean? You heard me instructing her to leave?"

Javier shrugged. "She's my birth mother. I suppose it was an accident that brought us together and you'd want to be sure it didn't happen again."

Still smiling, Roman nodded his head. "When did you make her?"

Javier got to his feet and dusted the powdery snow from his canvas trousers. "As soon as she entered the room."

Roman's mouth dropped. "And you fed from her anyway? Knowing full-well she was your blood?"

Javier's mouth formed an impish grin that caused his eyes to smolder. "I was hungry. Why not?"

Roman laughed and put his arm about the boy's shoulders. "Indeed. Why not?"

The computer chimed and Roman opened his eyes. He had dozed off and the image of Javier drinking his mother's blood circled his memory. They didn't desire blood anymore, no longer living the Hedonistic lifestyle of their former people. Roman and Javier were children of God, their transformation proved it.

Sighing, he clicked off his email account and decided to hit the shower. He would warn Javier later, when he had something to say. Right now, the threats were vague and empty. Satisfied with his decision, Roman cleared his mind and did his best to avoid thinking on the past.

TWO

Montgomery, AL
October 31st, 5:30 p.m.

A miniature princess and the 6'4" king of the house entered the room smiling as Beth Rider-Stone looked up from the edits of her work in progress. Her latest published novel, *The Rabbit*, was selling well and she hoped the Rakum that remained were reading it. They needed to know how their race was founded, the origins of their bloodthirsty father, Abroghia, and about the God of the humans who loved them. Michael Stone, former Rakum, now her husband, adjusted their daughter's tiara and waited for Beth's remarks.

"Beautiful, Gracie! What a lovely costume. You'll be the prettiest princess at the ball!" Beth came to her feet and bent to peck her daughter's cheek. Michael grabbed her in a half hug and kissed her hair. Not-so-costumed in faded blue jeans and a long-sleeved flannel shirt, Michael had volunteered to accompany their daughter to the church's annual Fall Festival.

"We'll be back by seven," Michael said and allowed her to wriggle free of his embrace. At 5'6", she was dwarfed in his presence, but he'd always been as gentle as a lamb with her.

"Okay, sweetie. Ya'll have fun," Beth cooed and watched them file out of her study and head downstairs.

Now to business.

The blinking cursor beat steady time, dependable and trustworthy. If only the literary muse was half so. She'd written twenty thousand words on her new novel, but the last week, concentrating had become impossible. Her mind wandered across space and time from her childhood, to her encounter with Michael's former people, to the latest visitors of the Rakum race who stumbled to their house to ask about God.

Presently, Grace popped into her mind's eye, adorable and fragile as a butterfly in her pink and white princess costume. Then Michael, strong and handsome, yet still growing into his mortal skin; sloughing off the evil that was deposited into his genes at birth.

And tonight, this same man with the dubious past played the ideal father, escorting their baby to church. What did the other mothers think when he came in? Beth chuckled. They probably put a lot of effort in *not* thinking. Michael was a looker and he was comfortable being adored. *Just think of Jeremy.*

Beth shuddered. It was unfortunate, but because she met Michael when he was a Rakum, many of the flashbacks she forced down were ugly. Jeremy had been one of Michael's regular blood donors, and was brutally murdered by Michael's Elder, Jack Dawn, hours before God turned the entire Rakum race on their ear.

Beth wiped her face with her hand and took a deep breath. It'd been a nightmare, the entire ordeal, but they overcame. Michael was hers—human and whole—and they had a wonderful baby girl together. Didn't God work everything out for their good?

Beth smiled and closed the current document. She wasn't going to get anymore writing in tonight. Reaching for the photo of Michael that she kept by the monitor, Beth examined his features. Strong jaw, light brown hair cut short, military-style, the broad shoulders of a linebacker. What did he see in her that night in the airport? Moreover, what made him pursue her after she practically annihilated his way of life?

"Can you love a Rakum?" he'd asked her a couple of months after the High Father deserted his bloodthirsty children. Beth shook her head and closed her eyes, the memory of that night replaying clearly in her mind. Keeping her distance wasn't easy. He wasn't only her knight in shining armor, but her idea of the perfect mate. Except for the part about him not being human.

"Michael, I can't."

Beth blinked as her recollected words came to mind with power. He'd taken her to a party, gotten her home, locked the door, and kissed her. She was faint with the elation of it all, but she'd managed to push him away at the last second. He objected, feeling confused, frustrated, irritated, and whatever else went with such moments, but she couldn't continue with him until he was human, and her determination caused him to leave in a huff. Beth had prayed for him then. She prayed that God would watch over him and bring him back.

When he was human, of course.

The phone rang and Beth jumped. It was a telemarketer, by the caller ID, and she let it go to the machine. Wiping her eyes, Beth exhaled without realizing she had been holding her breath. Standing so close to Michael, wrapped in his burly arms, had been terrifying before his transformation, but not because of what he was. She didn't trust herself to maintain her own parameters in his presence. She was no angel. Part of her wanted him just as he was then—a blood-sucking earthbound devil. Thank God he transformed into a mortal that same night.

The phone rang again and this time Michael's cell showed on the screen. Beth answered before the second ring.

"Festival's rained out, hon. It's like cats and dogs over here." He was shouting over the din of sudden weather, and Beth looked at her dark window.

"Okay. Be careful."

"Are you crying?"

Busted, Beth sniffled and slapped her knee. "Just walking down memory lane. It's all good."

"It turned out real good, honey. I love you," consoled Michael.

"I know. It's wonderful. Ya'll be careful. See you in a few."

Beth hung up and stood from the desk. She checked the wall clock and headed downstairs to watch for Michael's truck. He was right after all; it was very good. Settling into her husband's chair, she focused on the positive.

Michael placated an irate Grace with an ice cream cone from the drive-thru at McDonald's and headed home. If Beth was crying again, he'd do whatever he could to soothe her bruised psyche. She'd been through a lot with his people and although several years had passed, now and then, she crossed those old paths and worked herself into a fit. Of course, he hadn't made it easy for her back then, pursuing her before she was ready. Before he was ready. And tonight, by the way she answered his question, he knew she was thinking of the night he became mortal.

He'd spent the night trying to seduce the poor woman and when her adamant refusals finally broke through, he had stormed off like a child and left her crying on the stoop.

It was embarrassing really, because he'd gone to one of his Cows, one that needed no encouragement to give herself over at the slightest suggestion. As Grace managed her ice cream like the little lady she was, Harriet's unwelcome image hit his mind.

Harriet Bissell—single, 32, a smoker, and a gambling addict. She spent her days at any of the local Indian-run casinos and her nights at home hoping Michael might jump schedule and visit. She had good reason to expect him; before the episode at the Cave that split up the Rakum, he often slipped in to visit her between donation periods. She was a lonely woman who was extremely grateful for Michael's attentions. The night Beth kicked him out, frustrated and shaken, he hoped a few minutes with the consenting Cow might lift his spirits.

Michael had walked up to her door and squared his shoulders, masking his emotional weakness. The door opened as his toe touched the fake straw welcome mat.

"Mikey," the woman clucked and opened the door wide. Her sheer negligee was purple and contrasted starkly with her doughy complexion. Michael entered and stopped at the door to the living room. Harriet bolted the front door and turned to strike a pose. Michael did his best not to grimace.

"You look…different," he mumbled, buying time. He needed to orient himself, clear out the cobwebs caused by hanging with Beth. Harriet fluffed her bottle-blonde hair provocatively and grinned. Michael looked about the foyer and sniffed the air. Her house smelled different, too.

"What, Mikey? Something wrong? Why you been gone so long? You got another girl? You wouldn't be tradin' up, would you?" Harriet walked toward him until she could place her hands to his chest. "I expected you last week. You haven't missed with me since we started this love affair. I'm hurt you didn't call…"

Michael barely heard her. The room was close now, pressing in. Whatever he had intended to do with Miss Bissell was now pushed to the bottom of the list. Harriet leaned closer, put her hands around his neck, and attempted to pull his face down to her level. Michael came back around and grasped her by her wrists.

"It's over, Harriet. You'll never see me again." Amazed at his words, Michael pulled her off and stepped toward the door. When he reached for the knob, there were arms around his waist from behind, and Harriet was beginning to sob.

"No! No! What are you talking about? Mikey, you can't just leave me. We're supposed to be together forever. Mikey, I love you!"

Michael unlocked the deadbolt, the urge to flee the house overtaking him from the inside out.

"Harriet," Michael whispered as he gripped her forearms more cruelly than necessary, and peeled her loose. "Release me."

"But Michael!" Harriet wailed and slid to her knees, hands clasped in front of her, openly begging at his feet. "Please, stay with me! I need you, Mikey." The door was open now and her neighbors no doubt overheard her hysterical display. "Michael! I can't live without you! Michaeeeel....!"

Michael jerked his shirttail out of her grip and crossed the porch toward his car. She followed him outside, oblivious to the fact that she was practically naked, and pounded on his car as he closed the door and cranked the engine. He caught a glimpse of her puffy face, distorted with anguish, and wondered how he'd never seen her before. Not really. But he could see her now. He saw Harriet's desperate, barely-hanging-on countenance and her unseemly attachment to him. Michael gunned the engine and drove away, leaving her in the road. In his rearview mirror, he watched her slump to the ground as if dead.

Cows.

What made them do it? Why did they voluntarily let their blood and give over their bodies to his people for centuries? Was it like Beth said? Were they crazy?

Michael slowed for a stoplight and Beth's face popped to mind. She'd kicked him out that night because she loved him. Because she knew something he didn't. Beth saw a potential in him for something greater—and when he returned to her home directly after leaving Harriet, Beth Rider shared with him the truth about God.

That very night, Michael became a new man.

Literally.

"Done, daddy!" Grace announced, holding the napkin-sans-cone for Michael to see.

"So neat. Great, honey," Michael said and mussed her hair.

It was because of Beth Rider that he discovered his Creator and was thus able to father a child. That crazy night, as soon as his head stopped spinning, he asked Beth to marry him. And what a wild ride it had been so far.

Smiling, Michael hurried home to kiss his wife.

THREE

Nashville, TN
October 31st, 9:00 p.m.

The Rakum were on the hunt, Father Damien was their prey, and he'd let them in the house. Damien considered his options.

He'd let them in. Why not? It was Halloween and they said the proper phrase. He'd been hearing it all night from the neighborhood children: *Trick or Treat!* But once these two burst in, they chased him to the stairwell of the tidy two-story colonial that he called home. Now on the second floor, he considered the three bedrooms and the toilet on the hall. Where could he hide? Could he hide at all?

Damien tracked hastily toward the furthest room and paused.

"Father Damien, this pursuit is trying my patience."

The taunt wafted up to meet him from the first floor. They were coming up the stairs, the picture of wicked nonchalance. The intruders were Brethren. Underlings. But which two? He hadn't gotten a good look at them when they burst in. He knew them all by name, but without seeing a face, he could only guess. He'd been god to them, for two millennia. One hundred thousand Rakum bent their knee to the Ten Fathers. It had been a glorious life. But now? He was an outcast. A traitor. An apostate.

Tonight, two subordinates, barely old enough to wipe their noses, had come to serve up justice of their own making. Or the justice of their new leader, *Rufus Delouve.* The oldest living Elder. Seven hundred and fifty years old with a deviously black heart. Damien knew him well, had overseen his discipling under Jack Dawn, and had personally taught the youth the more complicated feats of telekinesis and apparent teleportation. It was ironic that the skills of self-preservation he taught the young Rakum centuries ago were now coming back to bite him. Literally.

"Surrender. We can do this the easy way, Father."

The same voice. They were coming up the stairs calmly, side-by-side. Damien looked around, eyes wide, and then up to the ceiling. The attic access door was directly above him. With no express plan in mind, he yanked the cord and pulled down the mechanical step ladder. His knuckles rapped against his pocketed cell phone and he thought of calling for help. One name came to mind right away.

Canaan. A Rakum Elder on the fence. Not guaranteed to help, but neither was he a sure enemy. Living in seclusion with a mortal, the Rakum Elder escaped the wrath of God that night at Assembly. Now, years later, only Damien knew of his location. He knew because he was a Father; very little got past him when he was among the Rakum.

The last time he contacted Canaan was six months after the debacle at the Cave. At that time, Damien was taking stock, counting allies and foes, when he stumbled across the Elder's thoughts very close by. In a desperate attempt to keep her with him forever, the reclusive Elder from Britain was contemplating feeding his mate his own blood. To keep her young. To keep her virile. To keep her *period.* Such an act would transform her into a Rabbit and such intentions carried much weight. With Damien only miles away, he picked up Canaan's accidental transmission easily.

In response to what he'd overheard, Damien made one simple telepathic relay to the Elder: *"I'm watching you."*

The Elder had sent back, *"And who's watching you?"*

Canaan's response was hard to comprehend then, but he thought he understood now. The proof had tracked him down. They'd been watching him, and had obviously timed their attack for when he was at his weakest.

Call 911. The notion occurred to Damien and he pursed his lips. Why not? The humans swore by it. He fumbled for his phone and thumb-dialed the three tones without removing it from his pocket. He left the line open sought an escape route.

"We have other things to do tonight, Father. Plans. Come on."

This voice was different; higher and more sarcastic than the first. Damien narrowed his eyes. Suffering such blatant disrespect was difficult. Since that fateful night seven years ago when the Rabbit demoralized High Father Abroghia, Damien had been on the run. At the time, he didn't understand the woman's entreaty regarding her God, but he understood the threat. Those who refused to at least consider her words would perish where they stood. So Damien attended, stood on the stage right behind Beth Rider, standing abreast the leaders of their kind. Nine Fathers stood broken and sullen on the platform that night; Johann, Theophilus, Umbarto, Amos, Yuri, Wornal, Kin, Duris, and himself. Where were they now? Damien didn't know. They went their separate ways, never to look back, lest an unseen force rip them apart. And Damien was the one unanimously chosen to protect Isaac.

"Father, you'll give yourself a heart attack trying to outrun us. Don't be a fool."

Damien grimaced at the hateful words and sought an escape route. He was helpless; as helpless as that night on the stage, standing behind the Rabbit as she prayed for their redemption. If he'd only known then what he eventually figured out seven years later. His mind went to her Rakum supporters who stood by her that night; Dawn's Lieutenant Michael Stone, Tomás' errant youngster David Walker, a competent Elder named Roman and Damien's own blood-son, Javier d'Millier. All but Stone had been transformed by then. The odor of human flesh filled the Great Hall that evening and nearly drove Damien mad.

When the Rabbit gave them an option to save themselves by opening their minds to her words, he did so and was spared. Half of his brethren consented to her offer of redemption and began a slow walk toward humanity. Twenty thousand transformed to fully mortal in the first twenty-four months. But there were those who rejected her words entirely and slithered off into the night. Damien was one of these. He took little Isaac and fled. The Rakum were destitute and vulnerable for the first time in their lives. When Abroghia deserted them, he took with him the spiritual protection that carried them as a Race since the Great Flood.

"I can hear your bones creaking, old man. What a sorry state. What a pitiful end to a great long life."

Damien scowled at the derisive comments, wounded by them. He scooted up the attic ladder carefully and covered the distance to the far window. The brute was right—his entire body ached.

In the Cave's Great Hall seven years ago, he listened to the Rabbit and afterwards went on the run. Running from God and running from the truth the Rabbit so innocently deposited in every listening ear.

A short seven days ago by a hasty confession of faith, like Michael Stone and the others, he was transformed into a mortal man.

Ironically, if the two apostate hunters had come for him a week earlier, he could have defended himself. As a Rakum Father, he possessed powers beyond the imagination. He could burst a Rakum's heart with a thought. With a glance he could incapacitate any assailant. But now? He was as powerless as a babe. He was human and more than that, an old man. When he shrugged off his Rakum spirit, he was left a wiry and bent 70-year-old heart patient, taking diuretics and in need of a hearing aid. Damien had never been so frightened in his long life.

"Judas Priest, Father! The attic? Where're you going next? The roof?" The first Rakum taunted him as they climbed the ladder to the landing.

Damien took in the entire attic at a glance and crossed to a small decorative window in the peak. Across the street, Lorna's house—a neighbor who helped him finally meet God. On the lawn below, children played in the moonlight, enjoying the clearest Halloween night in a decade. Tiny ghosts and witches crisscrossed the sidewalks, their miniature bodies glowing with chemically enhanced bracelets and necklaces that resembled fireflies in flight. One of the cherubs, probably nine or ten, glanced up and Damien reflexively squint his eyes to focus on the features. For an instant, a split second really, the boy resembled Isaac.

Damien scoffed and looked away, hidden from sight by the lack of light in the attic. Isaac was no longer a child as he was no longer innocent. He had grown into the image of his father and that was bothersome enough.

Isaac Akaron.

In the Semitic tongues, the name roughly translated *He Laughs Last.* Damien smirked inwardly. Indeed, the boy was their creator's last laugh. The last Rakum ever born; High Father Abroghia's final effort to reproduce himself.

Isaac. The boy everyone secretly feared and openly abhorred.

Isaac. Who was foretelling the future before he could walk.

Isaac. Who was moved to the Chamber of Fathers at age thirteen to be trained up in seclusion. What an experiment. It had never been done—take a young Rakum out of group-lair to be proselytized in the Cave by the oldest of their kind. But there had never been a Rakum quite like Isaac. Where was he? Was he safe?

Damien grunted at his memory's flights of fancy and looked around the attic. There was no time to reminisce or mourn lost sons. He was on the run for his life and the Rakum below were heading up.

But wait... The small window opened out. He could fit his body through there. He could go onto the roof, but what then? He couldn't jump down. His arthritic knees ached at the thought.

The Rakum were in the attic now, only fifty feet away. Damien backed to the window and faced them. Would he see daybreak? He'd waited two millennia to see the last seven sunrises; was that all he was to have?

Although loathe to admit it, Damien longed to see Javier, the last of his natural-born offspring. And little Isaac, whom he considered a son. Rakum didn't develop parental bonds, but he was human now. His heart ached to know them once more and see them in the light of God and His kingdom.

"Rufus wants to see you, Father, for real. No tricks."

Tyson and Gage. Their names came to him as he studied their faces in the filtered moonlight. Yet these two had been hitting the dead buzz, eating the flesh of corpses. The tale-tell signs were evident in the unnaturally bulging eyes, the drooping jowls, and dripping saliva. They'd been at it a few months and Damien knew that if they didn't stop soon, they'd lose all skin tone and upright posture. They were morphing into the dead.

You are what you eat, after all.

A thousand years ago, he'd seen it often, but the practice was outlawed in the 16th Century. Yet who remained to enforce the code of the Rakum? No one.

Tyson, shorter, greasy, and rapacious nudged Gage roughly to get him moving. Gage gestured with a fat finger and spoke slowly as if addressing an errant child.

"We got Theophilus already. See, you won't be alone. You guys can rehash old times."

Damien fumbled with the window latch behind him. Tyson inclined his head and bumped his fellow with an elbow. They were on to him.

"Seriously," Tyson hissed, a thread of black drool hanging from his slack lips. He lurched forward and Damien held up his hand.

"Stop." His eyes flitted between the Rakum he once called servants. Damien took a deep breath. He was in terrible danger and he was all alone. Or was he?

"You're a pitiful old man. You can no more control us than you can your own bladder," Gage chuckled as he crept forward.

Damien looked to the ceiling. The rafters were old and dusty;

blue light danced on cobwebs set high for eternity. He was *not* alone. His confession a week ago proved it when he spoke to the God of the humans and was changed. Damien closed his eyes and lowered his upraised arm.

"Into your hands, Master," he muttered and dropped to his knees.

Then everything happened at once.

"FREEZE! POLICE!"

One uniformed officer cleared the attic opening and trained his gun on the two Rakum. Damien's eyes came open in time to see Gage charge straight for him and then shove past to wiggle out the small window, the odor of decay trailing behind.

"Freeze or I'll shoot!" The officer called again as another cop entered the attic behind his fellow. Damien darted to the side and fell onto his rump, his heart beating painfully.

"You better start runnin' old man," Tyson whispered as he too soared past Damien and shot out the window head first. Both policemen jogged after them in pursuit. Damien inched toward the window to peek out, but instead of trick-or-treaters, staccato-lit patrol cars dotted the landscape.

"You okay, sir?" A third police officer crawled into the space and headed for him. It was a woman, petite but intimidating with her firearm at half-mast. Damien nodded his head and put out his hand. "Nice and easy, sir."

With her strong feminine fingers in his, Damien was helped to his feet and supported on her shoulder to the exit. Another officer helped him down with gentle care and before long, he was tucked onto a gurney and loaded onto a waiting ambulance. The humans had come to his rescue, saving him from certain death.

Damien received the care of the frantic but professional medics and stared at the red lights flashing in his vision. Rufus wanted him alive and was holding Theophilus captive. Something evil was afoot.

Damien glanced at the technician on his right who gave him a huge smile and swabbed his brow. "You're going to be fine, sir. Just taking you to the hospital for a once over, but your vitals are great."

Damien smiled behind the oxygen mask. He was rescued just in time, but this wasn't the first time he'd been saved from death. He was saved the first time by God, Himself, a week ago the first time he spoke aloud to the Creator of the universe. Damien sighed and closed his eyes. He served a new Father now and this one had only his best interest at heart.

FOUR

Radnor, TN
October 31st, 7:00 p.m.

Canaan rubbed his eyes and nudged Marcy awake. "Don't you have to go in early tonight, Cee? It's almost seven. We overslept." Canaan covered his eyes and switched on his bedside lamp. Marcy groaned as the gravity of his words sunk in.

She slapped her forehead. "Not again! God, Canaan! Set an alarm!" she shouted and yanked off the covers to hop out of bed. More expletives trickled out as she stomped to the bath and slammed the door.

Canaan chuckled and turned off the lamp. Thirty-nine years together, and he never set an alarm. He didn't need to. His internal clock, though not error proof, was fairly reliable. Why didn't she set the clock radio on her side of bed when they went to sleep each day? Canaan smiled. She enjoyed the drama. Marcy was at her best when under stress. Fifty-six years old with the energy of a woman half her age.

"Canaan! You up yet?"

Marcy's edgy voice got Canaan out of bed. He pulled on the sweats he'd left on the floor and headed for the kitchen, shirtless. His reflection teased him as he passed the living room mirror. He was a big guy, well-muscled, with soft blond curls kept short by Marcy's request. His left side – shoulder, arm, and chest – were black with thickly arted tattoos collected over the last three decades.

Marcy encouraged him the first time. She'd been living with him almost three years, she was twenty, and the '70s were in full swing. He had to choose a crowd: the Hippies or the toughs. Canaan was no peace-loving beatnik. Leather chaps over jeans and a bandanna tied around his head suited him just fine. San Francisco, California; the place to find the best skin artists in the world and two of those were

Rakum. Canaan had to use a Rakum tattooist because of the risk of contamination. He would bleed, and an Elder's blood was nothing to leak lightly around humans.

"Let me draw it," she'd said, batting her long reddish-brown eyelashes. Never one to resist her wiles, he consented. When the artist lifted his needle for the last time, her creative input was stained in his skin forever. Marcy had drawn a stylized wolf, crouching like a man, preparing to strike with claws sharp as razors.

"This is where I shot you —right between his eyes," she'd told him as they studied it later in their hotel mirror. It suited him. When the novelty of it wore off a few months later, he went back for another. And then another. And yet another.

"Does it hurt?" Marcy asked him after his fourth trip.

"Yep," Canaan had replied, smiling. *"That's why I like it."*

Marcy didn't understand then, and now, thirty years later, the left side of his upper body was pretty much inked to capacity. Why not the right? Why not the lower body? Canaan shrugged whenever she'd ask. He had no conscious reason for only doing half. But it looked cool and it made him appear dangerous and unpredictable. Canaan laughed, flexed his biceps, and gave himself a wink.

"COFFEE!" Marcy boomed from the back bathroom.

Turning abruptly, Canaan reached the kitchen, laughing at the old girl. She had him wrapped around her finger and he regretted none of it. Four decades with the same mortal woman and he was still smiling. How many of his brethren could boast such a track record? None that he knew. Most Rakum who took a mate tired of their catch within a few years. And no matter how unsavory to his brethren, Canaan couldn't imagine life without his.

He yanked the pot from the coffee maker and filled it with tap water. As he went through the morning ritual, he listened to the sounds of Marcy's shower. She was singing an old Platter's tune, *Twilight Time.* Her voice was one of the many things he treasured about her.

She'd be scrubbing her back by now with her loofa on a stick. She was manic with the thing, but her skin was silky smooth. And then she'd wash her hair—twice. Marcy's shoulder-length dark red hair was curly, bordering on frizzy when the barometer rose. Canaan recalled that the first time he saw her, he noticed her hair.

And the gun she had trained on him.

The shower shut off in the back of the apartment, and Canaan leaned against the counter in the dark kitchen nook. He needed no light and she would flip it on when she came in. He could see every detail of the small space, and as he scrutinized the dust bunnies in the far corner, he pictured Marcy that first night. She was a hellion. But wasn't she also a lamb?

Canaan grinned, rubbed his face, and let the memories wash over him. He loved reliving the night Marcy Josephine Haddle shot him in the back.

"Freeze, scumbag!"

BAM!

Canaan was shoved forward by the thrust of the hit, and he went to his knees to catch his breath. Sneaking up to the farmhouse was turning out to be a huge mistake. He'd audibly located the father, the mother, and the little brother sleeping soundly in their beds. But even as he stealthily hunted the young lady that his nose told him was nearby, she'd been stalking him. Possibly distracted by hunger and the excitement of seducing a buzz from such a young female, Canaan didn't realize he'd been bested until he heard the shot. She shouted again for him to freeze and, still on his knees, he slowly turned to meet her eye, braving another round if she was so inclined.

"Don't try nothin' funny, mister, or I'll shoot you again!" She spoke with a mouthy Southern accent and gestured with her weapon.

Canaan remained as he was and smiled at the youngster; sixteen years old, if a day, and ornery as a mule. With the full moon shining through her crimson hair, Canaan wondered if he should get to his feet. Her big hazel-green eyes flashed with victory, and she called for her daddy through plump pink lips. Out of the corner of his eye, a light flicked on in the house. He and the girl were a good fifty yards away, outside the hay barn. If Daddy was coming, he'd be another minute or so.

Canaan nodded to the girl and caught her eye.

"You're a good shot. And brave. Ever shot a man before?" Humor in his voice, Canaan hooked his thumb toward his shoulder. "Look at my back. I want you to see what you did."

The teen took his offer as a challenge and stepped forward, the rifle aimed at his head. Canaan removed his button-down shirt and turned his shoulders as she cautiously circled behind. She eyed his muscular build and managed a scowl.

"You deserved it, Mister. Somebody's been poaching my daddy's livestock, and he said if I catch the guy, he'd buy me another horse."

Canaan nodded and she stared at his back, the full moon providing plenty of light. He knew from long experience that such a wound inflicted on a healthy Rakum Elder would heal in a matter of moments, and he listened for the girl's reaction.

It came seconds later.

"Dang," she whispered and stepped closer.

Canaan watched her, craning his neck to see her lean forward and reach out to touch his skin. Her cool fingers ran up and down the back of his shoulder several times before she withdrew.

"Doesn't that just beat all...?"

"Ever seen anything like that before, kiddo?" he asked, aware that the back door had opened and one or more Haddles were headed to their location.

"Sure," the girl said and gingerly put her fingers to his back once more, "in the movies."

Canaan remained as he was; shirt in hand, on his knees, his stomach rumbling now that she was within reach. He calculated his options as her father approached. In ten seconds they'd have company. He could feasibly grab her and sprint out of sight. Or he could murder whoever came around the corner and carry on with his initial plans. Or—

"So what are you?" the girl whispered, lowering the gun and stepping back for him to stand.

Canaan chuckled and came slowly to his feet, the shirt in his balled fist. He towered over her, but she didn't back off. She was odd. She was different. To Canaan, the combination coupled with the fact that she shot him in the back at close range made her special, and Canaan treasured rarity above all things.

"What do you say I am?" Canaan whispered so she would have to lean in to hear. She was fearless and that only intrigued him more.

"Hmmm..." The girl pondered his question and parted her lips.

"I'll visit you tomorrow." Canaan bowed a few inches and stepped back, allowing a huge maple to hide him in shadow. "Do not shoot me again," he said with a grin.

"My name's Marcy," the girl whispered with a curious smile, and Canaan backed out of sight. Her father reached her side with a shotgun balanced in his shaking hands. Canaan remained hidden as he watched the teen explain away her antics without ever mentioning a trespasser.

The next evening, he indeed visited her in her bedroom. He was a gentleman and took her blood with restraint, but she asked him back, and the more time he spent with her, whispering in her room or watching the moon move across the Kentucky sky from the hay loft of the old barn, the more attached he became. Until one day, she left with him and never looked back.

What did her parents think? She sent them a card every Christmas, but never let on her address. Her little brother grew up and went off to college. Marcy was a senior park ranger for the State Parks system. She carried a rifle in her truck and a Glock on her hip.

Although so far, she'd kept her bullets in her gun.

"In the dark again, Canaan," Marcy deadpanned and threw the light switch. "Oh! Hazel walnut! Thank you, sweetie!"

Canaan grinned as she fell into his arms. She was slender and tan and melted into him as if they were one. That was why he could never leave her. Even twenty years down the road, as she became bent and infirm, he would hold her close. Somehow, they had become one person. It wasn't very Rakum-like to have such human ideas, but—

Canaan shrugged mentally as he released his bride. Since the Rabbit debacle, he could pretty much do whatever seemed good in his own eyes. There were no Fathers to submit to and no brethren to match wits with on every issue. Canaan was no longer inclined to hide his affection for the woman he thought of as a wife.

"Be careful tonight," Marcy said as she turned to pour her cup. "I had a bad dream last night. I dreamed about bats and you know that's a bad omen. You need to stay home—"

Canaan objected with a shake of his head. "Cee, no way. I've stayed in three nights in a row. Your bats will just have to stuff it. I'm not a saint. I gotta have a buzz or I'll explode."

Marcy regarded him with that gaze of hers and Canaan shook his head again.

"I'm serious."

"Then let it be me. I'll call in." Marcy set down her cup and reached for the phone. Canaan stepped up and covered her hand on the receiver.

"I'll be fine. I'm going alone, to the Shell Zone." Canaan smiled at his rhyme, but his wife's eye was hard.

The Shell Zone was a bar for men, hidden in a dark corner of downtown, where the country music was live and had a decidedly cozy rhythm. When he could, it was safe to visit there and find a voluntary meal with a man he knew as Westley, a Cow in a world without Cows. The right to hold Cows went south when their race dissolved, but there were still plenty of humans out there willing to let blood to vampires. Since Canaan was gentle with the man, he'd never been turned down.

"Lighten up. I'll be careful. I always am." Canaan cupped Marcy's face in his hands and sang the first few words of one of her favorite show tunes. *"Beautiful girl, let me take a picture…"*

"Stop it," she cooed and covered his fingers with hers.

"Beautiful girl, let me call the preacher…"

"You don't even know the words." Marcy's retorts were spoken through a smile framed by the lines of happy times.

"I'm in a whirl…" Canaan sang off key and pulled her lips to his.

She returned the kiss and then hugged his back, burying her face in his bare chest. He kept it waxed at her request, and he rather enjoyed the discomfort the procedure brought. The sensations of pain and pleasure often melded together for his people and he sought stimulation constantly.

Marcy giggled as he dropped his hands and briefly tickled her waist.

"…over my beautiful girl…" He sang, finishing the chorus with aplomb.

"Call me on my cell when you get home, okay? Things are different now and we have to stay on guard."

"Hon, I'll know if they come around." Canaan resumed a serious tone and waited to meet her gaze. "Don't mistake my gentleness with you for weakness with *them*."

Marcy's eyes watered, but she quickly wiped away her tears and cleared her throat. She was an incredibly strong woman, a trait Canaan admired.

"You said they were re-gathering. Plotting a comeback," Marcy said and paused. "Heard anything else?"

Canaan shook his head. He used to be telepathic, but now his only mental connection to those who remained came in dreams and odd rumblings in his spirit that he rarely understood. But by the visions he received most recently, he knew enough to avoid contact for as long as possible. One name came through his last lucid dream and it was one he distrusted.

Rufus Delouve.

Canaan had spent enough time with Elder Rufus that he knew to avoid him now that there was no order among their kind. And he wondered about Father Damien. As of their last contact, the man was considering changing sides. Had Rufus gotten to him? Canaan realized he really didn't care. His only concern was the safety of Marcy and himself. The rest of the brethren could go to—

"Just stay on guard." Wrapped in his embrace, Marcy interrupted his thoughts.

Canaan nodded and kissed the top of her head, the fragrance of her perfume causing him to smile anew. He'd never brought trouble home since they'd been together, but recently, Marcy had become more cautious. She'd been having nightmares, usually about his dying race. But she needn't worry about his feeding ritual. Canaan had 365 years' experience. He knew how to take blood stealthily, and he knew how to avoid capture. Besides, with the Fathers out of the picture and Rufus far away, he was the strongest Rakum he knew.

"You can count on me, Cee. I'll call you before your break."

Marcy squeezed him tighter and let him go. "You better, old man. I get worried."

"Good."

Marcy slapped his rear and swigged her coffee again. "Now put on a shirt and go warm up my truck."

Canaan flexed his muscles and tossed her a Schwarzenegger pose.

"No need of a shirt, ma'am," he teased and headed for the front door. Marcy sighed dramatically and cut her eyes away, but the corners of her mouth turned up. She was in love; head over heels with a creature that would never die.

Canaan's smile faltered as he headed to the elevator that would take him to the building's underground garage. He was an immortal who had joined himself with a woman who'd lived half of her life already. The last forty years had passed like days and Marcy would reach retirement in a decade.

Canaan shook his head. It didn't matter. They were one.

The elevator reached the bottom and he stepped into the dimly-lit space packed with his neighbors' vehicles. Marcy had privileged Law Enforcement parking that she worked out with the super, and Canaan reached her Chevy in deep thought.

Why was he so concerned about her age? He was an Elder and

Elders had special proclivities…

"No!" Canaan slapped his hand on the icy hood of the truck and swore, his breath making misty plumes in the frigid concrete world below ground.

Such thoughts could put Marcy in danger. He'd avoided discovery by keeping his mind clear and his hands clean. But if he began to ponder the old days, think on ways to keep his mortal wife alive past her time, Rufus and his minions would become aware of him. He knew by experience that even with their diminished telepathic prowess, some thoughts carried more weight than others. When a Rakum Elder began to think about marking a Rabbit, the entire bloodthirsty community was inexplicably switched on.

Canaan cursed again and revved the truck's engine. Clearing his mind wasn't easy, but it was necessary.

…Still, he could do it. He had the ability. Marcy didn't *have* to die. Rakum Rabbits were immortal…

"Canaan!" He hissed at himself and got out of the truck. *"You've got the magic touch…"* He sang one of Marcy's favorite songs loudly, not concerned with the fact that he couldn't carry a tune. Canaan sang all the way to the apartment and then disappeared into their room to get dressed.

Blood,

blood,

blood.

He needed a fix. His mind was easier to manage when his gut was full. He could handle watching his beloved Marcy grow old and die when his belly was buzzing with a fresh hit. But until he downed that first sip, his mind invariably turned to his options. And how wonderful it would be to keep her with him forever.

FIVE

Montgomery, AL
November 1st, 1:00 a.m.

"Are you afraid of the Moon Men, Mommy?" Six-year-old Grace Louise held her mother's face in tiny palms and stared into her eyes with a serious expression. "Billy said they can't hurt you. They're only trying to scare you."

Beth smiled and kissed her daughter's glittery forehead. The princess costume had been shed, but the stage make-up which she refused to wash off remained. Anyway, maybe Beth overreacted; after all, her daughter's frightened scream awakened her from a horrible nightmare of her own. But the bad dreams that awakened her child had been chased off and Beth yawned. She eased Grace under the covers and tucked the pink ballerina comforter under her chin.

"Who are the Moon Men, honey? Are they in one of your stories?" Beth asked. Billy was her imaginary friend. They'd known about him since she could talk. But the Moon Men? That was a new one.

Grace's face went slack and her smile faded. "No, Mommy. The Moon Men are in the grass." Grace's delicate hand appeared out from under her covers, and she pointed toward the large picture window, her bottom lip swallowing the top. Beth followed her line of sight as chill bumps prickled her arms. *Were they real people?*

"On the grass? When?" she asked in a whisper.

Grace drew back her hand. "Any time they want. So long as it's dark. Billy said they're afraid of the sun. Isn't that silly?" Grace laughed, but continued when her mother didn't respond. "I'm not afraid of them. Billy said they can't get in." She pulled her stuffed bear to her cheek.

"Grace, this is serious. Are these real people or invisible people like Billy?" Beth crossed to the window and looked at the lawn below. Like her own bedroom, Grace's was on the second floor. The front

34

yard sprawled out beneath her in the clear moonlight, and the road was shiny with a fresh rain shower.

"I've seen 'em, right outside my window." Grace inclined her head, but didn't look at her mother standing against her rose-colored curtains.

Beth considered the sheer drop to the meticulously landscaped lawn below. "You mean they were on the grass outside, right?"

"No, I saw them on the grass the first time, then in the window, side-by-side. They waved at me." Clutching her bear, Grace turned to see her mother. "I told them to go away. I don't like them. Not at all."

Beth's hand went to her chest and she purposed to control her breathing. Men on the grass was bad enough, but men who scaled a brick wall to peer into their second floor windows was another matter altogether. Memories of her week among the Rakum seven years ago came to mind against her will. It couldn't be helped. Her nightmare tonight was about them after all.

Beth walked back to her daughter and sat on the edge of the twin bed. "How long have you been seeing the Moon Men, honey?"

"Huh?" Grace rubbed her eyes and yawned, but Beth was determined to question her while the subject was hot.

"When did you see them first?"

"The day I cut my foot," Grace said and pushed the blankets down by flailing her legs. She grasped her left ankle and pulled it toward her chest. "I stepped on something sharp."

Beth examined Grace's foot, top and bottom, but it was unblemished. "Did you *dream* that you cut your foot?"

"Billy said you'd ask that." Grace's answering giggle was like the sound of bells.

Beth shook her head and looked the tiny foot over once more. "If you cut your heel, why didn't I know, honey?"

"I started to get you, but by the time I got up, it got better."

Beth stopped breathing. "It got better?" She tried to catch Grace's eye, but the child had lain down and was busily tucking her legs beneath the covers once more. "Honey, what do you mean, 'it got better'?"

"It's okay, Mommy. Billy said it was okay. He said it got better because I'm special. You always tell me I'm special."

Beth took a cautious breath. "So, it didn't bleed, huh?"

"Oh, yes, Mommy. It bled a lot." Grace's expression darkened and she pointed to the floor. "I covered it up. I'm sorry. I was gonna

35

tell you. I forgot."

Beth reached a few feet behind her to pull up the small oval rug in the center of the carpet. Underneath, several quarter-sized dark red circles filled the space and tapered out on the edge. Her daughter had bled quite a bit before her wound closed, healed almost instantly, just like hers did after Jack Dawn marked her.

Grace Louise was a Rabbit. Like her mommy.

Beth swallowed and concentrated on maintaining her calm. Seven years had passed. Was it possible she was still a Rabbit? And if she was, could she have passed the mark to her baby in the womb? Beth bit back a moan for Grace's sake and kept a straight face. The Rabbit mark would draw the Rakum to their house. Was *that* why the Moon Men were haunting her sweet little angel? Did they *sniff her out?* The Rakum could detect a Rabbit's scent from miles away. Beth wanted to be brave, but fear for her daughter chilled her to the bone.

"Grace," Beth returned to the bedside and stroked an errant curl from her daughter's forehead, "tell Mommy what the Moon Men look like, okay?"

"They look like daddy."

Beth pressed her lips together and slowly came to her feet. "How do they look like daddy? Because they're men? Tall? Brown hair? What?" Beth's tone alarmed the child, but there was no helping that.

Grace's lower lip quivered and she hugged her bear. "No. Like daddy's eyes. His eyes."

"Honey, I'll be right back," Beth nodded and forced a smile. "Everything's okay. Billy's right. They can't hurt us. Don't you be afraid of them. I'll be right back."

Beth backed out of the room with the ridiculous grin her six-year-old saw right through and bolted for her bedroom. Michael would need to be warned. He would need to be put on alert. And he would need to take care of it.

◆ ◆ ◆

At the bathroom sink, Michael doused his face with cold water. Call it intuition or inklings from God, but he knew something was happening among what remained of the Rakum. No longer connected to them by spirit, he now suffered phantom pains and vague visions regarding the creatures with whom he once ruled his world. Michael looked into his reflection and shook his head. Would it ever end?

"Michael?"

Beth's tone was urgent. Drying his face with one swipe of the hand towel, Michael tugged open the bathroom door.

"What is it, hon?" His wife's eyes were round, her voice quivering. Michael grasped her gently by her upper arms. "What? Is Grace okay?"

"They found us." Her words barely audible, Beth collapsed into his arms.

"What? Tell me what happened?" Michael spoke with his lips pressed to the crown of her head as he caressed her back. She was an incredibly brave woman and seeing her coming apart caused his courage to slip.

"Two Rakum are hanging around the house and I know in my spirit they aren't here to learn about God. Grace has been seeing them a while now." Beth leaned out of his arms and met his eye. "What will they do? What will God *allow* them to do this time?"

Michael hushed her and pulled her close, his mind racing. "Are you sure she didn't make it up? She has that Billy character—"

Beth cut him off. "No! They're real." She brought her hands to her face and spoke her next words through her fingers. *"She's marked, honey. The Rabbit mark...I passed it on to her!"*

Michael nodded gravely, not surprised at his wife's admission. Beth Rider was marked as a Rabbit a week before his entire race was brought to its knees in the Cave seven years past. In the back of his mind, he'd always wondered if Beth's blood chemistry had returned to normal. Neither of them wanted to face the most obvious sign—Beth hadn't seemed to age since Last Assembly, and Rakum Rabbits were designed to live as long as the brethren desired them to. That meant not aging. It was easy to ignore, Michael thought, with Beth being so young and health conscious. But Grace Louise?

Didn't they subconsciously avoid asking that one question so they wouldn't have to face the possibility? Grace had always been a particularly careful child, her scrapes minor, and rarely requiring a bandage. Even if they had both subconsciously ignored Beth's condition, neither had imagined their daughter was infected.

Michael sighed; he should have known. How else did so many of his former brethren locate them to ask Beth about God? They followed their noses as he would have done when he was a Rakum.

"Honey, shhh. First things first." Michael pulled her under his wing and led the way to his daughter's room.

When they reached Grace's room, she was sitting on her narrow windowsill staring out into the night. It was clear and cold and the moonlight bathed the neighborhood in soft azure. Michael rushed comically forward and scooped Grace into his arms, turning her sideways and causing her to fly back to her bed. She didn't giggle, but was smiling when he arranged her head on the ruffled pillow.

"Daddy, are you afraid of the Moon Men? Mommy looks kinda scared, but I told her that they can't hurt us. I trust Billy and he said they can't get in."

Michael tousled her silky hair. "Mommy just told me about them. What did they look like?"

Grace lifted her pink fingers and covered his lower face with both hands. "Like you, daddy."

Michael's smile faded and Grace's hands fell to the covers.

"What else? Did they look as old as me? Or maybe younger? What color hair did they have? What can you remember?"

"You know Caleb at the library? They might go to school with him. He's a big boy, right? He goes to the big school."

Michael nodded. Caleb Dixon read to the children at the library and was a senior at the High School. So these visitors were young. If they looked eighteen, then they were probably nearing the century mark. Michael pinched Grace's nose and she laughed, obviously encouraged by her father's put-on mood.

"What else?"

"They look the same. There's two of them, but they look the same."

Michael flinched and caught Beth's eye; she paled instantly. Beryl and Meryl, two of the worst of his former Elder's posse. The twins were beautiful to behold, but a terror to anyone they set their sights on. Michael smiled to his daughter and turned to watch his wife pace slowly to the window, her hands clutched into fists at her sides.

"Michael," she whispered and gestured to him with one hand, "I see them. Right under the Thompson's tree. Look…"

Michael reached the window and followed her eye-line. He saw them too, Beryl and Meryl, plain as day, standing in the light of the street lamp. What did they have in mind? Why weren't they coming in? Michael felt a tug on his pants leg and Grace piled into the windowsill in front of them.

"Yeah, there they are. Sometimes they come right up to the window, but Billy said they're only trying to scare me." Grace hopped down and paced back to her bed. "I'm not afraid. You shouldn't be either. You can trust Billy."

"Honey," Beth began without taking her eyes off the Rakum below, "why do you trust Billy? You can't see him. What makes him so special?"

"Billy works for God, Mommy. If Billy says something is okay, then it's okay."

Michael looked hard at the two below and they stared back, their angelic faces calm and expressionless. A second later, they both nodded their heads in the greeting of their people and faded into the shadows. Michael focused on the shade under the tree, but could no longer see them. They were gone. Gone to return later, at an opportune time. Michael knew the drill. He'd lived it for over a century.

SIX

Jackson, MS
November 2nd, 6:00 p.m.

Elder Rufus had been taking the Dying Buzz for nearly six years aside from the nightmarish physical malformations; his mind was gone as well. Beryl held his thoughts close and watched their leader fume silently over the shortcomings of his minions. His displeasure went out telepathically and Beryl and Meryl were the only Rakum who retained the ability to hear his thoughts. Two nights ago, Father Damien had escaped and Elder Rufus was livid.

"Insanity is in, my brother."

Beryl did not find his twin's jibe humorous. Their leader grew more unstable every night without even a clue that he had gone mad. For Rufus it was all about power and how much he could garner for himself. The blood he drained from the dying indeed made him stronger. He allowed no other Rakum to take the Dying Buzz, and with Father Theophilus neutralized and subjugated, Rufus became capable of enforcing his novel laws. The brethren were to find sustenance any way they could. Unfortunately, because of their lack of spiritual protection now that the High Father had been chased off by the Rabbit, many of the Rakum who remained sought food among the dead.

Defeated and depressed, the live buzz was too risky for most of the brethren. Even one hour in a mortal lock-up, under guard, could prove fatal when the sun rose and lightened the room. Dozens of Rakum were killed the first few months as they attempted to carry on business as usual. A Rakum could take a bullet, but unless he was an Elder, *two* bullets would take much longer to heal, and many brethren met their deaths in sunny hospital rooms. Now, they feared the human authority to such an extent that they rarely drew from the living. The dead were the easiest prey.

"I'll never take a dead buzz, brother. Mark my words."

Beryl smirked. So far, they'd been lucky finding plenty of blood among the living. Both were experts at manipulation and rarely did they miss with a human target. To be sure Rufus didn't interfere with their extra-curricular activities, the twins worked overtime to stay on his good side.

"If only he had a good side, right?"

Beryl snickered invisibly at his twin's commentary. The policy was that when twins were born to the Rakum breeders, they were to be separated immediately and raised apart, but when Beryl and Meryl were born, their bond was so tight that the Fathers decided to watch them as an experiment. Now, decades later, they represented an anomaly that was never repeated. Beryl and Meryl shared a consciousness and stayed inside each other's heads full time. Rufus couldn't read either of them; before the Rabbit incident, he had been as telepathic as any Elder, but now—his mental ears had gone deaf.

"Too bad. So sad," Meryl taunted.

Beryl once again agreed without any outward sign. Rufus forbade them from communicating outside of his awareness, so they did so surreptitiously. Even in their heyday, with exception of Father Abroghia, the twins' telepathy was superior to any of their brethren. Jack Dawn was infuriated by his limitations in this arena, but Beryl and Meryl discovered how to control their superiors. They seduced him as easily as they did the humans they preyed upon.

"We're wrapping this one around our finger as well," Meryl sent over.

Beryl agreed. He watched his wild-eyed superior give a few arbitrary commands to his underlings and then tuned in his brother. Meryl was thinking about his next meal. Always hungry, he was busily planning where to collect the sacrifice for their master's dead club. Rufus was not one to go hungry and he insisted that every few evenings, the twins find him a human victim; someone not likely to be missed by society at large. Because of the homeless population in Jackson, they had no trouble finding people to fill the bill.

Meryl needn't be anxious; the twins were always allowed first draw. If Rufus went first, he'd be too full to drink the victim dry, but if someone else took a couple pints off beforehand, their leader would be left with the food of the gods; the very food forbidden by the Fathers for five centuries. But Rufus held the playbook now.

His own face slack, Beryl watched their ridiculous fuehrer fume. Rufus was a fool, but he was their leader. When the Rabbit disbanded the Rakum and scattered them to the wind, Rufus was the

41

first to rise out of the muck to call the brethren together. Out of one hundred original Elders, only Rufus sought to revive their decimated race. A few died that night; including their Elder, Jack Dawn. The others either chose to defect during the Rabbit's tirade, followed her shortly after, or were taken down at Rufus's command. In Rufus's mind, if you were a Rakum and transformed into a mortal, then you should die. Likewise, if you remained a Rakum and refused to bend the knee, you should die. Beryl and Meryl had no death wish.

As former captains to Elder Jack Dawn, they were the first to respond to Rufus's call. He appointed them to his right hand and put them to work organizing the stragglers. So far, five thousand had crawled out of the underbelly and assumed Rufus's yoke. Happy to be under the thumb once more, they pledged their allegiance to his absolute rule and their submission to his grandiose agenda. Scattered across the globe and situated in countries Rufus deemed appropriate for his schemes, the remaining faithful kept in touch via internet and cell phones. The loss of their species' telepathy prevented them from truly rising to their former glory, but that didn't prevent Rufus from doing all he could.

Early on with the twins in his employ, Rufus initiated the first of many pogroms against the traitors of their kind. Natural leaders, Beryl and Meryl organized the Rakum into ranks and set Rufus's plans into motion. Within the first five years, nearly ten thousand apostates had been eliminated in Rufus's name. Ninety-six Elders had been destroyed, as well as countless underlings who chose the way of the Rabbit's God. The most recent of their brethren to meet his glorious and heroic end by fire was Elder Yu.

"Ninety-six comes up short, brother." Meryl sent telepathically without meeting his eye.

Beryl admitted they were a couple short. The Rabbit's accomplice, Elder Roman, had not yet been found, and there was one other in hiding that neither twin could locate. But as far as Rufus was concerned, telling him he was the last was enough. If the other two should surface on their hunt for apostates, all the better.

"We should have counted the bodies."

Beryl ignored Meryl's last comment. A few of the Elders died and their bodies disappeared, stolen by Cows or religious nuts— Beryl didn't care. They were dead. Collecting bodies wasn't necessary and was frankly, too much work.

"One of those dead Elders could bite us in the ass one day. We should have

made sure—for each one."

"Shut it." Beryl dared a glance his way and Meryl rolled his eyes and changed the subject.

"Rufus is sending Geoffrey and Spinner to collect a human woman on the account of David Walker and Javier d'Millier. Why?"

"You mean, why bring in their human companions?"

"Yes. It would be easier to end these guys than draw them here. What's his reasoning?"

Beryl glanced at Rufus then set his gaze on the far wall. *"He's tired of waiting. If he can get these guys to come to him, he can finish this once and for all. He wants to rule, and as long as this enemy is out there, he's afraid."*

"Afraid? Is that the proper word? Look at him. He's insane."

Beryl looked at Rufus again as he responded to his twin. *"He won't consider his work a victory until the Rabbit is in custody and all of her accomplices are dead."*

The stupid Rabbit/novelist Beth Rider had a support group of converted Rakum whom the twins loathed. Meryl considered his conclusion and was quiet. When he replied, his mental voice was exasperated.

"So many times we could've destroyed them, but he insisted we wait."

"Rufus has a plan."

"Oh, I know. And staring at you appears to make his brain work better."

Beryl cut his eyes imperceptibly to his brother then away again. Last night found him alone with Rufus in his bedroom enduring an unpleasant hour under the Elder's gaze. He called Beryl in at midnight, commanded him to stand against the wall, and then Rufus did nothing but stare at him in the low light.

"I dozed off before you returned. Did he pet you, too?"

Beryl sneered and corrected his face instantly lest Rufus notice. *"It's a small sacrifice."*

"Better you than me. You have much more self-control than I do."

Beryl agreed and ran his tongue over his teeth. *"We've both endured much worse."*

"Still, you're his favorite. How sweet."

Beryl grunted in his mind showing his disdain at being Rufus's preferred companion.

"I couldn't resist," Meryl offered sincerely.

Beryl accepted his apology and continued, *"All in all, there are very few Rakum left to destroy or bring over."*

"He should be satisfied."

Meryl's telepathic remark whispered with irony. None of them were satisfied. Since the Rabbit destroyed their race, nothing touched the anger and desperation in their hearts. All of the blood in the world could not dull the pain of being utterly separated from their brethren. That night in the Cave, the Rabbit's God skewered every single Rakum, and those who remained alive had a scar across their spirits that only the return of the High Father could heal.

"Father Abroghia is gone for good; you're killing me with your whining."

Beryl smirked and immediately relaxed his face. His twin was exaggerating. Abroghia wasn't flesh and blood. He was a spirit. A *demonic* spirit. The Rabbit's book explained it all. Beth Rider did the Rakum a huge favor by putting her story into print. She changed the names, but every detail of her misadventure with his kind was documented in a novel marketed as contemporary fiction. She was turning a pretty profit while trying to convince the remaining Rakum to give up their deity and serve her God. If only the more intelligent brethren remaining would read the woman's book, they'd better know their enemy. Out of fear of the unknown, Rufus outlawed reading altogether. As a result, Rufus didn't understand his enemy.

But Beryl did.

He knew the God of the humans, and he knew how to defeat Him. If only Rufus would listen.

"First, we have to catch the Rabbit," Meryl hissed in his mind, breaking up Beryl's thought patterns.

Arguing with Meryl was vanity. His twin knew everything he knew about High Father Abroghia. They both knew how to destroy their enemies without Abroghia sitting on his throne.

"He's our High Father. When we need him, he will come to us," Beryl whispered mentally and this time, Meryl agreed.

Because of the peculiar method of reproduction among Rakum, High Father Abroghia sired relatively few offspring. And now, since the Apostasy began seven years ago, the only blood-child of the High Father that remained was Michael Stone.

"Why do you have to bring him up? He's human now. We'll see him tortured to death very soon."

"We'll be careful. He is Abroghia's son. Highly favored in his day. He may have some surprises left for us. Be on your guard, bro—"

"GET OUT!"

The sitting room rumbled with words growled in fury. The

space began to empty and Rufus pointed a slender, sharp-nailed finger at the twins. "Not you!"

Beryl and Meryl nodded simultaneously, their poker faces intact.

Elder Rufus's voice had changed along with his appearance. Now raspy and guttural, one had to truly concentrate to understand him. He could no longer be seen in public, although he had no desire to mingle with the cattle of the world. No, he preferred to see their terrified faces when they were presented to him in private. He delighted in their horror. That was Rufus's life now, lording his superiority over the doomed mortals he fed upon. Beryl couldn't imagine how it fulfilled him.

The smelly, decomposing grunts filed out, their instructions for the night bouncing around in their feeble minds. How they could bite into a cadaver and call it food was beyond Beryl, but he hid his disdain. They were so weak and pathetic that it would be a miracle if their race could truly be restored. It was a miserable realization that the twins covered with expressionless faces.

When the room was empty, Rufus's gaze fell on Beryl as he stood the closest to his giant throne-like chair.

"You will wipe that sneer off your face before I knock it off!" Rufus waited five seconds and then stood to grasp Beryl's black T-shirt in both fists and slam him into the wall. "You don't think I will?" Rufus spoke into Beryl's ear then flicked his gaze right to catch Meryl's eye. "You don't think I can?"

Beryl maintained his composure, self-control one of his greatest attributes.

"Master, I am your bondservant. I live to serve you." Beryl spoke softly, and as expected, Rufus leaned back a few inches to look into his face.

The twins controlled human and Rakum alike with their hypnotic gaze and Rufus was no exception. His monstrous red eyes softened, and his lips fell slack around elongated canines as he awaited his subject's next utterance. Beryl let the seconds drag, milking the moment to the utmost.

"Forgive me for this face. I know it is tiresome to endure night after night," Beryl remained expressionless, but his words garnered a silent laugh from his twin. It was widely known that there had never been more attractive Rakum than Beryl and Meryl. Perfect facial symmetry and comeliness combined with their physical allure and advanced intelligence made them unsurpassed in every area. Rufus was as hooked as the rest of them. He lifted his crooked fingers to Beryl's cheek.

"You are dreadful to look upon," Rufus muttered, his mind expressing an opposing view. Beryl endured the caress and switched to telepathy, knowing his voice inside his master's head would serve to further subdue him.

"My life for you, my master," Beryl ran his palm along Rufus's smooth skull and allowed his fingers to rest at the back of his neck. Rufus swallowed visibly and held Beryl's eye.

"I'll hear your update now, Lieutenant," Rufus whispered. Beryl gave him a smile and Rufus's breath hitched in response.

"He is so pathetic."

Beryl ignored his brother and held his master's eye, resuming his soft-spoken way. "The Elders are dead. Yu was the last. Father Damien will be collected very soon."

"And Stone? And the Rabbit?" Rufus mumbled, now lulled by Beryl's gentle hypnosis.

"Master," Meryl said, stepping to his brother's side, "we've been to their home, but we can't reach them."

Rufus flicked his eyes to Meryl, "Are you so impotent, Lieutenant? Go and get them. Tonight. I want that Rabbit alive and I want her right away. I want her blood running down my throat night after night after night. She will pay for what she's done to our people." Meryl shook his head woefully and Rufus snarled, "What?"

Beryl resumed the quiet explanation, "Master, the Rabbit's God doesn't permit us entry. She'll need to be drawn out like the others."

Rufus stayed where he was, inches from Beryl's face, his mouth turned up into a half-snarl. He didn't understand. He didn't get it.

"He needs to read the book."

Beryl agreed with his brother and exhaled dramatically.

"Master," he said as he drew his fingers to rest on Rufus's shoulder and knead the muscle there, "read the Rabbit's new book. For the good of your vision. For the future of our people and the restoration of the brethren—read her book. You'll understand our enemy. You'll—"

"Reading is forbidden," Rufus hissed with only a fraction of his earlier venom. "I'm still losing Rakum to that woman's earlier work. It's poison. No reading. Period."

Resigned, Beryl nodded and switched to telepathy once more. *"You know best, Master. We will bring you the Rabbit without delay."*

"And Stone. Dead or alive, Stone, too," Rufus said, openly begging.

"They have a daughter, Master," Meryl piped in probably looking to earn a few points himself, as if it mattered, "only six years old."

Rufus's red eyes glittered.

"She's also marked, Master," Meryl continued, "the daughter inherited Dawn's mark."

"I had heard such a rumor. Oh, yes," he said and looked back at Beryl only inches away, "bring her to me. I will reward you." Rufus's hand left Beryl's cheek and cupped his throat.

Do it now, brother.

Agreeing the timing was perfect, Beryl whipped off his T-shirt and leaned to his right, exposing his throat to their mad leader. He and his brother used feigned adoration and their own blood many times to subdue their superiors in the past. Rufus had been seduced this way before, and if he objected he showed no sign.

"Why can't all my subjects be as loyal?" Rufus asked aloud and tucked his face into Beryl's throat.

Beryl met his twin's eye as their master's sharp fangs pierced his skin. Despite his bluff and bluster, Rufus was as weak-minded as a baby. Beryl cradled the Elder's head with his right hand and watched Meryl move out of his line of sight to the other side.

As before, they would drink from their master as he drank from them. Their blood did little more for him than to temporarily fulfill his lust, but *his* blood transferred power. Rufus had been supping not only the Dying Buzz from humans, but drinking from every Rakum apostate they could bring him. He had the power of dozens of vanquished Elders in his veins, and more than a few of their Fathers. Even Father Theophilus, who was being held prisoner in the basement, contributed his blood regularly albeit against his will. Rufus's blood magnified the twin's every talent and availed to them many others.

Thus from a tiny knife wound in their master's left forearm, Meryl took his portion and without Rufus acknowledging their actions in the least, Beryl would take his as well. Hence they grew greater than their master. And because they could, they kept it to themselves.

SEVEN

Nashville, TN
November 2nd, 7:00 p.m.

After spending the night in the hospital under observation, Damien was home again. He stuffed an overnight bag with an extra pair of pants and a wadded dress shirt. The aluminum cane the nurse prescribed him on his way out leaned against the chair, its thick foam handle reminding him of his newly-acquired weakness.

"I'd rather fall," Damien mumbled and shook his head. He took a last look around the room and shrugged. He'd hide for now. He wanted to end Rufus's tyranny, but he was only one man—and a sick old man to boot. God would surely send someone else. Someone who still had their youth with which to fight. Perhaps Michael Stone and his crew. Damien shook his head. He was no coward, but to put himself in front of the Rakum's new leader could be a fatal folly, and he was not prepared to die carelessly.

Jonah refused.

Damien recognized the small voice in his spirit and winced. Was God calling him a Jonah? In the ancient story, the reluctant prophet had been commanded to go to Nineveh and warn the sinning village of the coming judgment of the Lord. Jonah refused to go and tried to hide from God. Was that what Damien was doing? Was he hiding from God or Rufus or both? Because of the terror in his heart from the near miss the night before, it was impossible to tell.

He had good reason to fear Rufus. The new Rakum leader had Theophilus in chains. If it were still in his power, he'd sneak in and speak with the Father; see if their goodwill remained lively enough to join forces against the megalomaniac Rufus. Under Abroghia, he had no particular affiliation with any one Father, but the old Greek Rakum the Elder held hostage had something going for him that none of the others had. Theophilus had walked with Jesus of Nazareth, sat under

His teaching in the early days of His ministry. They were all aware of this anomaly, but never dared to speak of it in their heyday. Damien's heart quickened at the thought of asking the oldest living Father what he heard at the feet of the Perfect One. Was it in his power to attempt such a thing? Damien rubbed his throbbing elbows and shook his head. Faith in God left his flesh weak and frail.

Damien's cell rang and he listened to the directives of the police officer on the line. *Stay close to home, lock your doors, keep the phone line open, and we'll contact you when we have something.*

Damien ended the call and dropped the cell in his coat pocket. The empathetic detective assured him that his case was a top priority, but Damien couldn't stay home. He had to get underground. If Rufus had a price on his head, his best recourse was retreat. There would be time for heroics after God fished him out of the belly of the whale.

Damien shouldered the bag and headed for the front door, still arguing with himself and God in his heart. He couldn't face Rufus alone. It would be suicide. He would need help. He'd been a monster himself long enough to know that Rufus would stop at nothing to attain his goals.

Damien eyed a book that sat on the entryway table. *The Rabbit* by Beth Rider. It was a bestseller, but more than that, it was a map to the ways of the Rakum. The author described much in her book, and Damien had read it with interest. He learned that Abroghia was not born to a woman, but was a fallen angel—one that God cast down before the dawn of mankind. From Beth's book, Damien learned much about his former people, and much about spiritual warfare. But mostly, the text encouraged him to trust in his *new* High Father, the God of the universe. Damien felt certain that if he could join forces with the Rabbit and her army of confederates, he'd have a good chance of surviving the melee. But could he get to *them* before Rufus got to *him*? He knew the Stones lived in Alabama—should he head that way? Was God leading him that direction?

Go to Theophilus.

Into the lion's den? Damien shuddered. Surely, God hadn't punched his ticket yet. He'd only just become capable of serving Him. Why would God send him to be tortured by Rufus?

Damien pulled open the door and headed for his car.

With God all things are possible.

Damien nodded, his head tilted, as thoughts of victory teased him. What if he was able to somehow assist in Rufus's defeat? Would he then have a chance to speak to Javier? Make things right? Be the father he was never allowed to be in the world of the Rakum?

Damien swallowed, the notion misting his eyes. He misjudged the Toyota's lock, and his key ring fell to the driveway.

If he hadn't been distracted by a painful creak in his back as he stood up, he might have noticed the porch light blinking out behind him. If he hadn't been fussing with finding the lock in the newly darkened drive, he might have noticed the shape that crossed behind him and stopped just to his right.

Damien's key went home just as everything went black.

◆◆◆

Meryl's cell rang and he brought it to his ear.

"Father Damien will be at HQ by 2, sir."

The one man he and his brother knew they could count on had come through again.

"Good work, Dimple. Rufus wants him alive."

"He's alive."

"Good man. Anything else?" Meryl studied his fingernails in the low light. He and Beryl were waiting for Rufus to finish with his latest victim. Across the room, their illustrious leader was scarfing the last of a dying man's blood with grisly gusto.

"I'm gonna tap him. For old times' sake." Dimple's flat admission was not seeking authorization and Meryl didn't give it. Damien was human—no power left in the old geezer. If anything, his tired blood would make Dimple sick.

"Whatever. Just get him here." Meryl shut off the phone and turned to Beryl. "Rufus'll love this. Two Fathers in the basement by sunup."

"Damien doesn't count," Beryl countered, not really interested in the conversation.

Meryl shrugged and leaned against the wall. Rufus was just about finished, and the fat guy he was draining was breathing his last.

It was about time.

eight

Isaac Akaron sat up and looked about the tiny cubicle he called an apartment. His landlord was a commercial psychic, and for room and board, his talents made her a true one.

Tonight, as vivid as life, he telepathically witnessed Father Damien's capture. He'd also witnessed Tyson and Gage failing to nab him the night before, yet a late success was better than none. Spying on the lunatic Elder in Jackson had become a source of entertainment, and Rufus rarely bombed a performance. Beryl and Meryl were pleased with themselves and Rufus was ecstatic. Isaac saw all this from several states away without their knowledge. He was an amazing Rakum with unparalleled power. At least that was what Father Damien used to tell him when they shared quarters in the good old days. But now? Father Damien was human.

Isaac humphed and shook his head.

I need to get into the show.

His visions regarding the distant future were hazy at best, but he thought for sure he'd get to see the old Father once more before they killed him. Maybe he could spit in his face. Father Damien's un-Rakum-like behavior set Isaac in a spin and his anger simmered deep. The Father deserted him five years ago to search for the God of the mortals. Isaac's eyes glazed over as he rehashed the memories.

Born in 12 A.D., Damien was highly respected among the Ten. He had Abroghia's ear, which few, if any, of the others could claim. And three decades ago, Damien took 13-year-old Isaac under his wing and moved him into the Chamber. It was a necessary move as his peers had become too fearful of him to maintain amity. When Damien and the other Fathers took him in, Isaac truly began to grow and expand his extrasensory abilities to their fullest.

The Ten Fathers educated, discipled, chastised, and encouraged him daily, and on the advice of the High Father, they fed him as well—from their own veins. From the moment Isaac arrived at the Cave, their official underground headquarters in Nevada, until the Rakum were disbanded, he never touched human blood. He drank solely from the Fathers and as a result, his telekinetic and telepathic skills sharply increased. By his twentieth birthday, no Rakum, even among the Fathers, could outperform him in clairvoyance and foretelling. The only one he was forbidden to buzz from was the High Father and he expected that. Abroghia was above in every way imaginable. He was their god, their king, and their perfection.

And as such, he would have broken Tyson and Gage in two for failing to bring in the apostate, Damien.

The traitor.

A surprising turn of events to say the least.

Five years ago, Father Damien sent him packing. With very little explanation and much sermonic dialogue, the person closest to him his entire life completely shut him out. Pushing him gently out the door, Damien spoke of abstracts, mortal emotions, and the origins of the human species. Isaac thought him insane, but what could he do? Damien spent most of his nights at a monastery in the hills, communing with the monks, and learning from their books. The friars knew him for what he was, yet they looked for his arrival and kept him until nearly daybreak. So much so that Isaac would sit in their shared basement sleeping quarters anxiously watching the door, afraid that one morning, the Father would be burned to a crisp trying to make it home.

When Damien finally missed a return, Isaac hiked to the monastery at dusk to seek him out. What he found was a spiritually broken Rakum Father, humbled and pitiful, lying face down on a dusty floor before a wooden cross; not resembling in the least the mighty and frightening leader that he'd known most of his life. It wasn't long after that he and his guardian parted ways.

Isaac lowered his head atop his folded arms and closed his eyes. He concentrated on Damien, tried to pull him up, and couldn't. A week ago, he found he was no longer able to spy on the Father as in days of old. It had something to do with the traitor's new faith, his new God, and the spiritual forces that surrounded him that blunted Isaac's view.

Isaac sighed. If he never saw Damien again, it would be for the best. They were different species now, completely incompatible. If he laid eyes upon him now, he'd most likely shudder in palpable disgust.

He'd most likely kill him.

Who else is about?

Now and again, he would look in on Beryl and Meryl. The twins were under the impression that no one else was telepathic. It was sad, really. Isaac was half their age, and they didn't even know of his existence. But did any of them? Until Abroghia deserted their race, Isaac was kept shut up in the Chamber anterooms. He saw very little of their brethren and only when he left the confines of the Cave with Father Damien did he begin to meet other Rakum and their human companions.

Canaan…

There was an interesting fellow. Isaac hadn't met the man in person, but many of his vision-like dreams involved the intimidating Elder and his homely common-law wife. Especially the last ten days, Isaac was repeatedly shown a mighty battle between Rufus and this tough-exteriored brute. In the scuffle, Rufus annihilates Canaan, drains his blood, and leaves him for dead. It was the kind of prophecy Isaac would share with Rufus if he trusted him, which he did not. One of the last things Damien told him before he lost his mind to an unseen Deity was to avoid Rufus Delouve at all costs.

Isaac's stomach grumbled and he thought of Boris, the one Rakum in town who was willing to buzz him periodically so that he could maintain the purity he'd spent his life achieving. He'd be along soon enough. But first…

A knock sounded at the door and Isaac didn't budge; he'd seen her coming. She was a creature of habit.

Miranda—landlord, substandard psychic, all-around-nutcase—knocked again and her key turned in the lock. She was fearless. Isaac considered snuffing her out, but that solution would have him on the street as soon as she was discovered missing. He could suffer her attentions a little while longer.

She entered the room and Isaac remained as he was; head down at the card table. In a moment, she would speak—try to draw him out. Then she would attempt for the umpteenth time to seduce him. It was ridiculous, and by mortal standards, illegal. Close to fifty chronologically, Isaac's apparent age was just fourteen. He aged even more slowly than his brethren because of his specialized diet, and this woman's attraction to him was not motherly in the least. Isaac heard her approach and he sighed. It would be so easy to stop her heart.

"What're ya doin' in the dark, sweetie?" She clicked on the lamp as she drew near.

Her drawling voice grated on Isaac's nerves. She was drunk. Again. And now her hands were on his shoulders; massaging, kneading, irritating.

"I thought tonight's sessions went great. When you lifted that Georgia chick off the ground with your mind, I nearly tossed my lunch. What other surprises do you have in store for me, sweetie? Is there anything you can't do?"

Isaac grunted, and Miranda's hands slowed and were still, cupping his biceps now from behind. In their sessions, as she called them, Miranda sat at the proverbial circular table with the fake crystal ball fragmenting the light. Isaac stood to the side, dressed in black, blending into the dark purple curtains that surrounded the small space. When the show began, he'd go to work—throwing his voice, moving objects, flashing the lights and occasionally, mentally shoving a guest to the floor. It was great drama and the mortals ate it up like candy. Although bored to tears, Isaac would bide his time. His day was coming and he was patient.

"It's no effort for you at all, is it? You play with me, with them. You're above it all, aren't you? Isaac, look at me."

Isaac lifted his head and controlled his expression with extreme effort. His stomach grumbled again and she heard it, her eyes growing wide. She knew he was a blood drinker; the spiteful familiars she listened to helped her figure it out. But they obviously didn't tell her that he never drank human blood, for that was what she constantly offered him.

"You could stoop down to our level once in a while. Some of us down here worship you. Some of us would do anything for you. To please you."

Miranda pressed her abundant bosom against his back and ran her hands down his arms. Isaac's lip curled. He detested her wanton come-ons. When he refused to meet her eyes again, she came from behind to stand at his side. Producing a small knife from her copious skirts, she brought it to her throat. Isaac's eyes followed out of habit, but he had no intention of drinking anything she might draw out.

"Why don't you like me, sweetie? Is my blood not good enough? Am I too old? Do I look too much like your mommy?"

Isaac cut his eyes at her and she flinched, seeing his hate at last.

"How old are you, Miranda? How old do you think I am? Tell me?" Isaac hissed his words and she was offended by them. She lowered the knife and her face took on an inexplicable feminine grimace. "You're a meaningless blip on the screen of eternity, Miranda. In another fifty years, you'll be long gone. I'll still be here in fifty *thousand* years. Leave me be. Our contract is strictly business."

"How can you be so cruel?" Miranda dropped the knife and Isaac gestured for the door.

"Hit the road Miranda. My brother has arrived."

As he spoke, Boris entered through the open door and nodded a greeting. He looked at Miranda and smiled. He'd always had eyes for the dumpy matron and she knew it, although she didn't fully understand the nature of Isaac's dark compadre.

"Boss lady." Boris bowed to Miranda with flourish. She crossed her arms and stiffened her posture.

"This is my house. I refuse to leave before I am ready."

Isaac caught Boris's eye and nodded.

"Please come, brother. I couldn't care less if she watches. Come now." Isaac sent his plea mentally and Boris stepped forward, rolling up his sleeve. Isaac came to his feet and met him halfway. Boris was black as night and as strong as an ox, and Isaac was more than happy that his geographically closest brother was an amiable donor. Using Miranda's discarded knife, he shoved the tip into Boris's inner elbow. As he supped, he listened to Boris and Miranda's exchange.

"Oh, my god. Will you look at that!"

"What do you think, boss lady? Make you jealous?"

"Hush and be nice. I don't get it. In the movies, they can't get enough blood. But he won't come near me."

"I'll come near ya."

"Don't get fresh." (a giggle)

"This pup is too young, boss. He has no use for a beautiful, full-figured gal like you. In our world, it takes a century to become a man."

"What're you doin'?" (another giggle)

"I've seen three hundred birthdays, boss, and I'm always hungry."

Isaac moved with Boris as he stepped a few feet aside to put his free arm around Miranda's shoulders. He pulled her tight and Isaac was pressed into the stiff lace of her costumed bodice. She giggled a little more and he knew Boris was nuzzling her neck.

"Now? It has to be now?" Isaac transmitted, his irritation no doubt evident.

"The meat is fresh, little brother. Don't want it to spoil," Boris murmured over his head.

Angry, but not willing to stop his meal, Isaac pushed hard against Miranda with his inside hand and sent her sprawling.

"Tell her to be still or I will shut her up for good." Isaac knew how much blood he needed and he wouldn't take any less. Miranda screamed his name and came to her feet, but Isaac remained as he was, eyes closed and facing away from the furious old gal. Moments before his frustration reached its threshold, Boris spoke up.

"Boss lady…Boss. Shhh…"

"That monster! Ingrate! Spoiled br—"

"Shhh… he can kill you with a thought. Yeah. Uh-huh. Betcha didn't realize that, eh?"

(quiet pause)

"He's a god among our people. He can kill you like that." (snaps fingers)

Isaac finished his meal and smiled, appreciating Boris's allegiance.

"Okay," Boris said to no one and took back his arm.

"Thank you, brother…" Isaac sent telepathically, and then spoke aloud, cutting his eyes at Miranda. "Now take it upstairs."

The woman opened her mouth to protest, but Boris held up his hand and crossed to meet her where she stood, disheveled and red-faced. Isaac watched him lead her out the door by one flabby arm and then ascend the stairs out of the basement to her part of the rambling old house where Boris could romance her, drink her, whatever he wanted.

Isaac sighed, happy she was gone and glad he hadn't killed her.

Yet.

nine

Jackson, MS
November 2nd, 8:45 p.m.

Meryl dragged the night's unfortunate soul out of Rufus's room and down the hall. Beryl walked ahead of him, mumbling to himself. It was a man this time, obese and smelly. Meryl thought back to the old days. Days when he was free to choose his Cows, pick out the most desirable mortals and lure them into his clutches. The last was a matchless and stunning creature named Simon. He'd swiped him out from under that wimp Javier before their final night in the Cave. Simon had been young, strong, and oh so delicious...

"Simon? Judas Priest! It's time you let that moron go."

"That's not what you called him then," Meryl teased and Beryl made the tiniest grin.

"He was definitely pretty..."

"Oh, yeah," Meryl chuckled. "Let's find him when this is over. A Cow needs a master."

Beryl's dark cloud roll back into place. *"Bitching and complaining doesn't help anybody. Suck it up and stop pining for the way things were!"*

Meryl smirked at Beryl's telepathic reprimand. They were both on edge and grumpy, but it had little to do with the boy Simon, or Rufus and his idiotic attempts at leadership. No, they recently picked up an errant telepathic whisper from a foe they thought long-ago vanquished. The missing Elder had been overheard making some serious Rabbit plans. Worse, they'd lied to Rufus. This Elder could possibly be a threat to Rufus if not handled soon.

"How did he escape us? We've been hunting the Elders for five years and not a peep," Beryl said, speaking low before he switched to telepathy for a more private conversation. *"Elder Canaan is very powerful. I sense it. Even now, without the Fathers on the throne."*

"I don't suppose you can narrow down where he is?" Meryl yanked the fat

corpse hard and maneuvered him into the small elevator which would carry them to the basement furnace where Rufus cremated his victims. Thankfully, there were two junior Rakum on duty who would do the dismemberment. Meryl could think of better ways to spend his time than spoon-feeding chunks of a derelict into the mouth of hell.

"I might have an idea. I need to get to a computer." The door closed on the trio and the elevator started down. Rufus's house had two floors and a basement and the former owners ensured the entire estate was handicapped accessible. Of course, the former owners were the first ones to test out the crematory in the bowels of the house.

"We'll hit the Starbucks on Promenade. Less foot traffic and the girl there has the hots for me."

"For us," Beryl corrected and helped his twin get the dead man off the elevator and into the waiting arms of the brutes assigned below. They looked hungry and they'd probably find time to nosh on Rufus's leftovers.

Meryl averted his eyes in disgust and without a word, the twins headed back up. They'd make a lame excuse to Rufus; their leader didn't keep close tabs on them. He wasn't capable of controlling them, his hope being to merely manage them until his plans came to fruition. For now, they amicably filled their respective roles in tense harmony.

"What was that business about Kite? Did you get any more of that rambling?" Meryl hoped his twin gathered more information than he had because when Rufus thought about their slow-witted brother Kite, the transmission grew faint quickly. Almost as if—

"Almost as if he can still block us. At least to some extent," Beryl piped in as he led the way to the back door. *"I heard what you heard. 'Don't come back without it'. That's all I got."*

Meryl smirked and followed his twin out the exit and into the cool night air. Rufus was likely collecting another man's prize for himself. But it didn't matter. Their leader was constantly spouting ridiculous new edicts. He was insane, so Meryl wouldn't give it anymore thought. They had their plates full already.

The Starbucks was quiet and closing in ten minutes. Meryl sweet-talked the starry-eyed cashier into loaning out her laptop and Beryl was busy tapping away across the room, following leads that had not yet blossomed into useful information. Meryl glanced at his brother and picked up the latest search in his mind. *State parks.* Whoopee.

Sighing, he turned his attention to the teen behind the register and leaned on the counter. Blonde and buxom, the highschooler hadn't a clue about life, the universe, or anything important. And she hadn't enough sense to fear strangers.

"So, Hildy, how'd you get so cute?"

The girl blushed and tipped her head with a question of her own. "What's it like to have a twin?"

Meryl smiled. "It's pretty fantastic."

For no reason, the girl laughed one short burst and then put her manicured fingernails to her pouty lips.

"I can read his mind." Meryl tossed her a grin and she blushed deeper. He lowered his voice to a whisper, *"Watch this."* Meryl spread out a napkin on the counter top, grabbed Hildy's pen from her hand and wrote a message in block letters: WHAT ARE YOU DOING, BERYL?

Without looking up, his brother called out annoyed, "Buzz off, Meryl, I'm busy."

Hildy burst into a fit of giggles and covered her mouth with her hands. "He sounded like my boyfriend just then—"

"Boyfriend?" Meryl questioned and she fell silent. "What does he think about you working so late every night?" Meryl held the girl's eye and licked his lips. She was breathless and lost in his gaze. When she didn't answer, he winked and made a face. "Well? Hmmm?"

Hildy giggled and her tight corkscrew curls shook as she laughed.

"Is he the jealous type?" Meryl pressed and then settled his chin in his hand, giving her an adoring look. "Do you think I could take him?"

"He..." Hildy giggled again and glanced at her only co-worker, a shapely Latino girl a couple of years her senior wiping down the prep counter. Hildy's brown eyes flashed and she leaned on the counter, reducing the distance between them and making a shadow in the scoop of her shirt. She whispered, *"He's kinda wimpy."*

Meryl inhaled the aroma of her shampoo and fantasized about touching her impossible curls. She was plump and soft, her skin as pink as a rose, as if she never sat under the rays of the hateful sun. And she was young. When did they let these kids start work? Was she fifteen? Sixteen? Meryl wondered if he should ask. It had been some time since he touched one so clean, fresh, and unsullied. Across the room, Beryl made a noise and pulled him out of his thoughts. Meryl stood up slowly and smiled again to the young Hildy. If only...

"Don't start that again. Look. Come here."

Beryl's mental voice was annoyed and excited at the same time. Meryl didn't have to see to absorb the information his brother had obtained. Elder Canaan finally slipped up and left them something they could use. On a reunion web site linked to the Tennessee State Parks Community page, a familiar name popped out at them.

"Ranger Marcy Haddle. That's Canaan's mate. We met her at Assembly in '82. She was peculiar," Meryl sent thoughtfully.

"Annoying."

"Cute, though. She gave him a hundred percent, remember?"

"Huh," Beryl agreed with a chuckle. In the photo, the Elder leaned against her like a love-struck school boy. *"...and she's still giving it to him."*

"Why stay with her? He seemed like such a brute..." Meryl touched the monitor as he spoke. The few times he'd crossed paths with the Elder they sought, he'd bullied him out of the choicest Cows in holding during Assembly. Meryl went hungry more than once because he was no match for the Elder's brawn.

"Tough, yeah, but amiable," Beryl sent still eyeing the monitor.

Meryl nodded with a hum. Back in the day, the lumbering gorilla stood up for Meryl when he was too hotly pursued by Elder Dawn's contemporaries. Beryl chuckled and Meryl punched his arm.

"Jack would never have loaned you out, don't worry," Beryl sent, his silent voice smiling. Meryl didn't respond; all of the Elders sought possession of the twins, but Jack Dawn never once shared them.

"Jack respected Canaan," Meryl surmised. *"That's enough for me."* In the old days, Jack, Tomás, and Canaan were inseparable at Assembly.

Beryl sighed. *"Canaan didn't attend the last few Assemblies."*

"I wonder how he stayed under the Fathers' radar. He must have had help. Another Elder sympathized with him and covered his duties."

"Good point," Beryl said, his brow furrowing. Each Elder closely supervised ten lieutenants, a hundred captains, and a thousand brethren. Someone would've had to cover for him.

"Is it possible he stayed away from the brethren so that he could spend all of his time with this mortal?"

Beryl nodded. *"I sense that this is exactly what he's been doing."*

"Hiding," Meryl admitted.

"Hiding among the mortals. He's gotten good at it."

"So we're going after him before the Rabbit? Is that wise?" Meryl questioned Beryl's plan, but his brother was resolute.

"We told Rufus he was in the clear. Let's make our words true, and then go to Montgomery again. Stone has seen us. We'll give him a few days to freak."

"Cool. So..."

Beryl closed the laptop and stood up from the tiny circular table. *"It's a seven-hour drive to Nashville."* He checked his watch and swore under his breath. *"That'd put us there too close to sunup. I do not want to go back and look at Rufus tonight."*

"What're our options?"

Both twins searched their memories for alternate spots to sleep away the day, but Rufus's estate was the safest place in Jackson. Meryl shook his head and glanced at Hildy who was pretending not to watch them from the counter. Meryl's hand went to his pocket where he kept his knife.

"That girl needs to come with us wherever we go, Beryl. Please."

Beryl's smile turned up on one side.

"Ask her to come with us. Hell, we're leaving town. Who'll know? This place has been deserted since we arrived." Beryl's gaze fell on Hildy's petite coworker busily scrubbing the counter. *"Let's take them both."*

The second girl looked up then and blushed at the attention. Meryl nodded and returned the computer. Getting her to consent to a ride in his BMW was a breeze and by happenstance, her friend needed a lift home.

In the car, Beryl drove with the second girl on the passenger side. She admitted that she needed a ride because she loaned her car to her roommate for the week. Maria, her name tag read, had the apartment to herself for seven days.

Beryl caught Meryl's eye in the rearview mirror and didn't have to hear his reply in his mind. The twins had always been lucky. Tonight they'd do whatever they pleased, enjoying the company of Starbuck's finest. Tomorrow night, they'd head for Nashville to deal up some death to the last Elder resister.

Beryl smirked. No worries.

TEN

Tuscaloosa, AL
November 2nd, 9:45 p.m.

Javier reread Roman's email and sighed. Even though both of them were fully human, his former Elder still received information in his spirit regarding what remained of their people. Acting as his adopted father, Roman perceived that a great danger was headed Javier's way and he was flying in to protect him, if he possibly could. He checked his watch; Roman's email was several hours old, and he'd probably already arrived.

"Dave!" Javier called to the front of the apartment and shut down the computer.

David Walker was also a former Rakum, and they shared a two-bedroom condo in Tuscaloosa. When they walked out of the Cave seven years ago, fully human, they clung together and the Rabbit, Beth Rider, helped them build a mortal life on the outside.

Neither of them had held normal jobs in their Rakum existence, although they were both practiced at playing human. When Beth got them home to Alabama, she worked tirelessly to get them plugged into society. David was most accustomed to campus life, so Beth enrolled him in classes at the University of Alabama. Javier knew seventeen human languages, so she helped him set up an online translator service. Her last generous move was to co-sign for them to purchase a condo in town, and that was six years ago. David worked part-time at the LifeWay bookstore down the street and took classes on the side. Javier worked from home four days a week, translating job orders that came in from all over the world.

Javier rose from his computer chair and turned for the door. "David!"

"Yeah?" David asked, coming down the hall, oven mitts on both hands. They were the same height, but where Javier's build was a muscular medium, David's was more lean and athletic. The kid was always smiling, and Javier hoped one day he'd be half as jovial as his nerdy roommate.

"Did Roman call while I was out?" It was nearing ten and Javier had spent much of the afternoon and early evening running errands. He watched his friend's face, but it was blank. "Roman. Did he call?"

"No. I…" David sounded uncertain. He headed away and turned into the living room, holding his mitted hands in surrender.

Javier was right behind him and joined him at the answering machine next to the couch. The light was blinking.

"Oh, maybe. Sorry."

Javier sighed and pressed the button. One short message in a familiar voice, Roman was waiting at the airport.

"I'll go get him," David started but Javier waved him off.

"You finish whatever you're doing. I'll get him." Javier pulled his leather jacket from the closet by the door. "What are you doing?"

"Baking cookies. Want some?" David smiled like a kid and Javier shook his head.

Although he looked twenty and acted like a goof, David was at least seventy-five years old. Would he ever grow up? Javier waved his fingers as he left. He was practically twice the boy's age, but he'd been a goofy kid, too, and Roman would likely remind him of that tonight. Javier warmed up his aging Camaro and wondered what the evening might bring.

Roman's email said they were in danger. What kind of danger? The Rakum were disbanded, the Fathers had no power, and God was watching over the remaining brethren who turned human. What could be wrong?

Javier sighed and pulled out of his parking space. Roman was never melodramatic, so he prepared his heart and spirit for the worst.

♦ ♦ ♦

Roman hadn't changed much.

Javier saw him off five years ago when his Elder moved to L.A. to start up his own accounting service. Unlike Javier and David, Roman had old money and didn't need to procure employment. But he was an extremely intelligent individual, and not one to sit idle. As soon as he had his bearings as a human male, he studied, became licensed, and proved himself an excellent businessman. And here he was again, in the flesh.

Roman walked in long strides, with a rolling effect that caused Javier to smirk as he awaited him. He no longer wore his wire-framed glasses for appearances—now he needed them for nearsightedness. All Rakum who became human suffered one major drawback: Their health diminished in accordance with their apparent age. Roman's apparent age was fifty, with grey intermingling in his auburn hair. As before, he wore it long, but he now kept it tied in a ponytail in the back. He still looked cool. Human or not, Roman was an extraordinary fellow.

"You look like a dog longing for a bone, Javie. Did you miss me?" Roman said extending his hand as he approached. Javier smiled and shook his hand enthusiastically with both of his own.

"Yes, sir, I did. You look good. How are you?"

"It's only been a few years."

"Time has slowed down. Human time seems like forever."

"Try to tell them that," Roman deadpanned. "Nonetheless, I'm fine. Take me home. I have a lot to share and none of it is pleasant."

Javier nodded and reached for his friend's carry-on. "Dave's baking cookies."

"Good," Roman chuckled and roughed Javier's short black hair. "I'm glad you guys are together. That kid needs a tutor. He was the first of our circle to turn human, but I doubt he's assimilated as seamlessly as he pretends."

"What do you mean?" Javier asked. He thought David was pretty together as far as making his new life work. Roman sighed.

"David was naturally altruistic, true, as well as empathetic, but like all of us, he needs guidance to transcend the old nature. Have you guys joined a church or pursued any other godly counsel here?"

"Besides the Stones?" Javier had been avoiding the human believers purposely. How could the mortals understand where he was coming from? Even if he revealed his past, how could they comprehend it? Roman frowned and shook his head.

"A hot coal grows cold when removed from the fire, Javie. When this current emergency is over, find a congregation. They can be former Rakum. That's an order."

"Yes, sir," Javier replied, not at all confident that he'd be able to carry out the edict. He redirected the conversation to his roommate. "David met a girl. They might be getting serious." Javier matched pace with Roman and steered him toward the exit.

"Oh? Have you met her?"

Javier nodded.

"What do you think?"

Javier shrugged and avoided Roman's eye. "She reminds me of Isabella."

Roman shot Javier a disapproving glare and shook his head. "Do not speak of those days. Do not think on them. Do not long for them."

"You're right. I know."

Roman caught his eye and winked. "Forgiven. How about you? Any progress in that department?"

Javier shook his head. "I can't meet women. I guess I'm not ready. I have a lot of baggage."

"Baggage? Huh. That's ironic, isn't it? Before we switched sides, we had no worries. No stress. No baggage." Roman put his hand on Javier's shoulder as they walked. "Just go slow. I have the same problem. One day at a time."

Javier nodded. In the past, in their old lives, Roman's sexual appetite was as good as any Rakum. For him to refrain from intimacy with women would take tremendous effort. A late bloomer, Javier had not reached sexual maturity before he was transformed. He wasn't a virgin, but he felt no sexual desire. And worse, when he did consider a particular female in such a way, Isabella came to mind. Isabella had been his first love, his first conquest, and eventually, his first murder victim.

He killed her with his lust for blood.

"I can no longer read your thoughts, but your face says it all. Drop it."

Roman's expression was grim and Javier nodded apologetically.

"Good. Now tell me more of David."

"David's working it out." They exited the terminal and Javier led the way to his car. "He created a past for himself; a mortal past. He swears he'll never tell anyone how he started out." Javier caught Roman's eye. "Is that what God would want us to do? Keep our Rakum heritage a secret?"

Roman shrugged. "Like you, I can only say what I have learned from their movies and TV shows, but women expect you to be honest with them. If God sends David a woman, he'll eventually tell her the truth to keep her."

Javier was quiet and they reached the car. He lifted the hatch and dropped in Roman's bag. Roman recognized the Camaro and laughed.

It had belonged to him before their transformation, and he'd given it to Javier when he moved out west. It made Javier think of better days, of happy decades under Roman's tutelage, and of Simon Miller, the last Cow he ever—

"You should sell this heap," Roman interrupted his thoughts before they became too gruesome.

Javier shook his head. "Not yet." He slid into the driver's seat and clutched the steering wheel. "I'm not ready to let go. I miss a lot of it. I can't help it." He looked out his window and didn't meet his friend's eyes.

"What do you miss? Being a slave to your lust?" Roman came off harshly and Javier was stung by his words.

"No—I don't miss the blood." Javier fell quiet and shook his head. What exactly did he miss? Roman deserved an answer. "I just don't fit in this skin. I feel like I'm wearing a costume—a mask. Will I ever feel human?"

Roman's hand on his shoulder brought him comfort.

"You will," Roman sighed, "you're doing great. Keep moving forward and you'll let go of the past. Trust me. You'll let go and it won't hurt a bit."

Javier nodded and started the car. It would need a few minutes to warm up and stay running, so he filled the dead air with stories about David and his many misadventures. The kid was constant entertainment, and even as he caused Roman to laugh more than once with such tales, Javier recognized that he'd put his Elder through the same in his youth. Funny how life comes back around on you. *The Circle of Life.* Javier hoped he was doing his part to keep it going.

ELEVEN

Tuscaloosa, AL
November 2nd, 9:45 p.m.

Chloe collapsed onto her bed face first and screamed into her pillow until she was out of breath. Living at home while attending college was the worst mistake she'd ever made. Her brothers had moved out and mom and dad were making her life miserable, constantly nagging her, and filling her free time with their own agendas. She was sick of it. Chloe exhaled and looked up from her frustration. When her gaze landed on Dave's photo, she smiled despite herself. If she could just disappear for a while. Head off and stay with friends. Go sleep over with Dave—

"We're leaving, Mina!"

Chloe's mom shouted up the stairs, calling her by her first name. No one in the whole world called her Mina except her mother. It wasn't a bad name, it was just the fact that her mother insisted on using it when no one else did.

Chloe grunted a reply loud enough to carry down to them and then heard the front door close. Mom and Dad were heading to the University's faculty Fall fling. They wouldn't miss this party, although they purposefully left late so they wouldn't have to spend much time there. But whatever.

David Walker...

She'd never slept with Dave. She'd never slept with anybody. But she was going to and she wanted it to be him.

Chloe reached for Dave's framed photo and pulled it close, still lying on her stomach long-ways across her double bed. Dave walked into her life three months ago and stole her heart. Chloe flirted with boys in high school, teased them, and kept them at arm's length. But college was a different animal. She was an adult now. And this guy from her Abnormal Psych class took the cake. The first time their

67

eyes met, she knew they'd hit it off. Plus, he came on pretty strong. She'd been scouring the historical reference section at the library when he entered the stacks behind her.

"You're trapped now, Miss Bushman. What're you going to do?" he'd said with a devilish smile and blocked the exit with his frame. Before she knew it, they'd exchanged numbers and made a coffee date for the following night. That was two months ago.

A part-time student, Dave was shy, sweet, funny, and odd. He could make her laugh with a reference she understood one second, and then confuse her with a comment so far from left field that even he couldn't explain himself. He was aloof but attentive; subdued but oftentimes ecstatic for no reason. He was a unique character that Chloe hoped to work into her long-term plans.

Was he handsome? Sure, in his own way. Chloe smiled and traced the photo of his face with her finger. He had a pale and freckle-free complexion, and he wore his reddish brown hair short and spiked on top. His green eyes flashed with humor in every glance, and his voice was gentle and soft. She'd noticed his athletic build right away. When he looked at her, she lost her train of thought and the few times he kissed her, goose bumps raced across her skin.

Chloe kissed the glass over the picture and reached for the cordless phone. He answered on the first ring.

"You got Dave. Speak."

"Hey, there. What're you doing?" Chloe rolled over onto her back, holding the photo in one hand and the phone in the other.

"Just baked some cookies. Feel brave enough to try one?"

Chloe giggled and sat up. "Is that an invitation?"

"Always."

"Cool. See ya in a few." Chloe blew a kiss into the phone and disconnected. Now to throw on her low-rise Levi's and the scoop-neck sweater Dave liked. Chloe scooted into her walk-in closet and began to shuffle through her extensive wardrobe. She had to look her best. What if tonight was the night?

You never know... Chloe chuckled and shrugged off her ratty sweatshirt for something better.

◆ ◆ ◆

Dave and his roommate lived in a community off campus. Twenty minutes later Chloe stood outside Dave's door, and he answered on her first knock.

"Roll Tide, sunshine," he whispered in what sounded like a sigh of relief as he pulled open the door. The Alabama Crimson Tide dominated life in the overpopulated college town of Tuscaloosa, and although neither she nor Dave was particularly interested, they'd undeniably joined the prevalent sports subculture by proxy. Chloe giggled and repeated his greeting back.

"You look lovely," he said, giving her a wink as he closed and locked the door. They stood in the narrow front hall and Dave regarded her with a friendly gaze.

"Thanks," Chloe replied and held his gaze until he made a small noise and turned away. He led her to the kitchen without any display of affection, but she didn't fret over it. It always took him time to warm up. Or was he gathering his nerve? Chloe didn't care which it was, just so long as he eventually reached for her with his strong hands. She realized she was blushing and returned to the moment.

The apartment was filled with the aroma of baking and when they reached the dining nook, she noted two large trays of sugar cookies on the table top. They looked perfect.

"How about some soy milk?" David asked, opening the refrigerator.

For some reason, he didn't like dairy products, although he assured her that he was not lactose intolerant. He also didn't like pasta or pizza which made him the weirdest college kid she knew. Chloe nodded her head and reached for the cooled cookie.

"Is this what you did today? Baked cookies?" Chloe ate daintily and watched David pour milk into a spotless glass from the cupboard. He was wearing old jeans and a plain white T-shirt that stretched across firm pecs and washboard abs. Chloe knew she was hopeless, but she studied him anyway. When he handed her the milk, he gestured to a chair on her right.

"I also went to the library. I saw your nemesis, Kiki."

Chloe laughed and finished her cookie. She still liked to meet David in the library, in the stacks. They'd whisper and try to make each other laugh out loud. Kiki was the librarian and she had her eye on David.

"She tried to get me to follow her into the historical fiction section," David teased, his eyes smiling.

"That brazen hussy!" Chloe hissed comically. The woman probably did try to drag her boyfriend into that darkest corner, but she didn't have a chance. The adoration in David's eyes was unmistakable. Chloe opened her mouth to make an additional comment, but David sat up with a jerk at the sound of keys jingling in the front door.

"You'll be meeting a friend of mine tonight." David came to his feet and stepped to the threshold. "Javier's brother, Roman."

Chloe stood as well and smiled, but inside her wheels began turning as in days past. David, Javier, and now Roman? For six weeks, ever since she read this weird novel entitled *The Rabbit*, she'd been making wild comparisons between the novel's characters and her friend's life. David and Javier reminded her of two characters from the book; the physical resemblances alone freaked her a little when she first noticed them. But each time she really considered her suspicions, she was more convinced that the author, Beth Rider-Stone, knew her friend David and his roommate personally and modeled her characters after them.

David was odd enough by himself, but when she met Javier—weird with a capital W. He was good-looking in a dangerous way, with blazing green eyes that she could barely meet without blushing. His wavy near-black hair touched his collar and he had dark, almost bronze skin. Most suspicious of all was that Javier only wore black. Did he not own a single white T-shirt or pair of blue jeans?

If she had to peg his ethnicity, she'd put him in with her lab partner, Zoli. He once told her his people were Gypsies from the Balkans, and Javier could be Zoli's brother. But where her lab partner was funny, articulate, and completely transparent, David's roommate was brooding and pessimistic. Although never overtly rude, Javier's eyes lingered too long on Chloe's figure for propriety. And now, she would meet his so-called brother.

"Roman's smart," David offered and shuffled down the front hall "You'll like him."

Chloe couldn't put a finger on it, but David's inflection gave her the impression that he was making it up as he went along. While she waited on the kitchen threshold, she straightened her sweater and fluffed her long dark brown curls.

When the door opened and David stepped back, she caught Javier's eye first. He gave her a purposefully tiny glance and then looked away before stepping past her and heading into the living room. Chloe rolled her eyes as the man with him, Roman, shook hands with David, pulled him into a quick hug, and threw her a genuine smile.

"So is this the woman who has stolen your heart?" Roman teased and Chloe could see that David was not offended. "What a charming little girl."

"This is Chloe Bushman. Chloe, Roman." David introduced them, and then finished the introductions whilst looking into the man's face. "Javier's big brother."

"Javier, did you hear that?" Roman chuckled and stepped past David to reach for Chloe's hand. "We're brothers now."

She put her fingers in his and like a character from a turn-of-the-century romance novel, he kissed the back of her hand. Roman seemed old-fashioned in other ways too. Even though he wore an expensive tailored suit, his hairstyle, wire-framed glasses, and lack of wrinkles made her think of the black and white movies of days gone by. Plus, he smelled nice. Chloe didn't recognize the scent, but he was wearing some killer cologne and her cheeks reddened as he returned her hand.

"You've always been brothers, Elder—" David stopped and glanced at Chloe who looked at him wide-eyed. Roman smiled and David repeated himself a little too loudly. "You're his elder brother." David followed him into the living room. "What's up? Everything okay?"

Roman reached the sofa where Javier had collapsed, and he looked at both of the men in turn, and then at Chloe. "Family business."

Chloe was unwanted. She puzzled a second about David nearly addressing Roman as "Elder," as the Wraiths did in that woman's novel, but it was time for her to leave. She reached for her purse on the kitchen table and David was at her side when she grabbed it up.

"I'm sorry, sunshine. I didn't think." David touched her cheek and then withdrew abruptly, his eyes sad. Chloe smiled to reassure him and in the distance, she saw Roman ruffle Javier's hair affectionately as he sat beside him on the couch. They spoke close, face-to-face, checking her position periodically. It was very familiar; like a scene from that book. Without thinking, Chloe blurted out her question.

"Dave, have you ever heard of Beth Rider-Stone?" She was watching the two in the living room and when she looked back, David's face had paled considerably. "What? Have you heard of her?"

"Rider-Stone?" David repeated and then turned to glance at the two men in the living room. They were still conversing privately and he turned back to Chloe, fully recovered. "I don't think so."

Chloe tilted her head to the side. "She wrote a book that I think you should read."

David stumbled over his reply as Javier spoke up from the living room.

"Dave, we're going to talk in my room."

Chloe watched Javier and Roman get to their feet and disappear around the edge of the wall. She returned her gaze to David, but he had reentered the kitchen and was stacking dishes in the dishwasher.

"Is something wrong?" She reached him and put her hand on his forearm. At first he looked at it unseeing, lost in thought, but then he looked into her face and forced a smile.

"No. Nothing at all. Just a little tired."

"You want me to go?" Chloe started to back away, but David stopped her with his hand on her shoulder.

"No. Come here." He pulled her to him and pecked her cheek before cautiously kissing her lips. Chloe returned the move and wondered about his behavior in the back of her mind.

Surely he had nothing to do with the novel. The odds were astronomical that the author knew him well enough to copy him for her book. But if it was a coincidence, why did David freak out when she mentioned Beth Rider's name?

David's kiss deepened and he held her close. Chloe flushed but wasn't concerned. She'd come for some attention, and she hoped it would go on and on.

TWELVE

Chloe was locked in David's embrace as a knock sounded on the threshold behind her. She opened her eyes languidly, and her cheeks reddened at Javier's stern expression.

"You have your own room for that," Javier said to his roommate and flicked his eye at Chloe.

David stepped out of Chloe's arms, ran his hand across his mouth, and shrugged noncommittally. "You guys need me?"

"Roman's making some calls in my room. Hey, you." Javier gestured to Chloe and she raised her eyebrows. "I finished that movie you loaned us."

"*Vampires Anonymous?*" Chloe asked and he nodded.

"If you can untangle yourself for a minute, I'd like to ask you about it."

Javier's voice was hard and Chloe couldn't tell if he was irritated, anxious or both. Maybe Roman brought bad news. She took a step for the doorway thinking David would join them in the next room. When he didn't move, she looked to him to ask why. Javier spoke up, his voice laced with impatience.

"He didn't watch it, Miss Bushman. He refused," Javier said and left the room.

Chloe looked at David questioningly. "I thought you wanted to see it."

David shook his head. "I don't watch horror movies."

His self-righteous tone was uncharacteristic and Chloe scoffed.

"It wasn't a horror film. It's a comedy. I laughed my head off."

"Vampires, Miss Bushman!" Javier's voice reached them from the other room. "He hates vampire movies. Now, please come here."

Chloe frowned and moved toward the door. It was awkward leaving David in the kitchen, but he'd crossed his arms and planted his feet. Sighing, Chloe rolled her eyes and went to join Javier. David's housemate sat on the near end of the large sofa and when their eyes met, he patted the cushion beside him.

"What do you like most about this movie?"

"Why?" Chloe sat on the couch, but allowed plenty of space between them. Javier held the DVD case outward so she could see the cover. "It's not rocket science. It's just funny."

"Do you like vampire movies in general?" Javier asked her, this time lowering his voice just slightly in deference to David in the kitchen.

"I guess. Why? Did you like the movie?"

"No," Javier answered abruptly and tossed the box to land in her lap. "My question for you is this: if vampires were real and a really cute one asked for your blood, would you give it up?"

"Javier! What are you doing?"

It was David and he entered the room at a jog, stopping at Javier's left. His face was red and his fists clenched. It was the first time Chloe'd seen him in such a state, and she sat up straight and tried to calm him.

"It's okay, Dave. We're only talking."

"Javier, just stop." David lowered his chin and threatened Javier sitting near her on the couch. Javier's response was to lean back into the cushion and smile.

"Miss Bushman, you'd do it, wouldn't you?"

Javier didn't look at her, but she answered anyway, still watching David stare down his friend.

"Yeah, I guess. If it didn't kill me. Sure." Chloe looked between both men and goose pimples broke out up her arms. "Why does it matter? It's not real. It's just fun. It's just fantasy."

"*Your* fantasy?"

"I warned you!" David lunged for Javier and grabbed his shirtfront. Javier didn't resist and David yanked him hard to his feet.

"I've heard just about enough from you on this subject, brother!"

"I'm just seeing if my assertions are right, Davey. I pegged that girl from the beginning. She's one of them. Even like this, you attract them like flies!" Javier laughed derisively and David slapped him hard across the cheek.

"Shut up!"

Chloe came to her feet and covered her mouth. David was inflamed and Javier didn't lift a finger to protect himself. He allowed the younger man to shove him violently backward, and then he grinned and caught Chloe's eye.

"His blood is up now, isn't it?" Javier huffed as David shoved him hard, this time into the drywall. A framed photo rattled when he did so. Javier only laughed again. "Don't bring anymore vampire movies over here, Miss Bushman. David here just can't handle it."

"SHUT UP!" David slugged Javier across the jaw and pushed him into the wall again, this time simultaneously releasing his shirt. A drop of bright red blood slipped from a cut on Javier's lip as he regained his balance.

Free of David's grip, he took a step forward finally to retaliate. Smiling with a mad glint in his eye, he stuffed his fists with David's shirt as the bedroom door behind them opened.

"Javie, David, that's enough."

It was Roman, his voice low and controlled. His face was calm, but his gaze intense as he focused on the raucous pair before him. Chloe took two steps for the hallway as Javier released David and straightened his shirt.

"Yes, sir," Javier mumbled and David nodded, his mouth turned down, his chest heaving. Roman turned his gaze to Chloe and caught her eye.

"I apologize, Miss Bushman. This is embarrassing." Roman popped both men on the head as he passed and came toward her. "Perhaps you'll allow me to see you home."

"Uh, no, thank you," Chloe said. Every passing second, the characters from the Rider novel came to her mind. But each time, she pooh-poohed the crazy notions that tried ever so hard to barge into her consciousness. "I drove, Mr. Roman. Thank you."

"Just Roman, please. Allow me to escort you to your car. These children," he glared at Javier and David who were scowling at each other, "are over-tired and we have a big day tomorrow. I apologize again for their unseemly behavior."

Chloe nodded hesitantly and backed into the hallway before turning for the door. By the time she'd grabbed her purse from the dinette, Roman was shrugging on his dark knee-length overcoat. Awkward and uncertain of what to say, Chloe allowed him to pull open the door, and she ducked under his arm into the night air. Once they had cleared the front stoop, the tall and willowy Roman stepped up beside her as she walked and put his arm across her shoulders. Chloe tensed but didn't object. So far, Roman was no odder than David and Javier. She'd become quite familiar with their brand of eccentricity.

"Are you okay? Have you never seen David lose his temper?" Roman's voice was gentle and when she didn't answer, he added, "Did he frighten you?"

"No, it's not that. It's nothing." Chloe stepped a little faster and Roman slowed her pace with his hand on her opposite shoulder.

"David would never hurt you, or anyone for that matter. I feel I need to tell you that. Your expression alarmed me back there."

"Tell me this. What was he so mad about?" Chloe stopped walking and turned to face Roman in the well-lit parking lot.

Roman's arm slipped from around her and he clasped his hands before him, his chin lowered. He didn't offer a reply and Chloe stomped her foot.

"If someone doesn't like vampire movies, so what? Big fat hairy deal! Why pitch such a fit?" Frustrated with her inability to find the right words, Chloe stomped her foot again. She swished her long hair off her shoulder pouting, knowing she resembled a spoiled child to the suave and sophisticated gentleman. It couldn't be helped and she took on a pleading expression. "Dave isn't insane, is he? Please tell me he's not insane."

Roman smiled a second, then laughed out loud. "No. Not any more than the rest of us."

Chloe tightened her lips and shoved her hands into her jeans pockets. The guy was smoothing things over. Didn't Beth Rider have a character like him, too? As she recalled the details of the novel, Roman removed his glasses to clean them and she gasped.

Storm gray eyes. Reddish brown hair that just reached his shoulders. Round spectacles.

Just like in the novel.

"He used to be a Wraith, didn't he?" Chloe whispered and watched a small grin touched the corners of Roman's mouth.

"A Wraith? Where did you hear such a word?"

"More like where did I *read* such a word. I read a book by a woman named Beth Rider-Stone. She described the three of you to a T. You're the Elder who raised Javier, and David is the guy that went to the author's house looking for the Rabbit." Chloe couldn't tell what Roman thought of her suppositions, but he was listening intently and had not laughed her off.

"So, you're putting two and two together and decided your boyfriend was a Wraith?"

A knife of doubt sliced through Chloe's mind. Now, she sounded like a nut.

"David doesn't like vampire movies because it reminds him of his past," she said matter-of-factly. This time, Roman's eyes definitely opened slightly. She had hit on something and the guy was denying nothing.

"Miss Bushman, David is the one to speak with about these things." Roman turned her by her shoulder and got the two of them moving. "We're leaving town tomorrow on family business, but when we return, ask him. Perhaps he will speak to you on these matters."

"Are you saying I'm right?" Chloe asked softly and stopped in front of her cherry red VW Beetle.

"I'm saying that this is a private matter between the two of you." Roman opened her door and waited for her to slide into the driver's seat. "Do you have feelings for David?"

"Yeah," Chloe retorted without reservation.

"Then, when we return you'll have much to share." Roman closed the door and turned to leave. Chloe switched on the car and let down her window.

"Where are you guys going, anyway? Is everything okay?" She watched him step away at a leisurely pace and he did not respond to her question. "Roman? Is everything okay?"

Without another word, he reached David's front door and entered the house. Chloe slumped over the steering wheel and released the pent up air from her lungs. What did it mean? If her questions were preposterous, the guy would have acted accordingly. But he took all of her outrageous questions in stride. What did it mean? What *could* it mean? There was only one explanation. As far as Roman was concerned, David may have been a Wraith at one time. A blood-sucking, immortal undead thing.

Chloe shivered and put her hands to her neck, Javier's question coming back to her. Would she voluntarily give blood to a vampire? Like the Cows in the Rider woman's novel? She had said yes, but now… Chloe put the car in reverse but didn't move. She'd said yes, but in real life? No way, José.

Still frowning, and suddenly cold, Chloe turned on the heater and backed out of the parking spot. The Cows in *The Rabbit* were crazy. Chloe was *not* crazy. She'd *never* be a Cow. Even if the Wraiths turned out to be for real, and the novel was not fiction at all, she'd never let anyone drink her blood. Bile rose in her throat as the thought passed and she shook her head. No way, José.

Thirteen

Jackson, MS,
November 3rd, 3:00 a.m.

Rufus watched with interest as Dimple half-dragged, half-carried Father Damien into the room. Things were finally falling into place; the last of his plans coming to pass. Only a few small odds and ends remained to tie off, and he could see his future forming before his eyes: the entire Rakum race reunified and re-empowered, and owing it all to Rufus Delouve. The preparations were tightly orchestrated, and even though Gage and Tyson failed to bring in the old guy, Dimple managed—and by himself.

Dimple served as a lieutenant under a large mook of an Elder named Yosef before the misery of the Rabbit's interference. When he answered Rufus's call to arms, the big Rakum went right to work. He preferred to work alone, but he did so quickly and without complaint. For the moment, Dimple was entering the study, holding the ancient Father up by his overcoat. He stopped a respectable fifteen feet away from his master.

"Anything else, Elder Rufus?" Dimple spoke with a thick Cajun accent that belied his fair skin and nearly translucent pea-green eyes. Rufus was unexpectedly curious.

"How old are you?"

"Cracked two hundred last year, sir."

"How did you avoid that mess Yosef fell into?" Rufus asked, ignoring Damien's pained questioning glares. The guy was hurting and that was a pretty sweet reward in itself.

"Got no tolerance for insurrection, Master. As soon as I saw him turning his back on his people, I blew the whistle," Dimple said, shaking Damien back and forth. "Told this sack about it first. Ironic, eh?"

Rufus grinned and nodded. Dimple opened his fist and the Father tumbled to the carpet. A decent healer, but not much of a diagnostician, Rufus wondered at the extent of the old guy's maladies. Dimple had buzzed off the guy; that much was evident by the raw wound visible at his throat, but what else? He was old for a mortal— was he on medication? The thought made Rufus chuckle.

"Father Damien, what's it like? Have a lot of pain, do ya?" Rufus teased. He didn't approach the man despite a strong urge to remove his head. What was stopping him?

"Rufus, my son, you look bad. Really bad," the old Father mumbled his words, his eyes unfocused.

Rufus laughed and gestured for Dimple to bring him closer. Dimple grabbed Damien's shoulder with one beefy paw and dragged him bodily across the floor. Rufus had beaten the defeated Father Theophilus within an inch of his life, but seeing the great Damien so mishandled brought joy to his heart. Life under the Ten Fathers was a living hell. He didn't know it then, but now that he'd tasted freedom, he realized what power-hungry and selfish creatures the Rakum Fathers were. It was good to be in charge for a change.

Dimple stopped three feet away and released the man once more. Damien landed hard on his hip and moaned. Rufus didn't think he could walk much less rise to his feet.

"You need a cane, grandfather?" Rufus teased and enjoyed the look of misery on Damien's face. His former patriarch was humiliated and afraid, which was a glorious turn of events.

"*I failed,*" Damien said under his breath. "*I messed up. Please help Javier…please protect Isaac…I'm sorry I tried to run.*"

After several long moments of staring at the old man's lips, Rufus tried to decide to whom he was speaking. Without an ounce of couth, Dimple cleared his throat and said plainly, "He's praying, Master. You should stop him."

Rufus gave the lieutenant a blank look. Why should he care if Damien prayed? No one was listening. There was no god to call upon. All they had was their flesh, and Damien had dumped his for an empty promise from an empty religion.

"When Elder Yosef prayed, things happened," Dimple announced, his voice flat.

"I don't see how." Rufus reached for Damien's chin. Inches before he made contact, a pain shot up his back and pierced the base of his skull. Rufus snapped to attention and rubbed his spine with both hands. The sensation lasted only a millisecond, but it was enough to awaken his every nerve.

"It'll pass, master. Shocked me twice already. It's the praying. It's magic." Dimple's poker face never changed as Rufus considered his explanation. Yosef's former lieutenant was large, broad-chested and tall—perhaps he could handle a few of those jabs to his nervous system. Rufus could not.

He stepped back and motioned with his hand. "Put him downstairs."

Dimple reached for Damien's shoulder and lifted him off the ground. There was a stifled pop, and the old father yelped once before clenching his jaw and falling silent. A smile toyed with the edge of Rufus's mouth. Damien's shoulder was dislocated. Served him right for casting spells in the presence of his new king.

When Dimple was gone, Rufus walked to his wide floor-to-ceiling window and looked at the night sky. Beryl and Meryl were off to collect the Rabbit's crew. A few of their subordinates were off to collect the rest of the loose ends. Things were indeed going to plan. Rufus's stomach growled and he rubbed his palms together. His system no longer tolerated solid food, and there was no human to feed on tonight. Rufus thought over his collection of available Rakum. Only Dimple was untouched by the dead buzz. He would have to do.

◆◆◆

Damien suppressed a groan as Dimple manhandled him to the basement door and shoved him through the opening. Thankfully, his hand found the metal railing as the door closed behind him and he didn't sprawl down the stairs. Damien took a deep breath, winced as his wrenched shoulder reminded him of his injury, and shuffled carefully down the steps.

At the bottom, he paused to catch his breath and look about the dark space. Other than traces of light filtering in beneath the hall door, the room was enveloped in gloom. Damien heaved his weight from the railing to the other wall and felt for a light switch. When thrown, the room blossomed into a hazy yellow glow. He immediately recognized his former contemporary sitting on the floor close by.

"Greetings, Theophilus," Damien stated without approaching. The man was a Rakum Father and that alone garnered a great deal of caution now that Damien was human.

"Dah-mien, béke. Jó dolog látni az arcát."

Damien nodded slowly. The Father spoke to him in Hungarian; had greeted him with peace and expressed joy at seeing him in the flesh. Damien considered his reply and answered as truthfully as he could.

"It is good to see you alive."

"*Alive* is relative," Theophilus shrugged, moving as if his veins were thick with syrup instead of blood. Carefully and methodically, he rose to his feet by rolling onto his knees and then bracing against the wall to hoist himself upward. Damien stayed put, unwilling to show fear or alarm. The man before him was not much older than he, and they'd ruled side-by-side for almost two thousand years. Damien saw no other option but to wait and discover the old Father's intentions.

"Damien, come close." Theophilus leaned his right shoulder against the wall and held out his left hand, palm down.

Damien swallowed and considered the familiar time-wrinkled face obscured by a grey beard peppered with the red hair of his youth.

"Eláte kontá," he repeated, this time in Greek.

Sighing resignedly, Damien supported his dangling right arm with his left hand and closed the distance between them. Theophilus's eyes were glazed and his voice slurred, but Damien recognized the Rakum's expression; the old Greek Father was willing to heal him. Damien nodded his head.

Theophilus's gaze softened at his approach. "What ails you, brother?"

"My shoulder is dislocated and my hip sprained." Damien refused to mention his chronic maladies. As he inched into Theophilus's space, gnarled fingers lighted on his painful shoulder and gripped securely. Heat flared under the Rakum's touch as the healing began.

"Lift your arm," Theophilus barked, his voice cracking.

Damien set his jaw and did as he was told.

"Lower it."

Damien relaxed his muscles to lower the arm and a new stream of electricity flowed from Theophilus's hand on his shoulder traveling down to his fingertips. When the energy finished its course, his pain was gone. Damien tested it with caution and then tried full range of motion; his shoulder was completely healed.

"Your hip." Theophilus dug his fingers into Damien's waistband and yanked him closer with surprising strength. Damien leaned back, as now their faces were only inches apart. He looked to the side as Theophilus put his free hand against his right hip.

"I admire your courage, brother," Theophilus said, his face now against Damien's throat. "I haven't fed in days."

Damien made no reply, but waited to see what he would do. If Theophilus wanted to attack him, he'd have no defense. But instead, the old Father grunted twice and shook his head.

"Cancer. The old demon is eating your bones from the inside."

Damien held his tongue. What did he expect? He'd only been mortal a week, and the sorrows of the flesh worked fast.

"You happy in this life, Damien?" Theophilus's hand remained against Damien's body, but he sought his eye. "Before I remove this malignancy, are you willing to stay and fight? Because there will be war, my friend. I see so clearly, now. I see so clearly the pain of war."

Resigned, Damien exhaled and replied, "Heal me, if you can. I have more work to do for the Creator. I will pass out of this flesh in His time, not my own."

Theophilus closed his eyes and hummed low in his throat. Damien's lids also fell and he leaned against the wall as a fiery sensation grew in his inner core. Soon, heat from a thousand fires scorched every cancer cell in his body. Damien jammed his fist into his mouth and bit down hard to prevent a scream. Then, as quickly as it began, it was over. He released a pent up breath and wiped the tears from his cheeks.

"It is done, old friend. Now, give me some room. That despicable pup upstairs finds great pleasure in starving me." Theophilus sank to the ground and cast his eyes to the floor. Damien backed two steps and went to his knees.

"How did he subdue you? I don't understand."

Theophilus shrugged. "It is not difficult to vanquish a slave. I served Abroghia with my entire being. I lost myself in him eons ago. Before you were yet inaugurated into the Chamber of Fathers, I promised my soul to that devil."

"I served him, too—" Damien offered and was cut off.

"No. You served him, but I was owned by him. You know this. All of you knew this."

Damien nodded his head wearily. He was speaking of his choices. "You chose Abroghia over the Man from Nazareth."

"Aye." Theophilus lowered his regal head.

"Old friend, that same Man lives in me. He is alive. The kingdom of God is near you once again. You have another chance to receive His promise. His gift of life eternal."

"You speak as a child, brother. I have made my choice."

"God forgives, Theophilus. Consider my words. God forgives. I promise to you right now, in the name of Y'shua, the King of all creation, that if you ask Him to forgive you—He will. Do it. Before the war. Consider my words." Damien leaned in to press his point and Theophilus sneezed and backed into the wall.

"Give me some room, brother, or give up your blood."

Damien scooted away, but the man had heard his words. Now God could do His part.

FOURTEEN

Radnor, TN
November 3rd, 10:00 a.m.

Marcy lay with her back to her lover, snuggled into his embrace, and stared at nothing in the dim light of the bedroom. Johnny Cash belted out a tune next door. A cat meowed adamantly in the apartment above. A cold November rain sloshed against her painted-over windows. The occasional sound of car horns reminded her that outside their four walls, people were going and coming, eating and drinking, playing and working as they did every day. She was here in bed with Canaan from sunup to sundown as if she, too, needed to avoid daylight, but she chose this life. Canaan never forced or even suggested to her that she leave with him and be his mate. It was her choice.

Sure, he had a way with words, and his eyes spoke volumes, but Marcy had joined Canaan because she was in love with him. Now, forty years later, her Adonis was still by her side. She was forever comforted by the sound of his rhythmic breathing and the reassuring feel of his strong arm draped across her waist.

Marcy glanced down to her middle and studied his knuckles bent into the soft mattress; fingers that could kill a man with very little effort, yet brought her only pleasure and security.

His hand opened and touched her upper arm, stroking it tenderly. He was waiting for her to speak, to share about her night, or maybe to vent. He hated when she bottled up her emotions, but how could she tell him how she felt? Work was crappy, as it was every night. Her job was interminably boring; the chance to chase criminals and unholster her firearm was the only thing that kept her going in day after day.

"Relax. Work time is over. This is *my* time."

Marcy grunted, but didn't turn. Canaan didn't ask for much, just small amounts of attention a few times a week. He was as faithful as

84

an old dog. Why did he care about her? He'd lived centuries and could have anyone on the planet. What did he see in her? Marcy sighed and Canaan stroked her hair.

"What's bugging you?"

Marcy bit her lip, thankful that Canaan had lost his telepathic prowess. Before the Rabbit fiasco, he was constantly in her head and her privacy was nil. But now, he read only her countenance and was understandably frustrated by his loss of ability.

"Talk to me."

Marcy turned a few degrees until she could make out his silhouette. A black flames-and-barbed-wire tattoo covered his entire shoulder from his neck, down his left arm to his fingertips. Like all Rakum, Canaan was perfect and unblemished—not a freckle, spot, or the slightest fault could be found on him anywhere. Smooth skin, a strong jaw balanced with intelligent eyes, and a healthy crop of feathery blond hair. He was an angel, an earthbound god. And what was she? A farmer's daughter with a lisp and a crooked leg.

Before she realized what had happened, a fat tear slipped down her cheek and Canaan pulled her onto her back.

"I can't hear your thoughts, but I can see. Stop it, right now. You promised me you wouldn't do this, remember?"

Marcy nodded with a single jerk, mentally commanding her emotions to get in check. Canaan knew her as a stout-hearted, capable woman. She reluctantly met his eyes in the dark room and he looked back with adoration in his gaze.

But why her?

Canaan wiped her tears with gentle fingers. "In 1770, I snatched a princess. Did I tell you that story?"

Marcy shook her head and held his gaze. He often redirected her pain with tales of his past.

"I'm British, you know," Canaan said and put on his accent, the same one she knew he'd weaned himself of over the last century as he blended into American society. Marcy smiled at the comical sound and he continued, exaggerating for her amusement. "And my master dared me to enter the Buckingham House where the king sent his family on retreat. My mission was to steal away with one of the princes."

"Who was king then?"

"George III. He had eight children at the time. Jack Dawn was my master—you remember me telling you about him?"

Marcy nodded and frowned. Before they met, Canaan admitted to being quite a monster. At 1200-years-old, Dawn was one of the Rakum's oldest Elders and the most violent of the bunch. She'd even met him once at Assembly years back. She was glad he was dead.

"Yes, you remember him," Canaan joked, seeing her face darken. "He gave us Brits quite a bit of leash, and the night he sent me into the palace, I found the children's rooms and intended to bring out the oldest prince to *er*...play with the boys."

"Canaan, is this going to be gross?" Marcy warned, hoping his story had a point.

Canaan laughed, "No, I wanted to tell you about the princess. I intended to bring out the boy, and I knew which bed he occupied because of my surveillance the night before. So, I scooped him into my arms covers and all, and stole out the window – I jumped down three stories. Pretty good, eh?"

"And then?" Marcy asked, prodding him along.

Canaan chuckled, "When I handed the screaming child to my master, he pulled back the sheet, and it was a girl. The kids had changed rooms. I had grabbed the oldest princess, Charlotte."

"You gave her to that monster?"

"Of course. But my master chastised me, had me look upon her, terrified and perfect, beautiful and defenseless, and he told me to leave her be."

Marcy was confused. "Why would he do that? You always described him as a total miscreant."

"That's a bit harsh," Canaan chastised, smiling, "he taught me well. No, his reasons were thus: taking blood from a princess was only profitable if she *offered* it. He and I could have taken our fill and left her to die, but her resistance affected her blood. It was not worth the trouble."

"You let her go?" Marcy was unconvinced.

"I didn't say that," Canaan chuckled. "The point is, Jack taught me that taking forced donations from females tainted the blood."

"Why did you tell me that story? Is it supposed to make me feel better?"

Leaning on his right side to face her, Canaan reached forward and grasped Marcy's wrist. "You remember the first time you gave me your blood?" He brought her arm to his mouth and kissed her hand.

Marcy shivered involuntarily. She had given her blood freely to Canaan that night, and any other time he asked her.

"You're my princess, Marcy. You are perfect and beautiful. You are the only you in the whole world, and you're the only you there will ever be. To top it off, you were made for me." Canaan kissed her wrist and pulled her close until his lips brushed her forehead. "I told you that story to illustrate this fact: without you, there would be no me. We are joined together. I can't imagine life without you, and when you leave this earth, I'm leaving, too."

"Canaan, don't talk like that. That's just stupid." Marcy regretted her words when she read the pain in her lover's eyes.

"Stupid? Then so be it."

"I'm sorry. I mean, you've lived so long and you'd probably go on forever if we'd never met. If you really feel this way, wouldn't I be guilty of killing you?"

Canaan shrugged. "We are a Greek tragedy. The god and the mortal, locked together in love and destiny."

"Tragic, huh?" Marcy laughed without smiling.

"Do you believe I am a god, Cee? Do you believe in me? In what I am capable of?" Canaan had lowered his voice and she strained to hear him, "If I told you that I could make you immortal, would you believe me?"

Marcy narrowed her eyes at his secretive tone. "What are you talking about?"

"I'm aware of a ritual that would render you immortal. I'd like you to consider enduring it…for my sake. Will you?" Canaan's voice wavered and Marcy knew he was serious.

"Canaan," she said, raising her hands to cup his cheeks, "I want to grow old and die. Granted, I want to do so in your arms, but I don't want to live forever. Life is hard and dirty and painful."

"It doesn't have to be. Look at me. Free, strong, and immortal. I want that for you."

Marcy sighed, still smiling sadly. "I'm looking forward to going to the next world, honey."

"What world is that, Cee?"

"I don't know, but it'll be different." Marcy pecked him tenderly on the lips and he responded. She giggled through a few passionate kisses and pushed away.

"Where're you going, princess?" Canaan mumbled in his put-on accent and buried his face in her neck.

"Canaan, did you get that buzz you needed tonight?" Marcy said, still giggling, and Canaan pulled back to meet her gaze. "Did you go to the Shell Zone?"

She watched his eyes as he nodded and read the unspoken offer in her eyes. Sure, he didn't take her blood anymore to protect her health. *But once in a while should be okay...* Marcy smiled and blushed.

"Marcy Haddle, you feeling generous?" Canaan brought his fingers to the pulse in her neck.

Marcy reached behind her and rifled through the bedside table drawer without looking. When she pulled out the small pocketknife, her old lover's eyes widened, looking exactly as he did that first night four decades ago when she was sixteen and a willing princess to a Rakum prince. The most wonderful creature she had ever seen.

She handed Canaan the knife and unlike a thumbnail, it sliced clean. He was gentle, just as he was then, and when he was done, he'd sew up her laceration with his touch. He was a healer. Like all gods, he took care of his own.

FiFTEEN

Montgomery, AL
November 3rd, 3:00 p.m.

Two days had passed since they'd seen Beryl and Meryl in the yard and the house had been thankfully quiet since. Perhaps the twins realized the futility of their efforts to harm Beth's family. Surely, God didn't pull them through hell seven years ago only to turn them into Rakum food today. Beth sighed and hoped she would not have to face the Rakum again. *Ever.*

Three o'clock arrived and Beth watched out her front window for Selene and Dae Lee. Selene met Jesse Cherrie as a Rakum during the nightmare that ended up finishing off the strength of the Rakum race. Beth didn't have the entire story, but she surmised that Selene started as a mate to one of the Elders before ending up in Jesse's gentle arms. Today, Jesse was human, residing with his family in Birmingham, ninety miles away. He spent many days of the week away from home with business ventures that spanned the globe. Tonight, Selene and their five-year-old daughter, Dae Lee, were coming to stay over while Jesse was in Europe overseeing the sale of one of his companies.

Beth looked forward to Selene's visit for Grace's sake, but the woman herself was a hard nut to crack. Drop-dead gorgeous with the face of a Nigerian princess, Selene seemed like a woman with everything. She had a husband who worshiped the ground she walked upon, a child in perfect health with a wonderful disposition, and thanks to Jesse's keen business sense, all the money she could ever need. But it was Selene's unhappiness that Beth found exasperating. She'd spend much of their time together biting her tongue. Also, Selene didn't take well to instruction. It was difficult for her to lend her ear to anyone with an opposing view.

Beth sighed and sipped her tea. Then with a glint of sun off a polished fender, Selene's white Lexus rounded the corner by their neighborhood sign.

"Dae Lee is here!" Beth called and upstairs, her daughter squealed. The girls were as close as sisters and she soon heard the happy sounds of her daughter clomping down the steps.

"Is she wearing her bow? I told her to wear her bow. Her daddy gave it to her last week, and she said she'd let me wear it today!" Grace hurried past carrying two large dolls.

Beth smiled and moved aside so Grace could see out the floor-to-ceiling window. The car stopped behind her Honda and the driver got out with purpose and poise. Selene was tall, slender, and elegant with a voluptuous black weave cascading down her back like an onyx waterfall. She leaned into the backseat to unbuckle her daughter and then turned toward the house, meeting Beth's eye. Surprise, surprise. She wasn't smiling. Dae Lee trotted for the front door and Grace pulled it open as she arrived.

"Daily!" Mispronouncing her name out of habit, Grace handed over the blonde-haired, blue-eyed doll in her right hand. She kept the dark brown one with the curls for herself and pulled her friend toward the stairwell. "Going to my room, mommy!"

To look at the girls, you'd think them as opposite as their dolls, but they had everything in common. Beth tried not to ponder their likeness: that both of them had former Rakum for fathers. Instead, she brought to mind their mothers and their God who brought all of them together.

Selene cleared her throat and Beth turned to give her a hug. The less demonstrative Selene murmured her greeting, slipped free of the embrace, and led the way to the living room.

"What a mess—that traffic!" Selene swished her long hair off her right shoulder and dropped her Coach handbag on a nearby side table. "Jesse said you had those evil twins over here." Selene's voice was mellow and sultry as she sauntered over to the sofa. "Please tell me he was joking."

"I wish I could," Beth said and gestured to the couch. "Is that why he sent you here? Is he headed back to the States? Are the boys working up a plan?" Beth poured Selene some tea and watched her eyes. She suspected Jesse opened up much more to his wife than her own husband did. But then, Selene had entered their relationship as a willing blood donor,

"Jesse told me everything. He has it on good authority that the Rakum are regrouping under an Elder who could make trouble for the rest of us. He said it could get ugly." Selene sipped her tea and dabbed her lips with the napkin. Beth shook her head.

"God in heaven. I thought that nightmare was behind us."

Beth leaned into the soft couch and closed her eyes. When she answered God's call seven years ago and brought all of the Rakum to bear with the words of Life, she'd hoped that was the end of it. Over the last eighteen months, fewer and fewer Rakum turned to them for help or sanctuary. Beth had started to believe that it was over, that the Rakum were gone for good. Selene's prophetic words caused Beth's eyes to water.

"Sweetie, the boys will protect us. Don't worry."

"You know they're just men now. They're no match against those who escaped that night." Beth's voice was hard, but she was unable to soften her tone. "I have to believe that God didn't pull us through seven years ago just to let us be conquered now."

"Unless their killing us brings about His purposes, right? Isn't that your gospel?"

Selene's voice carried a hint of sarcasm, but Beth squelched her offense. Jesse, Michael, and Selene had subjected themselves to her teaching as she shared with them the truth about God. Now, Selene was using her own words against her and Beth had no recourse. God's saints were often murdered in the course of working His will, but how could she explain the significance of that teaching while so utterly panicked? She couldn't.

Beth cast her eyes to the ground. "So what're they going to do?"

"Jesse and Michael are going to find them and confront them."

Beth pounded the sofa armrest with her fist. "I wish they'd consult us first. We have the girls to think about. We need to pray about it—all of us, together. It'd be just like them to go off half-cocked and forget who to trust."

Selene set down her cup and relaxed, her stylish pastel-yellow dress perfectly complementing her smooth chocolate brown skin. "I trust Jesse," she sighed. "He'll do what's best for our family. You should have more faith in your husband."

Beth met her eye and tried to smile. Was her faith in Michael insufficient? God had given her Michael Stone as a husband and father to her child and would surely empower him to guide the family on righteous paths.

"I'm sorry," Beth exhaled, "You're right. I'm freaked out that the twins came here." Beth shivered. "Beryl was one of those that attacked me, you know, when Jack tried to kill Michael." Memories of being pressed into the cold leather seat of the Rakum's limousine as four of the brethren drank from her at once surfaced unbidden.

Selene's focus went soft. "Meryl's no better, trust me."

She offered no more, but Beth imagined the fair twins took advantage of Selene in every way imaginable before Jesse spirited her away from the Cave that night.

"They all need to burn." Selene's eyes flashed now, as her own nightmarish memories poured in. "Jesse and Michael were the lucky ones. Lucky that they weren't blinded by the lust for blood and sex and..." Selene choked on her words and lowered her voice. "The Rakum are evil. I hope every last one of them burns in hell."

Beth exhaled and the room fell silent. Selene looked uncomfortable now, memories better left buried eroding her previously calm demeanor. When the clock on the mantle chimed the quarter-hour, they both startled.

"It has to end this time," Beth quipped. "I called Roman and told him about the twins. He's going to gather up Javier and David and bring them here. I think all the guys together can figure out a plan. I feel very strongly that you and I should stay here, at my house, set up a base camp. This house is protected and the girls will be safe here."

"You really believe that, don't you?" Selene's sarcastic tone stung and Beth again chose her response carefully.

"I *know* it. Beryl and Meryl couldn't enter because God is keeping them out." Beth didn't mention Grace's invisible friend, Billy, although she put a lot of stock in her daughter's unadulterated faith. As far as she knew, "Billy" was a 6-year-old's way of saying *Emunah*, an angel Beth had personal, physical experience with when she was battling the Rakum.

"Okay." Selene set down her cup and placed her hands on her lap. "I'll play along. Jesse arrives tonight in Atlanta and I'll tell him to meet me here."

"Michael will be home before dark. Roman and the boys should arrive tomorrow." Beth forced a smile, the image of Beryl's face outside her house finally fading. "I know everything will be all right." Selene nodded and sighed. The sound of giggling wafted down to them and Beth smiled. "I'm glad you're here. Thanks for coming."

"Of course. What are friends for?"

Beth grinned and hoped that in the events to come, friends didn't *die* for friends. That biblical teaching was one she hoped didn't apply to her. ...Or anyone else she knew.

SIXTEEN

Radnor, TN
November 3rd, 4:00 p.m.

The day marched toward night as Canaan watched Marcy sleep. Absolutely no light seeped through their thickly curtained and painted-over windows, but he sensed the sun as surely as he felt the cotton comforter across his hip. The sun was a hated thing; a destroyer of his kind; a monster that held him captive and restricted his movements. But what was the alternative? Burn to death? Canaan scowled; he had no suicidal tendencies.

Turn to God.

Canaan furrowed his brow at the unwelcome thought. Where it came from, he didn't know, but it wasn't any advice he'd give himself.

God.

Canaan humphed and shook his head. Many of his brethren turned to the God of the humans and lost their immortality, their vigor, and their deity. How? Whatever happened to his brothers was much more than they were letting on. Mumbling a couple of chosen phrases could change you into a mortal? Canaan swallowed. What a nightmare to wake up weak, naked and vulnerable. He grimaced and closed his eyes, still propped up on his elbow over a slumbering Marcy. The old-fashioned bedside clock clicked over to 4 p.m. and he opened his eyes.

Marcy Haddle.

In his eyes, she was still young, brave and rebellious; his perfect counterpart. She moaned in her sleep and rolled onto her back. Canaan took in the haggard lines the rotation of the planet gave her and the pale complexion in her cheeks. She'd almost taken ill this time. He'd drawn so little, but she was no longer capable of withstanding his appetite. The last time he accepted her offer, he made a mental note to make sure it was the last. But here he was again, his gut pleasantly full, looking down on her as she slept, waiting for her aging body to make up the blood she'd lost. Even with his potent Rakum Elder rejuvenation treatment, her body refused to replicate cells the way it used to. Why didn't she want to live forever?

Canaan didn't buy her reasons, not for a moment. Most likely, she just didn't believe what he promised her was true. She knew almost everything about his people, but he'd never let on to her about the marking of humans. He had never let on to her the legend of the Lost Rabbit, where a human is marked by a Rakum Elder and slowly morphs into a Rakum themselves. The Fathers assured them it had never been done, but it must have happened at least once because there were laws set in place and punishments assigned for anyone who attempted such a thing. Yet who would deal out that punishment now? If Marcy ingested Canaan's blood, then theoretically, she could join him in immortality. No one would hurt her; no one would hunt her down. The Rakum were disbanded. It was every man for himself.

Rufus Delouve.

The name came to his mind in a whisper and he shook his head. Was he a threat to her if changed? Canaan had sensed the Rakum re-gathering under the older Elder's reign, but discerned nothing else. Besides, they were far away in Mississippi; he knew that much from the rumblings of the few survivors he'd seen over the years. Would the new Rakum Brotherhood leave him alone and allow him to remain outside? Canaan had been avoiding them long before they disbanded; sneaking between the lines, living in the white space between the human world and his own. If he could stay hidden and keep Marcy hidden as well, why not mark her as a Rabbit? She wouldn't have to know. After all, it was for her own good. By the time she realized what had happened, she'd accept the idea and thank him. Hadn't he rescued her from bad decisions in the past without her knowledge? It was what he did; he took better care of her than she did of herself. *I even ended that disastrous pregnancy.*

Canaan blinked as the memory of that night came back to him. Only the Rakum Fathers were capable of procreation, so his and Marcy's relationship was childless. Marcy accepted that fact by word a few years in, but as she reached thirty and her maternal drive kicked in, she longed for a baby. When she pestered Canaan about it non-stop for six months, torturing him with long silences and a volatile disposition, he relented at last and she was artificially inseminated at the local clinic.

For six months, Marcy was in heaven. Her face glowed with joy every passing moment as the blessed event approached. But in her third trimester, something went wrong. The doctor ran test after test only to come to the undeniable conclusion that Marcy's baby would be born with Down's syndrome. Canaan expected her to schedule an abortion forthwith, but to his surprise she hugged her protruding belly and dug in with both heels, asserting that everything would be okay. Canaan could not disagree more. The best thing for Marcy was to end the pregnancy. The best thing for the baby was to save it from a life of suffering. And the best thing for Canaan was to not be tied to a woman with a handicapped child.

Two days later, as she slept beside him, peaceful and happy as a woman could be, he used his Elder abilities to stop the baby's heart. Healing was an art, murder a talent, and Canaan was an expert at both. Marcy was never the wiser.

In the morning, she had miscarried and after three months of crying, she was back to normal. Her heart was fractured, but her old countenance returned. She no longer wanted a baby and admitted some years later that the child's death had been a blessing. Since he'd known her, Canaan knew what was best for his mate.

Convinced beyond the shadow of a doubt, he slipped noiselessly out of bed and tiptoed to the bathroom where he stored a syringe acquired for this purpose; for the moment when he'd finally have the courage to take this important step.

Marcy would thank him later.

◆ ◆ ◆

Marcy screamed in agony and curled into a ball, her hands pressing firmly against her left breast. As soon as her lungs allowed, she inhaled for another scream and opened her eyes. Her heart was bursting and the pain was excruciating. The third distressed cry tapered, then slowly disappeared altogether as the pain settled into her chest cavity and faded out.

"Canaan! Canaan!" she hissed, still protectively clutching her chest. She was wide-awake now and her vision cleared steadily in the shuttered bedroom.

Canaan wrapped his arms about her from behind and kissed her hair. "What, Cee?"

"I think I'm having a heart attack!"

"Eh?"

Canaan wasn't alarmed, Marcy could tell, but why should he? He could heal any ailment with his touch. As she held her breath, he placed his hand over her heart and mumbled in her ear.

"You're fine. It was a nightmare. You're 100% healthy, Cee."

Marcy took a hesitant breath and had to agree. She felt marvelous; invigorated. Sighing, she relaxed into his embrace and closed her eyes, not bothering with the tiny sting that remained at her inner elbow. It barely registered with the horror of the earlier agony.

"Some nightmare, hell."

"Sleep, princess. One more shift and you're mine for the weekend."

Canaan nuzzled her neck and Marcy smiled cautiously, just in case the pain returned. Thankfully, it didn't and she fell off to sleep.

SEVENTEEN

Tuscaloosa, AL
November 3rd, 10:00 p.m.

Chloe covered her face with both hands as her watch beeped the hour. It was ten o'clock, the library was closing, and she hadn't heard from David since leaving his house the day before. Had Roman really taken them off on a family emergency? And if they were former Wraiths, did this family business have to do with their former people? Chloe chuckled, sat up, and collected her books. It was unreal; Roman knew she'd go bananas trying to figure out their mysterious dialogue. Perhaps that was how he got his jollies.

"Well, forget him," Chloe sighed under breath as she came to her feet, Jung's *The Red Book* and Freud's *The Interpretation of Dreams* under her arm. She looked around and caught the eye of Kiki shutting down her computer. The woman glared at her and then at the exit sign to Chloe's left. Forcing a smile, Chloe headed for the large double doors of the library.

The Gorgas library faced the gigantic quad, and up ahead in the light of a faraway streetlamp, a handful of students shuffled between buildings. A security guard zoomed past her in his golf cart and gave her a businesslike nod. He looked to be on a donut run and the thought made her smile.

Dave likes donuts.

Chloe giggled at the errant reflection, remembering how he scarfed the powdered donuts they sometimes had in the library's Java City. He only liked a handful of foods that she knew of, and he considered pastry a food group all on its own. Chloe pictured his smiling face, dotted with white sugar and his teeth gummy with dessert. He was a funny guy.

A funny guy who hates vampire movies...

Chloe scowled and dug her keys out of her purse.

Why did David freak when Javier started up with his stupid comments? Chloe stuck out her bottom lip and put her key into the lock, the yellow glow of the sodium lights glinting off her house key.

But then again, David had everything going for him, if he turned out to be normal and not a former monster. Chloe laughed to herself and shook her head, smiling.

At that moment, pain shot up her back and she opened her mouth to scream, but was mute. Her instinct to run fizzled as she realized she was also paralyzed.

The pain came again and her eyes bulged with terror as everything went black.

◆◆◆

"Careful, you idiot," Geoffrey warned Spinner, who slung the young woman into the waiting van. "She'll break."

"She's fine," Spinner hissed, hopped into the van beside the unconscious girl, and swung the door closed. "Come on. That guard won't be out forever."

Geoffrey frowned, but jogged to the driver's side and climbed into the aging Dodge. The stun-gun had been Spinner's idea and it worked like a charm. They disarmed the guard five minutes ago in his cart, and he never knew what hit him. Now this girl was putty in their hands. Technology – go figure.

He left the lot at a leisurely pace to avoid attracting attention, and when they reached the main road, he checked his companion in the mirror. Spinner had the girl in his lap, running his fingers through her hair with one hand and feeling the pulse at her neck with the other.

"Don't even think it, dude. Rufus'll kill you if you spoil that girl." Geoffrey didn't have to warn him twice. Spinner shimmied out from under her and left her lying across the rubber mat of the cargo area. He joined his partner in the front seat and kept his eyes forward.

"It's been so long since we had anything like that, Geoff. This really stinks."

"It's better than the alternative," Geoffrey responded.

They'd met the girl's boyfriend, David Walker, when he was a Rakum. Unfortunately, before they could bite the Rabbit he was with that night, a bossy and traitorous Elder incapacitated them in the bathroom of the Cave's Population. When they came to, the Assembly was over, their High Father was gone, and the world had gone to hell in a Rabbit-fur-lined hand basket.

"Remember how fierce that guy was in the Pop? He was ready to die for that Rabbit. What a nut-job," Spinner mused, shaking his head. "I wish we'd been allowed to bring him in. He's not so tough anymore."

"No, he's not. Why didn't Rufus let us bring him in then? Why are all of Rufus's rules so brainless?" Geoffrey hit the steering wheel as he spoke. "We tailed Walker all over town last week. I sat right behind him at the movies, twelve inches away. I could've snapped his neck. Why bring this girl in? It doesn't make sense."

"Makes sense to Rufus," Spinner offered in a neutral tone.

"Lookie here," Geoffrey muttered, eyes glued to the windshield. "Do you see what I see?"

Spinner leaned forward and grasped the dash. "I think that fella needs a ride, Geoff."

"By golly, I think you're right." Geoffrey turned on his signal to change lanes and pull onto the shoulder while Spinner jumped into the cargo hold and moved the unconscious girl behind the seat.

The hitchhiker walked toward them as they rolled to a stop and he smiled, waving a gloved hand. Spinner pulled open the sliding side door and put on his friendliest expression. The guy might notice his sunken eyes and sallow skin, but there was no hiding that his food of late hadn't been the most nutritious; more than once, he and Geoffrey had been forced to gnaw on the dead. But when he motioned for the guy to step up, he did so with enthusiasm and crawled in to squat on the rubber mat behind the driver's seat.

"Thanks guys, it's kinda cold to be walkin'."

"Brrr," Spinner offered and put on a shiver.

"Uh huh, it's way too cold for this time of year," the guy said, and stuck out his hand to shake with Spinner. "You guys came along just in time. My old lady kicked me right out of her car, so I'm hitchin' to the next exit. There's a hotel there where I can crash 'til tomorrow."

Geoffrey had pulled back onto the roadway and he nodded his head, catching their passenger's eye in the rearview mirror. Spinner was on his knees between the hitchhiker and the side door, his stun-gun inconveniently sitting on the front seat, out of reach. Geoffrey cleared his throat.

"Name's Geoff, that's Spin. What's yours?"

"Stan Rotich, nice to meet ya. Ya'll students here? My

girlfriend—my ex-girlfriend—is a freshman. Me, I work at the diner. I hated school as a kid, I hate it now."

"I feel ya," Geoffrey offered in a jovial tone. "Spin, why don't you show Stan your new toy? That girl in the parking lot was sure impressed by it." Spinner grinned and crawled the four feet to grab the stun-gun off his seat.

"A toy? Let me see." Their passenger eagerly leaned forward.

Weapon in hand, Spinner sidled up, whipped out the stunner and jabbed it into Rotich's middle. The man sputtered and shook a few seconds, eyelids fluttering, and then fell still.

"He's out; pull over. I'm not waiting for you." Spinner tossed the weapon aside and dug around in his pants pocket for his knife.

"There's a rest area ahead, I'll catch up. But don't go too far. Remember the rule." Geoffrey glared at Spinner in the mirror, satisfied that he recalled the edicts regarding taking the Dying Buzz. He peeked at his partner every few seconds, longing to be drinking the young man's blood, too.

One-half mile.

One-quarter mile.

When he pulled over, he'd jump in the back and join in. The van had no windows except those in the forward section. No witnesses. The stun-gun had been a good idea. The cargo van had been an excellent idea.

Geoffrey pulled off the interstate to the rest area and found a dark deserted corner to park his van. It wouldn't take long. At drawing blood, he was old hat and for a change, this one was alive.

◆ ◆ ◆

Chloe opened her eyes and stared straight ahead, trying to determine what had happened. One moment she was getting into her car, the next, she was lying in the dark watching—what *was* she seeing?

Chloe squinted and tilted her head to focus. She was in a van lying on her side on a grimy rubber mat, staring at someone on the other side of a seat. Was that a man up ahead? Chloe blinked several times and held her breath. Whatever was going on in the front of the vehicle was violent. As her vision cleared, she discerned that two men were manhandling a third only feet away. Chloe shifted her head a fraction so that she was more upright, and she saw what they were doing. The two men had their mouths pressed against the third man; one at his wrist, the other at his throat.

Omygod, they're drinking his blood!

Chloe's breath hitched, Beth Rider's book coming vividly to her memory. The two attackers had not noticed or heard her so far. As slowly as she could, she sat up, still ducking behind the only seat, and shimmied a few inches to the rear. If she could open the back doors and jump out, she might be able to run for help. She studied the handles only to find them chained and locked. Chloe sighed inaudibly and turned her attention to the side door. It slid open by use of a handle that was less than five feet away. Could she get to it before they grabbed her?

Chloe inched her way across the van until she reached the edge of the seat. A quick peek at the bloodsuckers and she could see that they were entirely engrossed in their present business. She dared one more inch, now in the aisle and possibly in their line of vision, and she saw a stun-gun lying directly before her on the floor.

That's how they got me! She thought miserably and reached for the gun. Chloe closed her fingers around the thick handle and examined the firing mechanism. It was similar to ones she'd practiced with in her self-defense class. She peered at the vampires without moving her head and gauged the distance between them.

I could get that skinny one and jump out of the van.

A plan more or less devised, Chloe gathered her nerve and her strength and then lunged. She fired the gun and jabbed it into the back of the Wraith nearest her. He screamed, arched his back, and whipped around to look at her with eyes full of fury. Chloe scuttled backward and slammed into the sliding door, feeling for the handle behind her. The other guy dropped the poor victim's wrist and came at her fast.

"GET HER!" The skinny one shouted, spitting blood. Paralyzed, he fell back against the seat, his arms seizing and jerking.

Chloe's hand found the door handle and she pushed it down. The door began to slide open as she shoved it with her body weight, but the bigger monster reached out and grabbed her leg at the knee.

"Get back here, you tease."

The brute was smiling, red drool circulating his gory mouth as he reeled her in with a grip as strong as iron. Chloe swung the gun around to stun him, but he knocked it out of her hand with one vicious smack.

"No, thanks; I'd rather be buzzed by you than a silly old gun."

Chloe rolled over onto her belly and tried to force the door open more. She yelled for help even as her attacker reeled her back in, pulling her thigh, her waist, and finally her upper arms. Once she'd been tugged to the opposite side of the van from the door, he leaned forward to slam and lock it. The vampire returned to pin her down with a knee on the small of her back. Chloe managed only a whimper, weaker now with her breath knocked out by the move.

"You'll need to keep quiet, missy. Shhhhh."

The dark-haired monster dug into his back pocket and pulled out a yellowed handkerchief. After stuffing it into her mouth, he hauled her up, yanking her arms hard behind her back.

"Let's see," he mumbled as his hand went to the waistband of the unconscious man with the oozing wounds. "He'll not be needing this belt anymore."

Chloe struggled and watched him shimmy the guy's belt loose with one hand, controlling her with the other. When he'd pulled it free, he tossed her forward where she landed directly on top of the still-stunned Wraith who leaned stiffly against the seat. She averted her face and her cheek was pressed against the man's panting lips. Chloe squealed through her gag as the other one tied her hands to her ankles with the braided leather belt and then jerked them tight, wrenching her shoulders in the process.

"Now," the bigger Wraith said, laying her on the floorboard. "We have a long drive ahead of us and you need to be still. We might just make it home before sunup."

Chloe watched with wide eyes as he checked his fellow and then took his place at the wheel. He looked at her in the rearview mirror and she shivered at her helplessness.

"If you can be still, I'll leave you alone."

Chloe thought of David; if only he were here. She'd seen him get angry. He'd give these two monsters pause.

"I'm okay." It was the other one. He scooted up with care and stood hunched over in the van. He turned only once to glare at Chloe before slumping into the passenger seat.

Chloe's back ached from being compressed by her bonds and her hips throbbed at being over flexed. She made an attempt to free herself and the belt seemed to be slipping, but when she lay still to rest, the driver cleared his throat and caught her eye in the mirror once more.

"Look, lady, my master wants you in one piece and alive. He never said nothing about you coming in a virgin. You get me?" Chloe's eyes widened as the one in the passenger seat started to rise.

"Give her this last chance, Spin."

Chloe watched "Spin" settle back into his seat, his eyes glittering hungrily. In her desperation, she considered Javier; his soulful eyes, sad and full of unexpressed anger. He'd probably help her if he were there. And Roman, he'd help. Roman wouldn't take any guff off these guys. But they were only human.

Humans against immortal cretins.

Chloe cried softly in her bonds and closed her eyes. If anyone was going to save her, it wasn't going to be any time soon. She relied on the promise of the monsters in the van; if she was still, they'd keep their hands and their mouths to themselves. Oh, please...

ЄiGhтєєn

Radnor Oak State Park
Nashville, TN
November 3rd, 10:00 p.m.

It was too easy.

Beryl stood hidden by an enormous oak and his brother was across the clearing, kneeling behind the bushes encircling the campground. Elder Canaan's woman was at the mossy cement bench between them, puffing away on a cigarette as if she hadn't a care in the world. What kind of law enforcement officer was she? According to their online search, the woman had nearly twenty years on the job, and she didn't hear Meryl break her partner's neck a few feet away. Beryl smiled and sensed his twin chuckling.

"Just grab her, brother. What's she gonna do? Shoot you?"

Beryl nodded at his brother's mental suggestion and flexed his fingers. The night was clear, the moon almost full, and the air cold. His joints would be a lot more nimble if they'd eaten beforehand, but sometimes you had to take life as it came. Plus, they'd tap the woman. The only reason she was located so quickly was because she was marked. Why the old fool marked her was beyond understanding, but Beryl was thankful for Canaan's decision now. There was nothing in the world tastier than a recently-marked Rabbit and Rakum Rabbits didn't have to consent to be delicious. Beryl snickered at his thoughts as Meryl nudged him again telepathically.

"Shall I grab her, Beryl? Are you done contemplating the weird, wild ways of the universe?"

Beryl smirked at his brother's teasing and stepped from his hiding place. Canaan's woman had finished her smoke and was crushing it out on the heel of her boot. Beryl closed his eyes and inhaled for one last tantalizing whiff of the Rabbit's scent. Smiling, he stepped forward only to watch Meryl cross the yard invisibly fast, and grab the woman from behind.

"You snooze you lose, brother," Meryl said aloud as he whipped out his pocketknife and jabbed it into his victim's neck.

Beryl reached the pair and secured her wrists, standing nose-to-nose with her and staring her down. She opened her mouth to scream, but Meryl's hand snaked up from behind to silence her. She was easy to subdue, offering only a perfunctory struggle.

"*She's accustomed to feeding Rakum,*" Meryl mused as he drew her blood as fast as it would come.

After several long seconds with his stomach rumbling, Beryl decided Meryl was taking too long. He released one of Marcy's wrists to pop his twin on the head.

"We have all night, Meryl. Let's get her in the car. Then we'll—"

A tremendous explosion rocked the clearing and Beryl was simultaneously punched in the groin. No longer holding the woman, he staggered backward and looked down as his blue jeans turned black with blood. Confused, he looked up and Canaan's woman had a large caliber semi-automatic weapon pointed in his direction. At that moment, Meryl released her, his lips crimson and agape, his eyes wide with surprise.

"Did she shoot you? For real?" Red spittle left Meryl's mouth as he spoke and Beryl nodded, pressing his hand to his crotch. The woman yelped and ran off, but neither Rakum reacted. As Beryl grimaced and waited for the wound to begin knitting back together, he regretted more than ever that neither he nor his brother were healers.

"We've never been shot before, brother," Beryl stuttered as their telepathic connection caused his twin to double over in pain.

"*Never,*" Meryl agreed silently. "*I don't like it.*"

"*Neither...do...I...*" Beryl gasped and dropped to his knees in the wet moss. The bleeding had stopped, but the mind-numbing pain refused to let up.

A few feet away, Meryl fell to the ground and bared his teeth, not spared a fraction of the discomfort. Being attached telepathically had its drawbacks.

Acquiring Marcy Haddle would have to wait.

Beryl slipped onto his back, his hands still clutching at his wound and Meryl followed soon after. They both hoped she was too frightened to return and shoot them again.

♦♦♦

Marcy sprinted to her truck parked under the sodium lamps in the uneven gravel lot and whipped out her cell phone. Holding her gun at the ready, she stared back the way she'd come. Forty years and she'd finally fired a shot, and ironically, it was at another Rakum.

"Are you okay?" Canaan answered in a terse tone. Had he intuited her trouble? Marcy opened her mouth to answer, but he beat her to it. "Rakum?"

"How'd you know?" Marcy grumbled, assuming Canaan knew enough that he should've been there to protect her. "Where are you? Weren't you supposed to keep me safe from them? 'You'd sense if they were around', remember all that?"

"Meet me at the hut in five." *Click.*

"Canaan!" Marcy screamed into the dead handset and pulled open the driver's side door. He was nearly there, so he *did* discern something was up. But he was late.

If she hadn't shot that monster...

If he hadn't gotten distracted by his fellow...

If they hadn't stabbed her in the neck—wait. Marcy put her hand to her throat and came away with bloody fingers, yet felt no wound. She slammed the truck door and turned over the engine. Did they heal her up that fast? Before putting the truck in gear, she put her left hand to the other side of her neck, just in case, but there was no evidence whatsoever that she had been stabbed so violently five minutes earlier.

Marcy tossed the truck into drive and peeled out of the lot, headed for the communications hut. Canaan would be waiting for her there and he had a lot of explaining to do.

Canaan stood outside the quiet com shed, hands on his hips and watched Marcy's truck careen onto the asphalt and skid to a stop a few feet away. She was livid and he took a deep breath to prepare for her wrath. Hopping down from the cab, Marcy sprinted toward him and he caught the aroma of her blood—*spilled.*

Now he recognized the feeling of dread that filled his core for the past half-hour. How was he to know what the odd rumblings meant? He wasn't accustomed to determining the meaning of the miniscule nudges he felt in his subconscious; life was much easier when he was a telepath. But one of the "impressions" he had while driving out to the preserve where Marcy worked was that Jack Dawn's twin captains, Beryl and Meryl, would threaten her tonight.

The twins were nice to look at; all the brethren enjoyed their company. They could talk a human into anything and Rakum were also fairly easy prey to their wiles. To add to their eccentric nature, they willingly let their blood to the brethren; Canaan had tasted them both in the old days. But they were conniving and coldblooded, even more so than Canaan himself, and so very much like Jack had been. And considering what they had just done to his mate, their time had run out.

Satisfied with his conclusions, Canaan cracked his knuckles and welcomed an angry Marcy into his arms. He soothed her with his words and caressed her hair, but inside he was planning the best way to punish the two misfits who dared mock him. Rakum code permitted him to *end* them for defying an Elder. Canaan's mouth formed a grim line—Beryl and Meryl were history.

Canaan remained calm as Marcy leaned out of his arms and began cussing him for real, full of the spit and fire he'd come to expect.

NINETEEN

"Take me to where you left them," Canaan said, getting into Marcy's truck. He didn't wait to see if she would comply. After frowning at him from outside the vehicle, she screamed in frustration and climbed into the driver's seat.

"You said you'd know if they were near. They could've killed me!" Marcy got the truck moving and sped down the dark forest road.

Canaan held his tongue. He hadn't found the right time to tell her she was marked and that she needn't worry about such an attack.

"They're probably gone now. Why hang around? They'll crawl into the night and come get me some other time. You should have been here!" Marcy cut her eyes his way, more frightened than angry.

"I am here now," he mumbled, a little late reading the fear in her voice. He reached for her forearm, but she yanked away and wiped her face with that hand.

"Here's where I was parked." Marcy stomped the brakes and Canaan braced himself on the dash. "Right through there, third camp site. I left one of them bleeding next to the picnic table."

Canaan opened the truck door, but turned back at Marcy to catch her eye. "I sensed something was wrong and I got here as fast as I could. Look at me."

Marcy forced him to ask one more time before she looked at him sideways, tears spilling down her cheeks.

"You want me to trust you? You want me to see you as a god? Omniscient and omnipotent you aren't! They almost killed me!"

Canaan suppressed an unkind reply and said, "Stay in the truck. I won't be long." He waited for her to give him the tiniest nod. "Hand me your gun."

Marcy's expression flickered, but she yanked it from its holster and handed it over, butt first. Canaan gave her a reassuring wink and exited the truck.

He jogged into the tree line and counted the clearings. Before he reached the third, he got a whiff of Rakum blood and skidded to a halt before he broke cover. Flexing his fists, he gathered as much information as he could before making himself known. As inferiors, and relative kids at that, the twins would pose him no threat. Plus, one of them was nursing a bullet wound.

Up ahead, Beryl lay on his back moaning, his hands covering his face and not his obvious wound. Next to him, separated by a few feet of wet leaves and mud, lay Meryl mimicking his position and making similar noises. Canaan stepped from behind the bushes that hid him and swaggered toward them, the gun tucked into his belt at the small of his back.

"*Tsk, tsk*, boys. Got yourselves in a pickle, eh?"

Meryl looked up to watch Canaan approach with no attempt to rise. "I thought I smelled a rat," the weakened kid mumbled, following Canaan with his eyes.

"If you knew I was coming, you should've cleared out." Canaan reached Beryl first and booted him hard with his toe. The kid coughed with the action, then fell still again enduring the pain. Canaan kicked him again, not satisfied with his stoic response. "Which one of you tasted my Marcy? Which one of you will die first for touching what he knew belonged to me, your master?"

"The Rakum follow Rufus now," Beryl sputtered. "You no longer have authority over us."

Canaan kicked Beryl more sharply in the ribs and he yelped with new painful fractures to deal with. Taking a step around him, Canaan peered down on Meryl. Beryl's twin had dried blood on his chin, precious crimson that belonged to Canaan alone.

"You," Canaan said softly before reaching down for Meryl's jacket and hauling him to his feet. "You buzzed my princess. Oh, you should never dip your hands into another man's treasure."

"Put me down!" Meryl gasped, still recovering from his brother's wound. Canaan braced the kid against the concrete picnic table and maneuvered until he had his hands on either side of his face.

"Ever had your neck snapped, buddy?" As the question left his lips, Canaan violently flicked his hands in opposite directions. Meryl's neck broke with a loud crack and Canaan dropped him to the wet earth, the twin's eyes now lifeless as a doll's. Beryl shouted with surprise and tried to stand, but Canaan turned and put the heel of his boot over the man's chest.

"Can you feel that, twinnie? Your neck starting to sting?"

"You can't kill us! We're your brothers!" Beryl grunted, his eyes wild.

"Oh, you're wrong there, baby-doll. There's the unforgivable trespass; or have you forgotten?" Canaan raised his foot and measured the distance to the Rakum's face. "You've tied my hands, little brother..."

"Elder Canaan, Master! Please!" Beryl cried, this time shaking his head back and forth and thrashing his legs seeking purchase.

"CANAAN, WAIT!" Marcy jogged to his side.

Canaan lowered his foot and glanced her way. Her face was ashen and he surmised she may have watched him dispatch Meryl.

"You got that other one. Let him alone. Let's just get out of here. The sun will finish him in a few hours." Marcy clutched Canaan's arm and he heard the pain in her voice. As much as she hated her attackers, she was too kindhearted—too human—to see them destroyed.

His rage passing, Canaan wrenched Beryl up and pushed him against the park table. He wriggled his bicep free of Marcy and produced the Glock. Flicking off the safety, he put the barrel to the twin's temple. Beryl looked him in the eye and gritted his teeth.

"What is Rufus up to, kid?"

Beryl grunted and looked to Marcy for mercy.

"She can't help you, kid. Daddy's talking. What's Rufus up to?"

Beryl rolled his eyes closed and swallowed. "He sent us to grab your woman so you'd come to him. He wants to enslave you; you and all the Rabbit's company."

Canaan nodded approvingly. "Are you heading back there? If you survive me, that is?"

Beryl grunted what sounded like a yes, but his eyes were still closed. Canaan lowered the gun barrel and shoved it into the youth's belly.

"If you can somehow recover from this..." Canaan pulled the trigger. Marcy screamed, but the kid only squeezed his eyes against the pain. "And if you can drag your brother to safety before the sun shows up, I have a message for your buddy, Rufus. You ready?" Beryl nodded, digesting new waves of debilitating discomfort. Canaan continued. "You tell Rufus to leave me out of it. I'll kill him and anybody who tries to interfere with me or my life here. Got it?"

Beryl shook his head as blood welled and spilled from his lips. "Rufus will never stop pursuing you," he sputtered. "He has plans for your blood. Plus," Beryl took a breath and grimaced, "no Rakum will be able to resist your Rabbit. It's true—" Beryl gasped and then resumed his sentence in a telepathic whisper. *"We found her because we smelled your mark."*

Canaan glanced at Marcy who looked on not understanding their exchange. Was Rufus *that* determined? Canaan was familiar with the twins' superior telepathy and now had evidence that they were still able to utilize it. He tucked the gun into his waistband and grabbed Beryl around the throat to lean into his face.

"Show me Rufus."

Like their Elder, Jack Dawn, tactile telepathy came easily to Canaan and after a few moments, Beryl began sending real-time images of his lunatic leader. Canaan witnessed the Elder's ravaged face, the insanity in his gaze, and even some of his high-brow plans regarding their people. But most of all, Canaan saw that Beryl was telling the truth; Rufus would never let up. He was drunk with the promise of power and he would stop at nothing to get his way.

"This isn't the way I thought it would be either, Master," Beryl whispered sympathetically.

Canaan released him and the kid slid to the ground.

"Will you heal me up, Master? You know I won't live if you leave me here. Do it for Elder Dawn..."

Canaan considered the youth's words. Jack had been his Elder, too, two centuries before the twins were even born. Had he been too harsh? Had jealousy caused him to behave so erratically against his brethren? Was he becoming human? The thought angered him.

Beryl was still begging for help and he looked into his face. *"I'll no longer hunt for you. Give you time to go back into hiding. I'll tell Rufus you're dead. He'll believe me. He always does..."*

The beautiful Rakum before him was broken, bleeding, and miserable. Canaan could sense the kid was trying to hypnotize him but he wasn't offended; Beryl wasn't the one who attacked Marcy. Canaan looked at his right hand and turned it over to examine his palm. If he laid it on the kid's abdomen, the gunshot wound would close instantly. Canaan felt power rush to his fingers at the thought.

Marcy squeezed his other arm.

"Are you crazy?" She put her fingers over his gently, and caused him to lower his hand. "What's done is done. He's made his bed, now let him sleep in it."

Canaan looked at Beryl a little longer and stepped back. He was satisfied that the kid wouldn't see another sundown, and the reign of Jack's twins would finally come to an end.

"Yes," Canaan agreed softly, not entirely content with the decision to leave them for dead. He was fully capable of healing them both and then helping them get to safety. If she hadn't distracted him, he'd have done it. He had made up his mind to do whatever the fair twin required of him. The guy's telepathic plea was that convincing.

Canaan took another step back and pulled his gaze from Beryl's with effort. "Let's go before the sun beats *us* to bed."

"Yes, sweetie," Marcy said and removed the gun from his belt and re-holstered it. "Let's leave them to their gods. They've had a good run."

Canaan blinked and turned away, as an uncomfortable twinge in his middle signified that the invisible cord that bound him to the two Rakum was still in place. What else could he do? Rufus was determined to kill the only person he cared for.

"Yes, they've had a good run," Canaan mumbled, hoping to convince himself. He trudged behind Marcy, shoulders stooped. He would have to kill Rufus, but he would need help. It was time to find the Rabbit, the one that bested their Fathers.

Canaan sighed and started making plans, his perfect life going to pot. And probably for good.

TWENTY

Raleigh, NC
November 4th, 1:00/2:00 a.m. ET

In the tenement apartment he shared with a grizzled black mortal named Freddie, Boris took a swig of his beer and spread his full house on the table top.

"Beat that, Dupe."

Dupe was Freddie's grown nephew; sloppy, hairy, and stupid as a log. In response to Boris's taunting challenge, the repulsive cuss slammed his cards down face up and stood from the table.

"You gotta be cheatin' to win like that every time!" Dupe turned toward his uncle leaning against the chipped Formica bar top. "Freddie, did you see that?"

Boris sent the older gentleman a languid gaze and awaited his reply. Freddie had long since figured out that his roommate of the past twelve months was not human. In fact, the man was mostly convinced that Boris was some sort of devil.

"You got a death wish?" Freddie snapped back. "Leave the guy alone. If he's cheating, so what? Keep your mouth shut!"

Boris smiled. He *was* cheating actually—and Fat Freddie was right; no one should ever question Boris. He inclined his head toward Dupe and looked at Freddie sideways. The flabby hippo continued to spout his indignation before the other guys; a Chinese mechanic from Slippy's Automotive and the plumber from two doors down. Freddie got Boris's drift. He slumped off the bar and clutched his nephew by one wiggly bicep.

"Time to go. Get out!" Freddie shoved the younger man toward the door and Boris licked his lips. If Dupe stayed, he'd end up dinner. Deep down, Freddie probably knew that.

"Freddie! That ain't fair! That's all my dough! I don't get paid again 'til next week, Freddie!"

Dupe complained all the way to the door. Boris watched the two men wrestling back and forth and longed to be in the fray. Life was so boring lately and he had to behave—it was increasingly difficult to get away with murder.

"Shut up!" Freddie screamed and yanked open the door.

Standing in the doorway was a familiar figure and Boris came to his feet. "STOP!" he shouted, loud enough to shake the glass in the stereo cabinet. All of the human occupants fell still and turned their heads his way. He pointed toward Dupe. "Come back to the table. Freddie, bring him back."

Confused, but not willing to disobey, the older man did as commanded and pulled a reluctant Dupe to the messy card table.

"Isaac," Boris said softly and nodded the greeting to his new guest. Isaac had never visited his home and he was taken by surprise. The kid who wasn't a kid entered calmly, considered each occupant in turn, and stopped well into the room. The boy looked to him expectantly, and Boris thought fast. Why was he here?

"Who invited Casper?"

An appropriate question from the mechanic since Isaac was the only Caucasian in the room, and an apparent baby to boot. Momentarily at a loss on how to react, Boris glared at the man to be quiet. Should he exert his control over the men and perhaps impress the youth, or should he send them all out to afford them some privacy? Boris stood dumbfounded, knowing that Isaac read his every thought.

"Had dinner yet?" Isaac asked. His voice could've come from a school boy, high and sweet, with a Midwestern accent. So the kid was hungry? Boris shook his head and Isaac gestured toward Dupe. "That one looks pretty big."

"Aw, man, Boris, look—" Freddie whined and took a step toward his roommate.

"Everybody out but Dupe," Boris said, his eyes on the blond youth before them.

"Boris, you gotta—" Freddie's voice wavered.

Boris turned his head and narrowed his eyes. "Now."

Freddie pushed Dupe's shoulder. "Stay put," he mumbled and grabbed a windbreaker off his chair. "I'll run you home later."

"Wait a minute!" Dupe yelled and started to rise.

With one hand, Boris forced him down hard enough to crack a chair leg. The mechanic and the plumber grabbed their winnings and maneuvered warily around Isaac who stood with his hands clasped behind his back, smiling and watching the show. The last to go was Freddie who instinctively made a wide berth around their blond guest and closed the door soundly behind him. Isaac waved his hand lazily toward the door and the bolt was thrown on all three locks. Dupe gasped at the magic trick, eyes darting between Boris and the kid.

"Take your dinner, brother. I have plans for us tonight and there's a time element." Isaac stayed where he was and thrust his hands in his jeans pockets.

Boris nodded obediently, wrenched his victim out of the chair from behind, and held him tightly. Dupe grunted and complained until Boris clamped his left hand over his mouth and dug out his switchblade. As his diminutive superior watched, he jabbed the tip into the man's throat and took his portion. Dupe strained against him, elbowed him in the solar plexus, and stomped his toes, but Boris didn't relent. By the time his gut was full to capacity, Dupe had been weakened enough that he collapsed when released. Isaac strolled over and looked upon the guy, face down, head to the side, and snoring through a deviated septum.

"That is one ugly dude," Isaac offered and Boris chuckled.

Then Isaac went to his knees alongside the sleeping boor and grasped his head. With one swift move, Freddie's nephew was dead, his neck shattered by the violent rotation of Isaac's palms. Boris's mouth dropped open, but he offered no opposition. He'd known the kid two years now and he'd come to trust his every decision.

"Now me," the kid whispered and approached Boris eagerly.

Boris sank down into a chair and presented his wrist to the boy he fed as regularly as possible. Isaac didn't drink human blood—and because of that he was extraordinarily powerful. Like the Fathers. And now that the Fathers were gone, Boris had an inkling that Isaac could take their place. The boy was a son—but he was the closest thing they had to a Father.

"See this, brother, I've learned something new. Figured it out while I was strangling Miranda." Isaac took hold of Boris's arm and opened his mouth wide. As he watched, the kid's eyeteeth lengthened into fangs and he sank them deep into the proffered wrist.

Boris inhaled and raised his eyebrows. Isaac was presenting fangs as if he'd been taking the Dying Buzz, but the kid never drank from mortals. How was it possible? Was the boy's power without limit? Could he transform into a vampire at will? Boris pondered all of his questions and watched Isaac feed. A sense of peace filled his mind as the minutes wore on. Isaac was a baby, but he was also a god. He'd finally hitched his wagon to the right horse.

◆◆◆

"I need to get to Alabama, immediately." Isaac peaked his fingers under his chin and studied the Rakum across from him. The dead man's body had been moved to Boris's bedroom and the table cleared of the earlier poker game.

"Anything you need," Boris replied, looking sincere, but clueless nonetheless. Isaac smiled, anticipating his fellow's intellectual shortcomings.

"Freddie will drive, I'm calling him back. He's afraid of you—good job." Isaac gave Boris a wink. "You tell him what to do and he'll get me there safely."

Isaac closed his eyes and concentrated on the odor of the fat loser Boris enthralled some time ago. He learned in his youth that the best way to telepathically track mortals was by their scent. Each man, woman, and child had a distinct odor and if a Rakum made note of it with purpose, he would be able to later find him again by seeking his scent mentally. Isaac found his mark two blocks away in a hazy bar.

Come home, now! Boris needs you! Isaac sent the command telepathically and vaguely saw the man start, hop off his bar stool, and head for the exit. It was funny really, how easily they were manipulated. The majority of his brethren could barely communicate with each other this way, much less with mortals, but Isaac's power grew exponentially every passing minute. He turned his attention to Boris who was still trying to figure out how best to help his master.

"I'll need money and a car."

Boris dug into his jacket pocket and whipped out his wallet. He handed its contents to Isaac and then scrounged in his jeans for the night's winnings. Isaac made a swift count and nodded.

"And a car."

Boris got to his feet and pulled open a nearby drawer. "Take the Hyundai, it runs the best. And Isaac…"

Boris stopped and Isaac could see he was choosing his words wisely. He wanted to come along, to help, even though he had no idea what was going on. He was a dedicated servant.

Isaac shook his head. "You may follow later if I need you." He glanced at his watch—1 a.m. "Don't risk the sun. I've seen my future." Isaac touched his temple with his forefinger. "I will arrive safely. But if you go now, you will die."

Boris nodded and handed over the keys. "I'll wait for your call."

Freddie's rapid step in the hall sounded and they both came to their feet.

"Leave town, brother. That corpse'll sing soon," Isaac gestured toward the bedroom as Freddie entered the front door.

"What is it?" he asked, beads of sweat on his brow.

Isaac put his hands in his pockets and watched Boris do his thing. He made arrangements and planted the appropriate protocol in the idiot's weak mind. Humans were so pathetic, it was almost sad.

Isaac sent his mind ahead to Alabama and looked for the Rabbit. He couldn't mentally lock on to her or any of her apostate pals, but he knew she was in Montgomery. And as soon as he got close, he'd be able to track Jack Dawn's mark. Rabbits were easy prey, easy game, always had been.

Within the hour, Freddie carefully loaded him into the trunk of the Azera and headed South, just under the speed limit. Boris's roommate would drive all night, he'd pee in a cup, and he wouldn't go near the trunk until nightfall.

Isaac smiled.

It was good to be god.

TWEDTY-ODE

Radnor Lake State Park
Nashville, TN
November 4th, 4:00 a.m.

"*Meryl? Meryl?*"

Beryl called his brother twice telepathically before calling him in a harsh whisper. The lines were down, disconnected, as if his brother were dead. But more than that, Beryl felt half dead. A broken neck couldn't kill a Rakum, but it could render him unconscious for hours. Sighing, Beryl realized the futility of his actions and relaxed against the cold earth. The sky was purple now, the sun only a scant ninety minutes away.

"*We're not going out like this, brother,*" Beryl sent over and watched the trees slowly wave at the waning moon. "*Someone will come. Someone...*"

Beryl sent out a mental beacon, seeking a like-minded Rakum who might be within range. His earlier gunshot wound had healed completely, but his second was still seeping. The tugging sensation of his organs and muscles reattaching and regenerating was nauseating, and he fought back the bile that periodically rose in his throat. He was tough, but taking two bullets had not been in the plan this night.

Leave them to their gods.

Canaan's woman's words floated to his memory and he focused on the thought. Her derisive comment was meant to demoralize him, but he had no gods. Yet, seven years ago, he had a Master.

Beryl closed his eyes and pictured High Father Abroghia, who sired their race millennia ago. Abroghia was the strongest of them all, one hundred percent spirit, and not at all tainted or limited by the flesh that bound the rest of the Rakum to the earth. Sure, he'd departed and left them unattended, but Beryl understood his reasons. His time had come. The spirit realm worked on a different set of parameters than the earthly one. The High Father—a.k.a. the spirit *Ta'avah*, a demon of ancient times—had a set time to rule before he returned to his world; his dimension.

Was he dead? No, he was a spirit.

Was he gone forever?

"No."

Beryl opened his eyes at the telepathic answer that carried a tone he didn't recognize. Glancing about the clearing, his gaze landed on the bench to his left. There might have been a shadow there, a shimmer, a slight change in the way the trees were viewed, as if through an invisible filter.

"I've been waiting for one of you to screw up."

Beryl squint his eyes and made an effort to prop up on his elbows.

"Oh, don't bother. Your brother will die soon. Send me into him and I will fix him up. He can carry me about. I will fix the mess you boys have made."

"I don't understand," Beryl whispered speaking in the direction of the wispy specter. "Send you in? Who are you?"

There was a telepathic sigh and in Beryl's mind, he had a sense of the ghostlike speaker shaking his head side-to-side.

"You waste my time."

"If you are who I think you are, then you're outside of time," Beryl corrected.

"But you are not. The sun is on its way. Even I will have trouble getting you to shelter in time if you do not hurry and do as I say."

Beryl's lips parted, but then paused. If he sent the spirit of Ta'avah into his brother, would he release him later? Or would he never again enjoy the intimacy he shared with his twin?

"Tick-tock, Ballerina. Tick-tock."

Beryl pressed his lips together and stared at the empty space above the bench. Father Abroghia assigned him that moniker when he was thirteen years old. Meryl was dubbed "Mary". The demeaning act taught the twins to attack without mercy anyone who referred to them by their alternate names.

"What do I do then?" he mumbled miserably. He wanted to live, he wanted to be restored, and he wanted to be rescued. But losing his brother was a hard, nearly impossible trade.

"Send me in. You are of one mind, are you not? You may consent for him. Do it now."

Beryl lowered himself back to the wet leaves and closed his eyes.

"I send you into Meryl, Ta'avah. I mean, Father."

"Call me 'Master'."

It was Meryl's voice now, loud and strong. Beryl's eyes flew open and he struggled to his elbows to look at his brother. Meryl was standing and he stepped to Beryl's side with haste.

"I'm allowed only the talents your brother enjoyed, so I cannot heal you." Meryl-Ta'avah bent at the waist and grasped Beryl under his armpits.

"But you healed Meryl..."

"You are much too simple-minded to comprehend our ways, Ballerina. Come." Meryl-Ta'avah shouldered him in one smooth motion and turned off the way Canaan and his woman had disappeared. "There is a cabin three miles west of here, deserted and used for storage. We can hide there until nightfall."

Beryl didn't reply, but watched the grass go by in his vision, feeling deep within the uncomfortable threat of the sun as she neared the horizon. As sure as Elder Canaan had left them for dead, his master Ta'avah would have none of it. The trade-off being, Meryl was no more. A numbing flare momentarily paralyzed his brain.

"Shut up. Your brother is better off. Quit whining."

Beryl grimaced as Meryl-Ta'avah leapt a log that crossed their path and landed heavily, causing his healing belly wound to split open. He clenched his jaw and took the pain like a Rakum. Their true father, the Father of their race, had returned, and he'd always been the most ruthless of them all. It wouldn't do to complain.

Meryl-Ta'avah chuckled and Beryl cleared his mind. Telepathy was about to lose its appeal. Maybe for good.

TWENTY-TWO

Chloe scrabbled to consciousness, her eyes gummy with tears and her throat dry from crying through the filthy gag. Voices, masculine and angry, nonsensically filtered through the haze as she made an effort to concentrate on the words. When her head was no longer swimming and she could focus on her surroundings, she realized happily that she was untied. Her shoulders ached from the earlier rough treatment, but she was free. A moment later, she realized that she was no longer in the musty cargo van, but lying on a short sofa in a dimly-lit suite.

"Traffic? That's the best you can do? Half-wit! I expected you hours ago!"

The voices again, behind her and to the right; this one raspy and hollow, as if spoken through a Halloween mask. Afraid to turn her head to investigate, Chloe remained still and looked ahead blindly to listen.

"I'm sorry, master. We—"

There was a crisp ring of a slap and a grunt of surprise. Chloe winced; she'd seen enough violence in the last few hours to last her a lifetime.

"Get out before I rip your face off. I've heard the last of your excuses."

Chloe squeezed closed her eyes and repressed an instinct to cry out. Oh, if only she could remain unmolested. Was there any chance at all? She heard a door close and held her breath, probably now alone with the monster in charge. What would he do to her? Chloe shuddered as her thoughts ran rampant.

Dave! Oh, how I wish you were here!

Then, without even realizing it, Javier's face came to mind and replaced that of her adoring beau. Javier, who hated the ground she walked on and disdained David's gentle nature.

Javier, who would likely fight for me.
Somehow, she knew it to be true.
I wish you were here, Javier!
"Are you quite finished?"

Chloe's eyes flew open and she gasped. Standing over her was the spitting image of Hollywood's Nosferatu. Her captor was pale, thin, and ghoulish with long, claw-like fingers that dangled from hands that shook as if with palsy. He looked down at her, his glittering eyes nearly invisible in the low light, sunken behind an eerily protruding brow.

"Precisely how many of my deceived brethren are you stringing along, missy?" A mist of rancid spittle rained down on her as he spoke.

Chloe shook her head. Was he responding to her thoughts? Wasn't that impossible? Not really, for hadn't she already determined that he was a monster? A real one?

"I'm Rufus. And yes, I'm a monster." Rufus smiled and his jagged fangs glinted in the available light. "Boo."

Chloe kicked her feet against the floor to scoot into the back of the couch. The vampire leaned in and reached for her as Chloe averted her face, screaming into her gag.

"I wish to hear you, little one. Be still lest I accidentally crush you."

Chloe emitted a muffled squeal as Rufus came down on one knee and drew near to her face. He smelled of sulfur and something else. Something dead.

Chloe closed her eyes and wrenched her face as far to the side as possible. Rufus's jerking hand on her shirt dragged heavily toward her collarbone, before his cold fingertips scraped up her throat. When he grasped her chin between his thumb and forefinger, he exhaled, "Let's remove this." The monster pulled the dirty cloth from her mouth and hissed, "Much better."

Chloe coughed in the vampire's face, but he didn't recoil. Rufus remained where he was, leaning into her, one knee on the cushion between her thighs and the other foot on the carpeted floor.

"Tell me your name." The vampire maintained his too-close position and his eyes darted rodent-like about her face.

Chloe's tongue touched her palate and she tried to swallow. Too dry to speak and too weak to struggle, she sank further into the cushion.

"Never mind, I read you like a book." Rufus inhaled and grinned in her face. "Chloe Bushman. Or is it Mina?"

Chloe moaned and looked away again. The monster's breath was horrid and even though the shock of his ghastly appearance was passing, she reviled at his proximity.

"Chloe Bushman." Rufus smacked his lips and put his fingers to the dark curls that spilled over her shoulder. "Welcome to my home, Miss Bushman. But alas, it is dawn and sleep beckons. You will spend the day with me. In my bed. How would you like that?"

A moan deep her in throat, Chloe rolled her eyes and did all she could to avoid looking at his face. Inches away, he had one hand in her hair and the other held up his weight by pressing into the back of the sofa. Was she about to be ravaged by a monster? Faint at the notion, Chloe swallowed painfully. If only she had some water and a large caliber machine gun...

"Water, you shall have," Rufus whispered in her ear and then lifted himself upright. "You must survive the day, young one. I need you fresh at nightfall."

Chloe rolled her head to the side to look his way, but he was gone. Faster than she could follow with her eyes, Rufus had left her side and was now across the room, running water at a sink in an attached bathroom.

"Please," Chloe whispered. "Please, let me go."

She blinked once and the vampire stood before her again, as if he'd never left. Except now, he held a small glass of water in his distorted hand. He put the rim to her lips and patiently watched her gulp down the contents. The water energized her as it hit her stomach and she dared another plea for release.

"Please, Mr. Rufus, please, let me go. I don't want to die."

The vampire laughed, more putrid spittle fluttering down on her as he did so.

"I will not allow you to die, Miss Bushman. Oh, no. I know the plans I have for you and they are all about me."

"Please..."

"Come." Rufus reached for her wrist and pulled her forcefully to her feet.

Chloe resisted, but the claw around her arm was like steel and he walked casually, as if she didn't pull against him at all. He dragged her into an adjoining room and the door closed behind them unaided. The single floor-to-ceiling window was curtained, and in the center of the room sat a king-size bed with a red satin comforter and thick matching pillows.

Chloe pulled away with more determination.

"Please, Mr. Rufus! Please, let me go!" Chloe pulled at the fingers that held her and shuffled her feet in the opposite direction. The vampire's reaction was to reel her in and wrap his left arm about her waist, tight enough to restrict her breathing.

"I'd like for you to whine and complain as long as you can, my sweet. 'Tis music to these old ears." The vampire yanked back the covers and crawled into the bed, dragging Chloe along behind him. Once he was tucked in, he pulled her close, her back against his front and he spoke again, right against her ear.

"If you would only beg me for mercy, I might relent."

Chloe had no more tears. She stared at the low-wattage lamp on the nearby table, and with a wave of Rufus's hand, it went black.

"Please, don't hurt me," Chloe whispered, shaking, but too terror-stricken to cry.

"How high is your pain threshold?" Rufus asked, speaking into her ear in the darkness. His arms wrapped spiderlike about her middle and his free hand twirled in Chloe's hair.

Where was her knight in shining armor? Why couldn't she scream or cry for help?

Rufus chuckled and shimmied closer. Chloe held her breath. What would he do to her? *I'll do whatever comes to me, Miss Bushman. I am king here.*

Chloe gasped and stiffened in his embrace. His words came across in her mind that time. He wasn't only reading her thoughts, but now speaking in them.

Her captor squeezed her tighter. *It's nice to have a warm body to hold.*

Rufus's telepathic voice chilled her to the bone and made her think of gravestones and decay. Chloe didn't believe in heaven, as her mother vigorously pushed it on her as a child. And she barely believed in God, as her mother made Him into a bossy overseer who insisted on constant slave work to be noticed. But tonight, she believed in hell.

Hell is a cold place. A ruthlessly cold place. And you will keep me warm.

Chloe clenched her jaw and wished she had the faith of the novelist in Beth Rider's story. When the Wraiths threatened her character's life, she withstood their attacks with a faith Chloe didn't understand then and definitely couldn't comprehend now. The woman's novel was true, not fiction. The Wraiths were real, flesh and blood, and she was in their leader's clutches. David, Javier, and even Roman couldn't help her. Why cry out to them when they were no danger to the monster that held her captive? Who was left?

Where's God when I need Him?

Chloe sobbed now, quietly without tears. She wished she'd read her Bible more. She wished she could pray. But more than that, she wished she believed it would help.

TWENTY-THREE

Highway 80
Alabama/Mississippi State Line
November 4th, 3:30 p.m.

Marcy checked her speed and set the cruise. The number one rule when transporting her sun-sensitive life partner across state lines in broad daylight was *don't get pulled over*. She'd transported Canaan this way twice before and both times, she was a nervous wreck on the other end. What if she had a blow-out, a collision, a speeding ticket? Any of those might require opening the trunk which, depending on the sun's intensity, could destroy the love of her life in a matter of minutes.

Marcy shivered. Right now, she missed his voice in her head. On the other two trips, taken long before the Rakum were disbanded, he telepathically spoke to her along the way. From his cozy nest in the trunk, Canaan sang to her in his distinctive warbling falsetto. He told her dirty jokes and made fun of her co-worker Erin…

Erin. Awful way to die. Canaan assured her that the woman never knew what hit her, but to die like that? Alive one second, dead the next? No goodbyes, no last wishes, no chance to make things right. Marcy had no real faith system, but she knew that when her number came up, she wanted some time to think it over; to speak a few choice last words to her lover; tell him things that she could never voice except under the threat of death.

Marcy looked in the rearview mirror, senselessly paranoid. The coast was clear and Canaan could no longer read her mind. She sighed, undeniably saddened at his loss of power. He was still the strongest of his kind, he assured her, but Marcy was afraid he'd lost more than he was admitting. It wasn't just the telepathy, Canaan had lost his *edge*.

Marcy inhaled sharply as a rush of memories flooded her consciousness. Late summer, 1971, her family's farm. Daddy Haddle had two hundred acres and farmed half of it with soybean and corn. On the other half, he kept Herefords for market. The night she shot Canaan while creeping around the hay barn, Marcy had just celebrated her 16th birthday, and what a gift the Rakum turned out to be.

That night, just before he disappeared into the shadows, he promised he'd come back. Marcy worried and fantasized all day long, awaiting nightfall. She rushed through dinner, complained of a headache, and hit the sack early. With her door locked but her window open, she awaited her caller. When Canaan finally arrived it was after midnight and Marcy had dozed off at her desk.

"Did you expect me to come through the window?" he had asked as he struck an imposing figure next to her four-poster bed. *"I'm not a bat."*

Marcy felt no fear. It surprised her now, forty years later, driving down I-65 with an earth-bound god in her trunk, that she'd never been afraid of him. From the moment their eyes met, she felt a kinship with him; that he was either her guardian angel or her soulmate—either way, she feared neither.

The first time he came to her bedroom, she half-expected—and half-desired—to be ravished by him, but he was a gentleman. He touched her cheek as they whispered to each other in her room, the radio disguising anything that might filter down to her parents. He chucked her shoulder as he complimented her bravery and prowess with a shotgun. The only time he put his lips on her was to take her blood, and of course she consented. Who wouldn't? He had more than proven his ability to magically heal any wound he might inflict while drawing it out.

Marcy put her hand to her throat and glanced at the speedometer. Across the wide, grassy median, a State Trooper peeled out onto the roadway chasing a red sports car. Marcy exhaled with relief. *Let them chase someone else today.*

Then, *Canaan—you had so much self-control.*

Marcy sighed and nibbled her lip. For over a year, Canaan visited her weekly; not always taking her blood, but more frequently just talking, laughing, and swapping stories. To teenage Marcy, it made perfect sense that a wonderful and beautiful vampire would fall head over heels in love with her. Why not? She was special—her daddy always said so. And finally, as her 17th birthday came and went, her Rakum courter revealed his romantic side.

Marcy recalled the night he secreted her out of the house and took her to the hay barn. It was April and she wore a thick cashmere sweater over her nightgown to combat the frigid spring breezes that whipped through the structure. Canaan had pulled her close, lit only by the moonlight that streamed down on them from the hay loft door, and he held her face in his hands.

"Will you be my princess, Marcy Haddle?"

She had to bend her head back to meet his gaze, as safe in his arms as she'd ever be anywhere on earth. She answered him without wavering.

"I already am."

"No, my sweet. You will be my mate. Come away with me. I will care for you, protect you, keep you close to me forever. I vow these things to you, if you would only consent."

Marcy swallowed hard at the memory and checked the mirror again. Her heart was racing and she took a deep breath. How could she say no to such an offer? Who in their right mind would refuse a chance to spend their lives with such a creature? She consented, by word and by deed, that very night. And a few short weeks later, he came for her and she left her parents' house forever.

Happily, Canaan turned out to be even more wonderful than she could have ever imagined. Within their first month together in California, he began allowing her into his world. He personally governed a thousand Rakum and kept close ten lieutenants who reported to him regularly. Marcy was assigned to one of them, a heavy-shouldered wrestler-type called Tork.

Canaan had warned that Tork was the only one of his brethren that she should go to if he was unavailable. What stuck in Marcy's mind was how Tork revered and respected his Elder; she'd never seen such devotion in the mortal world. Tork watched over her like a hawk for twenty years. Whenever Canaan was away on Rakum business, he was there to play board games, take her to dinner, and take her ice skating whenever she asked. And never was Marcy accosted by man or Rakum with Tork at her side.

But Canaan sent him away. He sent them all away. When was that?

Marcy searched her memory. One night as they snuggled in their rented San Francisco apartment, Canaan told her they were going underground. He swore up and down that it had nothing to do with the recent terrorist attack on 9/11, but Marcy wondered. All she knew was that another Elder came to see them as soon as the sun went down. Canaan asked her to wait upstairs while he firmed their plans with the handsome Rakum, and she heard everything through the door.

"What do you require? I could never say no to that baby face of yours."

"Brother, I'm taking a time-out. Be me before the Brethren. Only the great Kilmeade could be two Elders at once."

"Flattery, oh, how I love it... give me some more..."

Later that evening, Canaan informed her they were leaving and they soon began their new life; a life where he no longer supervised his brethren. He had essentially cut himself off from his people. Now his choices were making him vulnerable at a time when he needed to be stronger than ever.

But why am I complaining? It's my fault. He's spent too much time with me.

Marcy wiped a tear from her eye and slapped her cheek.

Two hours and ten minutes. Keep it together. You can do it.

She was more than half-way to the author's home in Montgomery, and if she could keep from crying, she'd give herself a pat on the back. She'd been bawling a lot lately. Canaan had no idea how many times she sobbed silent tears in the shower as she loofah-ed her back until it was raw. But why? Why the waterworks?

Marcy sniffled and hit the steering wheel with her fist because she knew why; their world was coming apart, crashing down around them. Sure, Canaan played his role well, her brawny champion. But even he had trouble hiding the uncertainty behind his eyes; that they'd soon be separated. Maybe forever.

Marcy hit the steering wheel again and fished out a Kleenex from the console between the seats. If only Canaan was as strong as he thought he was.

TWENTY-FOUR

Highway 82 South
November 4th, 3:30 p.m.

Before they hit the road for Montgomery, Roman warned them both sternly that the Rakum were regrouping and were out for blood, especially that of the so-called apostates. David had been surprised to hear it. He really hadn't given the Rakum much thought the past few years as he worked to forget his origins. Anyway, what were they expected to do about it?

Roman had a vague plan, get to the Stone's house, and take it from there. Vague or not, David was happy to follow the former Elder's lead; after all, he was a tremendous help back when they needed the most guidance. Living as a mortal didn't come naturally for any of them, but David had jumped in with both feet. He took classes part-time, worked part-time, and studied the Scriptures part-time. He had a decent ear for tongues, and although he didn't speak as many languages as Javier, he could read and write Hebrew, Greek, and Aramaic. Those aided him greatly as he worked to figure out who God was and what He expected from His children.

While David went through the motions of the average American college student, he spent hours devising a complicated and detailed background for himself. He dreamed up relatives to four generations, complete with intricate genealogies. By the time he happened upon Chloe Bushman, he'd memorized the entire novel-length tome. It should be a no-brainer, it should be easy as pie, but nothing could be further from the truth.

David didn't miss being a Rakum—he never fit in with them anyway. He'd been excommunicated for "excessive empathetic altruism" just before Beth Rider came onto the scene. But now that he was mortal, he struggled with guilt and shame. For decades, he'd lived off the blood of God's children, using and manipulating them to

130

satisfy his selfish desires. It didn't help when Javier reminded him that his blood donors volunteered to serve him. It didn't help when Beth Rider tried to convince him that God had wiped the slate clean. No matter how hard he tried, David couldn't shake the past.

So he pretended.

All the time.

On the bright side, Chloe Bushman helped more than he expected. She was all girl, full of unprovoked giggles and varying opinions. She made him laugh and without realizing it, taught him how to behave around their classmates. Most enjoyable, Chloe's innocent and playful flirting awakened David's dormant sexuality.

Most Rakum didn't mature sexually until their hundredth birthday, and he'd been transformed at seventy. Being asexual at an apparent twenty-one made him stand out more than anything, so David welcomed the education young Chloe unknowingly threw his way. Thinking of her more heated contributions tinted his cheeks pink, and he checked his watch as a distraction.

"We're half-way there, Dave," Javier remarked from the front seat, peeking back at him, his face lax.

David nodded absently and considered his roommate. Roman's former proselyte had been growing more depressed over the past few months, and when Roman told them they were leaving town for the Rabbit's house, Javier's countenance darkened considerably.

As he was still glaring at him from the front, David gave him a thumbs-up until he faced forward. His housemate didn't care much for Chloe, but it wasn't surprising. Javier hadn't shown any interest in females since they set up house together more than five years back. Maybe he was gay. David looked out the window and pondered the notion. Rakum did not recognize sexual orientation; for them, a sensation was a sensation, no matter who delivered it. As mortals, the brethren chose along the way which way they might lean. If Javier had made his choice, he'd made no announcements to that affect.

David's cell phone sounded the ring-tone assigned to Chloe Bushman, jostling him out of his thoughts. As far as he knew, she would be cramming for finals back home. His abrupt departure hardly fazed his instructors or his boss at Lifeway, and the only ones who seemed to miss him at all was Chloe and the library ditz, Kiki. David fished the phone out of his pocket. "You got Dave. Speak."

"David?"

It was Chloe's voice; small, broken and whispering. An

unexplained sense of dread churned his gut. Perhaps by intuition, Javier turned from the front seat at that moment and watched his face, his brow furrowed with concern.

"Chloe?" David spoke loudly over the sound of the rented Tahoe.

"Dave, I…"

There was a pause and David sat up in his seat ignoring Javier's animated gestures for him to explain what was going on.

"Where are you?"

"Dave, I've been kidnapped. Help m—"

Chloe's voice faded. Where was she? Who grabbed her? Was it a Rakum? Was Roman's damning prophecy happening already, with Chloe as collateral damage?

"Who—" David started to ask when Chloe screamed and then quieted, her voice moving some distance from the phone. "CHLOE!" David shouted into the handset and noticed Roman's rapt attention now as he piloted the vehicle.

"David Walker. I'd know that pitiful, whiny, girly voice anywhere. You sound concerned. Awww…how sweet."

The voice on the other end wasn't familiar, but it was a Rakum. David gulped and caught Javier's eye.

"Get here as soon as you can. Bring your traitor pals with you or I cannot attest to the condition of your woman when you arrive."

"Leave her alone! Who is this?" The blood drained from David's face as he bared his teeth and resisted an urge to put his fist through the truck window.

"This child is a hotbed of confused loyalties," the voice on the other end laughed. "She's been calling for all three of you intermittently since I've had her. Do you share her? That's bizarre behavior for mortals, isn't it? That's what you are now—mortals, correct?"

"Elder Rufus?" The name popped into his head as a dusty file folder fell open at just the right moment. Rufus was aged, telepathic, and ruthless. All of the Rakum were aware of his reputation.

"The one and only."

"What have you done with Chloe? I'll kill you if you hurt her!" David yelled his words and tears sprang to his eyes. He started to set in with more threats when Javier climbed half-way over his seat in the front and took the phone from his hand.

"Tell him to leave her alone! I'll kill him! I swear!" David unbuckled and slipped just behind Javier who pushed him back with one hand and spoke quietly into the handset with the other.

David cursed and Roman hissed for him to be silent. What would Rufus do to her? Covering his mouth, he tried to console himself by reciting Scriptures under his breath. After several long seconds passed, Javier set the now-quiet phone in David's outstretched hand and looked down. Roman glanced his way and David waited breathless for some word.

"Rufus knows we'll come to rescue her," Javier said and shook his head. "He wants a showdown and he wants to be sure we play by his rules."

With emotion that David hadn't expected, Javier's breath hitched and he looked out the windshield.

"Try Michael Stone. Give him an update," Roman said evenly, but David sensed he was working hard to remain calm. That was definitely a bad sign.

TWENTY-FIVE

Jackson, MS
November 4th, 3:30 p.m.

"Good job, Miss Bushman. Got them fired up." Rufus pulled the back of Chloe's phone off with his fingernail and popped out the battery. The girl had snuck out of bed moments before, and slipped into the suite's bathroom. He listened as she dialed her friends—she had no secrets from him, her mind completely open. As soon as she'd connected with Walker, he was by her side.

"Now, let's get back to bed. We still have a few hours until sundown."

Rufus led her back and she barely resisted, her will finally beginning to crack. He hoped that by the time he tapped her sweet blood, she would have given up completely. That was when the true ecstasy would come.

"Why is this happening to me?" The girl whispered her rhetorical question into the air.

Rufus hushed her and pulled her back into his embrace. Her skin was akin to fire against his, but he chose to bear the discomfort. Extremes of pain and pleasure were all he could register now that he'd chosen to adopt the vampire persona. Even sex had become a non-issue. In his day, no woman could resist his charm, but now? His internal *and* external organs had shriveled to near uselessness. He couldn't digest solid food and he no longer required a toilet, but the power that was transferred upon him following every delicious victim was well worth the trade.

"Which one is he? Which one? The High Father is dead, isn't he?"

Chloe's thoughts rolled past his and he furrowed his brow. What could she know of his people? Rufus knew one way to find out.

"Tell me what you know of the High Father," he demanded telepathically, knowing it played to her vulnerability. She didn't answer

134

him overtly, but her thoughts danced across a novel she'd read some weeks before. Rufus didn't have to ask to know that it was the Rider woman's work. The cursed Rabbit was *still* making his life miserable seven years later. Oh, he could barely wait to have her in his clutches.

"I don't want to die."

The girl spoke in a desperate whisper. Rufus had his arms about her waist, one arm pinned by her bodyweight and the other free to feel of her hair, her cheek, the hot skin at her throat. He pressed his finger there and absorbed her pulse until it resonated throughout his being. She fell silent and he realized that he sincerely enjoyed hearing her fearful words. If only she'd beg for mercy.

Being one to get what he wanted, Rufus smacked his lips in her ear and mumbled aloud, "I have told you, Chloe Bushman, I will not allow you to die. You may wish to, but I am going to keep you with me forever..."

"You're going to make me a Rabbit," she whispered as her pulse increased.

Rufus smiled. The notion must have come from Beth Rider's novel and the little girl in his arms knew exactly what hell the Rakum Rabbits endured.

"Yes," he hissed and enjoyed the shiver that ran through her at the sound. "But first, I need the blood of an Elder."

A few experiments a year ago taught him that his blood was no longer suited to transform Rabbits, so when he learned that one Elder remained alive and viable, he was actually relieved. His plans for the future required quite a number of Rabbits.

Rufus removed his fingers from Chloe's throat and put his hand beneath the hem of her T-shirt. He wanted to terrorize her and it didn't take much. She played the brazen hussy with the pitiful men he used to call brethren, but she was so far, unspoiled. She recoiled from his touch which only egged him on.

"I need Elder Canaan," he cooed softly. "Do you know him?"

Chloe didn't speak, but he heard her reply in his mind.

"No? I thought all those traitors hung together," Rufus mused. "No matter. My men are luring him here just as your beaus will come for you." Chloe moaned and Rufus tentatively touched the skin of her abdomen. "Can you imagine? A Rakum Elder shacking up with a bitter old woman? It's despicable."

"Please, don't hurt me..."

Rufus sneered at the girl's mumbled plea. "Frightened by the prospect of pain. That's original."

With his pinned arm, Rufus brought Chloe's throat to his mouth. He wouldn't take her blood until he could garner the most power from the move, but her heart rate increased and her despondency was delightful. His captive had no faith, in anything, and her despair was delicious.

"My fangs yearn for you, Miss Bushman." Rufus opened his mouth and pressed his teeth to her skin, just short of breaking through. The girl strained against him, trying to move away, but he held her fast. She wasn't yet broken. Just a little longer, just a few more frightening threats and damning prophecies.

Rufus maintained his position, his tongue dry and thirsty against her fiery skin. Oh, the self-restraint he had learned over the last few years. If he hadn't, he would have killed dozens of his own men by now. They were stupid, weak, and bumbling. It was all he could do to not rip their hearts out when they paraded past him night after night announcing their shortfalls. But he mustn't forget Kite, Jack Dawn's eager beaver.

The pensive youngster Rufus put to task was getting close to completing his mission. He knew where to find the Staff of Abroghia and he was busily digging it out. When the Last Assembly ended, the Cave collapsed onto itself within forty-eight hours. Nothing of any value was saved. So it was a true excavation, one that Kite orchestrated with the help of several greedy humans who he promised the world to if they'd only pull the staff from the earth intact.

Rufus smiled. Kite revealed himself to the foreman as a vampire. Now the foreman was working for the promise of immortality; the kind Hollywood assured him he could acquire if he did the vampire's bidding. It was fairly hilarious, and Rufus commended the kid for thinking of such a ruse. Now, within weeks, they should have the High Father's staff and Rufus's power would escalate. At least that's what he was hoping. Like most Rakum, he believed the staff imbued its bearer with the strength of the Fathers.

"No, no, no, no," the girl whispered and weakly pressed her palm against his forehead.

No, no, no, no was right. It wasn't time. The sun had to be down, and the girl had to consent. It was worth the wait.

Rufus remained where he was, his agitated tongue caressing her throat. He had just as much self-control as those arrogant twins. Unbeknownst to the pompous duo, he overheard every demeaning telepathic remark made against him. They thought him a fool, an ancient buffoon ready for the loonies, but they couldn't be more wrong. He permitted their condescension and allowed them to cajole him because he needed their cooperation for now. It didn't hurt that they were so willing to cater to his every whim. Especially Beryl. Meryl kept his distance, which mattered little. The twins thought of themselves as one mind in two bodies, but as Rufus's power grew, he could see their differences clearly: Meryl was devoid of any smidgen of humanity.

All Rakum were half human, and although they played down their weaker nature, each had it in them. Meryl's human nature was suppressed, as if in the womb, Beryl absorbed the mother's seed and Meryl his father's. But Beryl...

Rufus's gut tightened at the thought of drawing the kid's blood. Beryl retained just enough of his mortal essence that buzzing him was pure pleasure; a soothing balm on Rufus's cracked and chapped soul. Never in his seven hundred and fifty years had he tasted its like, even among the mortals. Beryl carried ambrosia in his veins and he surely didn't know or he'd never so cavalierly let his blood. It was a hot, pure, quicksilver that fed Boris's deepest parts.

"No. No. Please! No. No. No!"

Rufus opened his eyes in the dark room, sensing he'd dozed off and the sun was still not close enough to the horizon to set.

And he was feeding.

The girl squirmed in his embrace and he swallowed, downing the crimson fluid that kept his future alive. Rufus snapped wide awake and drew back, instantly placing his hand over the two large punctures in the girl's neck. A frantic thought, a surge of white electricity that flowed from his chest down his arm and into his palm, and her wound was healed.

Rufus sighed and lay on his back, staring up to the ceiling, his tongue reacting to the stale flavor of the stolen blood. He'd almost ruined everything. His plan hinged on the girl and all of his constructs were nearly brought down by a premature bite.

The girl sobbed beside him, curled into a ball, and wishing she were somewhere else. Wishing she were dead so she could stop being afraid. Wishing he'd bite her again and end it all.

That's more like it. Rufus smiled at her internal weeping and fell off to sleep. There would be time to tend to her needs at nightfall when he could finish what he'd started.

TWENTY-SIX

Montgomery, AL
November 4th, 3:45 p.m.

Michael Stone lowered his cell and caught Beth's eye. Jesse was snowed in and wouldn't be leaving Hamburg. Beth read enough in his gaze to throw her hands in the air in frustration.

"I can't believe this! What're we supposed to do? What is God up to?"

Michael held his tongue and pocketed the phone. He'd taken off work early to be home when Jesse arrived and seeing his wife upset did nothing for his personal confidence. Before the baby came, nothing could shake Beth's larger-than-life faith. She was molested, tortured, and nearly killed more than once while under the thumb of his people, and had barely bat an eye. But since Grace arrived, she questioned God often, and now that the sharks were circling, she complained a lot.

"Michael, what are we going to do?"

Michael opened his arms and she fell into him. "Hon, you know what we'll do."

Stroking her shoulder-length honey-blonde hair with one hand and holding her close with the other, he waited for her composure to return. She was a mama bear now and protecting her cub was her top priority. Michael had figured out what deep down Beth knew already: God ran the show, and it was ultimately up to Him who was to live, who was to die, and who would suffer in the meantime. Reminding Beth of this would only serve to frustrate her further. He'd let her vent, cry, bemoan, and object, and tonight when Roman arrived with help, they'd simply do what God led them to do.

"I can't do it again, I can't!" she said with tears on her cheeks. Under her breath, Michael heard her pray for her husband's safety.

Beth trembled anew and Michael tried to sooth her with his

words. She was small, her face barely reaching his chin, and he always felt unstoppable in her arms. He would protect her with his life, if necessary, and what she was most afraid of. God had used her to destroy a race of demonic beings run by the devil himself and now she feared He might exact payment.

Michael sighed. This was not the nature of the God they served. Somewhere along the line, Beth's faith had taken a hit and he would do whatever it took to make her feel safe again.

"Honey…" Michael waited until she lifted her face and met his eye. "Nothing's going to happen to me. Nothing's going to happen to Grace. I promise."

"…But they got that girl," Beth sobbed and buried her face in his chest.

Michael shushed her and held her tight. It was disturbing news that Javier had transmitted earlier; that young David's girlfriend was in Rufus's clutches. But even that must be part of the plan. Before he met his wife, he knew nothing of spiritual things. His people were raised to believe they were gods themselves. Nowadays he understood the basics and those who followed the Creator were required to put all things under His care.

"That girl'll be okay. She's part of this. Every piece of the puzzle will come together for good. You believe it, don't you?"

"Yeah, I do." Beth sniffed finally and hugged him tighter. Michael kissed her forehead as a knock sounded at their bedroom door.

"Come in," Michael answered knowing that Selene was watching cartoons with the girls in the living room and might need a break.

"Beth—" Selene said as she opened the door, but stopped when she saw them embracing. "Oh, sorry. I just got off the phone with Jesse. He wanted me to tell you that he was praying for us and that he's here in spirit." Selene repeated her husband's words without emotion, evidently unconvinced.

"Yeah, good," Michael replied and gave her a reassuring nod.

Selene remained in the door, one hand on her hip, her knee-length dress wrinkled from hours of sitting on the floor playing with the girls and waiting for news. Michael wondered absently if she was cold, wearing such a short skirt in November, but he let it go. Selene dressed to be seen and the weather had little to do with her wardrobe.

"We're ordering pizza. You hungry?" Michael asked.

Selene scrunched her face. "I'm going for a drive."

139

Beth whipped out of Michael's arms and stepped toward their guest. "No, you shouldn't. Only a couple more hours and Roman will be here. We'll work out a plan." Beth's voice was plaintive.

"Bethie, I'll be right back. I wish you'd relax." Selene tossed her hair. "I'm going crazy. You've got your family together, mine is split apart. I need a break." Selene lowered her gaze. "I'll be back in twenty minutes."

With that, the woman turned away and headed to the staircase. Michael watched Beth run after her, begging her to reconsider. His wife understood the woman better than he ever would. From the first time he saw her at the Last Assembly, he knew she was unusual. Sure, she was pretty, but temperamental. Jesse promised the woman a way out seven years ago and she took it. Not that there was anything wrong with their pairing, only Michael wished Selene would cater to Jesse's whims once in a while.

Scoffing at his train of thought, Michael sighed. What business was it of his? He headed for the bathroom as the front door slammed downstairs. His wife called out Selene's name in desperation, but a car pulled off as she did so. Selene was no dummy. She'd come back before sundown. She was the last person who would want to run into the Rakum again.

Michael took a cleansing breath and got ready for his shower. The show was about to begin and he hoped for the best.

TWENTY-SEVEN

Highway 82 South
November 4th, 4:30 p.m.

The truck's occupants had been silent for some time, and Javier wasn't about to break the quiet. A low but consuming flame burned deep within him and he hated that it was Chloe Bushman who lit the match. The pouty, spoiled waif that entered their lives two months ago had wormed her way into his subconscious and now she was in mortal peril. Life was easier when there were no females around.

Roman glanced at him and Javier looked back, guarding his expression. Roman used to hear his thoughts as if spoken aloud. Now? His Elder worried over things he couldn't control and anguished over Javier's safety. Yet, he was now as helpless as any human, given to the whims of anyone stronger in his path. Roman used to be the mightiest Elder he knew. How did he live knowing what he'd left behind?

Roman returned his eyes to the road, but Javier stared at his profile recalling how his Elder violently and capably disabled the Rakum who threatened them that night in the Cave. Roman protected and provided for him for decades, long after he'd graduated First Ritual. But now, Roman was his brother, his *mortal* brother. A brother Rufus could kill with one blow.

"Why do you hate her, Javier? Why?"

It was David. His eyes leaked tears of frustration and anger even though Chloe's phone call had been an hour earlier. They were rushing to Beth Rider's home and would arrive in less than an hour. Why did the kid have to ask such stupid questions? Javier didn't answer and instead turned away to look out his window.

"He doesn't hate her, David."

It was Roman, offering his two cents. Javier scoffed, staring at the trees zooming past in the waning daylight. Roman was right. He didn't hate Chloe Bushman. He couldn't. She really did resemble

141

Isabella, once the girl's hair grew out and Javier moved her out of her filthy cell and into a room in the main house.

For nearly a year, Javier made certain Isabella was as comfortable and happy as a kept girl could be. She was not permitted to leave the second floor, but she had books to read and he and Roman as company.

True to his word, Javier only drew her blood periodically, and her health was good. He grew so fond of her that Roman became concerned that their relationship would weaken him and prevent him from graduating the Ritual at the end of their hospital tenure. With all of the respect he could muster, Javier was able to convince Roman that keeping Isabella was good experience, teaching him to control his appetite and manipulate the mortals. But tragedy struck a few short days before they were to depart New York for good. Javier accidentally tapped her too hard and the next evening, she was dead.

Javier put his hand to his mouth and closed his eyes. Over a century had passed and the wound was as fresh as ever. The ridiculous Chloe girl physically resembled Isabella, sounded like her, and even reasoned like her to some extent. Now she was probably going to die and Javier was helpless.

If only, Javier thought, *if only I'd kept my distance, as Roman suggested, I wouldn't be so miserable now.*

"David, Javie, if you're not praying, you should be."

Roman's voice carried a tone of disappointment, but Javier didn't turn his head.

"We're not powerless. We've crossed from death into life. The King of the universe is looking out for us *and* for those we hold dear. You boys cease this negative attitude immediately."

"Yes, sir," David mumbled from the backseat.

Javier stiffened his jaw and switched on the radio. He didn't want to speak to God. Not just yet.

Roman held his peace and focused on the road ahead. Javier and David didn't know what he knew about their enemy. In a waking dream during the night, it was revealed that Rufus Delouve was more than a ruthless despot—he was also out of his mind with the Dying Buzz. Roman had first-hand knowledge of the effects. Over a century ago, his twin Kilmeade had been overcome by the lust for the dying, and subsequently judged by the Fathers. Roman looked back to the night he first saw the effects such prolonged transgression had on a Rakum's life.

It was New York City, 1897, and he'd been commanded by the Fathers to relieve Kilmeade of his position at a Rakum-owned hospital there. He and Kilmeade were born of the same mother on the same evening, three minutes apart. Among Rakum, no familial ties were acknowledged, so the boys were kept apart until their teens. But when reunited at the close of First Ritual, the two 17-year-olds became inseparable.

Being fraternal twins, they were able to play down their blood connection, and for decades they traveled the world as Rakum comrades. But politics among the brethren being as they were, when both were promoted to Elder only months apart, they were separated by the Fathers to settle different areas of the North American continent. In 1838, at 200-years-old, Kilmeade was sent to establish a Rakum presence in New York City and Roman to the villages and forests of Eastern Canada. It'd been sixty years since he'd last seen Kilmeade and when he reached the man's office, he knocked with no small amount of curiosity.

"Enter, brother."

Roman recognized the voice and wondered what he'd see. He'd been warned by the Fathers that Kilmeade had been taking the Dying Buzz and that he'd been disfigured by the effects of his erroneous ways. The Fathers would mete out punishment and Roman need only send him on his way. Now, as he opened the door and approached his brother, Roman readied for anything.

"Roman, having you here now, gives me great pleasure," Kilmeade said, facing away from his guest. Roman stepped up, waiting for him to turn. "I hope you're as strong as ever, big brother. I've been up to no good here at the hospital."

Kilmeade turned slowly and met Roman's eye, a devilish glint of humor shining deep down, and a smile playing on his lips. Roman's eyes widened, but he returned the smile and tilted his head to the side.

"You've looked better, my brother."

Kilmeade laughed aloud and leaned against the wall behind him. Roman marveled at his countenance. Like his twin, Kilmeade was naturally tall, but where Roman was slender, Kilmeade had always been broad-shouldered and thick-necked. Now he appeared hunched over and more muscular by inches. He'd always worn his auburn hair shoulder-length as did Roman, but now it drizzled down his chest on either side as long as a woman's. His smoky grey eyes were now an unnaturally bright robin-egg blue and his lips ruby red. Roman snickered and gestured toward his brother's face.

"Please, don't show this face to Javier. He'll have nightmares for years."

Kilmeade returned his grin and nodded. "Your pup is squeamish, then?"

"To say the least," Roman said. "This is from the Dying Buzz?"

"Nice, eh?" Kilmeade smiled wider and revealed his canines, now extended several centimeters and sharpened to a point. "Check these out."

Roman walked up to him, put one hand behind his head and the other in his brother's mouth. The tips were serrated and Roman's flesh was nicked as he made contact.

"Those must come in handy," Roman chuckled. "Wrong or not, I could use some teeth like that."

Kilmeade laughed and ran his tongue over and around his fangs. "I'll miss them. If they go away, that is."

"They will. The Fathers will put you in isolation, you'll drink only Rakum blood for a year, and you'll be completely restored. Trust me." Roman spoke with confidence, rehashing the same story the Fathers told him when he was ordered to report to New York. Their leaders were usually honest and their explanations reliable. Well, most of the time. They were the Ten Fathers and they did what they thought was best. What could a Rakum Elder do but comply?

Roman huffed and returned his attention to the present. Elder Rufus would look much worse than Kilmeade, and most likely, his condition was terminal. How would it play out? There were no easy answers, so Roman prayed. Now and then, for effect, he reminded the boys to pray, too. It couldn't hurt.

TWENTY-EIGHT

Radnor Lake State Park
Nashville, TN
November 4th, 5:30 p.m.

Beryl watched his brother come awake, a sinking dread deep in his gut. Meryl was indeed dead, but Ta'avah had reanimated him, given him new life. One question nagged him as the spirit of Abroghia caused his brother's flesh to stretch, yawn, and gain its feet. What if he hadn't sent him in? What if Beryl had said simply, *No, Ta'avah, you may not enter my brother?* What then? Would they have died, set aflame by the sun?

Not convinced, Beryl met Ta'avah's gaze and nodded a greeting. They probably would have found some way to survive. But it was too late for regret—

"The sun has set. Let's get going." Ta'avah interrupted Beryl's train of thought and stepped over a stack of rotted wood toward the exit. The two-room cabin was filled with various tools and implements layered in rust, and it'd been a good hiding place. Folded tightly together in the cabin's windowless lavatory, Beryl and Ta'avah slept safely away from the sun. Now his watch chimed the half-hour, and Beryl took a deep breath as they stepped out into the cold night.

"Let's see how you've healed." Outside the cabin, Ta'avah turned and tugged up Beryl's dusty black T-shirt.

The bullet wound in his groin had healed before they'd even left the clearing, but the belly wound was still seeping when they hit the sack hours before. Beryl gazed downward at his stomach, glad that the outward evidence had disappeared, yet the disrupted tissue beneath was knitting together much more slowly than normal.

"A little buzz will fix you right up," Ta'avah said, coming to the same conclusion. He dropped Beryl's shirt and stepped away toward the tree line. "The road is two miles this way. We'll get a meal and a car and head south."

"To Jackson, I suppose," Beryl mumbled. Reading Ta'avah was not like reading his brother. Now, he had to work at it just like any other Rakum. Beryl hoped the old demon had just as much trouble reading him.

"Yes, and stop moping. I'm bringing you with me to serve my purpose. If you want out, I'll relieve you right now." Ta'avah stopped walking and faced Beryl, his expression grave. "Two heads are better than one, but I can do this on my own."

Beryl flicked his chin westward. "I'm with you, sir. Let's get going."

Ta'avah stared at him a moment longer, then nodded and led the way through the thick brush.

Within a half-hour, they'd reached the road and the demon held up his hand.

"Now, wait."

Beryl looked down the road and then up the other way. The forest was silent and no vehicles approached from either direction. He stood quietly for several moments and finally sighed aloud.

"It's at least six hours to Jackson from here, sir. Don't you think—"

Ta'avah spun around and put a finger to Beryl's lips. "Either follow me or bow out. I'll not tell you again."

Beryl winced at the light in his brother's eyes. No—Ta'avah's eyes; Meryl would never look at him with such utter loathing. It was High Father Abroghia who gazed at him now; malevolent, proud, and every bit as evil.

"Good." Ta'avah faced the road again and crouched behind a wide oak. Beryl breathed shallowly and kept his mind blank. Meryl was gone and he was alone.

Alone with his creator.

That gave him no comfort at all.

Fifteen minutes passed before a yellow Dodge pickup came barreling down the two-lane highway that ran through the park. Beryl stepped into the road and waved his arms as Ta'avah limped along the side. They played their roles well enough that the driver slowed, pulled off, and then hopped out to offer assistance.

"Dang! What happened, son? Did you have a wreck?" Thick and muscular with an ample beer belly and cheeks full of RedMan, the driver helped Ta'avah balance and then noticed the copious amounts of blood staining Beryl's shirt and jeans. His eyes widened and he did a double take at the twins' faces. When he recovered, he spit out his chew and pointed at Beryl. "Ya'll get in the cab. I'm taking you to the hospital right away. Come on, son. Can you walk?"

Beryl hobbled to the vehicle unaided as the husky Samaritan carefully lifted Ta'avah into the passenger seat. When he came around to the driver's side to open the third door, Beryl considered how the attack would go down.

Subduing mortals was easy enough if you surprised them. The two seconds that it took to realize the threat was plenty of time to snap a neck or otherwise immobilize for feeding. The driver was a big man and would have leverage; Beryl didn't want to be shoved off his feet in front of his master. He limped toward the man and whimpered, his muscles tense as he prepared to lunge.

"You look all banged up, son. What happened to ya?" the man asked, his head to side, totally convinced by Beryl's performance.

Using supernatural speed, Beryl reached forward and grabbed him tightly by his arms. The man was shocked by the move, but as his predicament dawned on him, he began to curse and thrash against his attacker. Beryl allowed the man to struggle and met Ta'avah's eyes. His master leaned back in the seat, smiled, and crossed his arms. Undaunted, Beryl growled and spun the man around easily, grabbing him around the chest from behind. With a sneer aimed at his master, he violently stressed the man's torso to one side and fractured several of the driver's vertebrae. His victim screamed as his legs buckled and pain ripped through his body.

Eyes still glued to his superior hidden inside his brother's body, he held the paralyzed man up with one strong arm and stabbed him in the neck with the blade in his free hand. They weren't leaving him alive, so Beryl aimed for the jugular. He'd have his fill with or without the demon's help. His victim fell unconscious, and Beryl drew out his blood until he could hold no more. As he was finishing, Ta'avah slipped down from the truck and casually approached.

"Pretty good," he smirked and bent to drag their victim to the side of the road. "I mean, for a ballerina."

Remembering the power in Ta'avah's gaze, Beryl held his tongue and watched him pull the man out of sight by his wrists. He wouldn't live long with his spine severed and third of his blood drained into a hungry Rakum.

"Get the truck started, pup."

Beryl startled at Meryl's voice in his head, saying words only their

Father would utter. He climbed into the cab and turned the ignition. The diesel engine roared to life, and as he adjusted the mirrors, Ta'avah jogged into view and hopped into the passenger side.

Beryl glanced at him and then returned his eyes to the road. The demon had drunk the man to death. His long teeth and extended nails gave him away. But why not? Ta'avah wouldn't take commands. Not from him, not from Rufus, not from anyone. Why should he? He wasn't even Rakum. He was something else. Something other.

Beryl cleared his mind and got the truck up to the speed limit. They'd be in Jackson before midnight, plenty of time to do whatever needed to be done. Plenty of time to help Ta'avah with his plans, whatever they turned out to be. Beryl was with a new master now, and he wasn't foolish enough to turn against him.

Even if he did kill his only brother.

TWENTY-NINE

Montgomery, AL
November 4th, 5:00 p.m.

The sun hadn't yet touched the horizon when Beth entered Michael's study with a child on each side.

"Let's go find Selene. Maybe she broke down. We'll drive up and down the bypass and check Vaughn Road." Beth lowered her voice in deference to the children. "She's not answering her cell and I'm getting a bad feeling."

Michael covered a sigh and stood to his feet. Grace released her mother's hand and flew at him, arms open wide.

"Daddy! How do you like my bow?"

"It's my bow!" Dae Lee countered and ran to him as well. Both girls clambered into his arms to be pulled off the ground. Michael and the girls had an impromptu raspberries war as he carried them out the door and toward the foyer. Not at all amused, Beth's face was ashen, no doubt fearing that Selene had been abducted like the Bushman girl.

Michael glanced at the sky as they exited the house. The sun sat above the horizon, shining enough UV to blind his former brethren. He said as much to Beth who sent him an impatient glare.

"Please, let's get on the road, honey. "

He could've argued, but he knew better. Instead he handed Dae Lee over to be buckled in. Beth was furtively surveying the yard, the neighborhood, and finally the house as if she expected to see Rakum at every turn. It was impossible for the Rakum to be out before dusk, but Michael again held his tongue and fell behind the wheel.

"Honey, try her phone again," he said, turning over the engine.

Beth frowned at him and then softened her gaze. "I'm sorry, honey. Please, let's just look for her. It'll be full dark in thirty minutes. What could it hurt?"

"Nothing. It's a good idea." Michael pulled out of the driveway and started toward the main road. Selene was probably headed back as they spoke, but better safe than sorry was a human adage he was coming to appreciate after a century of carefree immortality.

♦♦♦

Roman pulled up to Beth Rider's driveway and scowled that the family sedan was missing. Michael's truck was on the right, but Roman knew if they were home, their Honda would be nearby.

It's almost dark. Where would they go?

Hiding his displeasure, he gestured for the boys to follow him and he rang the doorbell.

"Didn't you just talk to them?" David asked, his voice still shaky from weeping off and on the past hour. He was not taking Chloe's abduction well and Roman felt for him.

"Michael said they'd be here." Roman knocked on the door, and when no one answered, he pulled out a separate key ring. "We're going in."

Javier entered first, his faced pinched. He hadn't spoken since Chloe's call and Roman instructed him to sit in the living room. Fishing out his phone, he punched Michael's number and waited. After two rings it went to voicemail and Roman sighed, unwilling to hurry up and wait. If they left the house, there was probably trouble. Roman tapped Javier's shoulder.

"Stay here while David and I drive around the neighborhood."

"Whatever," Javier mumbled and sank into the leather couch.

Roman swallowed a terse retort and motioned for David to follow. He locked the door behind him and led the boy back to the truck. "I'm sure they're right around here somewhere."

Thankfully, David kept his thoughts to himself and followed obediently to the Tahoe. Worrying about Michael and Beth, Jesse and Selene, Miss Bushman, and now Javier's despondency was enough for one man to handle. Not to mention the possibility of facing off with Rufus Delouve. After all, that's what he was now—a man, and he would need God to help him keep it together.

Roman nodded at nothing and lifted up a prayer in his heart. It would have to be enough for now.

Thirty

Selene checked her watch and glanced at the setting sun. In Germany it was six in the morning. Jesse wasn't an early riser, which she attributed to his century and a half of sleeping through the daylight hours. Even if he'd adjusted to the European time change, she didn't think he'd be awake. Still...

She pulled out her iPhone and pressed Jesse's assigned icon. Sitting in her car outside the Texaco, she was waiting as long as possible before having to return to Beth's house and face their next move. Beth's blind faith got on her last nerve. Moreover, Beth obviously had no concern whatsoever that Jesse hadn't made it home.

A low noise escaped Selene's throat and she covered her mouth. Oh, how she wished she and Jesse could just disappear. She played brave and strong for Dae Lee's sake, but mostly she was scared of losing everything she loved. Worse, she was scared of being found once again in the Rakum's clutches.

Jesse, I need you.

Selene closed her eyes and waited for the call to connect. Jesse was her rock, her foundation. Without him, she was as fake as the highlights in Beth Rider's hair.

The phone chimed across the miles, then switched to voice-mail.

"Call me," she said and pocketed the device. Jesse would call soon; he was an excellent lover, father, provider, and everything a husband should be.

Unbidden and unwanted, Selene received a sudden image of Ira Montana, her first husband. He'd been a human monster that she married out of family obligation at seventeen. Beating his teenage wife was his favorite pastime. The last time he whaled on her, she landed in the hospital.

Selene closed her eyes, not happy that her mind was busily retelling the painful history of the events that followed her

151

hospitalization; including when she met her first Rakum and became his mate. The story played out as she succumbed to its pull, her pulse quickening. Jesse's strong arms would be perfect right about now.

◆◆◆

Posing as the hospital chaplain, the Rakum Elder who became her master and mate had sauntered into her room as she lay there—newly nineteen, battered, bruised, and only half-conscious. He was built like a linebacker, with a thick beard and curly brown hair. He wore a black fedora that nearly obscured fierce brown eyes, and although he seemed to be very old, there were no lines on his rugged face. Even in her pitiful condition, Selene felt her heart quicken at the sight of him, as an unexplainable peace came upon her when their eyes met.

"Mrs. Montana..." His voice rumbled through the room even though he had spoken in an undertone.

"Selene, please," she replied and watched him with wide eyes, knowing he was different, but not sure if she should be afraid. He was dressed like any other man; in fact, he was pulling off the rabbi bit fairly well. Selene's relatively light skin was attributed to her mother's mixed heritage—half-Nigerian and half-Caucasian Jew—and as her medical chart labeled her under Ira's religion, she expected her visitor to begin praying in Hebrew at any moment. But he only offered her a sympathetic grin and set her chart on the side table.

"He worked you over, yes?" the rabbi said finally, his voice soft. He put his hand out toward her face and his fingers made contact with her lacerated cheek. When she winced, he added with sincerity, "I'll take that pain away, my beauty."

Selene inhaled as her visitor closed his eyes briefly, and a curious tickle grew in the skin above her jaw line. The tickle slowly became an itch and Selene took a deep breath of surprise. Her cheek was healing—and rapidly.

"Rabbi?" she whispered, moving her jaw back and forth. "What power is this?"

"No, not Rabbi. I'm Yosef." He bowed slightly at the waist and allowed his hand to slip down the nearest forearm until they clasped hands. "You don't belong here, eh?"

Selene's eyes watered and she wiped away a tear with her free hand. "I really don't, do I? What am I going to do?"

Yosef grinned and released her hand. He positioned both palms over her midsection and maneuvered them underneath the sheet to rest heavily on the thin cotton hospital robe. As she watched, he concentrated on her injuries: a bruised kidney, two fractured ribs, and a perforated uterus. He was healing her, he was an angel. Selene's eyebrows arched as she realized she was in the presence of the divine.

When the job was done, her angelic visitor raised himself up and clutched interwoven fingers to his chest. He looked down on her with an adoring gaze similar to the one her deceased father reserved for her alone. Selene swallowed and awaited Yosef's next words.

"I've mended your injuries, my beauty. Do you realize this?" her angel asked and took a tiny step back.

Selene panicked and grabbed his sleeve. "Please, take me with you. I'll be good to you. I'm not garbage, I know I'm not." Selene pleaded with her eyes and after a long moment, he smiled and nodded his head.

"Remain here until tomorrow night. We'll see then what we will do with you."

Yosef pulled his arm from her grip and slipped to the door. Selene's eyes filled with tears but she didn't cry, hoping to impress him with her stoicism.

"Good evening, my beauty," Yosef said as he bowed low and backed out of the room.

When he returned the next night, she learned that Ira Montana was dead. Yosef invited her to come with him to be his mate for as long as she was wanted, which she hoped was a very long time.

Selene snapped back to the present and checked her makeup in the rearview mirror. She'd lived with the Elder as his wife for four years and he'd treated her well. Her hell began when the Rakum started wondering about God. When Yosef got religion, he put her out. He tried to make her safe, but once the trouble began, she was grabbed up by a few of Yosef's proselytes and taken to the Cave. There, they all took turns at her as she became a plaything to any and every Rakum who plucked her out of the Population for the night.

Selene shivered and wiped a tear from her eye, glad she didn't smear her mascara. If Jesse hadn't shown up and rescued her, she would have surely taken her own life. When Jesse brought her into his world of devotion and kindness, Selene discovered what love could truly be. Once again, she was reminded that above all things, Jesse was her savior. And didn't he adore their daughter with his entire being?

Since the day Dae Lee was born, Jesse was a different person. Stronger, wiser, more self-confident, and more determined to make certain his family had whatever they desired. Selene shook her head and lowered her eyes. Jesse wanted more children. "A houseful" he'd once said. She laughed and rest her eyes on the colorful dashboard. The one baby she carried nearly ruined her figure. Maybe when she was older, but now? She just turned thirty and last month, squeezed into her pre-pregnancy, size-two jeans. No way was she giving up her flat belly any time soon.

Selene pulled out her iPhone and pushed Jesse's number once more. It rang twice and just as she heard the familiar click of her husband picking up on his end, the driver's side door was yanked open and the phone swiped from her hand.

"Move over, sweetie!"

Selene reacted instantly and without forethought. Five years of Extreme Tae-bo were put to good use as she cocked her fist back into the man's face as hard as she could. With a yelp of fury, she pushed against him in the cramped space and brought the heel of her right palm to the bridge of his nose. Her attacker wasn't fazed and he shoved her viciously across the seat and settled into the driver's side, pulling closed the door. The sound of a rear door slamming shut barely registered as Selene screamed at the top of her lungs. Swiveling right, she grabbed the door handle as two strong hands from behind yanked her back and pressed her into the leather seat.

"Hold her tight, Tyson!" The driver shouted and peeled out.

Selene wrestled against the one who held her from the back seat and kicked her legs frantically. Within moments, and despite the restriction of her narrow dress, she was able to get her legs up to the level of the dash. Modesty aside, she lifted both legs high, wheeled to the left, and kicked the driver in the face.

"Tyson! Are you useless?" The driver shouted and dodged the sharp toe of her Prada pumps. Two more kicks and Selene's right shoe popped off. She landed a few good jabs into the driver's neck with her heels, and he drove his right fist into her face with power that stunned her.

"Now, be still!" he yelled as the car fishtailed onto the highway.

Selene's head swam from the blow. She watched the city flow into her past as her captors sped down the interstate and into the dark beyond. When her vision cleared, she twisted side-to-side with renewed vigor until she was grabbed her under her armpits and brutally dragged over the headrest, into the lap of her backseat attacker. She barely noticed the several strands of Fifth Avenue weave that were ripped from her scalp during her progress to the back. The man covered her mouth with one hand and secured her wrists with the other.

"Hand over your hanky, Gage!"

He bellowed his command and Selene writhed in his lap as he brutally shoved the cloth between her teeth. That done, Selene continued to contort herself with all of her strength until the man hopped out from under her, and straddled her on the long bench seat.

"She's still a little too feisty for my taste, brother," the one called Tyson said, breathing hard.

Selene was tiring, but his words gave her renewed energy. She raised her knees beneath him and he bounced, bumping his head on the cloth-covered roof.

"I'll have to tap her or kill her, Gage!" he said as his head hit the roof a third time.

"Tap her, she's no prize. We just need to get her there alive. Go ahead, man. Use my knife."

Selene froze and aimed her eyes toward the face that hovered over her. Sunken brow, glittery black gaze, and powdery complexion—these two kidnappers were Rakum, and they'd been eating some very bad food. Out of old habit, she grabbed a glimpse of the horizon. The Rakum couldn't bear the day. These two must have been hiding very close and come out even as the sun went down. It was a premeditated set-up and Selene only had a millisecond to regret leaving the Stone's house before Tyson flicked open the blade and stabbed her neck.

Falling still, Selene sank into the seat and exhaled slowly. The nightmare wasn't over. The Rakum had her, Jesse was nowhere in sight, and she hadn't finished paying her dues.

She's no prize, the driver had said. She was garbage. *We just need to get her there alive,* he'd said.

Latched onto her wound, Tyson gripped her upper arms, slurping like a frenzied animal. Selene curbed her tears and stopped struggling. Her anchor was thousands of miles away, a prisoner of an unexpected European blizzard. Selene was in a blizzard of a different sort, but she'd been here before and resisting never did help her one bit.

155

Thirty-one

Beth sent the children a strained smile and faced front once more. Michael had obediently trekked up and down the length of the eastern bypass and was now traveling Vaughn Road away from the house. The sun had set nearly twenty minutes ago and frankly, she was quite sure Selene was in trouble. It was full dark and the safest place to be was at home where she was certain God had stationed a platoon of angels. Beth considered her words before speaking so Dae Lee wouldn't know that they were desperately afraid for her mother. Finally, she touched Michael's arm.

"Honey, let's turn back. Roman's probably waiting for us."

"Wait, hon." Michael interrupted her with an upraised hand and gestured toward the gas station on the right. Three city police cars and one ambulance sat idling in the parking lot with all lights flashing.

"Do you see her car?" Beth leaned as far as the seatbelt would allow and grasped the door handle. Her heart fluttered at the thought of finding her friend safe and well, but Selene's Lexus was nowhere in sight.

"No, but I have a hunch." Michael pulled into the Texaco and stopped well away from the emergency response unit. "Wait here."

Beth nodded, flashed another unconvincing grin at the girls, and watched her husband step up to the nearest policeman. After a few brief exchanges, Michael waved for her to come over. Beth turned on the radio for the kids and locked them in before jogging the fifty feet to where Michael stood.

"What? Find something?"

Michael pointed to a plastic bag in the officer's hand. It was an iPhone.

"You think that's Selene's?"

156

"Look at who she dialed last."

Beth leaned forward and the officer pressed the flat screen through the plastic. It was Jesse's cell.

"Oh, God! Where is she?" Beth looked around, but Michael touched her arm and shook his head.

"Honey, it seems she was abducted."

"What happened? Did anyone see it?" Beth shrugged out from under Michael's hand and looked to the officer for an explanation. He started to answer, but Michael spoke up, his voice strangely calm.

"Witnesses said two men got into her car. She screamed and they drove off, headed northeast to the interstate. That's all, honey." Michael looked into her eyes, mouthed the word "Rakum" and she knew he hoped she'd keep it together. But all Beth could do was imagine her daughter kidnapped, or Dae Lee, or her husband.

"Michael, I—"

"Go back to the girls." Michael took her upper arm in his fingers and made as if to turn her toward the car. Beth resisted and shook her head.

"But—"

"Beth, go back to the girls. I'll join you in a moment and we'll go home."

"But—" Beth wanted to obey her husband but what were the police doing about Selene?

"The girls, Beth. Go sit with them." Michael lowered his chin and his voice. "Now."

Beth huffed, bit her tongue, and turned with angry aplomb back to the car. Michael knew how to speak to the police since he was Chief of Police at the airport. Michael knew the danger they were in and the strength of the Rakum they were up against. So why didn't she trust his ability to steer them? Was Selene right when she accused her of not having enough faith in her husband?

Jesse!

At the thought of Selene's husband worrying himself crazy for news, Beth rushed to the car, unlocked it and slid in.

"Where's mommy?" Dae Lee piped up, her expression curious and not yet afraid. Beth forced a big smile as she fished her cell out of her purse.

"She'll be back soon, sweetie. I have to call your daddy, okay?" Beth stepped back out of the car, closed the door, leaned on it, and dialed the familiar number. Jesse answered on the first ring.

"Beth?"

"Yes, Jesse, I'm so sorry—"

"I've spoken to the police. They have an APB out on her car and a description of the guys who nabbed her. They're definitely Rakum, but from the witness description, it sounds like they've been eating the dead."

"We'll get her back. Roman and the boys should be at my house now—"

"What's going on? Why take Selene? If they want me, why take her? I can't get there any faster!"

Beth heard the frustration and desperation in her friend's voice, and her heart broke for him. Helpless and faraway, he would have to put his trust in his friends and in his God to rescue the love of his life.

"Jesse, Selene is strong. She'll be okay. She knows how to handle herself around them. She won't do anything stupid."

"You don't understand. Selene never wanted to be part of that life. You think she chose to be a Cow? A servant to Elder Yosef? She had no choice. Her whole life, men have made choices for her. Abused her. Made *her* all about *them*. She's fragile, Beth. She's so fragile…"

Jesse's voice broke off and Beth knew he was weeping. But Selene—breakable? Beth blinked her eyes at the possibility. Had she misread the woman? Granted, since they escaped the Cave all those years ago, Selene seemed to be a woman of iron will, but Beth hadn't known her when in their clutches. Jesse knew her before she found God and before she found real love.

"How's Dae Lee? Does she know?"

"No." Beth answered. "I told her mommy was running errands. Do you want to speak to her?"

There was a pause. "No, I'll call in another hour. Let me check the counter again. I'm at the airport on stand-by. Cell service is sketchy here, too. God, help us."

"Okay. Michael's right here. And Roman and David and Javier. We'll have a group of Godly men to battle this evil. God will take care of Selene. He has to."

"Selene's been on the outs with God lately. She needs me. She's so precious…" Jesse fell silent. Beth licked her lips and nodded. If Selene was questioning her faith, it would explain her attitude earlier.

"God'll take care of her." Beth hoped she sounded convincing. She believed it, but she knew that God's ways were high above her own and there was no telling what He planned to do with the woman they sought.

"Listen. Stay on guard. There's an evil element that stands outside the mess with Rufus and his zombie patrol. I can't see it clearly, but trust me. You need to be careful. The devil masquerades as an angel of light. Don't be deceived."

Beth shivered. "I'll watch out."

"Yes. Please, God," Jesse agreed and was gone.

Beth slipped back into the passenger side and held her breath. *God is in control. God is in control. God is in control.*

The mantra soothed her spirit, and when the other voice whispered that Selene was dead and she was next, Beth shook her head. Selene would be okay, Jesse would catch a flight back soon, the plans of the enemy would fall through, and she would recognize any threat that came to their door. Because God was in control and there was no denying His power.

Thirty-two

Shivering and miserable, Chloe crawled out from under the vampire's draped arm and tiptoed to the bathroom. According to her watch, the sun was down, but the pale monster under the covers was as still as the dead. And oh, how she wished he *was* dead.

Chloe closed and locked the bathroom door and darted for the toilet. If he was going to barge in on her again, she hoped to be finished beforehand. As soon as she could, she flushed and stood in front of the mirror to scout the damage.

Gorgeous.

She looked like a person who'd spent the night with the devil. Her hair was going every which way, dark circles bruised her eye sockets, and the skin flaked where her lips were chapped seemingly beyond repair. Chloe swallowed hard and looked away. Any minute now, Rufus the Horrible would open the door with a wave of his hand and show her the way to hell.

Dave, hurry!

As David popped into her mind, Chloe's eyes fell on the wastebasket between the toilet and the sink counter. It was clean and unused, and sitting in the bottom by itself was her cell phone. Her heart skipping a beat, Chloe fished it out and ran her fingers along the groove where the back was missing. Rufus had popped out the battery. The memories were sluggish, but they were slowly filtering in. Filled with a spark of hope, Chloe fell to her knees and peered around for the missing parts. The slip of plastic that formed the back was against the tub, and feeling with her fingers underneath the rug, she found the battery.

Oh, please, please, please.

Chloe assembled the contraption and switched it on, cupping it

160

tightly in her hands to disguise the hello chime. Of course, Rufus would hear it, but she had to try. If she could just speak to Dave…

All four bars shot straight up and Chloe jabbed the keys rapidly. Before the first ring ended, her prayers were answered.

"Chloe! Where are you? Are you okay?"

"I'm scared. Are you coming?"

"Yes! As fast as we can. Did he hurt you? Where is he now?"

"He bit me!. He's a vampire. A real one. Why didn't you trust me? Why didn't you tell me where you came from? Why didn't you tell me you were a Wraith?"

"I'm sorry, sunshine. I'm so sorry."

Chloe's bottled sobs erupted then and she barely heard his reply.

"I thought I was done with them. I never thought you'd be pulled in like this."

Chloe heard the pain in his voice and she tried to regain her composure. "He held onto me all day. In bed with him all day. It was awful. Please, hurry!"

"Don't give in to him!" David's adamant tone answered her woeful plea. "Keep resisting. That's your number one defense. Do you hear me?"

"What am I supposed to do? He's got me in here tight. He said he's going to bite me for real later. He has fangs, Dave! Like Dracula. Not like in *The Rabbit*. Not like a Wraith!" Chloe sunk to the floor and sat on her folded knees. "I'm scared, Dave. Hurry!"

"Listen," David's tone sharpened, "he's been taking blood from the dying and it changes a Wraith's appearance. Rufus won't drink your blood if you resist. He'll try to wear you down, make you feel powerless. He wants you to give in. Chloe—are you listening to me?"

Chloe gulped and made a small noise.

"Just hang on and don't give up."

"He's not waiting!" Chloe couldn't control the desperation in her voice and she didn't try. "Are *you* listening to *me*? He bit me last night! I can't go through that again."

"You have to trust me. Rufus won't do it again until you consent. Trust me, I know what I'm talking about!"

David's anxious tone caused Chloe to raise her voice. "Just come get me! When are you going to be here?"

"We have to gather our forces. I'm bringing friends. We'll be there tomorrow. You can make it! You're strong!"

Chloe shook her head jerkily. Who was he talking about?

161

Certainly not her. "You're crazy!"

"Your resistance taints the blood. Listen—this is what you do. Submit to God, right now. Submit to God and Rufus will leave you alone."

Chloe looked at the closed door, tears running down her cheeks. David was spouting nonsense and she was in fear for her life.

"Did you hear me?"

"God's not looking after me, Dave!" she spewed, knowing her voice must have awakened the monster by now. "If He was, I'd be at home with my cat and not in here with a monster from hell!"

"No, you just don't understand God. He's been watching over you since you were born. Submit to God, resist the devil and—"

Chloe looked up from her place on the cold ceramic tile as the door swung in and she met the vampire's eyes. He was smiling, his sharp teeth barely disguised by his swollen lips. Reaching his needle-like fingers toward her, he took the phone away from her ear.

"He's back. Ya'll hurry…" Chloe mumbled and came to her feet. David's angry responses faded as the phone was lifted to Rufus's deformed ear.

"Are you coming, little David? Your girlfriend is tasty. I intend to show her my full hospitality tonight. Hurry."

Rufus didn't disable the phone this time but dropped it to the floor, and with a single violent move, crushed it with his bare foot. Bits of plastic shot out in every direction and Chloe stepped backward until she lost her balance and fell hard into the bathtub.

"I have a sweet spot for you, Miss Bushman, see? I allowed you to use the facilities and call your little friends." Rufus was in the small room with her now and he stepped to the tub. "How about a little payback."

He held out his hand, but Chloe pressed her arms to her sides and shook her head stubbornly. "Leave me alone! I'll never give in to you! Never!" Chloe glanced around for a weapon, but there was nothing.

Rufus reached forward, grabbed a handful of her hair, and pulled her to her feet. Chloe did her best to stay with him as he walked casually into the bedroom. "I believe you'll change your mind, sweet one."

Rufus reached the bed and tossed her down hard. Chloe's breath was knocked out by the move and when she flipped over, her neck throbbed from being forced to the side.

"I have many chores to tend to tonight." Rufus glared at her, his face contorted into a snarl and did not react when the door opened behind him.

"Master, we have Jesse Cherrie's woman. She'll be here by ten. Where do you want her?"

Rufus didn't turn, but answered, his gaze glued to Chloe's.

"Put her in my study." Rufus thought a moment and his lips curled into a smile. "And have everyone meet me there when she arrives. I'll introduce her to the boys. She knows the drill."

Chloe's eyes widened as the vampire's innuendo paralyzed her. Was she next? Whoever this poor woman was, she didn't want to end up in the same boat. As if reading her mind, Rufus laughed and gestured one bony finger in Chloe's direction.

"Yes—you're quite young. Some of the boys likely prefer the innocent ones. I'll let you know." With that, Rufus turned and left the room.

Chloe held her breath, her eyes trained to the door. He'd left it ajar; was he returning? Was someone else coming in? Chloe put one foot to the floor as a large, intimidating Wraith entered at a swift walk. Without a word and before she could shuffle away, he leaned forward, grabbed her around the waist and tossed her over his shoulder.

Chloe kicked and punched, but his step didn't slow or waver. As he made two turns and headed down a long hall, she stopped struggling to map out her surroundings. What if she got loose and had a chance to make a run for it? Chloe braced herself against the brute's back and watched the house go by backwards. When he stopped at a closed door and headed through, she knew right away they were in a basement. Down below it was dark, and when the Wraith reached the landing and dropped her to the floor, he didn't throw on the lights.

"Wait! Come back!" Chloe got to her feet. She waited for her eyes to adjust as the sound of the Wraith trailed up the stairs, the door closed, and a bolt was thrown.

Chloe looked around as her surroundings began to develop edges in the darkness. The center of the room was clear, but around the walls she discerned boxes and the looming shapes of discarded furniture.

A small noise to her left, like stocking feet on linoleum, caused her to turn and hold her breath. Someone was with her. The sliding sound reoccurred and seemed closer now. Chloe strained her eyes and spun 360 degrees in the center of the room.

"Who's there? Please, don't hurt me!"

The footsteps halted and a rasping exhale filled the room.

"Who's there? Please? Is there any light?"

As her queries ended, the room was lit by a single bulb hanging from the rafters. Chloe again spun all the way around, and she saw two old men against the far wall. One was tall and distinguished-looking in a shabby gray suit, with dark grey hair and stubble on his chin. The other one was shorter with hunched shoulders and a long, reddish-white beard. This one was wearing coveralls, socks, and a stocking cap. Near him was a light switch.

"Uh…" Chloe managed and remained where she was and clutched her arms at her chest. "Who are you?"

Coveralls shook his head and sank to the floor. He tucked his face into the wall and fell silent. The second man followed his lead and went to his knees, carefully collapsing on his rear like the old man he was.

Chloe backed to the opposite wall and sat pensively on the cold cement floor. How long was she to share this dungeon with the two mysterious grandfathers? Would she be able to resist the devil? Isn't that what Dave was trying to say to her? Submit to God, resist the devil, and he will flee from you?

The old man in the coveralls grunted just then and Chloe froze, the behavior so much like Rufus when he read her mind. She clenched her jaw, balled her fists, and sent out a loud mental test message.

"Are you reading my mind?"

The old man grunted again, face still stuck to the plaster.

Chloe hugged herself tighter and cleared her mind. Old man or not, he creeped her out.

Maybe David and his friends would hurry.

Thirty-Three

Montgomery, AL
November 4th, 5:45 p.m.

Riding in the trunk of his car wasn't entirely unpleasant; Canaan slept most of the way. Now that they'd arrived in Montgomery, he sensed the sunset without having to see it with his eyes. And fortunately, finding Beth Rider's address was a piece of cake.

Marcy's clearance to the law enforcement database allowed them to locate the Rabbit's residence in seconds from their home computer. And as there was some urgency with Rufus's cronies on their trail, Canaan risked his stowaway trick. He'd used it once or twice before when he had to skip town or escape in a hurry. At their current apartment it was easier than ever. Blue Creek Condominiums had underground garages with interior access for all of its premier units. So handy was this that in broad daylight, at noon precisely, Marcy had led him blindfolded—just in case—down the cement stairs and helped him into the trunk of their new Cadillac Seville. She covered him carefully with a thick canvas tarp, closed the trunk, and headed for Montgomery. Now that they'd arrived, Canaan would improvise.

He didn't have the heart to admit to his mate that he had no plan. He didn't trust the Rakum traitors that he was going to find surrounding Beth Rider, but he knew he could never align himself with Rufus and his ilk. To protect Marcy and hopefully seek a resolution to his problems, Canaan decided to see what the Rabbit and her army could do to help him. It reminded him of the popular human adage: The enemy of my enemy is my friend. Beth Rider had been very eager to excommunicate their High Father seven years ago in the Cave. She'd also been gung-ho to lead his brethren into her faith system afterward. If she had a pathological compulsion to help Rakum, then he would use her assistance. The only thing the remaining Rakum feared was whatever Force this woman carried with her. Canaan wanted that power on his side for the upcoming showdown with Rufus.

For the moment, he was settling Marcy into a laundry room off the back door. He'd entered using ancient methods to open two mechanical locks and newer skills to disarm the electronic alarm system. Marcy didn't possess the stealth necessary to scope out the house so he tucked her inside, blew her a kiss, and closed the door.

Now…who was home?

Canaan stood in the dark hallway and closed his eyes. It was unfortunate that his telepathy had been stunted when Abroghia was bested, but he still had his superior natural senses. Firstly, he detected the mark Jack Dawn had placed on the woman, Beth Rider. It was as if his Elder was still around, how heavy his scent hung in the air. Yet, Canaan listened for heartbeats and heard only three: his own, Marcy's, and one other. The third was accompanied by a masculine sigh.

Canaan proceeded down the dark hallway toward the intermittent light of a television. The sound was muted and when he reached the doorway of the large and lushly-appointed den, he spied a man seated on a long leather couch. Canaan remained where he was and leaned thoughtfully against the threshold. His quarry faced away, looking blindly forward, not watching the television, but deep in thought.

Taking his time, Canaan analyzed the man's scent. Perhaps he knew him; it was vaguely familiar, yet strange and human. Was this one of the traitors? Canaan's mouth went to the side, marveling at the whole misadventure. Why would a supernaturally powerful being long to be weak and powerless? What kind of Rakum would be so dim-witted as to barter such a transaction?

Canaan studied the man's black hair; it was short and wavy and readily reflected the light. There was an ethnicity to this one, a dark and swarthy countenance apparent in his skin, his well-formed neck and proportionately muscled right arm that lay across the back. This man had European origins, maybe even Eastern Europe. Canaan guessed a few seconds longer when, from the way he had come, a tiny sneeze emitted. Marcy, behind closed doors several rooms away, broke the silence.

The man on the couch jumped to his feet and spun around to face the door. He brandished a fearsome hunting knife and gasped with surprise as their eyes met. Canaan smiled. He knew this one; he'd met him a century ago.

He'd tasted his blood.

"Javier d'Millier. Well, I'll be..." Canaan stood up off the door. This was going to be interesting.

Javier startled at the Rakum that stood so casually before him. The man's countenance read that he'd been there for some time, studying him, considering him, and perhaps planning to kill him. Javier thrust the knife forward once for effect, but the stranger in the doorway only smiled wider. Then he winked and it all came back.

"Canaan?" Javier whispered, his weapon upraised, but his arm softening. The Rakum he'd known briefly in his youth took a step toward him and shook his head.

"You, Javier? You're mortal now? How in the world did this happen? You were such a delight," the man said, clucking his tongue. "You had such promise."

"Canaan...what are you doing here?" Javier took a corresponding step back, lowering the knife a few more inches. Should he be afraid? As the older Rakum opened his hands and shrugged, Javier realized that deep down, he was glad to see him; to see a real, hot-blooded Rakum in the flesh and in all his glory, like the good old days.

"It's *Elder* Canaan now, little brother. You're with them? The traitors?"

Javier lowered his arm to his side and dropped Michael's knife onto the sofa. He'd been fiddling with it since he picked it out of the collection on the wall, but this man hadn't come to kill him. He dared a small grin and Canaan crossed the floor. Licking his lips, Javier realized he was sweating; quite a different scenario from the last time the two of them met.

Back then, he was a twenty-year-old proselyte, lackadaisical and fearless, with his whole life ahead of him. A life of reigning alongside his brothers until the end of time.

And now?

Javier sighed and his visitor lowered his chin and held his gaze.

"I'll have your answer now, little brother." Exercising his authority in a way Javier understood from decades of subservience, Elder Canaan put a heavy hand on his shoulder. "How long have you been this way?"

Javier looked sideways at the hand on his right, and then returned to the Elder's liquid gaze. The guy was 360 years old, but could pass for thirty-five. His skin was not completely without color as if he'd retained the small amount of melatonin that all Rakum youth developed when undergoing the Ritual of the Stinging Sun. His hair, although shorter now with the current fashion, was just as full and as golden as it was when they'd last met. Only the tattoos sprouting from the collar of his button-down shirt were truly new.

Several seconds had passed without an answer, and Canaan brought his palm to the back of Javier's neck, pulling him a few inches closer.

"Did you make a mistake? Is that what happened?"

Javier swallowed. No, he definitely made the right choice. Being a child of God was infinitely superior to being a child of Abroghia, a demon. Javier paused a second more. If he didn't speak soon, Canaan would move on to his next question and Javier was afraid of just what that might be.

"No, it wasn't a mistake, Master." Javier regretted his choice of words. He was no longer a Rakum. He was not inferior to the Elder that held him close, hypnotizing him with his gaze. According to Beth Rider, he was, in fact, empowered by the Creator of the universe, not small and insignificant. No matter that he felt such in Canaan's impressive shadow.

"Come meet my Marcy." Canaan gave him a wry smile and stepped aside, still cupping Javier's neck as he gestured for the hallway. "I have told her of our days together in New York."

Numbly, Javier nodded and led the way down the hall toward the back door where the Rakum indicated. Once they stopped at the laundry room, Canaan rapped on it once and pushed it open.

"Marcy, meet Javier d'Millier."

Javier stepped to the threshold and remained there as his eyes met the woman's inside. She was fiftyish, thin, and stoop-shouldered with a shock of frizzy red hair that a wide barrette barely contained. He smiled and she did the same. How long had she been with this guy? She was completely at ease and moments later, she laid into Canaan like a mean old dog.

"Do you think you took long enough, Canaan? I have to pee and I told you that before you wandered off. I wish you'd keep my needs in mind more often because I nearly wet my pants waiting for you, and I had no idea who was out there with you and if it was safe to go out."

When she was finished barking, she circumvented Javier in the doorway, glared once more at Canaan, and disappeared down the hall, poking her head in various doors. Javier's jaw dropped and he looked for Canaan's reaction. The big Rakum shrugged and pushed the door closed with his fingers.

"Now that we're alone…"

"Is that your mate?" Javier asked incredulous, but Canaan only winked and crossed his arms at his chest.

"As I said, now that we're alone, little brother, what can you tell me about this transformation of yours? I've been wondering what would make a Rakum choose this life over what you had. Please, enlighten me…"

Canaan oozed sincere curiosity, but Javier was at a loss for words. Part of him nudged to shout aloud that God had saved him from an eternity of punishment, that he had never been so at peace in his whole life. But another part of him, the smaller and more familiar part, warned him to be quiet and mind his tongue. It also whispered to him little suppositions of what the Elder may or may not be able to do for him, to give him back a portion of his former glory. All of these things and more poured past his consciousness, and he stopped himself abruptly when he recalled the telepathy of the Elders.

Canaan's eyebrows went up and he chuckled. "I no longer hear your thoughts, little brother." He held up his fingers as if to frame Javier's face. "Now, I read countenance, and you're plenty expressive."

"No telepathy?" Javier asked, confused.

Canaan shook his head, still smiling down on Javier as if he was a child to be coddled. "Unfortunately, no. Since Last Assembly, I can only read Rakum I can *see*. And mortals? Forget about it. But I read your expression well enough. You're afraid of me, aren't you?"

"No." Javier shook his head. "No, I'm just tired and…"

"Confused," Canaan said and Javier nodded. "You know, I was good to you, Javier. You remember the gift I gave you?"

Isabella's tragic yet beautiful face came to Javier's memory and he nodded. "Of course."

"Pity what happened to her," Canaan whispered, holding Javier's gaze.

"It was an accident." Javier looked up, questioning the conspiratorial tone. "What did you hear?" News traveled fast among the Rakum back then, before modern electronics crowded the

169

imagination and the mental airwaves of them all.

Canaan allowed a tiny smile. "You didn't kill her, Javier."

Javier looked at him suspiciously. "It was an accident, but yes. It was all me."

The Elder shook his head. "Roman killed her, kid. If you were even the least bit telepathic, you'd have seen it. All of the Elders and Elder-candidates saw it; we talked about it for decades. We call it 'pulling a Roman.'"

"What?" Javier's voice rose an octave and he furrowed his brow. "You're lying. Roman would never—"

"Roman would never what? Protect you from yourself?" Canaan flicked his hand toward the hallway. "Why do you think I left the Brotherhood? I left before my superiors 'pulled a Roman' on Marcy."

Javier exhaled and dropped his shoulders. The night he found Isabella's body, Roman had seemed so surprised and saddened. Roman, his master, his adopted father, his brother, his best friend—a murderer? A liar?

Canaan cleared his throat. "I rode to Alabama in the trunk of my car, Javier. I haven't eaten in twenty-four hours. You remember the hunger, don't you? We're alone now."

Javier's eyes narrowed and another image flashed in his long memory. Over a hundred years ago, this Rakum took his blood at Roman's okay. Would he have the audacity to ask for another dose, this time with Javier's consent?

"I've never tasted an apostate's blood, little brother. What do you say?"

Canaan didn't have to ask, he could take what he wanted by force. Javier greatly appreciated the courtesy, his resistance slipping. What harm could it do? The incredible truth about Roman simmered in his heart and made him nauseous. Canaan needed a buzz. Wouldn't it ingratiate him further to the amazing Rakum that stepped out of time to see him tonight?

"Javier?" Canaan whispered.

Javier's chest tightened with the decision he was about to make. He should say no. He was a child of God now, a son of a different Father, and Canaan was no longer his brother at all.

"I'll sew you back up, Javie."

Javie. Roman's old nickname for him. It was a name that dredged up memories of good times reigning as gods over the mortals, and recollections of the many times Roman may have "protected" him in the past. How many Isabellas had there been? Javier never grew quite as close to anyone ever again, but there had been a few promising prospects who died or disappeared mysteriously. And didn't Roman openly hate his last Cow, Simon Miller?

"Javie, it's me, your old pal."

Javier mouthed *no,* but remained locked in the older Rakum's icy blue gaze. He wanted to consent very badly.

"No one has to know," Canaan whispered.

"Roman killed Isabella."

"Yeah, sorry, dude. It was for your own good."

Javier shook his head and rolled up his right sleeve.

"Don't blame Roman." Canaan closed the distance between them and put his hand to Javier's neck. Javier grunted, remembering: Canaan was a throat guy.

"Roman," Canaan whispered up against his left ear, "he loves you. He's always been an old softy for you. Now, shhhh."

Javier closed his eyes and tried to block out the screams of defiance in his spirit. Roman would be very disappointed and David would laugh at his weakness. But they'd never know.

And he'd never tell them.

Thirty-Four

They hadn't found Michael and Beth after searching for a half-hour, and now the sun was down. Another try at Michael's cell also went to voicemail, and Roman opened the Stone's house with his key, resisting the urge to curse. David looked up to him, expected him to be a hero, a mentor—and Roman wasn't quite ready to disappoint the boy with the truth. The painful fact was that as a mortal, Roman had no confidence at all concerning their upcoming fight against Rufus and his men. Sure, as a Rakum Elder, he was never one to take any guff from human or brother, but now? He was tired and frightened, yet he couldn't let the boys know. No matter what.

"Michael and Beth will be in right behind us, I'm certain," Roman stated sharply and led David into the foyer. "And they'll have a plan. Don't worry David; we'll get your friend back."

David made a noise of unsure agreement, and they both stopped at the entrance to the living room.

"And who are you?" Roman stood at the entryway staring at a middle-aged woman on the sofa. She was drinking iced tea and watching Jeopardy on television. Unfazed by their arrival, she hooked her thumb toward the hall behind her.

"I'm with Elder Canaan," she mumbled and returned to her show.

"Canaan," Roman mumbled under his breath and gestured to David. "Find out why they're here."

"A Rakum Elder is here?" David asked, sounding fearful. Then he added, looking around, "Where's Javier?"

"He's with Canaan," the woman spoke again and then fell silent, engrossed in her program.

Roman narrowed his eyes and pointed David to the couch again. "Get that information. I'll find Javier and Canaan."

Once David moved toward the woman who was still ignoring them both, Roman headed down the hall, his mind racing. Canaan

172

and Kilmeade had been companionable in the old days, but Roman's main memory of the man was how much he enjoyed pummeling the grunts until they cried uncle. What brought him to Beth Rider's house?

Roman pounded the door. "Javier? Canaan? Open the door. Now." If he was overreacting, so be it. He was human and allowed extreme emotions. "I will not ask again."

◆◆◆

Inside the laundry room, Javier leaned against the door with Canaan off his left side, his forehead pressed against the drywall. The Elder was smiling lazily and he snickered at the urgency of Roman's knock.

"Keep your socks on, old man," Canaan whispered, jovially mimicking Javier's voice.

Javier shushed him and spoke through the door sounding as normal as possible. Canaan had taken quite a bit of his blood and although he healed him up as promised, he was still dizzy.

"Hang on. Canaan was just filling me in on what's been happening." Javier struggled to make up a good lie. "Just a second…"

"Javie, come see me alone soon. I'll have something for you next time," Canaan whispered, his face only inches away as he leaned against the wall.

The coppery odor of the Elder's breath brought back memories that Javier was unprepared to face. He shook his head and made an effort to stand off the door and balance on his own feet. Giving blood as a mortal was proving substantially more debilitating than when he was Rakum.

"You'll take my blood, little brother. It'll be all right. We'll put your house back in order. You remember the Lost Rabbit? You can be the new Lost Rabbit."

Javier was still shaking his head. Canaan obviously hadn't read Beth's book. He had no idea that there never was a Lost Rabbit. That also meant that Canaan didn't know the true nature of High Father Abroghia or how he founded their race after the Great Flood.

"I have the power to bring you back, little brother. Do you believe me?" Canaan stepped in front of Javier and put a hand on either side of his face. "I have the power."

With a slight pressure that resonated through his skull, Javier absorbed the pure energy that Canaan sent into his body to rejuvenate him. It was a skill many of the Rakum enjoyed and the effect was instantaneous. Within moments, Javier's vitality was completely restored and Canaan released his head.

"I can bring you back," Canaan whispered and held Javier's gaze. "If you will trust me."

"Come out, Javier. Now!" Roman's aggravated shout came through the door.

Javier whispered his answer to Canaan, guarding his mouth with one hand. "No, you can't. You're mistaken."

"You won't even try, will you? You're truly lost." Speaking in an undertone, Canaan cut his eyes to the side.

"No." Javier rubbed his face. "You don't have a clue of what's going on here, Canaan."

"*Elder* Canaan."

"I can't call you Elder with these guys." Javier put his hand to the knob to unlock the door, his eyes still pleading with Canaan's. "We serve God now."

"*Come see me alone,*" Canaan mouthed the words and Javier read his lips plainly. "*We're not done here.*"

Javier looked away and pulled open the door to see Roman waiting in the hall, absolutely livid.

♦♦♦

Roman stepped aside and pointed back the way he'd come. "Javier, wait for us in the living room."

Javier nodded his head and left. He looked guilty, but Roman didn't want to make any wild guesses. He stepped into the laundry room, met Canaan's gaze, and crossed his arms at his chest.

"Why are you here, Canaan?" Roman kept his tone even, although inside he was experiencing an array of emotions, none of which were pleasant.

"It's Elder Canaan now, Roman."

Oh, the arrogance. Roman thought as he worked up a response. *Was I that haughty?*

"You're a relic, Canaan," Roman said when he found the right words. "You've obviously no home, no place among the Rakum, and you're not one of us. I'll ask you again, why are you here?" His words affected the brawny Rakum and his eyes flicked around the room before he answered.

"I want to bring Rufus down."

"Why?" Roman asked and the Elder paused again. It had to do with the woman. Why a powerful Rakum Elder would attach himself so long to a mortal confounded their brethren, but Roman's human heart understood. He hardened his gaze. "Why her? That woman is old. She has maybe two decades left, tops," Roman said testing Canaan's commitment.

"She'll live forever; I've seen to that."

Now it was Roman's turn to pause. His mind raced with possible scenarios that may have compelled Canaan to mark his mate as a Rabbit. It was unheard of, unimaginable, and after several long moments, Roman still didn't have it figured out.

"By marking her, you've made her a target." Roman spoke slowly and softly. "Do you love her or hate her? I find your actions confounding."

"I didn't know Rufus was on a killing spree." Canaan went on the defense and he took a step forward, his wide shoulders contrasting to Roman's.

Not cowed in the least, Roman uncrossed his arms. "Follow me," he said in a gruff tone and abruptly turned on his heel to walk down the hall. Behind him, the Elder considered his options only a moment and then was heard trailing behind.

Somebody would have to share the Truth with the guy. If he was to be welcomed by Beth Rider—God's own daughter—he would need a little educating. Roman hoped Beth would be home soon; no one could share the news of God like the Rabbit that started it all.

Thirty-Five

A new red Cadillac and a white Chevy Tahoe signaled to Beth that she would need her game face once she entered the house. The feigned joviality she showed the girls all the way home from the crime scene no longer fooled them in the least. Dae Lee was crying and Grace had turned mean, throwing her doll across the car and flailing her arms as Michael extracted her from her booster seat.

"Who are we expecting besides Roman and the boys?" Michael whispered as Beth gathered Selene's weepy child in her arms. He'd noticed the extra car, too, and led the way to the front door.

"Only the Lord knows." Beth paused as Michael's hand reached for the knob. "I don't see how we're going to go through it again. Poor Selene—" Beth gulped and Michael touched her arm with his free hand.

"Honey, hang in there. You're God's champion. There's nothing coming up that you can't handle."

Beth nodded her head and tipped her chin toward the house. "Let's go. God help us."

Beth adjusted Dae Lee on her hip and followed her husband into the house. As they cleared the foyer, she and Michael stopped at the living room threshold to absorb the scene before them. Roman, David, and Javier looked pretty much as they did the last time she saw them, but the other two occupants were strangers, and one was a Rakum. Beth caught herself before she gasped and Michael handed Grace over to her free hip.

If her husband had hackles, they'd be raised. He strode over to the strangers and nodded to the man. Beth shushed the children who grew increasingly loud and irritated at being held uncomfortably, and she watched to see what Michael would say.

"Hey, guys." Michael nodded to his friends and then looked to the couple who stood before the sofa. *"Canaan."*

Her husband's voice definitely carried a tone of warning and Beth wondered how well they were acquainted. With Michael's back to her, she could see the pair's faces and their expressions could not have been more dissimilar. The woman was fiftyish and her eyes narrowed at Michael's approach. The Rakum appeared no more than thirty and he was bigger than Michael with a dreadful tattoo snaking out the collar of his shirt. He gave her husband an exaggerated wink.

"That's *Elder* Canaan, Stone. But you're all squishy now; you probably forgot me." The Rakum stepped up, reached out his hand in the mortal fashion, and pumped Michael's hand twice.

Tersely, Michael replied, "Oh, I remember you. What do you want?"

"How about a rematch?" he jibed, his fists coming up. "I'll go easy." Michael didn't respond and undaunted, Canaan lowered his hands and continued while seeking Beth's eye. "I squashed your husband as often as I could. Used to be my favorite punching bag."

Michael moved to the side, blocking his view to the foyer. Beth set the girls down and held their hands. Dae Lee was sniveling and Grace began to fuss and yank at the bow in her hair.

"What's your business here?" Michael asked as the testosterone levels in the room rose. The Rakum thrust his hands in his pockets and offered another winning smile.

"Heard you've been busy, you and your little lady there."

"We were just about to get to the bottom of it, Mike." Roman stepped forward then and shook Michael's hand, his mediation bringing down the tension in the room. "He's out to get Rufus, but that's all we've established."

"Get Rufus? How do you intend on doing that?" Michael asked the Rakum in a measured tone.

"Any way I can, baby-doll," he answered, seemingly amused. "Any way I can."

Despite his condescending attitude toward her husband, Beth surmised then that he'd been sent to help them. How else did he get into the house? Hadn't God established angels to watch over them? The children wailed simultaneously and Michael turned to face Beth.

"Let me talk to the Rakum, hon," she said and gave Michael an unintentionally weary smile. Beth normally took the lead when it came to sharing God with Canaan's kind and after a few seconds, Michael gestured for the children to be handed off.

"Canaan, Beth speaks for me." Michael positioned a child on each hip. "Listen and try to learn something." His voice was still harsh

177

and Beth watched the Elder for a response, now more curious than ever about their history.

"Elders are always learning," the Rakum replied and bowed low.

Michael held the his eye another few seconds before turning to the staircase. "Beth, watch him. He's sneaky. I'll explain later." Michael kissed her cheek. "I'll get the girls settled and be right back."

Beth whispered her thanks and shooed him off. Canaan cleared his throat and Beth met his gaze. He was everything a Rakum was supposed to be, a perfect specimen in every way imaginable. Dashingly handsome with a deceptively charming aura, and worse, he knew it. The pride in his gaze was evident even from across the room. Beth took a deep breath and stepped forward, but David met her a few steps in and surprised her with a hug.

"Hey, buddy." She returned his embrace. "I'm so sorry about your friend. We'll get her back. God has a plan and it's not about killing that poor girl." Beth trusted her words were true and prayed to God even as she spoke them.

"I know. He's covering her with his wings, like in Psalm 91," David whispered in Beth's ear, released her, and looked toward the stairs. "That was Jesse and Selene's daughter, wasn't it?"

Beth frowned and fought back a tear of frustration. "Yes. Rufus has Selene."

"Oh, God," David whispered and fell into the Queen Anne chair behind him.

"Tried to get me last night."

Beth looked at the woman next to Canaan. "Pardon me?"

"Yep. Tried to snatch me at work last night."

"You got away?" Beth asked, skeptical, yet encouraged.

"I'm Marcy. Marcy Haddle. And yes, ma'am, I shot the jerk. Shot him where the sun don't shine. M-hm."

Beth's hand went to her mouth. "You shot Rufus?"

Canaan chuckled then and patted Marcy's shoulder. "No. Rufus doesn't leave the nest. He's completely disfigured. Been hitting the Dying Buzz. You know what that is?"

Beth nodded, her fingers still over her lips.

"Rufus sent a set of twins to get me. But I shot one of them right square, right there." Marcy used both hands to point towards her groin. "Man, that sure was rewarding." The woman laughed high and shrill, her Southern accent growing as her tale extended. "Then Canaan went to work on 'em. You should of seen him. Broke one of

178

'em's neck, lickety-split. So sexy."

Marcy put her hand to the Rakum's lower back, and Beth marveled at their intimacy as a mortal/Rakum couple. Before her mind could wander, Roman jumped into the conversation.

"Beryl and Meryl," he said, not asking a question, "they're dead."

Marcy nodded, but Canaan shook his head slowly back and forth. "Probably not, Elder Roman. I feel it." Canaan put a hand to his middle.

"You don't know that," the Marcy woman started, but her mate shot her a glare and she fell silent.

Beth cleared her throat and gestured to Roman. Time was short and she needed to get to business with the Rakum.

"Roman, you and Canaan please join me in the study. David and Javier, please pray for Selene and Chloe, okay?"

Her friends nodded as Marcy slipped into the couch and turned on the TV. Beth followed the short hallway to the study and took a deep breath.

It was going to be a long night.

Thirty-six

"Canaan—"

"It's Elder Canaan, Miss Beth, if you don't mind. I've earned it and it makes me more comfortable."

The handsome devil winked and Beth shrugged; she didn't care. She just wanted to get started.

"Or you could call me, Master," he said, his smile to the side. Beth stared him down a few seconds and then rolled her eyes.

"Ahem. Elder Canaan, you may call *me*, Mrs. Stone. Now, what do you think we can do for you? Did you come here to help us stop Rufus, or is your own agenda going to have priority over ours?" Beth settled into the desk chair, subconsciously happy to have five feet of oak between them.

"Mrs. Stone," Canaan cooed as he found a seat across from her. "As Elder Roman put it so aptly, I have no place among the Rakum. I know I look the part..." He smiled then and Beth shook her head at his narcissistic behavior. "...but I haven't walked with my people in many years."

"But your responsibilities—how did you manage?" Roman asked, seated and leaning over his knees.

"I have friends. I'm a nice guy. You remember that, don't you, Roman? I'm very charismatic."

"You've met before?" Beth asked getting a bead on their relationship.

Roman huffed. "Seldom did we cross paths; the last meeting was more than a century ago."

"An interesting time. Elder Kilmeade's recovery was a success, in case you ever wondered," Canaan said as he casually looked about the room. "I know you two were close, thought you might like to know."

Beth knew Kilmeade was Roman's fraternal twin brother, but remained mum. She sighed and Canaan turned his blue eyes on her with power.

"Kilmeade took the Dying Buzz for a year, Mrs. Stone, and

recovered after another two years of the good old Canaan buzz. I cured him, you see. Then I was promoted to Elder." Canaan turned to Roman and smiled. "Our old friend Rufus has been drinking the dying for several years. There's no going back for him. He'll continue to degenerate until he kills himself and everyone around him."

Canaan looked back at Beth and his gaze caused her breath to catch. She hadn't been in the presence of the Rakum for almost a year, and even longer since she'd been around one not searching for salvation. Canaan exuded a wanton sexuality that Beth actively resisted, but thankfully, after blushing the first few seconds in his gaze, she began to feel herself again. When Canaan noticed he had an effect on her, he smiled and sent her another of his famous winks.

"You talk like he's going crazy," she said, her voice more husky than she preferred.

"He's already there, Mrs. Stone," Canaan answered, holding her eye. "Making rash decisions and formulating extravagant schemes he'll never be able to bring to pass. Within a year, he'll be dead. It's like syphilis. He thinks he's getting stronger and stronger, but he's really pretty weak. It's a cruel disease that the Dying Buzz brings on, and it killed thousands of our brothers over the centuries before the Fathers outlawed it."

Beth nodded and closed her eyes, the Elder's gaze giving her a headache. She made an effort to look aside for the duration of their chat.

"I heard Kilmeade was killed in his sleep." Roman's voice was low and Beth heard the pain in it. Even as Rakum, the two brothers had a close relationship. "And he was still a Rakum."

Canaan sighed and nodded. "Aye, I heard the same."

Beth furrowed her brow as the Elder took on an accent that only added to his charm. She needed to get down to business and her patience was wearing thin, but Roman was preoccupied with the discussion regarding his twin.

"How did they murder a Rakum Elder in his sleep? Have you any notion?"

Canaan looked off in the distance, his gaze going soft before he hummed and shook his head. "Never heard how, just that they did."

"He's probably still alive." Roman's tone was hopeful, but Canaan disregarded him with a shrug. Beth jumped in as the topic seemed exhausted.

"Elder Canaan, our guys will head to Jackson in the morning and you can only travel by night. Did you expect us to wait for you? Two of our friends have been abducted. What did you have in mind?"

Canaan shrugged. "Simple. We leave at sundown, tomorrow night. We can drive to Rufus's place and get there by midnight; take the fight right to him. Plenty of time." He tried to catch Beth's eye, but she looked down. "Trust me. He's not all that. I could squash him with my pinky. I might kill a bunch of those guys worshiping him, too, bunch of losers."

"Or," Beth added, "the guys can leave now and you can follow along later. It makes a lot more sense to attack in the day than at night."

"Not so, Mrs. Stone." Canaan's accent remained. "I have on good authority that Rufus's pad is painted dark. Do you know what that means? No sunlight gets in. They can walk about during the day in there. He's recreated the Cave."

"How do you know this, Canaan?" Roman asked, suspicious.

"I see things."

"What do you see?"

"For one thing, Rufus has Father Damien in custody," Canaan returned flatly, his eyes expressionless.

"Damien?" Roman sat up. "Still alive? How is he?"

Canaan laughed. "He's mortal by now. He was on the fence many years, but I sense he's gone the way of the coo-coo bird. Just like you guys."

Roman sighed audibly and caught Beth's eye.

"What?" Beth tried to keep in step with Roman and Canaan, but their common history made it difficult.

"Damien is Javier's blood father," Roman said to Beth, excluding Canaan by angling away from him in his chair. "Just think of it. If *any* of the Fathers come to know God, it'd be a huge miracle."

Canaan grunted and leaned back. "Oh, he's mortal. Bank on it."

Roman turned to catch Canaan's eye. "You know this how?"

Canaan touched his temple and Roman's eyes narrowed.

Anxious to get back on track, Beth interjected, "So, Elder Canaan, I still think the boys should head on over as soon as they've rested. Rufus has Selene and Chloe Bushman and there's no telling what he'll do to them."

"He'll do nothing." Flippant, Canaan answered and leaned back, crossing his legs at the ankle. "At least nothing permanent. He needs them to get you there. He has plans for them, but no intention of killing them. Not by a long shot."

"That's not good enough, Canaan," Roman offered and the room fell still a few moments before the Elder's eyes flashed and he leaned forward.

"Mrs. Stone—Beth—I gather you're staying behind? Dodging the bullet?"

Beth was taken off guard by the insinuation, but he clarified in her silence.

"Marcy can stay behind with your little ones." Canaan put on a woeful expression. "Don't these boys depend on your strength? From what I hear, you are Rufus's primary objective."

"All the more reason for her to stay behind," Roman said, stepping on Canaan's reasoning. "Beth will remain here, where it's safe. She's done enough. This is not her fight."

"Ah, I see. You *humans*," Canaan used the word as an insult, "will take on Rufus and his pups? Do you have a death wish, Elder Roman?"

"They have the same power I had seven years ago, Canaan—" Beth caught the Rakum's irritated glare and she quickly added, "*Elder* Canaan. What happened to your people had very little to do with me. God wanted these men for Himself. God loves you guys, and it's not His will that any of you should perish."

"Perish? What perish?" Canaan's previously calm demeanor dissolved into something akin to exasperation and he dropped the accent. "I've lived over three hundred years and I'm still young. This is what I can't understand. Why would I want to be human?" Canaan looked Roman up and down. "You, Elder Roman—they said you were a smart one. Your reputation as a scholar preceded you everywhere you went. I had you figured as a candidate for Father one day. But look at you; weak, aging, frightened…pathetic."

"Roman is none of those things—" Beth began, but her friend wanted to hold his own ground.

"Canaan, I've heard from the Creator of the universe. When your Maker calls you, warns you of the soon coming judgment, and offers you a place in His kingdom, you accept. He's going to call you, too, mark my words."

"What makes you so sure?" Canaan's voice softened and Beth hopped on the opportunity to step in.

"Because you're here, now, with us. You didn't just happen by, Elder Canaan. God allowed you to waltz in here when I know He's been keeping the twins out."

"What's that? Meryl and Beryl were here? When?"

"They came to scare us—didn't work. And they couldn't get in. You will eventually learn that God pulls the strings, not you or me or anyone else. He wants you here, so here you are."

"Someone's pulling my strings, eh?" Canaan chuckled, but Beth was dead serious.

"Me, Roman, Michael, David, and Javier—we're willing participants in whatever He chooses to do. But you? You're a puppet. He places you where He needs you, when He needs you there. Nothing at all happens on this planet without His say-so."

"I am not a slave—" Canaan huffed.

"Yes, you are, and you're the saddest kind of slave there is. The kind that thinks he's free. You're bound by your flesh, Canaan. You're a slave to your lust. Can you go without human blood? Good food? Luxury?" Beth took a breath and then drove her point home. "Can you live without Marcy?"

Canaan's mouth turned to the side and he looked away. "I don't believe in a divine creator, Mrs. Stone."

"Oh, yes, you do," Roman countered and leaned a little more forward to touch the Rakum's knee. "I discerned lies for two centuries; you've heard His voice. What did He say?"

Beth watched as the Elder grew more uncomfortable, shifted in his seat, and then stood to pace to the window.

"Canaan, He only wants what's best for you," Beth pressed gently. "You don't have to agree with us right now, or even tell us what He said, but don't pretend that you don't believe in Him. If He's already touched you, just accept it and move on."

"He hasn't touched me."

"He hasn't? Then why are you so upset?" Beth came to her feet and went to stand beside him. "Just accept that He's real."

"And lose everything?" Canaan turned to face her and lifted his hand as if to touch her shoulder, but just before he made contact, he thought better of it and dropped his arm. "Mrs. Stone, are you trying to trick me into becoming a mortal? I'm pretty sure these guys said a few words and magically transformed. I'm not going to let you trick me."

"It doesn't work that way, Canaan. God doesn't deceive people. You can say anything at all and remain just as you are—wicked, immoral, and abominable. Roman and the others were changed

184

because their heart changed."

"God doesn't accept devils, Canaan," Roman added from his seat a dozen feet away.

"*Elder* Canaan," Canaan interjected and fell still.

Beth could see his wheels spinning and she placed her hand on his tattooed forearm. "Do you recognize the fact that there's a Creator? Just admit it. Be truthful and you can join us. If you want to keep being obstinate, you can go your own way."

Canaan looked at her hand on his arm and pulled away slowly.

"I don't think you should touch me, Mrs. Stone," he said, stepping back. "Don't do it again unless you want me to return the favor."

"Does it hurt?" Ignoring the veiled threat, Beth reached for the same place on his arm. He jerked away and walked to Roman's side.

"Bugger! Okay! I have heard a voice in my head that I know is this God you speak of. I'm not interested, okay? Satisfied?"

Beth smiled and Roman nodded approvingly.

"Great. Yes, very satisfied. Okay." Beth walked toward the door. "I'm going to check on my guests and make sure you have a place to sleep. Welcome to our home, Elder Canaan. I'm very happy to have you on our side."

Canaan's frown deepened and Beth left the room. Roman stayed behind and she imagined they would speak more about the upcoming plan of attack. Whatever they decided, she'd go along prayerfully. For now, she was looking forward to getting some rest. The Rakum may stay awake all night, but even at almost seven, she was thinking about bedtime, and perhaps a long dreamless sleep.

ThiRTy-SEVEN

Beth was startled by the doorbell chime as she crossed the foyer. A dozen feet away, David started to rise, but Beth shook her head with a smile.

"I got it, David. Just relax."

The doorbell chimed again, one ring, and she pulled it open without looking through the peep hole. Why should she? God was keeping the Rakum out.

The bad ones, at least.

"Uh…h-hi?" a small voice on the stoop wavered.

Beth's hand went to her chest. It was a boy—a Rakum boy—she knew it as well as she knew her own name. As she looked upon him, an arrow of dread pierced her heart and she wondered why.

"Mrs. Stone?" The boy spoke gently and shyly averted his baby blue eyes. "Beth Rider-Stone?"

"Yes," Beth whispered, her mind racing. Why was she so terrified?

"My name is Isaac." The boy looked into the house over her shoulder as he introduced himself. "I-I heard you harbor my people. I heard you would keep me safe."

He met Beth's eye with his last word, and she glanced behind her to the crowd in the living room. Roman stepped out of the hall and started toward the door.

"I promise not to hurt anyone."

Isaac spoke more softly now, perhaps because Roman was almost upon them. Before she could answer, the invisible knife turned in her spirit with ferocity.

"Isaac, I—" Beth stopped herself, unsure of what to do. Her mind screamed multiple warnings, but her heart softened at his pitiful plea. He was so young, barely a teenager, her height and weight, with a humble stance and sorrowful gaze. His bright blond hair was shaggy

186

and unkempt, and it dangled in his eyes, causing him to flick his head periodically to send it back. He wore only a thin windbreaker against the bitter November wind and her mothering instincts went on full alert.

Roman reached her side and nodded to the kid like a Rakum; Beth's stomach turned.

"Where're you from, Isaac?" Roman asked taking a stance slightly forward Beth's. The boy acknowledged Roman's seniority by bowing a few degrees at the waist.

"All over, sir."

"Roman. Call me Roman."

"You're an Elder," the boy said tilting his head to the side.

"I *was* an Elder. Who're you staying with? You haven't been alone," Roman asserted and the boy pondered a response.

"I stayed a while with a Rakum named Boris." Isaac wrapped his arms around himself tightly. "But he beat me a lot."

Beth clenched her jaw. She wanted to let him in, to ignore the glaring red-lights in her spirit that told her to send him packing. Thankfully, Roman was the suspicious type and he continued his questions.

"Where is Boris now?"

"On his way to Jackson. He wants to help Elder Rufus. I'm afraid and I had nowhere else to go." Isaac shivered and rubbed his palms together. "In Harrisburg, two guys told me you helped them." He caught Beth's eye. "Mr. Stone let them stay here, kept them safe. Will you help me like you helped them?"

Roman looked at Beth, but she was watching the boy. He played his role so very well that she was almost convinced. Yet his baby-face and puppy-dog eyes were a façade, hiding something hideous. Beth shook her head and put her hand to the door jamb.

"No, Isaac. You can't stay here." Beth heard Canaan and Marcy come up behind her and she firmed her resolve. "Not in my house."

"Are you outta your mind?" Marcy spoke up and craned her head to see their visitor. "Let the kid in. He's freezing, look at him. How cold is your heart, missy?"

Beth exhaled and spoke carefully. "I have to do what's best for the house, Ms. Haddle. God protects this house and He has told me in no uncertain terms not to let this Rakum in."

"When were you born, Isaac?" Canaan looked at the boy between Beth and Roman.

"I'm The Last, Master." Again, barely audible, the youngster whispered his answer.

"The last," Canaan laughed, tapping Roman's shoulder.

"*The Last?*" Roman echoed, pronouncing the phrase as an official title. Canaan puffed his chest and this time, knocked Roman's elbow.

"You scared of him, Elder Roman? He's the last Rakum conceived." Canaan gave Beth a sidelong glance. "You do realize that makes him a baby, right?"

Beth absorbed Canaan's patronizing remarks and shook her head. "It doesn't matter what you see with your eyes. He's not coming in." Beth licked her lips and hardened her gaze. "You can take him somewhere safe if you feel so inclined."

"Did I hear that right?" David had joined the cluster in the doorway and he leaned left and right to see what he could of their visitor. "The Last? Wow. Is he The Last, like the legend of 'The Last'? Really? Can I meet him?"

"Everyone who wants to speak with this Rakum will have to do so outside. He's not coming in and my word is final." Beth's voice was laced with irritation and everyone fell silent.

"Michael Stone is the head of this house, right, Mrs. Stone?"

Beth's gaze returned to the youth on her stoop and she frowned. The kid maintained his meek tone, but there was a sneakiness there as well.

"Yes, and I'm sure he would agree with me."

Isaac shook his head, his eyes forlorn. "No, Mrs. Stone, no. You're wrong. Michael Stone would let me in. He'd help me in a heartbeat. He grieves for his people. Michael Stone is a hero to me. I wish you would ask him. Please."

Beth shook her head even as the crowd around her variously agreed with the boy. Her husband would be down any minute, but she was certain he would sense just what she did—that if not contained, this child was even more dangerous than Rufus.

"No, Isaac. Michael respects my opinion. He trusts my judgment and you're not welcome in this house."

"No offense, Mrs. Stone, but you're not nearly as brave as your reputation. Look at me." Canaan took a step back and Beth glanced his way. "I am a Rakum Elder. I have powers and abilities that you can't even imagine in your precious little human mind. I'll be here to protect you. I'll protect all of you. You said I was led here, that I'm a puppet in God's biggest production. And here's this kid, needing help.

Coincidence? Hmmm. So where is your faith? I'm unimpressed."

Beth considered his accusation, not breathing. She had faith. She knew what God wanted. Her instincts were trustworthy.

Weren't they?

"I-I promise to behave, Mrs. Stone. I'll subject myself to Elder…Canaan is it?" He waited for Canaan to nod before he continued. "Elder Canaan can handle me. You give me shelter and I will serve your purpose."

"We could use another Rakum on our side, Beth," Roman said.

"I understand, Mrs. Stone. You're tired and you've been through a lot. You want to keep the children safe. You're worried about those Rufus has taken hostage." Isaac touched his temple and lowered his gaze. "Don't worry, I'm not reading your mind. I don't read humans. I do read Rufus, though, loud and clear. He has plans for your entire group. Bad plans."

A murmur traveled around the cramped space and Beth nibbled her lip thinking.

"And I read your novels," Isaac added softly. "I want to know about this God of yours. I'm not a lost cause."

Beth looked sideways at the faces of the group that surrounded the door. Only Javier stayed put on the sofa. She could see the back of his head and his feet poking out from where he sat ignoring the show. Beth looked back at the kid and finally her spirit relaxed a fraction. She was fatigued and wanted the nightmare to end. For that dream to come to pass, they would need to destroy Rufus. With two Rakum on their side, their odds should be better.

Taking a deep breath, Beth stepped back and motioned with her arm for the kid to enter. Isaac did not advance, but lingered on the threshold, looking about the large foyer.

"You have some parameters for me, Mrs. Stone. Please, tell me what they are before I enter."

"Yes," she agreed, "you will drink no human blood here. None."

Beth looked at every face and met their eyes. Only Canaan looked away, and she was in no position to give him orders. "And you will not go upstairs for any reason. You will not speak to or touch the children at any time. Is that clear?"

Beth couldn't believe her ears, but she was letting the imp in the door. She shooed away her conscience and exhaled dramatically.

"Michael will set up a room for the Rakum. The rest of you can stay upstairs, just pick a guest room." Beth looked to each person in turn and tried on one last grin. "And if you will excuse me—I'm going to bed."

Isaac nodded and entered cautiously. As soon as the door closed, Beth watched the others clamor around him, bombarding him with questions as they led him into the next room. Upstairs, Michael would need relieving and she'd send him to fix up the basement for Canaan and now Isaac.

She'd put on her most carefree expression and tuck the girls into bed. Explaining Selene's absence to Dae Lee would be easy for one night, maybe two. But if the boys didn't bring her home, Beth dreaded telling Dae Lee her mother was dead.

A shudder shook Beth's spirit and she sent up a prayer in her heart for Selene, for David's friend, for all of them. She needed faith. She needed peace. But most of all, she needed Michael to get out of this alive.

Please, God. Please, keep Michael safe. I don't want to live without him. I need him. Please…

Her friends thought she was a godly Colossus, but she was as frightened and paranoid as the least of her cohorts. Beth prayed the rest of the night, and even as she slept, her heart knocked on heaven's door.

Thirty-eight

Isaac hunched his shoulders to appear as meek as possible as the curious bunch hustled him into the Rabbit's den. Even as they fired questions at him a mile a minute, he took note of the lone figure on the couch. In contrast to the frenetic attitude of the room, Isaac found this one's despondent posture appealing. The guy had been a Rakum, no doubt, but now his blood was diluted, like all of the apostates, mutating into something not quite either. Isaac memorized his unique odor as he sensed they'd have some sort of interaction in the coming hours. The vision was indistinct, but he made note of it just the same.

Stepping gingerly toward the guy, Isaac pointed loosely to the cushion beside him. The man shrugged and moved against the armrest, barely making eye contact. It was enough. Isaac saw the despair in the man's eyes and a shadow of the marvelous and beautiful Rakum he'd been before his fall. It would be good to bring him back around, if that were possible. Smiling at the imagined challenge, Isaac settled into the sofa's middle as the Elder's woman sat on his other side. Roman remained on his feet, but Canaan and David took up positions across from him in arm chairs. He hadn't answered any questions and put on a bewildered expression he knew would elicit sympathy from the group.

"One at a time, people," Elder Roman said, taking charge of the room and waiting for everyone to quiet down.

"Okay," a man called from the top of the stairs. "So, we have a new addition?"

Isaac turned in his seat to watch him descend the stairs. From a hazy transmission he hijacked from Elder Canaan, he knew it was Michael Stone. Isaac came to his feet and clasped his hands behind his back.

"Sir, thank you for letting me stay. I promise to behave. I didn't know where else to turn." Isaac watched the big guy's eyes. He was as wary as his wife, but he forced a grin and nodded his head.

191

"Don't worry about it, son. I'm headed downstairs to prepare a room for you guys. We have beds down there already, but I'll need to check that the windows are still shuttered. We haven't had any Rakum visitors in months."

"Thank you, sir," Isaac said and bit his lip. He played his part well, for the man's gaze softened and he ruffled his hair as he passed.

"You got it, kid."

A whiff of Stone's scent and Isaac knew he had adapted fully to his human existence. He made a furtive note of the other apostate's conditions and found only Roman and the guy on the sofa still clinging to miniscule vestiges of their former lives. He made a mental note and checked his expression: doe eyes and a frightened countenance. The group was much easier to manipulate with the Stones out of the room.

A few feet to his left, Elder Roman cleared his throat.

"Isaac, allow me to begin. As I remember, the rumors of The Last were hard to confirm. Who is your blood Father?"

"Theophilus," Isaac answered easily. It would do no good to let on that the most powerful Rakum of them all sired the child before them.

"I see. Who was your Elder before the Last Assembly?"

"Rufus," Isaac lied. Rufus was Boris's Elder, and he had enough borrowed memories from his buddy to carry him through the interrogation. He could see the news worried Roman, but he awaited the next direct question to play up the fact that they saw him as such an innocent.

"How and when did you become separated from him?"

"Within a month after Last Assembly, he put me out. Said I was slowing him down. He called for me later, two years ago, but I didn't want to be with him. I've been on the run since then." Isaac watched the apostate's eyes and knew he was being believed. Boris was the one who ditched Rufus and hid out in various North Carolina towns until meeting Isaac and dropping anchor in Raleigh.

"How did you learn of Beth Rider?"

"A Cow loaned me his copy of *The Judging* about a week before the Last Assembly." Isaac thought fast, using terms from the Rabbit's book that the traitors would recognize. He hadn't actually read the books, but reading the reviews online and the blurbs on the book covers, he had the gist. Everyone nodded sympathetically, all except for the quiet man next to him who stared at his own hands.

"Where were you during Last Assembly?"

"I was with Elder Rufus and Boris in the crowd." Isaac spoke his fabrications flawlessly. Indeed, it was Boris who stood in the high rafters with the hundred thousand brethren. Isaac had been under the stage where Damien stashed him moments before the Rabbit and her posse entered the Great Hall.

Satisfied, Elder Roman nodded and took a step back to allow the others access to their guest.

"What have you heard regarding Rufus's plans?" David spoke up, his voice soft.

Isaac turned to look at him and gave him an apologetic shrug. This apostate was younger than the others, and Isaac liked the look of him; his face, his build. But he read a lot of pain in the man's eyes— human pain. He couldn't have been much of a Rakum to begin with; the guy looked too miserable. Isaac waited an appropriate interval and then threw the guy a bone.

"I sometimes get visions of Rufus."

"Visions?" It was Elder Canaan, the only Rakum in the group. Isaac turned to look at him and his stomach rumbled.

"I see the future, Elder Canaan." He spoke quickly to cover his weakness. "I have seen you and Rufus in mortal combat."

The Elder's pupils dilated a touch and his mate touched Isaac's knee, frowning.

"What do you mean, mortal combat? As in *deadly*? Canaan and this Rufus guy fighting? Is this what's really going to happen or what might happen?"

Isaac tipped his chin and kept his gaze in the Elder's. He was tiring of the show. Putting on the little boy act was losing its luster as he thought of drinking Canaan's blood. The Elder straightened up then and cleared his throat as Isaac looked down. He was busted; the Rakum clearly read his intentions.

"Well, kid?" The Marcy woman tapped his knee again, and Isaac looked blindly at her hand. The Rakum across the room dramatically rumbled a correction in his throat.

"Cee, don't touch him. I know it's been a long time, but Rakum aren't accustomed to being handled."

Isaac looked up to meet Canaan's eye and the guy nodded. He was going to let his blood. He had absolutely no reservations whatsoever. Isaac exhaled, relieved, and got to his feet.

"Well, he doesn't need to be so sensitive. We need to bond

together if—"

"Cee, chill." Canaan stepped backward toward the hall. "Roman, I'll take the boy out for some fresh air. We'll return before sunup."

Isaac watched him catch Elder Roman's eye, as if seeking approval and the tall traitor consented after a long pause. Their interim leader knew Isaac needed sustenance and surely chose what he thought would keep the mortals safe. A secret smile came to Isaac's face as he stepped away from the couch toward the Elder.

"Pretty tales from a pretty boy," the dark-haired man on the sofa said, his voice low. "Who's your Guardian, Isaac? See if you can answer without lying."

Isaac met a few glances and then admitted the truth. "Father Damien."

His accuser looked up and met his eye. Isaac saw misdirected hate there, but another emotion as well—one he'd have to work on to name.

"I thought so," the man said under his breath. "Father Damien slipped your name to me once. *Yitzhak Akaron*—Isaac The Last. He saw you in a vision a century before you were born. He told me Abroghia would father the last Rakum, name him Isaac, and teach him the ways of the Fathers."

The room fell dead quiet and Isaac held his gaze. He'd heard that the rumors surrounding his existence bewitched their race, young and old. But no one had the hard facts and what they did know was extrapolated and distorted. What was this one's angle?

"Javier d'Millier. He's Father Damien's blood-son and used to be Roman's proselyte." Canaan offered telepathically. The humor in his gaze belied his affection for the dark-haired apostate. Grateful for the heads-up, Isaac began to pick up more the two men's history from the Elder as he glared at Javier.

"If you've been serving under Rufus, then Damien's vision was false. If Theophilus is your blood Father, then Damien's vision was false. Is that possible, Isaac?" Javier's words were delivered in a quiet but frosty tone.

Isaac licked his lips and his mind went back to Canaan and his delicious offer. He had no desire to walk down memory lane with one of Damien's traitorous offspring. He wanted to eat, and Javier's icy glare was dampening his enthusiasm. In response, Isaac held his tongue and crossed his arms at his chest.

"A Father's vision can't be false, can it, Isaac?"

Javier was relentless and he didn't blink. Isaac sucked his teeth dramatically and rolled his eyes for Javier's benefit alone.

"I'm heading out with Elder Canaan, sir. Perhaps while I'm gone, you can explain your theories. I haven't lied to your people; I'm on the run and I need their assistance." Isaac tore his gaze away and caught Roman's eye.

The former Elder was pondering Javier's words and was inclined to believe him. They had a close bond and Isaac was just beginning to pick up how thick their connection was when his stomach growled noisily. All human eyes looked to him and Isaac was out of patience. He monitored his tone, and spoke to their leader.

"I'm hungry, Elder Roman. I'll accompany Elder Canaan out, and then I'll return and do whatever you command. Agreed?"

If anything, the former Rakum would empathize with him. As far as they knew, Isaac could've gone days without a blood meal and it wouldn't do to reveal that he only drank from the Rakum. The less they knew about him the better.

Roman nodded again and gestured for the exit.

"Come on, kid," Canaan mumbled and headed for the front door. He grabbed his leather jacket off the chair and pulled it on. "When we return, Isaac will bunk with me. Cee, you stay upstairs."

"What? Wait a minute—"

"Cee—"

Canaan's voice hardened and Isaac watched the woman pale in response. She loved him, but she feared him, too.

"You sleep up here. Don't come to the basement." Canaan glanced around to all those present. "None of you should enter the basement during the day, understood?"

All present, except Javier, nodded as Isaac crossed between them and met Canaan at the door. He pulled a thick parka out of the closet and waited as Isaac shrugged it on. Once he was bundled up, he followed the Elder outside and didn't look back. The grumpy gus on the couch might spread rumors about him while he was gone, but he wasn't worried. The guy was right—visions were one hundred percent accurate, and he'd had a vision that he would travel with the Rabbit's party all the way to Jackson.

Canaan directed him to his car and opened the door. Once Isaac was seated, Canaan bent down and caught his eye.

"Can you wait 'til we get a piece from here?"

"I can wait until you've fed."

Canaan chuckled amiably. "That gloomy character on the couch in there? I tapped him barely an hour ago. I'm good."

Isaac smiled at the double meaning and Canaan closed the door. Once he was settled behind the wheel he switched on the car.

"Why don't you take blood from the mortals?"

Isaac raised his eyebrows. Canaan was handy enough with what little telepathy remained in him. He made an effort to block his thoughts and shrugged.

"I've *never* had human blood."

"I find that hard to believe," the muscled Elder countered as he pulled the car away from the house.

"Sir, you don't doubt your senses, do you?" Isaac returned, staring out the windshield. The big oaf would be able to smell his blood and know it was different. Plus, Canaan had him pegged as something extraordinary and playing dumb had grown tiresome.

"No, I don't," Canaan chuckled good-naturedly. "I haven't spent much time with our people lately."

"You slipped off the radar ten years ago." Isaac read the date in the man's mind, getting a bead on his particular mental signature. He doubted Canaan's telepathy went much past hazy impressions of those in his immediate presence.

"Yeah," Canaan nodded, looking forward.

"Why have you consented to me tonight?" Isaac watched Canaan's profile and waited while he worked up an answer. Rakum didn't normally enjoy buzzing others and his willingness was puzzling. But, *easier is better*, the Rakum's favorite saying.

"Uh," the Elder ran his hand through his hair. "I've always been different, Isaac. I do whatever comes to me, whatever pleases me. I have no qualms answering your need. You asked, I said yes, end of story."

Isaac made a noise of approval and his stomach rumbled once more. Canaan switched topics.

"Do you have a knife?"

"Sort of," Isaac replied flatly.

"Fine." The Elder gestured to an upcoming rest area. Within minutes, he'd pulled into the corner spot, furthest from the glare of the lot's sodium lamps. Parked and locked down, he turned and removed his leather bomber.

"You can take it now, little brother," he said raising his sleeve.

Isaac took hold of Canaan's beefy tattooed forearm with both

196

hands. For a split second he considered using his knife—after all, fangs were not part of the Rakum's normal repertoire. But Canaan was an odd guy. Isaac had peeked into his mind enough to see that he didn't fit in among the brethren for many reasons, the long-held mate being the least of his outsider traits. Canaan was a rebel, a malcontent, and his separatist attitude would actually serve Isaac's purpose on his current mission.

"Elder Canaan..." Isaac mustered his most respectful tone, and the big guy met his eye. "I've learned something new."

As the Elder watched, Isaac forced his teeth to elongate into fangs and he sank them deep into the proffered arm. The Elder's eyes widened only momentarily; images of another Elder that Canaan favored who manifested fangs filtered toward the forefront. Isaac shoved the snippets aside, his hunger overcoming his curiosity.

"I'm impressed," Canaan said finally with meaning and turned his gaze to the night sky.

Isaac drank deeply and closed his eyes; the Elder's blood was the sweetest he'd had in some time. Boris was nice, but an Elder was always better. *"It wouldn't do to tell the others my new talent,"* Isaac sent his suggestion telepathically and the Elder nodded again.

"What they don't know won't hurt 'em. Don't worry, little brother. It's our secret. You and I will stick together; help each other avoid the trap that stole our brothers from us."

Isaac grunted in agreement and allowed the Elder's blood to feed his thirsty cells. The only blood that was better than an Elder's was the Fathers'. That's what he wanted next. But Rufus and the Rabbit's God had killed nearly all of them.

Yet, Theophilus is alive.

Isaac saw the Father in Rufus's mind, incarcerated beside Damien in the basement of his Jackson headquarters. Weakened, demoralized, but still completely Rakum. Another good reason to go to Mississippi.

Isaac finished his meal and leaned back with a contented sigh. Canaan didn't acknowledge him, lost in his thoughts.

Theophilus will feed me again.

Isaac smiled. Everything was going according to plan and according to his vision. A hundred percent accurate like the Rakum prophet that he was.

Thirty-nine

Changed from his bloody clothing into a flannel shirt and cinched-up slacks from the dead man's truck, Beryl jogged alongside Ta'avah heading east, away from the accident scene. Fifteen minutes ago, following a brief lapse in attention, he'd lost control of the Dodge, swerved into the left lane and into the median. If his truck had merely been upside down, he'd have righted it and continued on, but he'd struck another vehicle as he left the road. The occupants of the Volvo—there were at least three—were dead, and the twins slipped out of sight before the other drivers had a chance to bear reliable witness to the hit-and-run.

Now, running at a good clip, hiding in the shadow of the tree-line that ran along East Shelby, Beryl regretted more than ever his choices of late. The roar of a jet engine sounded, grew, careened over them, and then faded as they reached the end of the tree cover at the edge of the airport property. Ta'avah stopped abruptly and gestured across the street.

"We'll catch a ride there and be back on the road in no time," he whispered, not even trying to speak silently.

Hidden inside Meryl's body, Ta'avah was finding telepathy an effort. It was just as well; Beryl's mind was no place for his master to be wandering as he became more and more embittered against him. Ta'avah's visage had returned to normal, his sharp teeth and nails a faded memory. Beryl was thankful, for very soon, they'd run into the humans and he needed to pass as one of them.

Across the road, a battered and collapsing clapboard building had somehow remained open as a bar, and behind that, corralled by chipped privacy fencing, a large trailer park sat sparsely-lit among wide-branched oak trees. Either place would be fine hunting grounds for what they required to resume their current mission.

Ta'avah watched for traffic on the busy four-lane road and then trotted across when the coast was clear. Beryl was right behind him and at the opposite curb they both paused, casing the smallish lot. Threatening thunderclouds obscured the moon and the air was crisp, keeping the patrons inside instead of hanging near their cars. Ta'avah made the first move and whispered to Beryl as he shoved past.

"Follow my lead in there, pup. You're on a very short leash, and I'll not suffer you any longer than I must."

Beryl tipped his head and Ta'avah made for the sagging entrance. A cloud of cigarette smoke washed over them as they entered and Beryl took in the joint at one glance. Several men lounged at tables scattered around the edges of the room and a lone woman sat at the bar, her back to the door. Ta'avah shot a look Beryl's way, an almost imperceptible smile on his lips.

"Meryl's keen sense of smell tells me there's a Cow here...you smell him?"

Ta'avah's telepathic voice grated Beryl's nerves, but he nodded and maintained his poker face.

"First, I'll taste the local brew," Ta'avah mumbled and settled his gaze on the female figure sipping from a wine glass.

Beryl vaguely intuited arousal from his twin and then remembered Meryl was dead. His brother had been a man of many needs, and it would appear that Ta'avah inherited his fondness for forgettable trysts.

"I beg your pardon, Master, but we haven't time—" Beryl attempted to speak reason, but Ta'avah grunted and cut him off in a harsh whisper.

"Go to the back of the room and wait for instructions."

Beryl headed away, his eye twitching. Maybe Ta'avah would hurry and they could leave this place. The old demon didn't care that the local police were no doubt searching for them. Even if the authorities didn't know who was driving the truck, they'd have the sense to search the surrounding area for strangers. Beryl shook his head; Ta'avah was incorrigible.

With nothing better to do, Beryl sniffed the air in an attempt to pinpoint the Cow. It'd been years since his people called upon these voluntary donors, but their scent lingered on no matter how long they'd been out to pasture. It'd been only a few hours since he drank his fill of the truck driver and he wasn't hungry in the least, but Ta'avah wasn't one to let an opportunity to feed pass him by. Then again, neither would've Meryl.

Beryl leaned against the wall next to the payphone and watched his master across the room. Ta'avah settled one stool away from the woman and began to sweet-talk her, compliment her eyes, her hair, and as soon as she smiled, he told her how much he'd like to bed her. She was a working girl, by her corresponding giggle, and they were about to close the deal.

Beryl scoffed and looked away. The man closest to him sat alone, hunched over a whiskey. The table next to his supported two Latino day workers, sipping frothy beer from dirty mugs. None of these men was the Cow. Beryl let his eyes glide over the remainder of the patrons until he reached the last, a single man, early forties, with shaggy black hair and a handlebar mustache. This man was watching Ta'avah like an eagle. His back was erect, his drinking arm resting on the table top, and as Beryl studied him, he noted the man was holding his breath.

He was the Cow.

As the realization hit him, the man stood up and crossed to the bar, stopping just behind Ta'avah. Beryl remained as he was and had no trouble overhearing their conversation.

"Oh, thank God. You-you-you're here for me?" the Cow burbled, his eyes darting from Ta'avah to the woman beside him.

"Go see my brother," Ta'avah replied without making eye contact and hooked his thumb Beryl's way. "He's by the phone. Now get."

The Cow met Beryl's eye and relief crossed his face as he hurried over. He came as close as he dared—which was plenty close as far as Beryl was concerned—and ran a hand through his hair, nervously tucking in his shirt-tail.

"Master, you're so beautiful," the man said in a whisper. He glanced at the other patrons a moment and leaned in closer. "Please, I've been alone a long time. What's going on? What happened?"

Beryl regarded the Cow, sending his thoughts to Ta'avah. *You want me to milk this guy? Where? The men's room?*

"No, stupid. See if he has a car. We need a ride."

"What's your name?" Beryl asked, his voice low. The drinker nearest them looked at them briefly and Beryl gave him a stern glare. The guy opted to move away and as he left, the Cow whispered his answer.

"Ardell. Mac Ardell." The man rubbed his face with both hands. He had it bad and Beryl couldn't help but be impressed. The Rakum

Cows of old were desperate to give blood and this one was about to pop with anticipation.

"Do you have a car, Mac?" Beryl asked, now allowing his voice to soothe the man, like the glory days; he and Meryl were so good with the humans. Mac's head bounced and he shoved his right hand into his jeans pocket.

"Got a van, master. It's yours. It's parked at my place." Mac's tone rose an octave as he completed the thought. "Just on the other side of the fence. I'm real close. Less than twenty yards yonder..."

Beryl took the offered keys, regarded the man with a wry grin, and respectfully waited for Ta'avah's response.

"Go, you idiot. I'll meet you there. I'll bring my girlfriend."

Beryl sneered at Ta'avah's condescension and then met the Cow's eye once more. "Take me to your place, Mac. Right now."

"Oh, thank God," Mac exhaled and turned away. "Thank God."

"Mac," Beryl said softly, so only he would hear.

Mac turned to face him, clearly agitated, but holding it together. "Yes, s-sir?"

"Drop the God-talk, 'kay?" Beryl said and Mac froze in place. Beryl pressed him further, "Thank *me*, Mac. Thank *me*. Let's get it right." Beryl's head went to the side and hoped his icy stare conveyed his meaning. Mac's expression fell, as if he disappointed his dad at the baseball championship.

"Oh, Master, I don' mean nuthin' by it. Oh, I'm so sorry." Mac's eyes watered and Beryl touched his shoulder.

"Dude, relax."

Mac eyed Beryl's contact and gave him a deprecating grin. "Yes, sir. Sorry, sir."

Beryl dropped his hand after a few more seconds and used his finger to prod Mac into turning around. Once he was walking again, Beryl fell in behind him toward the door.

"Mac, my brother will be joining us," Beryl said. "How will he find us?"

Mac swiveled left to catch Beryl's eye, a look of glee on his face. The thought of having two Rakum over really made his night.

"Through the gate and to the right. I got a silver Dodge van and a Mustang with no wheels out front. He can't miss it."

Beryl nodded flicked his hand to get the Cow moving again. A few men by the door snickered as they passed, but Beryl ignored them, following Mac into the cold night and then behind the building to a broken gate.

The moon peeked from behind the clouds as Mac picked his way across the littered lawns of his neighbors. He glanced back at Beryl repeatedly, but Beryl wouldn't meet his eye, too many things on his mind. Something was different. Mac Ardell loved him with his entire being, but Beryl didn't want the guy—didn't want his blood. He didn't want food, he didn't want sex, and he didn't want power. What did he want? As Beryl trailed behind the Cow, it came to him, loud and clear: He wanted Meryl back, plain and simple.

"Just through here, Master," Mac mumbled and led him to the back of a leaning manufactured home surrounded by cracked lawn furniture and one child's tricycle.

"You have a family here, Mac?" Beryl asked abruptly, but the old guy shook his head.

"Only on the weekends. I'm divorced. Thelma left me last fall," Mac said as he unlocked the rear door and showed the way in. "Please make yourself at home, Master. Can I get you something? A drink? Something else before we...before..."

Mac's sentence faded out as Beryl looked around the dingy space and then met the Cow's eye. Ardell was studying him, puzzled by his demeanor and afraid that he might not get the milking he so eagerly desired. His head to the side a few degrees, Beryl watched the man watch him, wondering what would make a human offer his blood to a Rakum. The thought never occurred to him before, but tonight, it was all he could think of. After nearly a minute of scrutiny, Ardell whimpered and his shoulders drooped.

"Master, what's wrong? What's happened to you guys? I wish I understood." Mac covered his face with one bear-like paw and slumped down on the ripped yard-sale couch.

"Hell happened, Mac, hell. Our lives shot to hell. How's that grab ya?" Beryl spoke softly and watched the man try to figure him out. Finally, Beryl said, "Sit up, Mac. Just sit up."

Mac straightened his shoulders and leaned back, his eyes red. "I waited so long, Master. I can't sleep, I can't work, and I can't concentrate. Then I see you guys in my bar—God." Mac winced at his last word, but Beryl didn't chastise him. Mac continued, simpering, "I saw you tonight and for the first time in years, I have hope."

"I know," Beryl replied and stepped over to the sofa. "What do you hope for, Mac?" Beryl pulled his pocket knife from his jeans as he spoke and Mac's moist eyes glistened.

"Sir?" he asked, his voice faraway.

"What do you hope for?" Beryl repeated, coming closer.

"That-that I might stay with you, sir."

Beryl laughed, "Oh, I don't think so, Mac. Look at my face. Would I keep an ugly old Cow like you around?" The man had no answer and Beryl laughed again. Mac was much too old and used-up to be considered worthy of Beryl's and Meryl's attention. But that was in the old days; Meryl was dead, and the Cows had been permanently turned out.

Beryl's smile fell and he got back to work, studying the way the Cow sat on the couch, and planning how to proceed. Ardell had fifty pounds on him and four inches so Beryl opted to keep him sitting. He rest his left knee beside Mac's right thigh and fell onto the man's lap, straddling him.

"How now, old Cow, what'cha got for me? Is your blood any good? Did your former master find you appealing?" Beryl pinched one tip of the Cow's moustache and gave it a yank. "Did he like this Mexican-cowboy-thing you have going on?"

Beryl didn't expect the guy to answer, and he didn't. Why was he playing with his food? In the past, he and Meryl enjoyed the sport, but tonight, he was only delaying what he didn't want to do. He didn't want to milk the guy and he desperately wanted to kill him. But why? Beryl grabbed a fistful of the man's oily hair and looked him hard in the face. Ardell's eyes grew wide, but he wasn't afraid.

"You look old, Mac," Beryl accused. "Is your blood old, too?"

Ardell unbuttoned his over shirt and shrugged it off as he nodded his head. "Yes. I mean, no. My blood's good. My master loved me best," he said, still sniffling.

"I hope so, because Mac," Beryl leaned in close to the man's face and pressed his blade a few inches north of his left shoulder, "if I'm not satisfied, I'm going to kill you and steal your van. Got it?"

Beryl didn't wait for a reply, but plunged his knife deep, making a gash much wider than necessary. The Cow started at the move, but remained still, well-trained and well-instructed. Beryl held him tightly and pulled the blood out of him, but instead of the pleasant buzz he expected, only a growing sense of unease sprouted in his brain. After another few moments, Beryl stopped feeding and spat in Mac's face.

"Dead blood, Mac. You've let it go bad. Your life is what we want—not this sad, empty shell." Beryl snarled now, angry at Ardell and his whole breed. "I'm afraid I can't cut you any slack, Mac."

Laughing at his rhyme, Beryl looked the man in the face, his left hand holding him by his long hair. The man's wound oozed a thick crimson rivulet that stained his yellowed undershirt.

"Master—I don't…I mean…" Mac began, but Beryl covered his mouth with his other hand.

"Hush now, old Cow." Still rhyming, Beryl moved his hand to cover the man's nostrils as well. Within seconds, old Mac realized the danger he was in and he began to thrash and buck. Unaffected, Beryl held his gaze. "I'm going to whack you, Mac. Tell me thank you. I want you to thank me for ending this pitiful existence of yours."

Mac strained against him as Beryl watched the sclera of his eyes tint pink, then red. When the struggle was over, and Ardell's pupils were fixed and dilated, Beryl rolled off his lap and sat beside him, thigh-to-thigh, on the couch.

I hope you're happy now, Master, Beryl thought privately, his eyes on the trailer's back door. *I got us a van. Let's get moving.*

Ta'avah didn't hear him, but he'd be along soon. He'd have that woman on his arm and she'd freak when she saw the dead Cow with the gaping hole in his neck sitting on the couch. Beryl smiled. It was going to be a good show.

FORTY

"*I'm cornered, Beryl! Get over here!*"

Ta'avah called him by his name for the first time since his resurrection; that had to count for something. Beryl sat up on the couch and rubbed his eyes. He'd been waiting for his master to arrive with the prostitute and dozed off against the corpse of Mac Ardell. Not until the demon repeated himself along with a string of telepathic expletives did Beryl come fully awake.

"Who's cornered you?" he said aloud and stood to stretch. Ardell's body slumped over as he rose.

"*The police, you moron! The bar! Come, now!*"

Beryl stepped dutifully for the door, but stopped as his hand reached the knob. What if the police nabbed Ta'avah? Would that be so terrible? Without intentional forethought, a few possible scenarios crossed Beryl's mind.

One, they successfully arrest and bind him, and tote him to jail. Ta'avah breaks out and makes a run for it. He desperately eludes police while seeking retribution on Beryl who abandoned him.

Two, his reanimated and possessed brother resists arrest and murders every police officer in sight, barely avoiding capture. Then he would have to flee, but he would come after Beryl first.

Three, the police manage to shoot him repeatedly before he kills every last one. Ta'avah loses consciousness and the reinforcements trot him off to the hospital under guard. Morning comes and burns the unconscious Rakum to a crisp.

Possibility number three was the most desirable, but also the biggest gamble.

"*What are you waiting for?*" Ta'avah's panic was barely disguised and it was good he hadn't peeked into Beryl's thoughts.

Beryl turned the knob. No matter how they handled the cops tonight, Ta'avah would kill him if he deserted him.

Setting his jaw, Beryl left the trailer, jogged over to the privacy fence and paused at the gate. The moon gave some light, and the single halogen above the establishment gave a little more, but Beryl saw every detail perfectly. The place was surrounded. From his vantage point, he saw three police cruisers, lights flashing, with five officers, weapons on the ready, covering the back door and the side emergency exit. Beryl poked his pocket and it jingled; Ardell's van keys were stashed and safe. If he could somehow extricate Ta'avah unseen, they could make for the van and slip away.

If only.

Beryl studied the faded pastel pink cinder block of the back wall, the flimsy rain gutter that ran the length of it, and the two wide ducts that emptied steam into the night sky. A sixth officer came around the side, plumes of mist floating above him as he called out orders to his fellows.

"Got any ideas?" He sent his thoughts, preparing to be verbally abused upon reply. For several seconds, nothing came over, and then a somewhat gentler Ta'avah responded in a telepathic whisper.

"No."

Beryl sighed. *"I see six cops surrounding the back. What do you see?"*

"I'm behind the bar, have a hostage. There—"

Ta'avah went silent unexpectedly and Beryl waited. Their link was only as good as any other Rakum's now, his two-as-one connection with Meryl lost forever.

"Three cops inside. I don't want to get shot."

Beryl nodded in enthusiastic agreement, even though he was alone behind the gate. If Ta'avah was wounded, would he feel it? Meryl was dead, but his body was alive. Beryl truly didn't want to take a chance.

"I can take out the ones I see. You kill your three. Meet me behind the gate. I have a van." Beryl paused making sure his every word translated across.

"Yes?"

"We'll make a run for it."

Silence. Beryl smirked unintentionally, sensing hesitation in his master that Meryl would never have suffered. Maybe Ta'avah was not as strong as he pretended. Then a gun fired, muffled and from inside the bar.

Beryl jumped into action.

Faster than the eye could see, he gained on the policeman closest to him and snapped his neck. As the officer was falling to the ground, two of his buddies turned and rallied to his aid, their guns beginning to come up. Beryl didn't allow them to complete their arc. As quickly as possible, he rushed them with arms wide, cupped the heads of each with open palms and slammed them together so hard that their skulls cracked like egg shells.

In a flash, a cop rounded the corner, weapon trained at Beryl's chest. The sudden recollection of being shot the night before caused his pulse to increase. He so didn't want to be shot again. The officer's finger tugged at the trigger as Beryl leapt off the ground and scrabbled onto the roof. The spent bullet ricocheted harmlessly on the cement wall, but the radio chatter increased exponentially. Beryl sensed more units being dispatched from all over the city. Things were getting out of hand.

Peeking over the roof edge, Beryl checked the ground forces. One uniformed officer disappeared into the bar, but there were at least two left outside and a dozen sirens heading their way. Had Ta'avah finished off his targets or had he been shot? Should Beryl make a run for it alone?

"I'm at the gate. Come down off the roof. Hurry!"

Beryl hunkered down and peered back the way he'd come. Ta'avah was waiting for him behind the broken gate, pale but otherwise unharmed. The remaining police officers were working out how to get on the roof—and they were radioing in for reinforcements. The phrases "extremely dangerous" and "shoot to kill" resonated in Beryl's mind.

"Head north twenty paces and you'll find the Cow's trailer." Beryl sent his thoughts with precision, his adrenaline pumping. One quick search for the remaining mortal authority found them securing a ladder to the south side of the building, but none of them had made it to the roof as yet.

"Catch!" He cocked back his arm and tossed the van keys to land in Ta'avah's hand.

He didn't see Ta'avah seize the keys or make for the van, but he sensed it just the same. Now, he had to get off the roof. Stooped over, Beryl checked the far side of the building, jogging along the rough tar surface. The sound of the police scanner filtered up and he knew their physical descriptions were being broadcast. If they were to escape, he needed to get off the roof *now*, and without being seen.

Translate to the trailer.

The notion popped into his head and he almost laughed. Very

few Rakum mastered it and to his knowledge, only three of the Fathers had the ability; Abroghia, of course, then Damien, and Theophilus was the last.

Theophilus. Beryl's sank into the shadow of the wide tin vent protruding from the roof, picturing the old Father wasting away in Rufus's basement. Theophilus had the ability to move from one place to another instantaneously, and Rufus had been drinking his blood for some time. Beryl and Meryl drank from Rufus. Had the talent been passed down through the blood?

Police Officer number one was climbing the ladder and shouting warnings at the top of his lungs; Beryl was out of time.

Squeezing closed his eyes, and furiously focusing on Mac Ardell's living room, he did what he'd seen Father Theophilus do a century ago while instructing the Rakum youth at First Ritual. When he performed feats to demonstrate to the proselytes how powerful their leaders were; to wow them into submission, reverence and awe. Beryl pictured Ardell's lumpy couch and willed himself there. With the shout of the cop who just gained the roof still ringing in his ears, Beryl was translated.

He opened his eyes and saw Ardell's corpse. With a sigh of relief, Beryl looked at his hands marveling, but there was no time to rejoice or even ponder exactly what happened. They had maybe three or four minutes to limp the van along the neighborhood alley to the north entrance and be added to the traffic, before the cops turned their eyes toward the trailer park. They'd drive until an hour before sunup and then find a place to hide in another town. Get out of Memphis.

Beryl crossed to the front door of the trailer and stealthily joined his master in the waiting van. They were going to make it.

Just barely.

FORTY-ONE

Jackson, MS
November 4th, 10:30 p.m.

"All right. You're done. It's all me, now, fellas."

Selene rolled her head toward the one speaking. She knew that voice. It was a long time ago, in another life, but familiar just the same. The three filthy Rakum who'd been taking turns at a jagged incision in her wrist, made a few disgruntled sounds and lumbered out of the room. She'd been in their clutches since she arrived at the Rakum's headquarters, and although she'd heard no such command, she assumed she'd been turned over to them—to all of them—just like before.

But what would Dimple do?

"You hanging in there, missus?" the wide Rakum asked, his vivid green eyes searching hers.

"Big Dimp?" Selene whispered, afraid to know if he was friend or foe. When Yosef was with her, Dimple promised to protect her with his life. He promised his Elder, his master. What about now?

"I don't like seeing you like this, missus," Dimple said softly, his gaze hard. "It ain't right."

Before Dimple came in for his turn, Rufus's minions had toyed with her mercilessly. None of them laid a hand on her sexually, but they did their best to weaken her by letting her blood. These Rakum were different. They were just as foul, but their lust was concentrated on intimidation and blood. Wincing with every move, Selene was too exhausted to appreciate the change.

"Will you help me?" Selene asked, but the big Rakum shook his head.

"You remember my talents, missus. Healing ain't one of 'em." Dimple turned to lock the door.

She'd been stashed in a good-sized den with two large desks on

209

either end of the room and three soft couches making a "U" between them. Selene was on the center couch facing the door and she watched Dimple's movements, still unsure of his motives.

"I can get you some water," he offered, without softening his voice.

Selene shook her head. "Forget it."

"You never should have changed your hair. If it weren't for your scent, I wouldn't know you." Dimple paused and narrowed his eyes. "It was I who turned Yosef in."

Selene had no reply, her feelings for Elder Yosef long since purged. Instead, she watched Dimple's face as he worked to express himself.

"But I refused to collect you," he said, tone as unreadable as ever.

Still, the flat denial gave her a measure of comfort. When Yosef left the fold, and they tried to recruit his lieutenants to clean up the pieces—of which Selene was one—Dimple declined. He guarded her as long as he could. Maybe he would help her now.

"You had a baby," Dimple remarked, loosely insinuating that she was heavier than when he last saw her.

"I grew up, Dimp," Selene replied. "It's been a long time."

"This hair is wrong." Dimple stepped closer and gestured to her head. When she was with Yosef, she had an afro, "simple and foxy," as her mate often remarked. When she married Jesse, she changed her look to symbolize a rebirth into her new life.

"My hair," Selene began, putting a hand to the dozens of loose and unraveled extensions.

"You need to cut that crap out of there." Dimple fished around in his pockets until he found his knife. He pulled open the blade and its wide six-inch blade gleamed in the lamp's light. "Sit up."

Selene didn't move, her mind wandering back. How many years? The number didn't matter. What mattered was that when she was with Yosef, Dimple handled her hair frequently. She might die from embarrassment if mentioned now, but more than once, the Rakum before her actually *bathed* her. It was a different life, a million years ago.

Dimple stepped up to stand before her and she still hadn't moved. He wiggled his knife hand and scowled her way. He'd always been gruff, hadn't he? Selene inhaled sharply and sat up straight, her forehead inches from Dimple's blade.

"Be still," he grunted and grabbed a handful of hair in his right hand. His left hand disappeared outside of her vision, but was at the hairline above her brow. With a deft sawing motion, he carefully shaved the extensions out, right against her scalp. Selene remained stock-still and barely breathed, not at all sad to see them go. The lovely human hair she'd paid ten grand to have added to her own was a liability while in the clutches of the Rakum. Dimple worked at the job unceasing until her entire head was shaved. When he stepped back, Selene thought she recognized a tiny glint in his eye from the old days; back when he watched over her when Yosef was called away on Elder business. She watched his face as he studied her, and before too long, the corners of his mouth turned up a fraction.

"This is much better, yes?"

Selene offered a small smile and ran her hands over her scalp. A fine layer of fuzz covered her head, and as far as she could tell, the job was even.

"Thank you, Dimple."

"You're welcome," he replied, milliseconds before he resumed his guarded disposition. "Rufus expects you to remain here until he sends for you. I'll look after you until then."

"Thank you."

"I'll bring you something to eat." He turned for the door, but faced her again once his hand was on the knob. "Stay *here*."

Selene nodded. Where would she go? She watched Dimple lumber from the room and heard him giving instructions to someone in the hall. She overheard three words, "*watch this door.*" He was still trying to protect her. How much he could do was left to be seen, but at least he hadn't hurt her, and that meant a lot.

Selene rubbed her almost-bald head, regarded the pile of shiny black hair at her feet, and leaned back into the sofa. What would Jesse think of her new style? Would she even see her husband again? What about Dae Lee?

Selene wondered if God was keeping track and fell off to sleep.

FORTY-TWO

With the light bulb extinguished, it was dark enough, but sleep never came. Chloe dozed fitfully and was thankful neither of the basement's other occupants paid her any mind. Now and then, she overheard them whispering in a strange language. Looking at her watch for the millionth time, Chloe trembled at the thought of being returned to Rufus's care. It was nearing midnight. How could she wait another whole day for her knight in shining armor to arrive?

Chloe drew up her knees and wrapped her arms around them. Her life had become a nightmare and there was no one to turn to.

"Submit to God," David had said. Chloe buried her face in her folded arms.

How can I submit to God? If He's real, He's abandoned me.

"You don't understand the nature of God. He loves you, Chloe." David's earlier advice trickled into her consciousness.

Chloe closed her eyes and tried to remember a time when she believed in God. When she was little? Sure. Her parents took her to church. She heard all of the stories in Sunday school. She'd made an announcement to the entire youth group that she wanted Jesus to be her Savior. That was when she believed.

Yeah. He was real then. He was so real.

Chloe and her friend Tammy used to have long talks about Him. They would sometimes debate other kids about Him at school. She was so sure, so confident. What happened? Why did He pull back?

Maybe He didn't.

What if she was the one who walked away?

Chloe lifted her head and wiped a fresh crop of tears that had escaped her notice. What if God was only a prayer away? The thought of picking up the phone line to the Almighty scared her to death. What would He say? She'd been gone a long time. What could she possibly say to Him now? And why would He listen?

Across the room, the two old gentlemen had fallen silent and were looking her way. She saw their outlines, sitting cross-legged and nearly touching, leaning over their laps with their fingertips brushing the grubby tile floor.

"A father had a son..."

Chloe gasped; one of the old men was speaking to her telepathically. She covered her mouth and looked between their silhouettes nervously.

"One ran off to another town and did all manner of horrible things. But the father missed him. The father didn't care about all that stuff. He only wanted the son to come home. The father watched for him every minute of every day, praying, wishing, and hoping his son would push through that door and come home."

Chloe recognized the paraphrased story of the prodigal son, but remained silent, hoping he'd stop speaking in her mind.

"The son ran out of money, got sick, and started thinking about his father again." The bearded old man in coveralls spoke aloud, his inhuman voice rumbling around the room with substance. "He worried his father would be angry and reject him, but the father's deepest desire was to be with his son once more."

Chloe dropped her hand and lowered her knees. The other man nodded his head in agreement with his fellow and she took a deep breath.

"When the boy came home, the father welcomed him with open arms and cherished him all the days of his life. And the son never left his father's house again."

"But how can God be like that?" Chloe asked. "It's too good to be true."

"God's ways are not man's ways, child." The other gentleman spoke this time, his voice as gentle and aristocratic as her history professor.

"He made you because He loves you," he continued. "What you have done is irrelevant. Submit to God, resist the devil and he will flee from you."

"That's what Dave said," Chloe whispered. "But how do I submit to God? What does that mean?"

The man with no beard glanced to the man in the coveralls and carefully rose to his feet. In the dim light, she watched him cross to the light switch and illuminate the space. Coveralls shielded his eyes as the professor stepped her way and offered his hand.

"Allow me to introduce myself. I am Damien. I was once a leader among the Rakum. This is Father Theophilus—still Rakum, but there is hope yet."

Chloe allowed him to help her to her feet. He was stately and she could easily see him ruling the Wraiths with an iron hand. Her sweet Davey once served this man and the realization made her sad.

"The way to submit to God is first to acknowledge Him. Do you, Miss Bushman, acknowledge Him? That He exists?"

Chloe swallowed and nodded her head, but the old man lowered his chin looking more like her professor than ever.

"Aloud, Miss Bushman."

"Oh, yeah. I mean, yes, I do believe He's real. I just don't know how to submit to Him and make all this go away."

"This isn't going to go away, Miss Bushman," Damien warned. "There's a battle coming between good and evil and you will play an integral role. Go ahead and speak to God. He's listening."

Chloe looked up at the ceiling and then at Father Theophilus who listened attentively a few feet away. "What do I say?"

"Whatever you were thinking earlier."

"I was thinking that He abandoned me," Chloe replied in a whisper.

"Then ask Him about that." Damien gave her an encouraging smile and took her fingers in his. "Say, Father…"

"Uh…Father…"

"I feel like you abandoned me."

"Don't I need to repent or something first?" Chloe asked, but Damien shook his head.

"Get the lines of communication open. The rest will come. 'Father, I feel like you abandoned me…'"

Chloe nodded her head and closed her eyes. "I'm so alone, God. I know you didn't abandon me. I left. I'm that bad kid who ran off to see what the world was like. I want to come home. I want to run back into my father's house. I'm sorry I'm such a mess…"

Chloe took back her hand and covered her face with her fingers. A fresh shower of tears began and she couldn't stem the flow. Soon her sobs were coming with more power, and she struggled to breathe through clogged nasal passages. Damien draped his arm across her shoulders and snugged her close. Chloe leaned into his chest, the old gentleman smelling like her grandfather: Irish Spring soap and Old Spice.

"God, I don't want to sleep with that Rufus again, and I don't want him to bite me again, and I want to go home."

"Father, please give this little girl strength and faith," Damien whispered over her head. Chloe looked up at his profile and wiped her eyes with the heel of her hand. This ancient creature was praying for her, speaking about her to the Creator of the universe. Chloe realized for the first time in a decade that God was listening.

And then He spoke back.

"God works all things for the good of those who love Him. If God is for you, who shall be against you? God is your rock and your fortress—whom shall you fear?"

Those and many more verses popped into her mind and gave her comfort. Chloe stood away from Damien and took a deep breath. Everything was going to turn out all right. God loved her and she was back in His house. Chloe exhaled and looked up, a sublime tranquility massaging her spirit. She turned to the former Rakum and gave him a small smile.

"What do you think will happen now?"

"It will get ugly," he answered truthfully. "We'll be put to the test. But remember to trust God. No matter what you see with your eyes, God is controlling this show. Faith is trust. Being faithful is trusting God to take care of you."

Chloe nodded and tightly hugged herself. From across the room, Father Theophilus mumbled something in another language. Damien nodded and looked down on her kindly.

"You'll be relieved to know that Rufus will no longer be able to hear your thoughts," Damien said, nodding.

"How do you know?"

Damien gestured to his partner, "Father Theophilus can no longer hear them. That means they belong to God now."

Chloe sighed and thanked God in her heart. Damien couldn't exactly promise her that she wouldn't be bitten by the vampire again, or that she was going to avoid sleeping up against him again all day. But his words gave her confidence. The monster wouldn't be in her head. God really was in control and if He wanted her to do a little battle for His cause while she was here, why resist?

No, she'd resist the devil.

And maybe, just maybe, he *would* flee from her and leave her alone.

FORTY-THREE

Jackson, MS
November 6th, 12:00 a.m.

Selene opened her eyes groggily, grey-streaked walls passing her vision. She bounced along, draped over Dimple's meaty shoulder as he toted her from the study to her next destination. Earlier, he'd brought her a stale sandwich and a Coke that preceded a short but mercifully deep sleep. Where was he taking her now? Selene thought to ask, but why bother? She was in hell, and unlike before, no one had swooped in to save her.

Dimple turned down a long hall and her head bumped against the wall. Selene grunted at the sensation, but he continued on without a word. When he pushed open a door and headed down a set of stairs, she rubbed her head, sufficiently coherent now to see that the space was a basement. When the Rakum dropped her semi-gently to the ground, she lay on her back, resigned, and stared at the hazy bulb in the ceiling.

"Hey, you."

Dimple's voice, detached and professional, echoed about the room and Selene looked at him upside down from the floor. He wasn't speaking to her. He gestured across the room to her right, and she angled her head to see a teenager with gigantic eyes and curly long brown hair. They made eye contact and Selene took a double-take; the girl wasn't afraid. She stepped toward Dimple and tossed Selene a gentle smile.

It's going to be okay, her empathetic glance said, and Selene watched amazed as the youngster led the way up the steps with purpose. At the top, Dimple grabbed the hem of her shirt and she stopped. He turned to face the basement and spoke, again not addressing Selene.

"Father Theophilus, this woman is for you. Rufus said you'll be hungry."

That said, he nudged the teenager forward, left the room, and locked the door. Selene sat up with a grunt and looked about, wondering at Dimple's words. Someone was down there with her, and if his name was Theophilus then they had a lot in common: Father Theophilus was her husband's natural father.

Across the room, sitting against the wall were two elderly men. The first man shook his head when their eyes met. The other man didn't raise his head, but stayed where he was, cross-legged on the bare cement floor, gaze cast down and to the side. He looked older by decades and Selene regarded him with a mixture of exhaustion and cautious interest.

He wore new gray coveralls, still creased from being folded on a store shelf and he wore no shoes; only a pair of white socks, stained with dirt from their basement prison. His orange and gray beard looked to be shorn off, straight across at mid-chest, and she imagined it had probably reached his belt in another life. Still, none of it added up. If Theophilus was bloodthirsty as Dimple indicated, then he was still a Rakum. Who would cut off a Father's beard? And how could he be Rufus's prisoner?

Selene held her questions and studied his profile in the low light. He made no move toward her, nor did he acknowledge her presence. The irony was rich; this two thousand-year-old Rakum was her father-in-law. Selene smirked and the old Father spoke up.

"Jesse Cherrie is alive, then?"

His voice was strong and even with a curious inflection on each consonant. It echoed off the sheetrock and caused gooseflesh to break out on Selene's arms. He appeared wizened and used up, but she had the impression he was anything but. Selene held her breath and his eyes met hers slowly and with purpose. Emerald green—so much like those of her husband.

"Your husband...he is mortal, then?"

Selene nodded, still working up a response. Theophilus beat her to it.

"Do not fret, woman. I am no danger to you."

"Are you mortal, Father?" Selene whispered, as confused as ever. If he was Rakum, he was mighty polite. Or mighty impotent. Theophilus scoffed and looked away.

"I am nothing. I am the walking dead. An animated shell who cannot cease to breathe."

"I don't understand," Selene muttered.

Theophilus rolled to his knees to push himself to his feet. With the strength and balance of a much younger man, he stepped lightly across the floor and laid his gnarled hand on the top of her head. Selene would have drawn out of his reach, but her bruised spine screamed with pain with the slightest movement.

"Animals, my children are animals," he muttered and placed his other hand atop the first.

Selene grew still and rolled her eyes up to see him. The scene was a familiar one and she waited for the jolt of electricity she knew was coming. Seconds passed and her scalp began to grow warm where his hands lay.

"A proud and respectable people—that is what Abroghia promised me. Better than humans, stronger, faster, smarter, longer-lived. Then he said, 'give them time,' 'they're evolving,' 'won't be long now'..."

Selene closed her eyes as the heat spread to her face, through her chin, to the back of her head and down her spine. The old man was healing her, and more than that, he was giving her back the strength the blood loss stole away.

"Oh, he was the father of all lies..." Theophilus's voice wavered, and he exhaled as the job was done. "Your child is safe, and I have no intention of taking your blood."

Selene looked at him then, relieved at both of his statements. "Thank you," she said and he backed away.

"Your *unborn* child is safe, woman. Jesse's seed grows in you still. You will have a son. You will name him Theo, after his grandfather."

Selene's face dropped and she shook her head, one hand subconsciously covering her belly. Of all the times to be pregnant.

Jesse would be thrilled.

FORTY-FOUR

Montgomery, AL
November 5th, 4:00 p.m.

It was Montreal, 1885, and Javier was 8-years-old. The group-lair, his home as far back as he could remember, had been burned to the ground by political zealots. They'd not been targeting the Rakum, but because of their actions, Javier and his fellow youths were transported hastily under the cover of darkness to new homes. As the youngest of three, emergency measures required shipping Javier off by horse cart to abide with an Elder named Roman.

Soon enough, his grumpy Rakum chaperone turned the mare down an overgrown lane and pulled up to a humble log cabin nestled in the trees. Without a word, Javier was hauled from the cart, brusquely dusted off, and maneuvered to the front door. When he was shoved into the room and left alone with his new guardian, Javier crossed to the center of the room and waited to be acknowledged.

Elder Roman was tall and lean, wearing a ruffled white shirt under a royal blue tail coat. No one dressed so fashionably back home and Javier was suddenly self-conscious in his hand-me-down cotton trousers. After several long minutes, his new guardian still had said nothing, staring down on him with an unfathomable gaze. Just when he'd thought he'd been quiet long enough and was about to speak, Elder Roman gestured with his hand and called him close. Javier jumped to his side.

After the Elder asked him a few questions about his language skills and his experience at group-lair, he offered Javier his blood. Javier's gut churned at the thought. On the one hand, he was assured by his instructors that the first few times he drank an Elder's blood, he would regret it for days. The aged and purified fluid would seep into his system and leech his energy, causing queasiness and cramping until it dissolved and melded with his own genetic identity. Still, his

219

tongue tingled at the thought and his fists clenched with anticipation.

It was what he was made for.

The race he was born into.

And the destiny of all he called brother.

Javier awoke in a sweat and sat up in the soft guest bed. He was in the Rabbit's house and it was nearing four. Canaan and Isaac would rise at sundown and they would all head for Rufus's headquarters.

Javier moaned and put his palm to his forehead. Nothing about his condition made sense and he was dizzy from his dreamy walk down memory lane. The first time he tasted an Elder's blood—the recollection still caused his stomach to flop uncomfortably. And how many hundreds of times did he feed off his Elder-Guardian? They lived alone for nearly twenty years, and there was no one else to buzz him for the first fifteen.

But that was when he was a Rakum. A child of the devil, according to Beth Rider.

No, according to God. Javier corrected himself and leaned over his lap in the dusky light. His shades were open; he no longer feared the sun, unlike Canaan and the mysterious Rakum kid who were in the basement asleep.

And what about Canaan?

He wanted to bring Javier back into the fold. Was it possible?

But I can't go back into the muck God pulled me out of. Javier – get a hold of yourself!

Javier exhaled loudly and slapped his cheek. He'd been 130-years-old, king of the universe, taking whatever he wanted and walking the earth as a god. Canaan still had that.

Wasn't Canaan doomed if he didn't repent and come to God? Wasn't that how it worked? A year ago, Javier understood God well and shared His truth with other Rakum who were freshly leaving the brotherhood. But the last few months had been hard. Watching David romance the nutty Chloe girl, hating himself for the many fantasies her face brought to his beleaguered mind, feeling absolutely no draw for the rest of the females he came in contact with throughout his boring existence. At least as a Rakum, whether or not he wanted sex, he visited brothels as a matter of course, but God's children disdained such things.

I am a child of God.

Javier scoffed. He was, but he was leaning away; pulling back from the hand that comforted him and gave him peace.

"I don't want peace. I want..."

Power.

Javier blinked and sat up. This voice he heard was not his own, and not God's.

And blood.

Javier came to his feet and turned a circle in the spacious borrowed bedroom. The carpet was soft under his bare feet and he looked at it, unseeing, as it caressed his toes.

"No, I want God," Javier mumbled after a silent moment and took a few steps toward the lavatory.

Liar.

Stiffening his jaw, Javier headed instead for the door. Could one of the Rakum below be manipulating him? If so, he wouldn't stand for it. Not taking the time to put on a shirt, he quietly opened the door and peeked down the hall. When ready, he took a deep breath, held it, and covered the distance to the stairwell. He descended the steps without a sound and jogged the carpeted first floor hallway. When he reached the basement door, he tried the knob; it was locked.

Javier's heart skipped a beat and he stared blindly ahead. He never considered they'd lock their door. Standing in the hallway in his pajama bottoms, Javier pondered how to proceed. Should he knock? Wouldn't someone upstairs hear him? What if—

Click.

Javier tried the knob again. It was open and he slipped through, closing it behind him. In the basement, thanks to Michael Stone's efforts, it was pitch dark. Javier stood at the top of the stairs, hand on the cool metal railing, and exhaled.

"Took your sweet time, little brother."

It was Canaan's voice and Javier's mind went blank. Why had he come?

"Can you see your way down?"

Javier felt for the step with his toe and grunted that he could. The empathy in Canaan's voice made him feel hopeful. Maybe he could return to the old fold and also keep a foot in heaven. How could God expect him to change so easily? He needed more time. He'd professed his faith too soon. Could he turn back the clock?

By the time he reached the bottom of the steep staircase, a hand landed on his shoulder.

"Isaac's here, too, Javie. Say hi, Isaac."

"Hey." The kid's voice was higher, but just as subdued; they'd been discussing him.

"If you want to work your way back to us, you'll have to trust me," Canaan said softly and Javier felt his breath on his cheek. "Can you do that? Trust me?"

"I should go back upstairs."

"You remind me of the caged bird." Isaac's voice, as soft as a child's, but filled with wisdom beyond his years.

Javier didn't understand. "What?"

"A bird in a cage. You think the bars of its prison are the worst torture?" Isaac paused. "It's not the bars. And it's not imprisonment. Do you know what tortures the bird more than these?"

Javier sighed, shaking his head and looking in the direction of the voice.

"Man keeps him low."

Javier furrowed his brow. "What are you talking about?"

"Man keeps him low. The bird is meant to fly, to soar, to seek the highest branch of the tallest tree, and look down on the children of man. Can he do that in a cage?"

Javier pictured a pet-store parrot and then the same bird in the wild, living in rainforests as old as the earth itself. To his left, he heard a friendly chuckle. On his right, Isaac continued.

"You were meant to live high above this plane. Born to reign, born to subjugate any mortal you saw fit. This religion, this blind faith, this is your cage. It has made what was extraordinary into something common."

Isaac stopped abruptly and Javier discerned it was for effect. When he began again, his voice was louder and it made Javier jump.

"Look up to the treetops, brother. You're a Rakum, you belong above. This is why you're so miserable. You've been shackled by those created to serve you."

"No." Javier shook his head, memories flooding back. Memories of his long conversations with God, with Beth Rider, with Roman—conversations that brought him peace such as he'd never known. Being human was a gift; being Rakum, an unrelenting curse.

As familiar as a lover, Canaan rest his palm around Javier's neck. The contact shook Javier awake from his thoughts and he inhaled sharply.

"I don't know," he stammered. "I just—"

"Isaac's been buzzing the Fathers." Oblivious to his disconcert, Canaan pulled Javier toward him. "For decades. His blood can bring you back."

"The Fathers? That's impossible," Javier mumbled, knowing instinctively the Rakum's statement had merit. Then his feeling of violation returned. "Wait, was he in my head? Isaac—was that you in my head?"

"You have to consent, Javie," Canaan continued, his voice stern, but gentle. "This needs to be your idea."

Javier's mind raced. If anyone could release a caged Rakum, it would be the kid. Father Damien believed in his vision completely and stressed the prophecy more than once in their brief meeting a century ago. But what of God?

Javier exhaled and waited for a word in his spirit. None came and the Rakum remained quiet on either side. Why wasn't God shouting at him anymore? Correcting him and pressuring him to head back upstairs? For seven years, God steered him in the way he should go, chastised him at every wrong turn. Where was His steady hand now? Had He given up on Javier entirely?

How long will I strive with man?

Javier exhaled and pondered those words in his spirit as Isaac laid a tentative hand on his opposite shoulder. High Father Abroghia's last child could possibly do it. Ta'avah, the demon who birthed the Rakum race could have empowered this last gifted son. And wouldn't God forgive him if he messed up? Beth assured them all that He was a forgiving God.

I'll never leave you nor forsake you…

"And there's more," Isaac's sweet voice whispered in his right ear chasing away the last words of his conscience. "You have to reject this new God to receive my offer."

"No, I-I won't do that."

"Then it won't work. Not the way you want it to," Isaac whispered again.

"I don't care. I can't do that." Javier was certain that if he uttered a curse against God, that he'd not be able to ride the fence any longer. He'd be doomed to an eternity of darkness. He shook his head one more time, resolute. "You do your part. I'll do mine."

"Do it, Isaac. We'll see what happens," Canaan said with urgency.

Javier waited, sightless, as there was movement on his either side, until his lips brushed up against the boy's wrist. No one spoke again and Javier knew what to do. The kid's blood burned in his gut like acid, and he took four long pulls before he pushed away and collapsed onto the cement floor, gagging.

The two Rakum snickered over his head and he heaved violently, ignoring them. It'd been a stupid experiment—a maliciously false hope put in his mind by the enemy. What made him so dense? The Rakum weren't just another race of beings—they were half demon.

And demons were from hell.

Javier groaned and wiped his wet eyes, happy that he couldn't see his tears hit the ground. But the Rakum saw him clearly and he soon felt Canaan's strong hands lifting him to a standing position. The Elder held him gently against his chest and ruffled his hair.

"You're fine, little brother. Go upstairs. We shall see what happens."

Javier nodded at nothing and turned clumsily back the way he had come. Unseeing, he felt around for the handrail and Canaan's cool fingers gently guided him until he grasped it. Words were caught in his throat—curses against Isaac and placations toward Canaan. Holding his tongue, Javier climbed the steps and left the basement.

As he padded back to his bedroom, he looked briefly to the prickled ceiling plaster. *"Father, why do you even bother with me?"* With a numbness in his mind and dizzying nausea in his belly, Javier's flesh scolded him for making the mistake of drinking the imp's blood. Closing himself into his room, he collapsed on his bed, still speaking to God in an urgent hiss. *"Why put up with me? Why?"*

Javier pressed his hand to his aching stomach and watched the room dim as the sun set outside his window.

God didn't answer, but Javier hadn't really expected Him to. For why would a holy God speak to a man who played with monsters?

FORTY-FIVE

I-55 South, TN
November 5th, 5:30 p.m.

"You can get off me now, the sun is down."

Responding to Ta'avah's patronizing tone, Beryl braced himself with strong arms and worked his way to a semi-standing position. It wasn't the first time he'd been squeezed into a small place with another Rakum.

Twelve hours ago, minutes before sunrise, Ta'avah directed them to an abandoned house on an overgrown patch of land three miles north of the interstate. Once a proud three bedroom country abode, the house was presently more a shack with a battered roof and various missing sidewalls. It was far from light-tight, but Ta'avah was certain no one would disturb them during the daylight hours. With the horizon pregnant with yellow light, Beryl helped him scout the place until they settled on an interior closet, crammed their bodies inside, and pulled the door to. With a floor space no bigger than 3' x 5', they began the day squatting side by side, knees folded to their chins. But sometime during their slumber, Beryl had fallen to the side and awoke stretched out atop Ta'avah on the dusty floor.

"We'll need a different vehicle. We'll jog back to the main road and catch a ride." Ta'avah shimmied past him through the closet door and stretched his arms toward a ceiling they could see right through in spots.

Beryl dusted off his pants, then his shirt, and shook his head violently to dislodge the insects that may have used him as a bed. Ta'avah was still making plans aloud as Beryl swatted a grass spider from his shoulder.

"May I ask," Beryl said softly, "how did you get out of the bar without them seeing you?"

"Same as you," Ta'avah said, taking the cue from Beryl and

shaking his clothes. "You didn't know you had it in you, eh?"

Beryl shook his head. Teleporting from one place to another was something he didn't think he could do again. He was fairly certain that his panic had a lot to do with his success.

"There's a lot you could do if you'd only work on it. You and your worthless brother always set your sights too low. All Meryl wanted to do was eat, sleep, and copulate. All you ever wanted to do was keep up with him. What a waste."

Beryl didn't care much for Ta'avah's spurious rant, but he said nothing. His master sneered and laughed aloud.

"You hungry? I'm starving."

"How can you be hungry?" Beryl asked without thinking.

"What do you mean?"

"You've had more blood in the last thirty-six hours than Meryl and I had in a week." Beryl did his best to temper his tone, but Ta'avah's expression was indignant. He barreled on. "The best thing for us to do is steal a car *without* a person in it, drive to Rufus's house, and get this over with."

"Get what over with?" Ta'avah teased.

"Your plan. Whatever you have in mind for Elder Rufus. The plan. Get it over with." Beryl exhaled, knowing he was on thin ice.

"You want me to tell you my plan, Ballerina?"

Beryl paused, expecting a reprimand.

"Do you think I will keep you alive once my *plan* comes to pass?"

Beryl nibbled his bottom lip then nodded his head. "Why not? I'll serve you in whatever capacity you require. I'm an excellent soldier for our people. I stand on my record."

"No, you're soft, and so much weaker than your brother." Ta'avah shook his head. "You're a poor excuse for a Rakum. I'm sorry it was Meryl who was incapacitated and not you."

Beryl ground his teeth and worked up the proper response. He could deny being soft. He could admit he wished he'd been the one Elder Canaan broke in two. Which would most please Ta'avah? Finally he sighed, "I will serve you, master. Do with me as you will."

Ta'avah nodded appreciatively and held Beryl's gaze, smiling like the devil he was.

"Take me to Theophilus. Through him, I will begin again, on a smaller, but more powerful scale. I will repopulate the Rakum race with supermen. All Rakum who do not make the cut will be destroyed. If you prove yourself capable, you will live."

"You'll assume Theophilus's body?"

"Indeed. He is loyal and once he gives control over to me, I'll take our people to a new level with no room for other leaders. I will rule supreme. This way I can assure our success."

"Pardon me, Master, but why didn't you do it that way to begin with? Didn't you start collecting Fathers more than two thousand years ago?" Beryl asked, honestly puzzled.

Ta'avah scoffed. "There you go again, trying to understand things beyond your comprehension." He turned and headed for the broken back door of the dwelling. "We operate within allowed parameters. Can you comprehend that, stupid pup?"

"Yes, you only do what the God of the humans allows you to do," Beryl said and Ta'avah's face darkened.

"For now."

Beryl didn't understand the intimation so he remained silent. After another few contemplative moments, Ta'avah sighed and exited the house toward the van. Beryl had backed it against the house amidst an envelope of grasses that reached the windows. The only way the humans would find it was by air, and it wasn't likely that they'd see it even then.

"How far to Jackson, pup?" Ta'avah asked while gazing up at the stars. The wind whipped through the field, zoomed past them, and continued east. Beryl shivered and set his jaw. It was going to be a long night.

"No more than two hours, Master. I hear the road. Rush hour in a small town." Beryl didn't move until Ta'avah did, but then fell in slightly behind as he walked eastward.

"Small towns have small police forces. Follow me."

Beryl matched his pace as Ta'avah fell into a slow jog. Would his master find a car without killing anyone? It made sense to avoid the attention of the authorities as long as possible. They were wanted already for the murder of cops in Memphis, and they may well be linked to the deaths of the people in the Volvo and the dead Samaritan and Forest Ranger in Radnor Lake Park. Why was Ta'avah so reckless? As their High Father, Abroghia was the most responsible of them all, setting law and punishment for the slightest violation. What made him so unreasonable upon his resurrection? Ta'avah broke into a laugh and tossed Beryl a quick glance.

"I'm not getting all of it, but enough is trickling through, Ballerina. You're a miserable milquetoast, a whining infant. How did

Jack Dawn tolerate you? Or are these personality traits blossoming forward for my benefit?"

Beryl had no answer and the sound of their footfalls in the grass filled the silence. Finally the demon grunted with victory and turned his attention elsewhere. Beryl did his best to keep his mind clear. Ta'avah was going to destroy him when their mission was accomplished, this was certain. But what could he do about it? Nothing.

He ground his teeth again. It was all he could do for now.

FORTY-SIX

Montgomery, AL
November 5th, 5:15 p.m.

Canaan buttoned his Levi's and shrugged on a freshly-ironed red oxford that Marcy left hanging on the basement doorknob. She was sore at having to sleep alone, but there was nothing to be done about that. Plus, Canaan enjoyed spending a few hours with one of his own. Not that he and Isaac spent the long daylight hours chatting; the only excitement had been Javier's brief visit. But there was a comfortable, ancient camaraderie between them that Canaan hadn't realized he missed.

For the moment, Isaac was in the bathroom taking a shower. The stall had been too short for Canaan and obviously a hasty addition the Stones put in to accommodate the Rakum apostates that passed through their home on their way to their transformation. Canaan scoffed, still amazed that he was among them; the strange, hopeful and stupid Rakum that ditched their divinity for a life of servitude to an unseen God. How nuts was that?

"Pretty nuts."

Canaan sniffed at Isaac's telepathic agreement. The boy was amazing. He operated in the gifts of the Fathers like no Rakum before him, and Canaan found it more than a little unsettling. So much power inside such a young, inexperienced Rakum was irresponsible. What were they thinking?

"They didn't foresee the Rabbit."

"True," Canaan replied aloud, buttoning his shirt. Three from the top, he heard a soft step at the basement door. It was locked, he knew, and he glanced at his watch—5:15p.m. The sun was on the horizon and the Rabbit's army would be amassing for their road-trip to Jackson. So who was tip-toeing around the door? Canaan resumed buttoning his shirt as the door at the top of the stairs opened and closed. He looked up and his jaw dropped.

"What does she want? Don't they keep that thing on a leash?"

Canaan hushed Isaac in his mind and closed his mouth. Coming down, one careful step at a time, her right hand on the rail and her left encircling a plush bear half her size, was six-year-old Grace Louise Stone. She squint her eyes in the dim light and peered in his direction.

"She's a Rabbit," Canaan sent to Isaac unintentionally.

"That explains why she stinks," the kid responded.

When she reached the landing, she felt along the wall in the dark until she found the light switch and flipped it. Was this her playroom when there were no Rakum present? Unable to think of anything to say, he remained mute, standing beside the unmade twin bed, his fingers frozen at the top button of his shirt.

"Watch out. I heard those things bite."

Isaac was having fun spying on him telepathically from the shower. Canaan ignored him. He was, after all, still a child in most respects.

The little girl approached, barely hip-high to Canaan, and stood right under his nose. He raised his eyebrows and waited for her to speak. In another circumstance, he might have thought someone was playing a prank, but these were serious times and the tiny human's face showed no humor. She wore pink footie pajamas and her jumble of loose blonde curls encircled her head like a halo. Canaan held his breath and wondered why.

After studying his face like David eyeing Goliath, Grace put both arms—her free hand and the one with the bear—on the bed and crawled slowly up, her feet scrabbling for purchase between the box spring and mattress. Canaan almost gave her a hand, but restrained himself, afraid to make contact. Isaac was snickering jovially on the other side of the bathroom door, but Canaan was filled with unexplained dread.

Once the little girl was standing on the bed, her eye level with his shoulder, she tugged on his shirt. Relenting, Canaan sat down and watched her face. What was she up to, and did she even have a purpose? Children were dumb and simple and basically—easy prey. Since the beginning of time, they made an easy dinner for Rakum on the hunt. A century ago when he and Kilmeade ran the hospital, he fed on waifs smaller than this one regularly. He never drank them to death—Fathers forbid—but plenty of times his nocturnal visits weakened them enough that they died the days following. Never had a child seemed so wise and frightening at the same time.

Shape up, Canaan! She's just a stupid kid. Geesh! Canaan mentally shook himself.

As he watched dumbfounded, the little girl put down her bear, placed her left hand on his shoulder, and climbed into his lap.

"Ugh," he groaned, uncomfortable in so many ways.

Isaac was moments away from leaving the bathroom to watch the show, but with a quick thought Canaan commanded him to stay put. He took a deep breath and snarled imperceptibly; the child was a Rabbit. As an Elder, Canaan was above chasing Rabbits, but the aroma was heady and he clinched his jaw. Finally, when she was as settled as she was going to get, Grace looked him right in the eye and put her tiny palm against his cheek. A low-voltage jolt coursed through him from the contact and he flinched.

"What?" he whispered, his throat strangely parched.

Grace licked her pink lips. "My mommy and daddy don't realize that you're going to make a big difference for everyone. You're going to make everything right again, Mr. Canaan. You have been a wasteland, a place where evil men walk and practice vain things. But soon, you'll be made into a promise fulfilled. A place worth saving. A place worth treasuring forever…"

Canaan furrowed his brow and stared back into the child's bright eyes. Wasn't she just six short years old? Where were those words coming from? Her gaze read like a child reciting a nursery rhyme, but her declaration cut him deep to the core. He vainly parted his lips, feeling a compulsion to reply. Then, before he could react, the tiny child wrapped her arms around his neck and held him tight. The butter-soft skin of her cheek pressed against his neck and her powder-smooth arms grasped him with the shivering strength of a newborn.

Canaan held his breath, his body making a mental imprint of the moment. The longer it wore on, the more deeply the details would be etched into his subconscious. He usually used this talent for recording the pleasures of life—feeding his hunger, releasing his lust, filling his gut with fine food—but tonight, he was saving up these few seconds to nourish his spirit in the time to come.

Just before his heart began to pain him for real and a speck of emotion welled up behind his eyes, Grace released him, grabbed her bear, and hopped to the ground. He watched as she adjusted her PJ's and trotted to the steps.

"See ya later, Mr. Canaan!" she sang and ran up the stairs with the clumsy agility expected of a child her age.

Canaan sat where she left him, dazed and bewildered. As she closed the door behind her, Isaac exited the bathroom and walked to his side. Dressed in the same jeans and T-shirt from the day before, and his wavy hair dripping from his shower, he gave Canaan a tight smile.

"I think you have a fan, Elder Canaan."

"Did you understand any of that?" Canaan asked the boy, still looking toward the stairs.

"What? I didn't hear anything. What'd she say?"

Canaan turned to Isaac. "What do you mean you didn't hear anything? That whole long speech about a wasteland and a promise or something like that. You heard that."

Isaac's eyebrows went up and he shrugged.

Canaan shook his head, looked up and exhaled. "Judas Priest, I'm ready to get this over with."

"You praying, Elder Canaan?" Isaac asked grinning, his head tilted to the side.

"Shit," he chuckled, hating the nervous titter of the sound, "I'm all the god I'll ever need. Let's get upstairs. I'm ready to get this show on the road."

Isaac nodded and gestured for the door. "After you, Master. After you."

Canaan got to his feet and straightened his shirt. He hoped no one would mention the little girl's visit. He hoped no one would know about it. And he hoped he'd soon forget her haunting words—a prophecy he had no intention of fulfilling.

FORTY-SEVEN

Going to face Rufus unarmed seemed like a bad idea on the surface, but the more he and Beth discussed it, the more they were convinced that God would fight for them. Plus, Michael stored his firearm at work and only his backup piece remained at home, unloaded, uncleaned, and unfired in over a decade. Even if the gun worked properly, a bullet from a .22 wouldn't faze a healthy Rakum. It was safer to leave it with Beth and Marcy than to take it to Jackson and count on it too heavily.

Mostly convinced by his logic and Beth's prayerful advice, Michael ushered the stragglers into the living room for last minute details. Just before sunset, Beth had taken Marcy aside in private and convinced her to stay behind. That had been Michael's idea, for what good could she do against Rufus with no faith and a separate agenda? He knew by her every word that she was serving her own purposes— to protect her man and her way of life.

But wasn't Canaan doing the same thing? Michael scoffed. Canaan's strength and hatred of Rufus was the Rakum's ticket to Jackson. No more, no less. Michael would trust that God was their travel agent, and pray the two Rakum they took along didn't turn on them along the way.

"Where's Javier? Somebody round him up," Michael snarled, not hiding his impatience. The plan was to get on the road immediately. Roman nodded and disappeared down the hall toward the stairs, presumably to fetch his pal. Michael's gaze fell on the two Rakum standing together in the foyer threshold. Arms crossed at his chest, Canaan surveyed the bunch, currently looking away, his mouth in a permanent smirk. The boy, Isaac, was looking dead at Michael, expressionless with a gaze as old as time itself. The child was an odd one; one to watch. Michael cleared his throat and looked away from the kid with effort.

"Come on, Roman! Javier! We're leaving!" Michael shouted toward the stairs, happy his voice carried as well as it did. He was human now, but he still worked on controlling his temper. It was probably his last and greatest challenge.

Footsteps clomped down toward them and Javier entered the room, freshly showered, wearing black jeans, and a familiar black T-shirt. Michael gestured toward his middle.

"Yeah—" Javier pulled the fabric out, his mouth turning up a fraction. "Miss Beth loaned me some of your clothes. Thanks."

Michael's eyes narrowed before he turned back to the group. The kid had borrowed his clothes before, when they were on the run seven years ago. But he let it go; he had many more things to think about than whether or not he'd get his T-shirt back.

Roman followed Javier in and Beth entered from the foyer. Michael could see her face over Isaac's shoulder and a phantom pain filled his gut. He bid her join to him with a flick of his fingers, not wanting her near the boy. With everyone in a semi-circle around him and Beth on his right side, Michael pulled out his cell phone.

"Everyone check your cells. Charged up, I hope." There were various nods around the group as Marcy walked in from the hallway and raised her eyebrows. Ready to get started, Michael filled Canaan's woman in on what she missed and she listened with a dead-pan expression.

"Okay, here are the traveling arrangements. Canaan, you, Javier, and I will ride in your Caddy. Roman, Isaac, and David will go in his truck." Michael tried to ignore the disapproval evident on the Elder's face. Canaan wanted to ride with Isaac, but Michael didn't trust them together. Apart, he and Roman could steer their conversations and monitor their behavior. Javier's uncharacteristic aloofness had something to do with Canaan, and Michael wanted to keep an eye on their interactions, too.

Roman jingled his keys. "Let's ride, boys."

Michael turned to his wife and grabbed her into his arms, considering the way their bodies fit together, as if they were made specifically for one another. What if he was never to hold her again? What if he'd never see Grace again? Before he could prevent it, a groan escaped his lips and Beth pulled back to look into his face.

"Honey, what? Please, what is it?"

Michael shook his head and offered her a warm smile. "Nothing, hon. Everything will work out. I know it will." He kissed her forehead and she forced a tight grin.

"God bless you, Michael Stone, and may He bring you back safely." Beth hugged him again as someone, probably Javier, impatiently cleared his throat near the door. *"I love you,"* she whispered and stepped away to face the foyer where everyone assembled. "All of you—I'll pray for you every minute."

Michael passed Canaan who whispered goodbyes to Marcy. He couldn't hear the exchange, but their expressions were identical to his and Beth's. No matter what went on between the odd pair, they were devoted to one another.

Canaan tipped his head one last time to his mate and as Michael came near, he grasped his upper arm.

"I should ride with the boy," Canaan said in a low voice only Michael could hear. "He's under my jurisdiction. It's for the best."

Michael ran his tongue over his teeth and looked at Canaan's fingers on his bicep. "I have my reasons." With a small movement, Michael pulled his arm out of the Rakum's light grip. "You ride with me. The boy rides with Roman. That's the way it is."

Canaan held his gaze for a few seconds until slowly, a smile spread across his lips and he winked. "You're the boss."

"Good," Michael said and walked out the door into the cool night air. The Elder was going to comply for the moment. Relieved, Michael fell into the passenger seat next to Canaan and tried not to think about how the night might end. Maybe God would continue to control the strong-willed Elder.

FORTY-EiGHT

Mississippi State Line
November 5th, 9:00 p.m.

"**R**est area in fifteen minutes, guys," Roman said as he changed to the right lane. They'd been on the road for three hours and as it was nearing nine, they were right on schedule. Isaac had been quiet most of the way. The first hour, Roman attempted to draw him out, to find out more about his past, but the boy was a closed file. The only information he would share was what he'd already given them when he arrived, and Roman was fairly certain that those stories were full of holes. Javier's accusation against the boy also bothered him. Was it possible that the kid was raised by the Fathers? Did Abroghia hide this one, The Last, to make him into some kind of demonic clone? Roman spoke Hebrew and Aramaic as well as any scholar and to his suspicious ears *yitzhak ackaron* —'he laughs last'—resembled a threat. Was Abroghia—no, Ta'avah—working on a comeback? Would God allow it?

Ta'avah. The name resonated through Roman's mind, echoing off the memories of the *old* Roman; Rakum Elder, fearless, ruthless, and completely self-serving. Full of every lust known to mankind. Roman scoffed unhappily, for the very name Ta'avah meant *lust.* How appropriate that the father of the Rakum race was the demon of lust.

A gurgling noise sounded from the passenger side and Roman eyed the boy.

"Do I need to remind you that we aren't making a blood stop, Isaac? You'll eat what we brought with us or buy snacks. Understand?"

The youngster gazed back, his face slack, and Roman had no idea what he was thinking. He suppressed an errant notion that popped into his mind. A phrase really.

This boy could kill me with a thought.

236

Yes, Roman would tuck that information down—deep down. Whether the warning came from God or the kid, he'd not venture a guess.

Roman swallowed and faced front. In his peripheral vision, Isaac smiled. It was not a good sign.

Not a good sign at all.

♦♦♦

Behind the white Tahoe, the Cadillac followed from a safe distance. Michael had been unsuccessful in connecting with the Elder, which didn't surprise him. As Rakum brothers, Canaan had been a brute. During Assembly, he'd been thrown together with the blond Elder for Jack Dawn's impromptu wrestling matches. It was for Jack's entertainment, because as a mere proselyte against an Elder, Michael never stood a chance. The grinning creature in the driver's seat had pummeled him senseless many times and by Michael's careful design, they crossed paths as infrequently as possible.

He shook his head once, glad the Rakum couldn't read his thoughts. Canaan looked right, caught his eye a millisecond and faced front again, a new smirk on his face.

"You remember me now, don't you," he said, not asking a question.

Taken off guard, Michael didn't reply, but wondered how he guessed so accurately what he was thinking.

Canaan grabbed another quick look at his face and chuckled under his breath. "I'm smart, Michael, that's all. You're staring at me all quiet-like, and that tells me you're walking down memory lane. You know it wasn't personal. At Jack's place. It was just for fun."

Michael scoffed, "You don't need to explain anything to me." He didn't like being spoken down to and he knew he had come off harshly. But so what? The guy was altogether too full of himself.

"You seem kinda spooked, that's all," Canaan said, watching the road. "Like I'm going to grab you in a headlock any minute." He laughed aloud. "I'm not grabbing anybody in a headlock, Michael. You're safe."

"Change the subject," Michael said, irritated at the man's every word. Conversing with Canaan was like speaking with his total opposite and everything about the Rakum rubbed him the wrong way.

"Suit yourself." Canaan removed his hands from the wheel to

form a surrender, and Michael looked out his window. Their headlights illuminated the green rest area sign and Michael shifted in his seat. He'd been holding it for over an hour and relief was minutes away.

Aware of everything and leaning casually back with one wrist lazily steering the car, Canaan chuckled. The man laughed a lot, but Michael had no illusions that he was joyful. Canaan mocked them—he mocked their cause, their goals, and especially their God.

"Javie, toss me one of those sandwiches," Canaan said and lifted his free hand to close it around the fat turkey breast club that was delivered from the backseat.

Michael watched out of the corner of his eye as the man noshed noisily. He finished in a few huge bites and swallowed dramatically.

"That Marcy makes a mean sandwich. Lotsa mayonnaise." Canaan licked his fingers and tossed the plastic bag into the back seat. "Still mighty hungry, though. Hit me again, Javie."

Michael caught the look the Elder tossed Javier, one filled with unspoken innuendo. They had made a strong suggestion to the Rakum to avoid buzzing while on their current mission. What Canaan thought of the idea, was obvious. Javier's hand appeared between them, this time with a smaller Ziploc bag; peanut butter and jelly.

"Last one, Canaan," Javier offered in a sympathetic voice. Canaan looked into the rearview mirror and made eye contact.

Michael again watched something pass between them, but decided not to ask any questions, assuming their odd glances and inappropriate jokes were a result of their history. Using the baggie as a holder, Canaan shoved the entire Wonder Bread sandwich into his mouth and tossed the bag backward as before. Michael sighed and looked out the window to hide his exasperation.

"Mmmmmmm," Canaan mumbled as he chewed the oversized mouthful. "Your wife makes a mean PB&J," he said around the lump of food. "Still really hungry. How 'bout it, Javie?"

Michael snapped.

"His name is *Javier*. Hah-vee-air!" Michael shouted and looked at their driver. "Can you manage that, Canaan? One more syllable—do you think that's at all possible?"

Canaan stopped chewing and met his gaze. The exit loomed and without paying attention to the road, Canaan merged seamlessly off the interstate and onto the ramp. His eyes half-closed, he swallowed and sucked his teeth with flair, still regarding Michael with his eyes.

"It's a nickname, Michael. That's all," Javier offered and moved forward to speak between the front seats. "Roman's called me that since I was eight years old."

"Well, I'm sick of it. Canaan, Javier's not your kid, your brother, or your pal. Just call him by his name, okay?" Michael trained his gaze on Canaan's profile as he piloted the car to park beside Roman's truck. "I'm running this show and as soon as you give me some respect, I'll feel a lot better about having you along. If you can't get behind me, then get out."

Canaan swallowed and switched off the car. He looked out the windshield where Roman's group had gotten out to stretch. Michael glanced at the men and caught Isaac looking at Canaan, a familiar smirk on his little boy face. The two Rakum were communicating telepathically.

"Canaan! I'm speaking to you!" Michael punched Canaan's shoulder hard and the big guy nodded to the boy outside before looking at Michael, his gaze languid as before.

"You seriously need to chill, boss," Canaan cooed, showing his palms. "I'll call the kid whatever you like. I'm not your enemy."

Canaan was right; he over-reacted. Michael lowered his eyes and tried to lower his guard.

Javier jumped out of the car. "I'll see you guys in a minute."

Canaan watched him walk away from the others and head for the men's room. Michael gritted his teeth and just watched Canaan until his own nature call forced him outside.

Stone was an anxious pussy cat who thought he was a lion. Canaan crawled out of the car and reached for the night sky, his back popping with delicious fervor. He caught Isaac's eye and sent him a wink. The boy was hungry, but that was to be expected. Weren't they all?

When he'd cracked his knuckles and stretched his stiff driving muscles, he met Roman's eye. Whether or not Stone realized it, the true human authority among them, as far as Canaan was concerned, was Roman. As a former Elder, he had the leadership training necessary to understand their party's Rakum complement. Roman held his gaze several seconds, as before, giving a little thought as to what he was about to approve, then he sighed and nodded his head.

Canaan turned on his heel and approached the building. Thankfully, the facility was overrun with travelers.

The hefty female attendant wore a uniform, but no firearm. Canaan gave her a friendly smile and flipped through the dozens of brochures that covered the far wall. Three women, all in their sixties, ambled close, smelling of Vick's and Dentyne. None of them paid him a hint of attention. Strike one.

Canaan moseyed across the room toward a framed state map on another wall. Two men stood there, tracing a route with their fingers and glancing to the handheld map in the shorter one's hand. Canaan met the eye of the tall one a fraction of a second and he returned his attention to the map. No-go. Strike two.

Undaunted, he turned, stretched, cracked his back again, and headed for the coffee pot in the corner. A father with his teenage son got in line behind him and waited their turn. Canaan poured himself a finger of black coffee and stepped aside, catching the teen's eye as he did so. Nothing. Zippo. Another strike out.

Deflating, Canaan downed his coffee and crossed to the trashcan by the exit. Attracting Cows had never been his problem; in fact, he excelled in it back in the day. Tonight, he expected out of the forty-or-so mortals wandering around the property, at least one of them would have the propensity to fall for his Rakum charm. He toyed with the idea that he might not find a willing donor at the rest area. The thought roiled his gut, leaving him angry and anxious. He could go days without a blood meal, weeks, months. He didn't *need* human blood.

But dammit—he wanted it.

Canaan dropped the Styrofoam cup into the bin and turned abruptly, knocking into a man carrying a vending machine danish. The pastry hit the ground and the man growled an expletive in a distinct Aussie accent before meeting Canaan's eye. Then his mouth dropped open.

Bingo. Canaan held his eye.

The man was in his thirties, a transient type, probably an artist—maybe a musician or an actor waiting for his big break. He was slightly built, scruffy, and unshaven with huge brown eyes that probably drove the women wild when he was gainfully employed. Right now, he looked to be on his last nickel and Canaan reached into his pocket and pulled out his wallet.

"Let me buy you another one, mate," he said, speaking low and using the British accent he was born with, assuming this down-on-his-luck expatriate would sense a kinship. He pulled out a five-dollar bill and the man was lost in his gaze.

"Change machine's outside," the man said, his voice monotone, his eyes unblinking. Canaan lowered his head an inch or so and flashed his smile.

"Lead the way," he said and the man made an about-face, military style, and exited the building. Canaan followed him two steps behind and didn't look at his traveling companions as he passed their position.

Isaac sent him a telepathic word, "*Score!*"

Canaan smiled and kept walking. The man led him past the vending area, past the building, and toward a rusty Chevy pickup at the end of the row. Without a word, he unlocked the passenger side, climbed in, and slid across, leaving the door open as an invitation.

"This good, Master?" the man asked in a whisper.

Canaan's eyebrows went up. The guy was a seasoned Cow who knew at least some of the ropes. Hauling himself into the cab of the truck, Canaan pulled the door closed behind him. When he pressed down the lock with his elbow, the man finally blinked.

"So you recognized me, eh?" Canaan asked, plain old curiosity delaying his meal. The man shrugged without replying. "Who's your master?"

"My master's long gone. Not seen him in years."

"You knew him here, in the States?" The man nodded, transfixed. Canaan traveled Europe and the Americas, but had never been Down Under. He grinned again, liking the guy already. He couldn't help but snoop a little more as his stomach complained with a loud grumble. "What was his name?"

"Tork. Tork Furlong." The man whispered the name with pain in his eyes. Canaan nodded knowingly. Tork had been one of his lieutenants. A good man and a great leader. Canaan's stomach spoke again and he dispensed with the questions. He put his hand to the man's shoulder.

"What should I call you, mate?" Canaan asked and scooted close. To anyone outside the truck, the men would appear to be in an amorous embrace. Canaan was fine with that as they'd never guess what was actually about to transpire.

"Stuart," the man grunted and turned at the waist as he realized Canaan was going for his throat. "Stuart Loudon."

"You play guitar, Stu?"

"Yeah," he breathed and relaxed his posture to allow Canaan to maneuver him into position. "Lead guitar, actually."

"You gonna be a big star one day, Stu?" Canaan whispered his question, now speaking directly in the man's left ear. Not expecting a conversation, Canaan pressed his long thumb nail into the man's prickly neck, opening a deep furrow. Stuart grunted to mask the discomfort and stopped talking. Canaan covered the wound with his lips and pulled the man tight against him. Shaved or not, the Aussie's blood was scratching his itch, and he hadn't a complaint in the world. Let the poor, deceived apostates have their abstinence, their holiness, their *religion*. His god was his gut and it had served him well his whole life.

Canaan supped leisurely and only let up when his watch chimed the half-hour. Bracing his left arm around the musician's shoulders, he pressed his palm against his throat and sewed up the wound with minimal effort. No worse for wear, Stuart let out a pent-up breath and remained still as Canaan sat against him, his smooth left cheek against the Cow's whiskered one. Tork's Cow behaved exactly as he should and Canaan grinned at his good fortune. When was the last time he went hungry? *Really* hungry? He couldn't recall. He was the luckiest Rakum he knew. When the delightful tremble finally filtered out of his belly, Canaan shoved his weight back into his seat with a contented sigh.

"Master?" Stuart mumbled, staring out the windshield into the dark sky. "What happened to Master Tork?"

"Well, Stu, he's gone. Most likely for good. It is what it is." Canaan spoke with his eyes closed, one arm still on the back of the bench seat, that hand on Stuart's shoulder. "Tork was a good leader. I knew him well."

"Master?" Stuart's tortured tone was more desperate. Intuiting his concerns, Canaan turned to meet his eye.

"Give me your address. If I can, I'll stop in on you from time to time," Canaan offered.

Without delay, the man dug around in his back pocket, fished out his wallet, and handed Canaan a tattered business card. A vegetable with a guitar neck sat next to the band's name, The Turnip Trucks, the raised lettering saying they hailed from Louisville, Kentucky. Canaan nodded and tucked the card into his billfold.

"You need some dough, Stu?" Canaan noted the man's eyes on

his wallet and the bills peeking out of it. "Here, take this and go home."

Canaan pulled out all of the cash and handed it over. He'd withdrawn five hundred dollars before the trip, but he could get more from the ATM in the building. He wasn't feeling particularly generous, but having a willing blood donor was unheard of since the Last Assembly. Maybe when the ruckus died down, Canaan would look Stuart up. Might be like the old days.

The Cow took the money, rolling his lips in, his eyes cast down. "Thank you, Master."

"Don't mention it. Just be home when I come over, eh?" Canaan roughed the guy's greasy hair and opened his door.

Checking his watch, and then the position of his friends across the parking lot, Canaan sent Stuart one more wink and exited the truck. He strolled to the sidewalk, caught Isaac's eye and gestured him over. He'd hit the ATM, buzz The Last, and get on the road for Rufus's headquarters. They'd still be there by midnight.

Plenty of time to squeeze the life out of the old monster.

Canaan clinched his fists as the kid jogged to his side, his eyes shining with anticipation. The pup had a lust for blood, all right. More than most Rakum he knew. But oh, well. He was an odd one, after all.

FORTY-NINE

Montgomery, AL
November 5th, 9:00 p.m.

Grace and Dae Lee fell asleep before the Barney video ended and Beth joined Marcy downstairs. Sitting across from her in the living room, she did her best to draw her guest into a meaningful conversation. It wasn't easy. After a few false starts, Marcy blurted out a question of her own.

"Why did those Rakum from your book want to be human?" Marcy asked, her tone none too friendly. Beth started to answer, but Marcy barreled on. "There was nothing wrong with them. If I didn't see it with my own eyes, I would never believe that a creature like Elder Roman would throw away his power for the sake of religion. It doesn't make sense."

Beth remained mum, awaiting a direct question. Marcy looked up, her shoulders stooped forward.

"Well? What do you have to say?"

"Do you want me to tell you why they changed or why they wanted to change?" Beth had to prevent Marcy from going on the defense. She held her relationship with Canaan sacrosanct and when Beth mentioned it in passing earlier, the woman became extremely angry.

"Well, yeah, if you know. Your husband, for one. He and Canaan were discipled under the same Elder. Michael was a star, a favorite. I got the impression that he was to be an Elder one day." Marcy's face reddened as she continued. "But now he's mortal. He's a nothing!" Hands now punctuating her words, Marcy raised her voice an octave. "He's gonna get old and die..." Marcy swallowed, realizing she'd overstepped. Beth lowered her eyes.

"It's okay. I know what you mean," she said, taking a few seconds to recover. Then, she stiffened her spine. "I'll tell you what happened with Michael. It's different for each man, but I understand Michael the best."

"That'd be great," Marcy said and leaned back into the couch.

"Michael's blood father was Abroghia, so big things *were* expected of him. His mother was actually royalty, a French Duchess who was being groomed as an Empress consort before the Rakum scouts abducted her and brought her to America to be bred. He—"

"Wow, that's interesting," Marcy interrupted.

Beth nodded. "Any Rakum they intended to be an Elder had to come from royal blood and Michael was supposed to be the best of the best. I imagine all of the Fathers assumed their seed had the power to create the ultimate Rakum, but in actuality, only Abroghia had what it took to make a Rakum the caliber of a Father. So Michael was special. He excelled early and his strengths caught the eye of his superiors long before First Ritual. You know what that is, right?" Beth waited for Marcy to nod. "He was paired up with Jesse Cherrie to complement the secondary gifts he lacked, healing and telepathy, but these deficiencies didn't hold him back."

"Canaan has strength, healing, *and* telepathy—well, before the Rakum busted up," Marcy interjected and fell silent. Beth continued without revealing her annoyance.

"But to hear him tell it, Michael was only doing what was expected of him. He was like a child protégé who is plucked out of public school at five to graduate college at eleven. Michael was the preeminent Rakum at his level. They gave him the best of everything and Abroghia coddled him."

"Coddled him? Really?" Marcy asked in a low voice.

Beth raised her eyebrows. "If Abroghia had been more firm with Michael when he met me, none of God's plans would have come to pass. Abroghia didn't punish Michael when he broke their rules with me. He let him alone and hoped Jack would work it out. Thank God that old demon was too arrogant to notice what was really happening with his people."

Marcy shook her head. "None of this explains why Michael would want to be human."

"Michael didn't take to lust the way some of his brethren did. Michael did what was expected of him—including their many murderous deeds—but it never *owned* him. When he went out on his own, he settled into a pretty boring life by Rakum standards. So when the Spirit of God touched him the day he saw me in the airport,

Michael responded."

"Yeah, I read about that in your book. He took one look at you and fell in love. How convenient," Marcy said sarcastically.

"God caused his heart to worry for me, and the reason God was able to communicate with Michael was because he already had a softer heart than many of his brethren. You see, Marcy, God created all of us and He knows who belongs to Him. Michael lived over 130 years as a Rakum, but when he was given a chance to become a child of God, he accepted."

Marcy shook her head, her eyes narrowed. "But why? Why a child of God? What does that even mean? I'm certainly not part of your religion. Do you think I'm missing out? Do you think I'm going to hell because I don't follow your God your way?"

Beth bit her bottom lip and proceeded carefully. "Michael wanted to be a child of God after God spoke to him and invited him. Michael made a choice. You're asking 'why' when the answer is just that simple. Michael liked what God had to offer and he accepted. As for you…" Beth paused a second and then continued quietly. "God will be speaking to you soon. You'll wonder whose voice you're hearing, and you'll wonder if you're going crazy, but I'm telling you in advance that it'll be God. He's going to talk to your spirit and you'll feel the quickening that all of us have felt. Canaan has felt it."

Marcy's eyes flew open and she sat up straight. "What? No way. You're crazy."

Beth shook her head slowly. "No, God has been speaking to him. Canaan will come around. I've seen it dozens of times, and God always wins. Marcy—don't be mad. God offers what the world cannot. He'll offer Canaan redemption and salvation. These things are only offered by the Creator of the universe. He will offer Canaan peace and love and joy and completeness."

"Canaan has no need of these things. They're just words, Beth. He won't be fooled like Michael and the rest of your guys. He's too strong to be sucked in."

Beth waited to reply. Marcy didn't believe her own words and her concern was evident in her pinched expression.

"I don't want to hear from your God, Beth. Tell Him to stay the hell away from me. I like things the way they are and I want my Canaan just the way he is."

Marcy arose and paced toward the cold fireplace. Then, in a shrill shout, she released a trail of expletives at the top of her voice, some of which Beth had never heard before. She slammed her fist against the brick mantle and shouted some more. Beth stood and crossed to her, but Marcy stepped hastily away, circumnavigating a reading chair along the wall and then tripping over the magazine rack. Unable to dash to her aid fast enough, Beth watched Marcy tumble to the floor, falling hard, and raking her left arm across the sharp edge of the adjacent side table.

"Marcy!" Beth called and dropped to her knees beside the woman's head. Marcy stayed put, face down, her arms out above her head and her hands open. She uttered a few more colorful words as Beth gently turned her over. Blood poured out of a three-inch gash in her forearm.

"Oh! Hang on! I'll get the first aid. Put pressure on it." After molding Marcy's free hand around the wound, she hopped up and jogged to the front bath. The first-aid kit was kept handy and she grabbed it, returning within seconds. When she reached her friend, Marcy was lying on her back, her left arm in the air, the wound toward her face. She was no longer stemming the flow. Beth hurried to her side and whipped out the white gauze. Marcy frowned and sat up.

"What the shit..." she whispered, staring at the soft underside of her arm, blood-stained, but completely devoid of injury.

Beth gasped. "Canaan marked you?"

Marcy gave her a blank look mixed with confusion and the edges of horror.

"You're a Rabbit. Like me. It's okay..."

Marcy closed her mouth and furrowed her brow. "Oh, Canaan, you did it anyway..." She wiped her bloody right hand on her blue jeans and rolled to her knees. Fat tears welled in her eyes and fell onto her blouse as she stood. "I need a cigarette," Marcy muttered and left the room for the hall.

FiFTY

A half-hour later, Marcy flushed the unused toilet, washed her face for the third time, and prepared to face Beth Rider. She plodded up the hall, dragging her bare feet across the Stone's thick carpeting. The house was huge, the appointments luxurious, the electronics top-notch. What kind of green did they pull down? Did Stone have old Rakum money or did Beth actually sell enough of her silly books to pay for it all? Why didn't she and Canaan live in a big mansion?

"Marcy? You okay?"

God! Marcy winced. Beth was calling her from the living room, sincerity in her every word, her every glance. Why did this woman care so much about their business? What did Canaan reveal to her in private the night before?

"Marcy?"

"I'm fine. Just great," Marcy mumbled and entered the room.

Beth was standing by the mantle, tiny hands clutched in front of her, huge watery eyes longing for some kind of female friendship. Marcy just didn't think she had it in her. They were total opposites. What did they have in common besides the fact that they both fell in love with Rakum?

Maybe that was a good starting place.

"Beth, tell me about when you met Michael," Marcy said and headed for the sofa. Beth's gentle face softened at the sound of her husband's name. She was crazy about him and Marcy could identify with that emotion.

"Oh, it was just like in the novel, really. I didn't embellish anything on purpose." Beth lighted into a soft chair across from her and sat upon one folded leg.

Marcy tried to remember the details in the book. She told Beth that she'd read it, but in actuality she barely skimmed it. In chapter one, Beth started praying and that was enough for Marcy to know that it wasn't her kind of book.

248

"In the airport. Remember the scene in the airport?" Beth asked, helping her along.

Marcy tipped her head to the side. "You left your purse on the plane and he helped you retrieve it."

Beth nodded and smiled as if the sun had just come out.

"When did you learn what he was?"

"You didn't read the book, did you?" Beth asked without sounding accusatory.

"Not all of it. Just tell me. I'm trying to connect, Beth. You and me—there's nothing to tie us together. No meat. No interest. We're total opposites. Just talk to me about Michael. Help me out." Marcy took a deep breath and waited. She had so few relationships over the years with women. Her partner Erin was only a friend at work. The rest of her time was spent with Canaan. He was her whole world. Who else did she need?

"Okay, yeah, I'm sorry," Beth said while arranging her soft silk blouse and unfolding her leg to cross her well-formed ankles.

Marcy knew Canaan noticed her. His eye never missed a lovely face or a shapely figure. It was meaningless—all of his ogling and mooning, but it stung nonetheless. Marcy had never looked like that. If Beth was the Homecoming Queen, Marcy was Stephen King's *Carrie*. She'd been Plain Jane her whole life. The question loomed again in her mind, even as Beth began her tale: *Why me? Why would Canaan choose me?*

"…cushions on the floor in my laundry room."

Beth laughed and Marcy snapped back to the present discussion. She hadn't been listening.

"I had a pretty good idea that he was something *else*, if you know what I mean. But he pretty much told me the entire story that first morning. He stayed by me the whole time and was almost killed by Jack Dawn."

Marcy nodded, not comfortable speaking of Canaan's deceased Elder.

"Jack Dawn is the one who first came after me, you know. He was a true devil," Beth said, her eye far away. Despite herself, Marcy snickered.

"He discipled our boys and they turned out all right." Afraid she'd come off defending the monster, Marcy added quickly, "All things considered."

Beth smiled in uneasy agreement, her dazzling white teeth making

Marcy wish she had stopped smoking.

"So you and Michael got together before he turned human?" Did they have that in common? Did this goodie-two-shoes have bloodletting in her closet? Marcy sincerely hoped she did. But Beth caught her drift and blushed like a school girl. It was pretty sickening.

"Oh, no. No, Marcy. I could never get close to him when he was like that. No, we were friends a while."

Marcy made an expression of offense and Beth began backtracking hastily.

"But I'm not saying I wasn't attracted to him like that. I totally understand how you feel about Canaan, really. Michael and I, well, we took it slow. He asked me about God and over time, he was transformed. I'm no saint—it wasn't an easy thing to resist him."

"Canaan waited over a year to touch me," Marcy recalled wistfully, looking away. Then she caught Beth's eye once more. "But I offered him my blood right off the bat. You think that's disgusting, don't you? That maybe I'm crazy, like one of those Cows?"

Beth paled and didn't reply.

Triumphant, Marcy continued, "Canaan was a gentleman. He treated me as if I were made of glass, and when I was old enough, he asked me to be his mate. That was forty years ago." Sudden emotion seized her chest and Marcy stopped.

The same old struggle squeezed within—why did he stay with her and how long until he was gone? A tear spilled down her cheek, but Marcy didn't wipe it off. Beth jumped to her feet and sat beside her on the couch. At first, Marcy drew back, but was defrosting rapidly. Beth seemed so sincere…and Marcy never had anyone with which to share her private pain. Whenever she opened up to Canaan, he would force her to shush and just "trust him." Beth draped an arm around Marcy's shoulder. The tears were coming and she decided to let them flow.

"Why is he still with me?" Marcy burbled. Sharing her worst fears aloud made her cry harder, and Marcy launched into confession mode. "I'm old now, Beth. I'm old and he's still a kid." Marcy sniffled hard and Beth handed her a tissue. "He's going to leave me if he turns human, Beth. I can't…I…"

"Shhhh," Beth said and rubbed her back. "Hush that nonsense. You and Canaan are attached at the soul-level, Marcy. That's why he chose you. That's why he's still with you. That's why he'll never leave you."

Marcy blew her nose and wanted so much to believe Beth's encouraging remarks.

"Listen, I'll share something with you. God designed in the beginning that when a man and a woman cleave together, they become one flesh. It doesn't make sense in the natural, I know, but it happens nonetheless, at the soul level. This is the closeness you have with Canaan. That I have with Michael. We're tied together at the soul-level because of God's design. Michael's not going anywhere any more than Canaan is leaving you. Understand?"

Marcy blew her nose again and wiped her eyes with a fresh tissue. "He told me that once; that we are one, that we're meant to be together. But I don't believe all that Bible stuff. How am I supposed to rationalize it if I don't believe it?"

"Canaan believes it."

Marcy's eyes flashed. "You said that before. Canaan no more believes in God than a monkey can sing opera."

"I asked him." Beth stopped rubbing Marcy's back and leaned away a few inches to see her face. "He told us that God's been speaking to him for a while now. God told him to come here."

Marcy's throat tightened and her tears began afresh. Canaan would turn into a human soon. She'd be married to a lover who looked like her son. Somehow it didn't matter when he was Rakum, but mortal? She'd be the worst kind of Cougar.

"Hey, it's not a bad thing. When Canaan comes around to God's way of thinking, he'll be transformed and he'll love you even more, I promise."

Marcy cried harder and pressed her face into her folded arms. Through a watery glaze, she noted her freckled skin and the area that had been sliced open earlier. She was a Rabbit now, regenerating endlessly. She could never die. If Canaan became human, would she no longer be a Rabbit? Or would he begin to age and eventually catch up?

Beth followed her line of sight. "I don't know how long we'll be Rabbits. My daughter has it, too. Maybe when the very last Rakum is transformed or killed, the curse will be lifted. I don't know, but I trust that God has us this way for His purposes."

"I don't understand that kind of faith!" Exasperated, Marcy was nearly shouting. "Why do you trust God?"

"Because I dwell under the shadow of the Almighty," Beth replied without raising her voice. "Whom shall I fear?"

Marcy stared back at her wondering from what nuthouse she escaped. Still, she was earnest and so confident. Her faith was attractive, even if it was kooky.

"But I don't 'dwell in' whatever you just said," Marcy whispered. "Where does that leave me?" Beth looked at the ceiling a moment and then smiled, pulling Marcy into a full, two-arm hug.

"Right next to me, Marcy. You and I are a team now. Until you understand, my angel is your angel."

Marcy found it hard to swallow. "Why? Why would you care about me? Why would He let you do that for me?"

"Because we love you, Marcy." Now Beth's voice choked and she squeezed Marcy tighter. "Because I love you so much, I would die for you. Right now. And that's exactly what God did for you already. You just don't know it yet."

"No…" Marcy wept and held onto Beth desperately. "No, I don't understand. But I want to."

"Then Marcy Haddle," Beth whispered in her ear, "you're practically there already."

Marcy held her breath and thought over what Beth's said.

"I love you."

The soothing words echoed into her ears.

"I love you."

So deep down in her mind, they could not possibly be from Beth's mouth.

"You were My princess first."

Marcy recognized the voice. She'd heard it as a child, saying her prayers before bed time. Before Mom lost her faith and stopped taking them to church. This voice spoke to six-year-old Marcy and told her that it loved her. It was God. And for the first time in fifty years, Marcy returned a small reply in her heart.

"Help me find You."

"You just did."

Marcy stopped crying, but held on to Beth for a long time, wondering what might happen next. And wondering if God was talking to Canaan, too.

FIFTY-ONE

Michael settled into the Caddy behind the wheel as Isaac filled the passenger seat. Roman stayed put in the Tahoe and exchanged his passengers. It was a desperate attempt to develop a semblance of comradeship before they reached their destination, because so far, both men had failed to connect with the Rakum muscle they'd brought along. For the last leg of their trip, they'd try another tactic.

Always clueless to tension and dissention, David leaned between the seats from behind and asked the obvious.

"So, you're driving us the rest of the way?"

"That's right, Dave. Gives me a chance to get to know little Isaac, here," Michael said as he turned over the engine.

"Good luck. He doesn't say much, do you, Isaac?" David stayed forward and playfully shook Isaac's shoulder. The boy shrugged and flashed his little-boy smile at them both.

"We'll see." Michael backed the car and headed toward the interstate access ramp. When the Cadillac was up to the speed limit and Michael set the cruise, Isaac volunteered a question.

"What do you think will happen when we arrive at Rufus's estate?"

Michael paused. Isaac was really asking, *do you have a plan*, and he didn't. He and the guys were pretty much relying on God, hoping He'd show them the way when the time arrived. It was how Beth confronted Abroghia seven years ago, and they had no reason to doubt God now.

For an answer, Michael nodded his head and said, "We'll see when we get there."

"Michael, your wife is going to be abducted."

Michael's head swung right and he caught the boy's eye. Isaac was dead serious and not at all amused at his grim admission.

"You saw this in a vision?" Michael croaked and attempted to control his anxiety. Back when he was a Rakum lieutenant, the rumors of *The Last* circulated as readily as any other, and the main thing The Last was supposed to be capable of was foreseeing the future even more accurately than the Fathers. Now that he'd met this mythical child, he figured the rumors about him must be true.

"Yes. I saw her walking out of the house into the waiting hands of a Rakum."

"Tonight? Now? Which Rakum?" Michael asked, masking his growing panic. Isaac shrugged and that was enough for Michael. He yanked out his cell and hit speed-dial; Beth picked up on the second ring. "Hon, it's me. There might be a Rakum outside the house. Don't go out for any reason, do you understand?"

"Michael, why would I go outside? That'd be suicide. What is going on? Everything all right?"

"Listen, Isaac saw you walk out of the house and get grabbed. I know it sounds crazy, but now that you know about it, just don't do it. It should be easy." Michael tried not to recall all the Hollywood movies where the protagonist did the opposite of what he or she was warned. "Promise me. Don't set foot outside."

"Michael, I promise. I'm definitely not going outside."

Michael sighed, relieved, and cut his eyes to Isaac. The boy shrugged again and lingered with his head to the side. *It won't make a difference,* he seemed to say. Michael huffed and turned his attention back to his wife who was in the middle of telling him about Canaan's woman.

"...and she might be praying now. I just hope she is. This poor woman is so mixed up." Beth sounded tired and Michael commiserated.

"Good, hon, good. Get some sleep. You sound exhausted. You hear me?" Michael waited for her to agree and then disconnected the call. He was afraid to see what Isaac thought, but he glanced over finally. "Well? You still think she's going to go outside?"

Isaac frowned. "Timelines are not my thing, but I see her plainly. She walks out the front door and gets into a red car with a Rakum. Voluntarily."

"Never happen," Michael mumbled and prayed Beth would stay inside. Isaac allowed thirty seconds before he sighed to break the silence.

"Michael, sir," he said politely, "how did Elder Jack Dawn die? In my mind, I see him confronting you and Mrs. Stone, but I can't see what killed him. It's hazy."

Michael blinked and looked at the kid briefly. His eyes were wide, his face the picture of youth and innocence. Did he actually read Beth's books? Michael was in no mood for confrontation so he gave the kid an answer.

"Elder Dawn came up against the power of God in Beth Rider," he answered, hoping the issue was settled. Isaac's brow furrowed and he turned his mouth to the side, thinking up a new question.

"Miss Beth's God killed him? Is that what you are saying?"

Michael sighed. "In a nutshell."

"Like with His mind?"

"Isaac, Rakum Fathers kill with their minds. The God of the humans is nothing like them. He is spirit with no limitations. Which of my wife's books did you read?"

"Some of *The Judging,*" the boy answered, and then added, "I didn't understand any of it."

"You didn't understand what?" Michael's irritation grew as he became more and more certain that Isaac was not what he seemed. The boy looked away and fell silent. After a few long moments, from the back seat, David offered up a plan.

"I think we need to break into Rufus's house and rescue Chloe and Selene. That should be our first objective."

Michael thought it sounded like a good idea and was happy to turn his attention away from Isaac. "We'll split up. The three of us will rescue the girls while the other guys go straight for Rufus."

"Canaan will fight Rufus, there's no doubt." Isaac offered his prophecy once more.

Michael nodded slowly, not caring for the boy's assured haughtiness. "And once the girls are safe, we'll go help them subdue or destroy Rufus, depending on what the Lord wants us to do." Michael's phone chimed and he answered it immediately. "What's up?"

"We have a flat." It was Javier, as sullen as ever.

Michael looked into the rearview mirror and the Tahoe was nowhere in sight. How long ago he lost them, he didn't know. It never occurred to him that they might become separated. "So, are you changing it?"

Javier replied, but the line cut out before he was finished. Michael slowed the Caddy, rolled onto the shoulder, and called him back.

"So, are you changing it?" he repeated when the call connected.

"We'll be back underway in a few." It was Roman and he was all business. "You three go on ahead. See if you can get to the girls. Isaac should be able to pinpoint their location as well as protect you. If at all possible, get them out of the house. When we arrive, we'll confront Rufus and see what God would have us to do."

Michael nodded. "Great minds think alike. David just had the same idea."

"Did you know Canaan brought a gun?" Roman asked with disdain.

"He what?"

"His wife's handgun. Against my better judgment, he gave it to Javier to carry."

Michael noted the hardness in Roman's tone and wondered what was taking place between the three men.

"We must need it then," Michael offered, trying to lighten his attitude. "God wouldn't send it with us if it wasn't going to come in handy."

Roman grunted. "I set Canaan to changing the tire, so we'll catch up with you soon. Go ahead and we'll be ten minutes behind you. Go with God, Michael."

The connection crackled and Michael peeked at his signal bars. They were in an iffy reception zone and he started the car.

"Okay, you, too. And hurry," Michael said and dropped the phone into his jacket pocket. He caught David's eye in the rearview mirror and the kid nodded with understanding. He looked to Isaac and the boy smirked. "What?"

"Nothing," Isaac said and looked out the window.

"Can you help us get the girls out safely?"

"Most definitely," Isaac replied without turning.

"Will you?" Michael added by reflex alone. Isaac turned slowly, his face slack, and then allowed an exaggerated grin to fill his features.

"At your service," he said, and Michael felt a chill.

"Okay, then," he said, rubbing his arms to dispel the goose-bumps. "We'll be there in forty-five minutes."

Please, let this night end quickly! Michael prayed and fell silent, studying the black ribbon of interstate aglow in his headlights. Within the hour, he'd be confronting a very angry and powerful Elder who wanted him dead. How did Beth handle her fear when she was handed over to his brethren? How did she so bravely face the Rakum as a small and fragile woman?

"God gave them a flat tire, then, right?" David asked softly.

Michael didn't answer right away, but then nodded hesitantly.

"He allowed it, at least. If we believe He's in control, then He's in control." Michael could see David was comforted by his response, but Isaac made a small noise of amusement. He didn't react, but kept his mind on the plan. Get in, get the girls, get out. Then confront Rufus. Didn't sound too difficult.

If God was truly in control.

FIFTY-TWO

I-20, just east of Meridian, MS
November 5th, 9:45 p.m.

A cold drizzle filtered down from the night sky and Roman turned up his collar against the wind. It was just above freezing and thankfully, Canaan was not affected. He'd unpacked the spare tire and was currently jacking up the truck. The flat occurred on the rear right, so the Rakum could work from the safety of the shoulder and not have his back to the traffic. Javier sat in the back seat, looking straight ahead, and Roman stood on the stiff brown grass a dozen feet behind Canaan.

The air between Javier and Canaan was thick with something Roman couldn't identify. The two men didn't speak to each other, but they exchanged plenty of mysterious glances. The only thing he knew for sure was that Javier was suffering spiritually. He'd been complaining about his "new mortal skin" even before their current emergency, but now being around Canaan made things worse, not better.

He absently watched the Elder remove the flat tire and position the new one as the rear door opened and Javier stepped out. He leaned against the car near Canaan who looked up at him from his kneeling position on the gravel. They were whispering.

"Javie, I prefer you wait in the truck," Roman said, calling over the intermittent traffic and the wind that periodically lashed exposed skin. Javier didn't look at him, but remained as he was, head down, eyes locked with Elder Canaan's. Roman tried again, "Javier, please wait in the truck."

Javier squatted down to Canaan's level and was hidden from Roman's vantage point. Roman inhaled and reminded himself to remain calm. Javier was an extremely obedient proselyte for as long as they were Rakum, but he was human now, and rebellion was doing its

258

work. He approached the two men and they stopped talking. Roman had had enough.

"Javier, wait in the truck. I insist." Roman stood directly behind Canaan and neither man acknowledged that he'd spoken. Sighing, he removed and pocketed his leather gloves and walked toward the duo. When he was close enough, he put his bare hand on Javier's shoulder and shook him roughly. "Javier! Get in the truck!"

Javier leaned to the side, dislodging the contact and stood up.

"Don't order me around, Roman!" Javier warned, piercing him with his gaze. He'd never been confronted by Javier, but Roman didn't miss a beat in his response.

"I'll order you around so long as you behave like an insolent child!" Roman stepped into Javier's space and reached for his shoulder again. Javier stepped back.

"Oh, you wish I was a child so you could control my every move. You had me so fooled, Roman. All these years. All these years and you had me so fooled."

Roman paused and tried to understand the boy's accusations. They had a perfect relationship. They never fought nor disagreed, in over a century, they never had a cross word.

"You strut around, high and mighty, you act like you have it all figured out. But you've lied to me, to David, to yourself. I trusted you, Roman." Javier growled the last.

Roman's lips parted. Water came to Javier's eyes as Roman shook his head and approached him again. "Javier, what's gotten into you?"

Javier gestured toward Canaan who was still squatting on the gravel, crowbar in hand, an amused look on his face, watching their interaction.

"Elder Canaan opened my eyes, Roman." Javier waved his hands in the air. "All of them. You killed them. And Isabella. You made me believe I killed her. How could you? How could you murder that innocent girl and then make me think I did it?" Javier was openly weeping now, but his anger was not assuaged in the least.

Roman looked at Canaan for a guilt response, but the goon smiled on, showing white teeth now that Javier was so worked up.

"How can I ever trust you again? You're a liar. A murderer. How many did you kill, Roman? How many of my friends did you destroy in your jealousy? Markus? Kevin?" Javier caught his breath a moment and grasped the lapel of Roman's long coat. "Philip and Alana?"

Roman eyed Javier's fist on his coat and then back into his

blazing eyes. All of the names he mentioned brought up faces—mortal faces—of men and women that Javier grew infatuated with as a youth. Roman had destroyed them all as a matter of duty. He was a Rakum Elder and he fulfilled his obligations to the letter. He was murderous and deceitful, Javier knew that. Why was the kid bent out of shape over it now? Roman didn't have a reply and Javier only grew more infuriated.

"Say something, Roman... –*Master!* Go ahead. Canaan said you killed them because you loved me. Can't you at least try that one out? Can't you just say that you did it for my own good?" Javier grabbed the opposite lapel and shook Roman as he spoke.

Roman held his tongue and looked over his shoulder at the Elder on the ground. Canaan only grinned and shook his head. He was useless.

"Say something!" Javier shouted again and this time released his coat long enough to strike Roman across the jaw with a balled fist. Roman shook it off and shoved Javier violently away with both hands.

"That's enough, Javier!" His own rage barely bottled, Roman stepped toward Javier who was rising from the frozen ground and dusting off his pants. "That Rakum is not one of us." Shouting now, he pointed angrily toward Canaan. "You have listened to his lies, his whisperings. Now I know why you've been so upset since Canaan showed up. You're slipping away, Javier. Straighten up or you will *fall* away."

Javier rushed forward then and shoved Roman with both hands. Roman flipped backward over Canaan who still knelt at the tire, and he fell to the hard gravel. Barely affected, he jumped to his feet and threatened Javier with his fists.

"You try my patience, boy." Roman didn't advance, but Javier came toward him, his own fists up, boxer style. They were both behind the Tahoe now and Roman waited for Javier to close the distance between them before he took another swing at his cheek. "If you won't get in the truck, I'll put you in!"

Javier dodged the blow, but not fast enough to miss it altogether. Roman's fist collided with his left shoulder and he ran forward to grapple with him bodily. Locked together in a furious knot, Javier and Roman tested each other's strength alongside the highway. A diesel truck zoomed by in the right lane sounding his booming air horn, and both men were astonished by the force of the wind created.

Roman held Javier with both arms and although the boy

struggled to gain the upper hand, he restrained him easily. Javier was bigger and more muscular, but Roman's decades of Elder combat training were no match for the younger man's brawn. He held him in place and spoke in his ear, his voice as soft as possible in his exertion.

"Javie, I do love you. I murdered those Cows, I admit it. But everything I did, I did for you. Of all the people in the world, you have always been my favorite. I love you like a son, Javie. You know this."

Javier continued to struggle and he rotated right so that his heels were now on the white line delineating the roadway. Roman looked down and noted the danger and attempted to pull him away from the road. Not caring, Javier continued his wrestling maneuver, attempting to bring Roman to his knees.

"Javie, please. I killed those Cows out of duty, not to hurt you."

"Friends! Roman, they were my friends! You've never understood me! You're a cold-blooded murderer!" Javier shouted the last and with a new burst of strength, pushed Roman away with all of his might.

Roman released him, thinking he might be able to keep the boy from falling, but Javier's body was thrust backward by his own momentum. He crossed the line into the road, waving his arms to catch his balance. Roman rushed forward to grab his sleeve, but before either of them even realized the danger, a car zoomed by in Javier's lane. The silver sedan honked and swerved, but clipped Javier, sending him sprawling into the ice-hardened shoulder.

"Javier!" Roman yelled as he ran to the boy's side. He'd been thrown at least twenty feet and he lay face down in the damp grass. When he didn't respond, Roman called Canaan. The Elder rose to his feet, only slightly interested, and ambled over. The driver of the silver car was also coming and they both reached Roman at the same time.

"Oh, God! Is he okay? Why was he in the road? My wife called 911. Hang on, buddy! Help is coming!" The driver spoke rapidly, in obvious shock.

Roman caught Canaan's eye and his jaw twitched. The Rakum could heal Javier, heal him right up. They had a job to do. They were needed in Jackson. Michael and David were counting on them, not to mention Beth and Jesse.

Canaan stood above him, hands in his pockets, leather jacket open to the elements. His expression read, *whatever you want me to do, just say it.* Roman couldn't decide. The driver was pacing and

261

gesticulating around Javier's inert body. When they were Rakum, Roman could diagnose any human ailment instantly, but now, he could only guess. He gently turned Javier onto his back and grabbed Canaan by the pocket of his jeans.

"Dr. Smith, see what's wrong with him." He said the first thing he could think of and Canaan got his drift. The Elder stooped down and placed his hands on Javier's chest.

"Fractured his spine," he whispered, "and both femurs," Canaan continued in a low voice, then moved his hands to Javier's face. "There is some bleeding in the brain."

Roman swallowed and ignored the driver above them shouting to his wife to bring some paper towels. "Heal him up, Canaan."

Canaan looked at the driver and then back to Roman. "Right here? Under that guy's nose?"

Roman considered the driver and now his wife who had approached, her hands full of paper. What would they think? Would they notice? Roman didn't care.

"Start with his head. Canaan—his head. Now!" Roman hissed. The big Rakum nodded, his mouth still in that perpetual smirk. If he cared at all about Javier, Roman couldn't tell. In the back of his mind he wondered if he'd been like that, cold and unfeeling, when he'd most likely been worse.

"Here's the ambulance!" the driver yelped above them. Then, "Yeah, stabilize his neck. Good idea."

Roman and Canaan ignored the man although the sirens were close now, the bus pulling up behind the Tahoe. With a very stealthy movement, he reached into Javier's jacket pocket and retrieved Canaan's gun. Now it looked like *he'd* have it for their trip to Rufus's estate.

Javier made a noise, but remained unconscious, a trickle of blood leaking from his nose.

"Well? Well?" Roman pressured Canaan to give him an update. Canaan released Javier's head and sat back on his knees. The paramedics arrived a few seconds after and Canaan stood up out of the way.

"Guys, I'm a doctor." Canaan spoke quickly and Roman was impressed at his put-on professionalism. "His spine is fractured at T8 or T9 with simple fractures in both femurs."

The paramedics went to work, a cervical collar and immobilizing frame were the first things applied. Roman stood and backed to

Canaan's side.

"His brain...you were able to stop the bleeding?" he whispered. Canaan nodded. "Good. Now, as for all that garbage you filled his head with—"

"Don't start with me," Canaan threatened in a whisper.

"Just get that tire changed," Roman growled. "Michael and David need us in Jackson. I'll speak to the paramedics."

Canaan walked back to the truck without replying and Roman approached the closest medic. He gave all of Javier's information and said they'd be at the hospital soon. In his heart, he wished the kid the best. If they survived their meeting with Rufus, he'd come back to get him. If not, well, then Javier was in God's hands.

It was the best he could do.

FIFTY-THREE

Beryl closed his eyes and reminded himself to hold his tongue. He had no fantasy that his hellish evening was headed for improvement. When they left the abandoned house in search of a car, it took them two hours to hike into the next town. Not a soul stopped to pick them up no matter what theatrics they displayed, and they didn't pass a single store or domicile along the way. By the time Beryl saw the lights of a city ahead, he'd begun pondering the reach of Beth Rider's God. Was He keeping them under His gigantic thumb? Notions he and Meryl laughed off a year ago were slowly beginning to make more sense as Beryl struggled with the demon he served. He didn't want to change teams so much as he didn't want to die in Ta'avah's service.

At least they had procured a vehicle from an old man in the town. It was a Volvo station wagon, not too old and well maintained. Ta'avah had unnecessarily and messily murdered the guy for it, of course.

Yanking him out of his thoughts, Beryl's superior punched his arm and pointed toward the large white building ahead. They'd reached Rufus's estate. Not all of Meryl's thoughts belonged to Ta'avah and he looked at the house as if he'd never seen it before. Beryl slowed at the gate that surrounded the property and closed his eyes to collect himself.

"Let's get in there," Ta'avah whispered at once.

Beryl sighed and tempered his tone. "What's your most pressing goal?"

"Theophilus," Ta'avah said, his gaze intense and focused on the house.

"Not Rufus?"

Ta'avah scoffed. "Meryl's no match for an Elder hyped up on the

264

Dying Buzz. Or have you so soon forgotten what I told you from the
start? I'll get Rufus. In my own way, in my own time."

Masking his vehemence, he pointed toward the house. "Father
Theophilus is in the basement. Meryl and I have full access to the
whole place. Just let me do my thing." Beryl punched the secret code
into the box and the gate inched open on mechanical rods.

"How many Rakum are here?"

Beryl glanced at his watch. "Seven or eight depending on who's
out on assignment."

"I sense there's a young woman here—but also an older, familiar
one. Meryl knows this other one's scent. But I can't see..." Ta'avah
narrowed his eyes and licked his lips. "I don't fully see Rufus's plans
for them. Do you, Ballerina? Do you see?"

Beryl didn't flinch at the insult this time. "Rufus collected the
teenager as part of his long-range plan to repopulate the Rakum race.
The other woman was with Yosef for a time."

"Ahhh," Ta'avah murmured, "Yosef. He's dead." Simply stating
the obvious, his master quieted again, looking thoughtfully away.

Beryl continued, "She's with the Rabbit's people now, and we
collected her to draw them to Jackson. Meryl would recognize her.
She was one of his favorites at Last Assembly."

Ta'avah smiled, lips closed and nodded his head. "Good. Get me
to Theophilus. Wait. There is one more, in his presence." Ta'avah
hummed and shook his head. "I cannot read him..."

"It's Father Damien. He's an apostate."

"Ah, yes, I see him now." Ta'avah smirked and leaned back in the
car seat. "The fool."

Beryl parked by the front porch and put his hand to the door
handle as Ta'avah stopped him.

"I'll follow you to the basement, but once there, I'll take the lead.
Understand, pup?"

Beryl nodded and got out of the car. Taking a deep breath, he did
his best to resume his normal, confident air. He walked to the door
and Ta'avah swaggered behind, looking up at the second floor in
apparent wonder. Without planning to, Beryl shot him an irritated
glance.

"Master—you know this place, right? I assume you've been
watching us. Why are you so disoriented?"

"I've watched you from my own realm, idiot." Ta'avah cut his
eyes to Beryl and narrowed them evilly. "We do not share this

dimension. Everything in this plane is distorted in mine, light refracts differently, surfaces do not maintain solidity. When will you learn that you're not intelligent enough to understand our ways? Bound by flesh, limited by three dimensions—you're barely alive and you think you can comprehend my kind? Imbecile. In the future, refrain from asking stupid questions."

Beryl absorbed the barbs emitting from his brother's beautiful face, imagining Ta'avah dying a million deaths in the Christian hell. As he opened the door, Dimple was passing the foyer and he sent them a nod.

"Dimp—where's Elder Rufus?" Beryl asked and the big guy stopped. A single telepathic image was no doubt unintentionally transmitted and Beryl saw Rufus latched onto Dimple's right arm, drinking his blood. Beryl sympathized with a grimace, but Dimple laughed.

"Don't hurt none. Anyway, Rufus is in his *throne room*." Dimple held up finger quotation marks at the last.

"Where're the women?" Beryl asked and Dimple looked at his watch.

"He just had them taken upstairs. He's expecting the Rabbit's crew here within the hour. Supposed to be a big showdown." Dimple acknowledged Meryl before continuing. "Damien and Father Theophilus are in the basement. What does he have you guys doing when they arrive?"

Beryl thought fast. "He wants us by his side as usual. How about you?"

"Gotta guard the basement." Dimple swabbed his brow with his right hand and turned for the hallway that led to the cellar.

"We're headed that way," Beryl said, and followed behind him. Ta'avah stayed close and when they reached the basement door, Beryl touched Dimple's shoulder. "Do me a favor, will ya? Go to my room and grab my overnight bag? I'll watch the Fathers for a second."

Dimple nodded without hesitation, completely trusting his Rakum brother. Once he rounded the corner out of sight, Ta'avah smiled and headed down first.

At the bottom of the stairs, the old devil met the imprisoned Fathers' eyes, giving each a good long stare. Beryl watched their responses with interest. Damien recognized them as Beryl and Meryl, shaking his head and resignedly lowering his gaze. Theophilus's reaction, however, was much more peculiar. The ancient Father stood slowly to his feet, and by the time he was fully standing, he tilted his head to the right and gestured with his pointer finger.

"Abroghia," Theophilus whispered as he saw the High Father's spirit through Meryl's fawn-colored eyes. Damien's head snapped around, mouth agape. Ta'avah laughed, the sound making Beryl's skin crawl. He stood in place as Ta'avah approached the old man, arms extended.

"Theophilus, you look horrible. And you've allowed our children to fall into decay in my absence."

As Beryl watched, Ta'avah wrapped one arm around the Father, whipped his knife from his pocket with the other, and jabbed it violently into his neck. The old man made a noise of surprise and gripped Ta'avah's arms. It was a surreal sight—seeing his brother ruthlessly attacking one of their oldest. Beryl shuddered and averted his eyes.

Damien didn't rise from the floor, but watched the violent display and shook his head, his lips moving inaudibly.

"Ah! Ah—! Abroghia, stop!" Theophilus squeezed out the words, and Ta'avah showed no sign of letting up.

Beryl clenched his jaw and looked toward the basement door. Dimple would return soon and wonder what they were up to. How did Ta'avah want to handle that? Then, like bees buzzing deep inside his head, he heard a car engine approaching the lonely road that led to Rufus's private property. The Rabbit's army had arrived and would be at the gate within minutes. Beryl put his hand to Ta'avah's shoulder.

"Do you hear? Someone is driving up."

Ta'avah pulled away from the Father's wrinkled throat with a loud smack and buried his fingers in Theophilus's long reddish hair.

"What does Rufus have in mind for you, old friend? Tell your master." Ta'avah held Theophilus close and spoke into his face.

Theophilus caught his breath and briefly touched his neck, but it had already healed. He looked Beryl's way and then closed his eyes to answer.

"As far as I can tell, he hopes to breed more Rakum."

"Oh? Aren't you a lucky guy," Ta'avah hissed and looked to Beryl for confirmation. Only the Fathers had the ability to procreate and Beryl had surmised the same thing without hearing Rufus say so expressly. He nodded to Ta'avah as Damien grunted and came to his feet against the wall behind them. Ta'avah tossed him a wicked grin.

"Damien, you know I won't leave you alive. You're the worst of all traitors." Ta'avah looked at Beryl and flicked his head toward the former Father. "Kill him."

Beryl blinked. "Wh—?"

"Break his neck. Can you manage that, imbecile?"

"Wait, Abroghia, wait." Theophilus managed a weak whisper, his head flexed rearward in Ta'avah's cruel grasp. "I will go with you willingly. I am your slave. Leave Damien. He is no danger to your plans."

Ta'avah seemed to mull it over before his grin reappeared. "Kill him, Beryl. Right now."

Beryl shook his head as the door to the basement came open.

"Meryl? What are you doing? Have you lost your mind?" Dimple trotted down the stairs and reached the group in two big strides. "Father Theophilus, you all right?"

Beryl opened his mouth to make up something half-way believable, but Ta'avah beat him to it. Releasing Theophilus, he whipped out his pocket knife and opened it one-handed. With a blur of fluid motion, he sliced Dimple's throat ear-to-ear. The Rakum's eyes opened and his jaw dropped before he had the foresight to clutch both palms to his spurting neck.

Beryl was dumbfounded. Torn between wanting to help Dimple and throttle Ta'avah, he stood where he was, his mind numb. Barely aware of his surroundings, Ta'avah tugged his shirt hard enough to pull him down.

"Come on, you dolt!" Ta'avah barked as he scooted past Beryl for the stairs, dragging Father Theophilus behind him. Beryl caught himself and stumbled backward, his eyes still fixed on Dimple writhing on the dirty floor. Ta'avah was up the steps and in the doorway when he hissed again, this time telepathically. *'Now! Or I'll kill you, too!'*

Dimple moaned, his eyes roaming blindly in shock. Father Damien knelt by his side as Beryl turned for the exit and bounded up the stairs behind Ta'avah. Would he make it? A Rakum could survive a throat wound such as that, but he'd need someone to feed him fresh blood and protect him until he healed. What would Damien do?

Beryl jogged behind Ta'avah and wondered over all that had taken place since the night he and Meryl tried to kidnap Elder Canaan's woman. As Ta'avah used Meryl's perfect body to tote their last remaining Father out the front door, Beryl wondered how his life had taken such a turn.

"Oh, how I wish you'd stop whining, Beryl," Ta'avah said in his mind. *"Get the car started. We must be gone before the Rabbit's folk get here. You miserable babies are no match for the force they're packing."*

On auto-pilot, Beryl zipped past Ta'avah to reach the Volvo and slide into the driver's seat. Within seconds, headlights approached the iron gate and he revved the engine. Ta'avah slung a defeated and dazed Theophilus into the back, crawled in beside him, and slammed the door. Without an order, Beryl stomped on the gas and peeled out toward the exit only to be stopped to wait for the gate to open. As soon as ample room was provided, Beryl zoomed through, coming nose-to-nose with a new Cadillac.

"Go around them, idiot!" Ta'avah shouted from the car's backseat and Beryl slammed the brakes and then the gas to whirl off to the other car's right.

"Yitzhak," Father Theophilus said from the back seat, pointing to the other car's occupants. Beryl kept his eyes to the dark road ahead, but Ta'avah began shouting.

"It is Yitzhak! Go back! I want that kid!" Ta'avah barked and gripped Beryl's shoulder hard, fingers digging into his skin.

"Who is Yitzhak?" Beryl bellowed in reply, Ta'avah's fingers like barbs in his flesh.

Beryl thought about the wreck back in Memphis. How they were almost nabbed by the authorities. He thought of how difficult it was to reason with his master. And then he pictured poor Dimple, sliced open for simply following orders. There was no way this Yitzhak was worth throwing away their last chance of success. Lastly, Beryl didn't want to face the Rabbit's army at Ta'avah's side. His main fear? That when the fight was on, he just might side with them.

"Go back!" Ta'avah barked and boxed Beryl's ear, knocking him out of his rambling thoughts.

"No!" Beryl shouted back and dodged another blow. "Retrieve him later! Listen to me. You're too rash. Stick to your plan. Father Theophilus, reason with him!"

Beryl ducked to his left as Ta'avah swung at his head again. He glanced in the mirror hoping to see Theophilus engaged in their current skirmish, but he was leaning on his side, staring out into the night, worthless.

A telepathic image wavered in his mind just then, but he couldn't tell if it was sent by Ta'avah or Theophilus. Either way, it was of a young Rakum boy with blond hair and blue eyes. Beryl inhaled sharply, and worked to keep the car on the road and watch the vision at the same time. In his mind's eye, the boy smiled at him and opened his arms. Beryl moved toward him and the boy's mouth opened, full of sharp teeth, *"Now you, Ballerina."*

With dread filling his every pore, Beryl snapped out of the trance and checked Ta'avah's position. The vision was clear: The demon inside Meryl would assume the blond kid's body and be stronger than all the Fathers combined.

"Worthless fool!" Ta'avah screamed and lunged into the front seat.

Beryl did the first thing that occurred to him. He whipped the steering wheel to the right and aimed for the nearest and thickest tree trunk. There were plenty to choose from and he chose wisely.

FIFTY-FOUR

Michael watched the silver Volvo screech to a halt and they both waited for the gate to open fully. The window tint was too dark for him to see the occupants, but Isaac ducked down as they passed, dust flying in their combined headlights.

"What—?" he began, but the other car accelerated and careened past them on the right. Michael turned in his seat to follow their progress until they disappeared around a curve in the moonlit road ahead. "What is it, Isaac? Who was in the car? The girls?"

Isaac worked his way upward and faced front, his expression finally a little pensive. "No, Beryl and Meryl."

Michael took a deep breath and pulled the car through the gate only to pause on the other side. He turned to Isaac and placed a heavy hand on his shoulder.

"Something's got you spooked. What're you not telling me?" Michael searched the kid's eyes, but like watching a veil fall, his arrogant demeanor rolled back into view.

"I told you everything. Now, let's get to the house." Isaac looked at Rufus's mansion a hundred yards away.

"I couldn't see who it was, but I saw at least three heads," David offered from the back seat, his voice higher than normal. Michael held Isaac's eye and flicked his head rearward.

"Who else did you see, Isaac? 'Fess up because I've just about had it with you."

"Or what?" Isaac hardened his eye. "You need me. I don't need you. I'll help you get the women out, but beyond that, I make no promises."

Michael started to reply, but stopped himself. There was a warning in the kid's tone that he almost missed. He'd been out of their game a long time, but he recognized the sinking queasiness that accompanied a serious threat. Michael swallowed, leaned back into his seat, and quashed a groan.

"Isaac? Can you tell us where the girls are? I mean, right now?" Oblivious to the tension in the front seat, David asked his question while staring up to the house. Isaac cleared his throat and placed both hands on the dash, eyes closed.

"Hmmm," he murmured, "I can hear the younger one speaking. She's not in the basement. She's on the second floor. Possibly in Rufus's presence." Isaac opened his eyes. "Wait—the other woman. She's with her."

"Michael, the plan was to sneak into the house and get the girls out of the basement. If Rufus has them with him, what now?" David leaned between the front seats and spoke closer to Michael's ear. "Should we wait for Elder Canaan?"

Isaac snickered. "I am more than capable of getting you in there and helping you get the women out. If you're up to it, let's go."

Michael looked at both passengers, then back to the house. Lights were lit in every upstairs window, but on the first floor, only the front door was illuminated. How long before Roman and his crew arrived? Was Isaac bragging or telling the truth about his abilities?

"Isaac, what do you want? Why did you come, really?" Michael asked with as much respect as he could muster. Isaac paused only a moment and then shrugged.

"I came for Father Theophilus, but he's no longer here. I'll help you because of Elder Canaan, but as soon as your mission is done, our alliance is terminated."

Michael tried to read his eyes, but Isaac was as closed as ever. Still, he had no other choice but to trust him. Putting the car in gear, he drove up to the front door. They weren't going for a stealthy entrance—Roman and Canaan would try that. Michael's plan was to walk right in and have Isaac use his talents to get them to the girls.

"Hey, guys," Isaac caught his eye and then David's. "If you follow my lead and stay out of the way, this'll work fine." Isaac smiled, his baby-blue eyes twinkling. "And don't be alarmed at anything you might see me do. I'm going to wing it."

Michael nodded, but the sinking feeling in his gut remained. With a whispered prayer and an amen from David, they exited the car and stepped to the front door.

Once inside, no one came to meet them. Isaac, Michael, and David stood in triangle formation with the kid at the front. The foyer was lit, but shadows reached for them from all directions. Straight ahead was a flight of stairs that ended in a gloomy landing going left and right. Upstairs, to both sides, were hallways that darkened to nothing as they petered out. The rooms were lit but the doors closed. Michael tried to listen, smell, intuit everything around them, but his meager human senses left him feeling vulnerable. Speaking to God in his heart, he watched Isaac. The kid stepped animatedly to the stairs and started up.

David walked shoulder-to-shoulder with Michael as a small noise filtered down to them that may have been a woman's voice. When they reached the landing, Isaac looked back the way they'd come. Two droopy-eyed Rakum were below them, smiling and clenching their fists.

Michael started to speak, but David beat him to it.

"Geoffrey? Spinner?"

He took one step down, but Isaac came to his level and pressed his chest until he was against the thick wooden railing.

"Allow me," he whispered and jogged down the stairs.

Michael expected the three to exchange words, but none of the Rakum spoke. Geoffrey and Spinner rushed Isaac in unison, fingers ready to grab his arms and throat, but the kid was too quick for them both. Grabbing the taller of the two by the face, Isaac flicked his wrists, and Geoffrey's neck was broken. As he tumbled to the marble floor, Spinner shouted with surprise and backed down.

"Hey, dude, hey." He held up his hands and continued backing for the door. "I don't want no trouble. Wait." When he reached the front door, he wrenched it open, his eyes on Isaac, his voice submissive. "I'm leaving, man, no worries. No worries, right?"

"Come on, Isaac—let's get upstairs," David urged and took a step forward. Michael grabbed his arm but he jerked away. "She's right up there. We have to hurry!"

As soon as the front door closed behind Spinner, Isaac smiled and trotted back up the steps. "Okay, Dave. I hear five heartbeats up here. At least two downstairs." He tilted his head to the right and his grin faded. He met Michael's gaze. "A human and a Rakum are in the basement."

"We get the girls," Michael said under his breath, and Isaac turned for the hallway on his left.

Three strides later, a door opened and two big Rakum stepped out; Michael didn't recognize either of them. Isaac rushed forward and with a flash of movement, rammed his forearm into the chin of the one on his right. The Rakum yelped with surprise and stumbled backward, his jaw fractured. He hit the carpet, groaning and fell silent. His partner rushed Isaac with hands open, but as Michael shouted for the kid to watch out, the second Rakum was found in Isaac's deadly grip. With his palms framing the big guy's shocked face, Isaac opened his mouth wide and long fangs erupted from the top and bottom. With a groan of unmasked anticipation, he pulled the taller Rakum down to his level and sank his teeth into his throat.

David's hand flew to his mouth and he caught Michael's eye. It was a new thing—to manifest fangs on cue, and such zealous cannibalistic ferocity was rarely seen among the Rakum. Michael understood now why deep down, he hadn't trusted Isaac. The one they called The Last, if left to mature, would be far worse than the ten Fathers altogether. Neither man spoke, but waited until Isaac released the now quiet Rakum to the carpet and gestured for the open door.

"Rufus's quarters," he whispered and pointed for the door nearest them, his face a mess with near-black blood dripping from his chin. "I'll distract the Elder while you rush the women out. Count to ten then do your thing. Ready?" Isaac's labored breathing wasn't from fear. On the contrary, he was exhilarated and ecstatic.

Michael watched warily as Isaac slipped into the room.

Game afoot.

Fifty-Five

There was a commotion in the hallway, but Chloe's back was to the door. A short time ago, Rufus had both she and a woman introduced as Selene transferred to his second floor suite. Selene resembled a bald Halle Berry and Chloe said so at least once before Rufus bellowed that they remain silent. He commanded she and Selene be bound, back to back, with vicious silver tape while he resumed position at his throne.

For the moment, Chloe's fingers gripped Selene's; stuck together as tightly as Siamese twins. She could see Rufus in his overstuffed chair, sitting forward, elbows on his knees, impossibly long fingers dangling, watching the door with anticipation. A few minutes before, he'd gestured for everyone to keep silent, and Chloe hoped to God that it meant David had arrived.

There was a bodily thud in the hall followed by silence and Rufus came to his feet. Chloe leaned as far to the right as she could, but still couldn't get the doorway in sight. She whispered to Selene to report what she saw and listened closely. There were a few more unidentifiable noises before Rufus stepped out of her line of vision.

Oh, let it be Dave! Chloe prayed and strained her back to see their rescuers enter the room. Selene must have been uncomfortable by her movements, for she bent at the waist and cried out softly. Chloe was about to apologize when Rufus's gravelly voice filled the room to the high ceilings.

"What is this? And a child shall lead them, Stone? Is this the best you can do? Dredge up a little baby to do your dirty work?"

Turned as far right as possible, Chloe could make out the back of Rufus's long coat.

"I am Isaac Akaron, Elder Rufus. The Last. We've met before."

This voice was high and sweet, like her 13-year-old cousin's. Chloe nudged Selene and she whispered back.

"It's a boy. A Rakum boy. He looks really young. But…"

"What is it to me?" Rufus's throaty monotone sounded then.

"What are you doing with these traitors? Are you searching for a god?"

Chloe heard the boy laugh, the sound of children playing in the park. The contrast was hard to picture. If only she could see. Chloe pushed the ground with her feet and was able to turn the both of them a few inches. She saw all of Rufus and he gestured toward someone with a dirty face and bright blond hair that hung in his eyes. Her head began to throb with eye-strain and she relaxed back into position.

"Is David Walker with him?" she urged Selene in a whisper.

"Yeah. Michael and David are behind him."

"Funny," the high-voiced Rakum replied. "What use would I have of a god when I am one myself?"

Rufus laughed derisively. "You're ill-informed, young one. I am king here. I lead the Rakum now. Bow to me or be destroyed."

Rufus's words dripped with evil intent, but Chloe heard the youngster giggle. He must have moved forward because Rufus backed three steps, finally comfortably in view.

"What's this?" Rufus stammered and backed again. The blond-haired boy advanced, hands on his hips, his eyes locked with the crazed Elder. "You're challenging me? A boy? Against an Elder? You waste my time." Rufus's voice wavered with what sounded like fear.

"All you have is time, Rufus. Approximately five minutes. Shall I prophesy for you?" The youth spoke confidently, his eye hard. Chloe felt goose bumps on her arms at the kid's malevolent manner.

"You? Prophesy?"

"I've seen your neck in my hands, squeezing. Squeezing."

Chloe watched the kid bring his hands up to eye-level.

"I've seen my teeth ripping your flesh—"

"Never happen!" Rufus screamed, his anger evident, yet he didn't advance on the boy. "So you have what it takes to be a Father, kid? I have no need of such. I have Theophilus at my disposal. And I'll have you—"

"What would you say," the kid interrupted him, "if I told you that tonight, High Father Abroghia ran off with your prize?" Rufus snorted and the kid laughed again.

Chloe felt a tug at her wrist. The two Rakum continued to threaten each other in measured tones as a wide-shouldered man with kind eyes busily cut through their bonds. He gave her a tiny "shh" gesture as her arms popped free. Chloe whirled around and met

David's eyes.

Every emotion she'd kept in check the past few hours spilled into her chest in silent heaves. David rushed forward and grabbed her up, lifting her off the ground and backing toward the wall. Chloe held tightly to his neck and looked for Selene who had draped her arm around the other guy's shoulders beside them. He inclined his head for the exit and Chloe held her breath as their heroes began inching them toward the hallway.

Rufus was facing the door. How would they escape?

"You had big plans, Elder Rufus. Eh?" the youngster said teasingly only fifteen feet away, his back to them now as they hugged the wall. Chloe had the impression that the kid was checking their position. Then in a flash, he lunged forward, slammed into Rufus full force, and tumbled to the floor with the monstrous vampire pinned beneath him. Rufus roared and thrashed, but the kid jumped to his feet and kicked him hard enough to send him sliding across the floor. With new urgency, Chloe struggled out of David's arms to the ground and the four of them escaped into the hallway.

"Chloe, this is Michael Stone," he whispered as they walked hurriedly for the stairwell. Chloe looked at the other man and he smiled.

"Beth Rider's husband," he said and she nodded, recognizing the name. Just as the man's life story from the Rabbit book began to rise up in her memory, a large shape started up the stairs toward them.

Michael put his body in front of Selene and Dave stepped before Chloe.

"Where're you headed, traitors? You wouldn't be taking Elder Rufus's women, now would you?" The Rakum tromped up slowly, his fists clenched and his face still in shadow. As Chloe watched, Michael charged forward and shoved the Rakum in the chest with both hands. Shouting, they tumbled backward and then down the last few steps as David grabbed Chloe's hand and tugged hard.

"Follow me!" he yelped and skirted the wrestling men, reached the foot of the stairs and made as if to open the front door. The latch moved on its own and Dave wheeled right, hauling Chloe after him. She glanced back to the stairs where Michael was taking a fist to his face and Selene was screaming, trapped by their position.

"What about Selene? We have to help Selene!" Chloe pulled against him but he managed to reach a side door. Once open, he pulled her into the dark space.

"Shhh," he whispered, and leaned against the wall. "I'll get you safe and go back for her. Shhh...we won't leave either of you behind."

Chloe nodded and strained her eyes in the dark. "Where are we? Are we in a garage?"

"I think so. They've painted over the windows, but it smells like gasoline. Now, shhh," Dave whispered in her ear. "Reinforcements are coming and if I read Isaac correctly, they'll be here in less than five minutes."

"Roman and Javier?" Chloe asked, happy that her hero held her so tightly.

"Yes," Dave breathed, "and another Rakum."

"Oh," Chloe said and fell silent. Maybe she could close her eyes. Maybe for just a moment she could pretend they were safe, back home, in her room. David repositioned her until she was up against the wall and facing his front. He was shielding her. It was good. Chloe let her eyes fall closed and she asked God to help them and to give her strength.

FIFTY-SIX

Canaan heard the wrestling match on the stairs before he opened Rufus's front door. He warned Roman to be cautious and pushed it open to leap to Michael's aid.

Ten feet into the house, he spotted an immobilized Rakum curled up off to the left of the bottom step. Isaac probably disarmed him when he arrived. Canaan listened for the kid's voice as he approached the straining couple in front of him. Stone was holding his own, most likely because of his years of fighting under the tutelage of Elder Jack Dawn.

Stone grunted as the air was knocked out of him by a recumbent body blow and Canaan stepped forward. He didn't recognize the Rakum pinning Stone to the bottom step with huge hands, but he didn't wait for the guy to look up before twisting his shoulder violently upward. The Rakum grunted and bounced right back. Instead of continuing his beat-down on Michael Stone, he turned for his real competition and came at Canaan, bellowing indignation at being attacked by one of his own.

"How dare you—" the Rakum began, fingers closing around Canaan's windpipe. He stopped short as he met the Elder's eyes. Canaan wrapped his own hands about the inferior Rakum's throat and regained his leverage instantly. The mere thought of coming up against an Elder was enough to cower the toughest underling, and this Rakum was no different. The lumbering Neanderthal released Canaan and wrapped his fingers atop those that threatened to snap his neck. Whispering pleas of forgiveness, his knees buckled and he sunk to the floor.

"Thank God. Not a moment too soon," Michael sputtered, coming to his feet and massaging his bruised neck. Selene jumped into him from behind and clutched him around the waist.

"Please—get me out of here. Please!" she cried, her shrill voice grating on Canaan's nerves. The attacking Rakum began to beg for mercy.

"Master, please." Choking on his words, he stared up at Canaan, his eyes bulging with the pressure applied to his trachea. Canaan relaxed his fingers slightly, no real desire to end the guy. Upstairs he caught a snippet of Isaac's exchange with a very angry and indignant Rufus. Oh, how Canaan longed to get into that skirmish. He regarded the Rakum at the end of his arms with a tilt of his chin.

"Rufus's reign is coming to an end tonight, brother. How does that make you feel?" As Canaan spoke, Roman circled around him to reach Michael Stone and the woman.

"I don't want to die, Master," he said, as sincerely as possible while in mortal terror. Canaan considered his words and allowed his fingers to relax completely. The Rakum scrambled back until he was against the railing, and he warily regarded the faces around him.

"I can appreciate that. What do they call you?" Canaan remained in place and the Rakum didn't attempt to stand.

"Hoss."

"Okay, Hoss. These guys are here to get these women out. I'm here to stop Rufus. What are you gonna do?"

Roman, Michael, and the woman remained silent, watching to see what the Rakum would decide. Canaan wanted the guy to run off and disappear into the night. He didn't want to have to break his neck. The brotherhood count had dwindled enough without him adding to the deficiency.

No matter what Hoss' strengths and weakness, telepathy wasn't a problem. He remained in Canaan's gaze and whispered with sincerity. "I'm gonna go out that door and disappear until all this dies down."

Canaan smiled and gestured for him to stand. Hoss rushed to his feet, keeping his eyes locked with the Elder's.

"Good answer, brother. Now, look," Canaan said as he walked the Rakum to the front door. "Please don't have a sudden change of heart, come back here and cause me any trouble because then I'll have to snap your neck. *Comprende?*"

The Rakum shook his head. "I promise, Master, you won't see me again tonight."

Satisfied, Canaan nodded his head, watched the Rakum open the door and fade into the night. He turned toward the trio on the steps and caught Roman's eye. They'd gotten this far and right upstairs, Isaac was holding Rufus on his own. It was time to get up there and finish the fight. Roman looked like he was about to speak, but he didn't and Canaan gave him an understanding nod. The guy was war-weary and more than a little despondent over the incident with Javier.

"You guys, leave Rufus to us." Canaan stepped aside, standing next to the unconscious Rakum on the floor. "Isaac has Rufus distracted, but it's time I got up there to do my part. You guys get on out." Then he held his hand out to Michael. "But take Roman's truck. I need my Caddy."

Michael fished the keys from his pocket and handed them over.

"And Canaan," he said, "we got separated from David and Chloe. Can you locate them?"

Canaan listened more purposefully to the noises in the house and thought he heard a feminine whisper off to his left. He opened his mouth to answer when he heard voices from below as well.

"*Father Damien...*" A weak, gasping Rakum voice. "*What's going on?*"

"*Quiet, son, just rest. We shall see what we shall see.*"

"David and his friend are down that hallway." Then Canaan pointed to the floor. "There are two men in the basement. One of them is Father Damien. The other is injured, a Rakum." Canaan was curious about the duo below, but not enough to distract him entirely. As he pondered, Roman broke the silence, handing the truck keys to his friend.

"Michael, take Selene out front and start the Tahoe. I'll send David out to you and get Father Damien from the basement." Roman pulled Marcy's gun from his waistband, his finger just to the side of the trigger. "If the Rakum downstairs gives us any trouble, I'll use this on him."

Canaan agreed and touched Roman's arm. "Tell Marcy I'll send for her when the coast is clear." He waited for the former Elder to nod and then heard Isaac's childish banter in his head.

"*I'd like to finish him off, Elder Canaan. If you want to play, you'd better come on up.*"

Canaan turned his attention upstairs as a loud crash of furniture sounded and the three people around him leapt into action. Roman disappeared down the hall, Michael and the woman headed out the front door and Canaan put his hand to the banister.

"*Save a piece for me, little brother,*" he replied and bounded up the stairs. Rufus was wailing now, screaming in extreme fury and intense pain. What was the kid doing to him? Canaan shook his head with amused wonder as he reached the closed door at the top of the stairs. With The Last, there was no telling. He had powers none of them understood and his behavior more unpredictable than the Fathers. There was just no telling.

Canaan filled his lungs and prepared to jump in with both feet.

FIFTY-SEVEN

It was the least he could do.

After carefully slicing open his arm with his knife, Damien flexed his fist twice over the prostrate Rakum's mouth to encourage blood flow. It wasn't proper to leave him for dead when it was in Damien's power to help him recover. The Rakum's lacerated neck healed quickly, but Dimple had lost a great deal of blood, evident on his clothing, his hands and the floor around them. After a minute, he grasped Damien's arm and brought it to his lips to draw the blood actively. Damien's head swam as he settled onto his rump and closed his eyes. He should pull away, but not yet. Dimple was meant to live and Damien prayed for strength.

"Father Damien!"

A man called him from the basement steps and Damien looked up, recognizing the now-mortal Elder instantly.

"No. No. Stop," Roman said as he reached the pair on the floor.

"It's okay," Damien whispered, but Roman was separating them and rolling the Rakum onto his back. Dimple didn't resist and lay still, struggling to breathe. "It's okay, Roman. It was my idea."

"Who is it?" Roman asked, and Damien looked upon the sad creature mournfully.

"Dimple, Yosef's lieutenant. He could be good. He has a decent heart. I feel he will join our ranks one day." Damien paused and then nodded, even more convinced in his spirit. "Yes, in his time, he will change allegiance as we have."

"You believe that?" Roman asked, and Damien nodded again.

"Then, Dimple? You may need this." Roman showed him the gun and placed it a few feet from Dimple's lax fingers. "Can you hear me?"

The Rakum groaned and met Roman's eye.

"Upstairs, your leader is facing judgment for his evil deeds. Do you hear me?"

Dimple's focus wavered, but his head made the slightest nod

283

before Roman continued.

"The God of the humans cares about you, Dimple. He's willing to forgive you, restore you, and place you among His children. The monster you served all your life was a wicked and evil being that God destroyed to bring us closer to Him. You've never known love, Dimple, but you will with Him."

"Traitors," Dimple managed before his lack of air caused him to quiet, his severed trachea still healing. Roman looked toward the door and then back to the Rakum.

"Use this gun to protect yourself until you heal sufficiently. God is offering you His peace and His covering. I sincerely suggest you consider His offer." With that, Roman got to his feet and helped Damien do the same. "All right, Father, it's time for you to leave. Come. We have a car upstairs."

"Where is Javier?" Damien asked, sensing that Javier was still a big part of the former Elder's life. Roman's eyes turned sorrowful and Damien's breath hitched. "What? You must tell me, Roman, I demand it."

"Javier was struck by a car on the way here." Roman resumed moving Damien toward the exit, his voice filled with emotion. "We had to leave him."

A sense of calm replaced the initial panic in Damien's mind as he pictured Javier, young, strong and on top of the world, just as he was at their last meeting over a hundred years ago. It had been brief, but even then, he felt a connection with the boy that was not common among their kind.

"He'll be fine, Roman," Damien whispered, allowing the former Elder to lead him a few paces toward the stairs. "I will see him again. There's a reason he was prevented from coming tonight. God is doing something extraordinary with him. I just know it."

Roman nodded his head as if dealing with an incognizant elder, but Damien wasn't offended. Roman didn't have to understand it; only accept it on faith.

The floor rumbled above them, shaking loose the plaster. Damien looked at the ceiling.

"And what of Rufus?"

"It's as I said to Dimple. Elder Canaan and Isaac Akaron are dealing him his hand as we speak." Roman resumed toward the exit, but Damien remained in place.

"Yitzhak?" he whispered. "He's here?"

Roman's jaw flexed, but he didn't answer immediately. Damien understood. The boy they called Isaac was on the road he and the other Fathers prepared for him decades ago. Was there any hope for him? Damien gave Roman a sidelong glance and spoke in a guilty whisper.

"If he follows my teaching, he'll do everything within his power to rule the Rakum."

"Your teaching?" Roman's indignant expression spoke volumes and Damien sighed.

"Before I realized the truth, before…" Damien choked and swallowed hard. "I rebelled against God. Like all of them. I took Isaac with me. I instructed him on how to assume control. To take Abroghia's place. He's doing precisely what I told him to do."

"He's going to kill Rufus, Father Damien. Is that what you told him to do?"

Was Roman dense? Damien shook his head and monitored his tone. "Ta'avah, the spirit of Abroghia, is back, Roman. Did you not know?"

Roman's normally rigid face fell and his eyes squinted to half their size. Damien woefully bowed his head.

"Yes. He does as he pleases. He came here in Meryl's body and took Theophilus with him. Ta'avah plans to regain the Rakum's favor. He will no doubt try to rebuild our former people into a murderous army to carry out the demon's initial goal."

"Destroy as many of God's people as he can," Roman mumbled, his head lowered but still making eye contact.

"Yes. He'll assume Theophilus's body and have the power of the Fathers behind him. He will come after us worse than Rufus ever did."

"Isaac will join him?"

"You're not listening, Roman. I taught Isaac how to assume control of our people. He'll control them. He will not allow Ta'avah to interfere."

"Are you saying Isaac is more powerful than—"

"Yitzhak is more powerful than us all."

Roman's bottom lip moved and he looked to the side a moment. After a few false starts, he met Damien's gaze. "So what do we do? Isaac and Ta'avah both want to take over the world. How do we respond?"

"Know your enemy, for one. Ta'avah would *like* to rule the

285

world. Ask any demon. It's his greatest desire. But Isaac's a Rakum, and just a boy at that. He only wants to feed his lusts. You remember what that is like, eh, son?" Damien tempered his tone with his next ugly admission. "And Roman, he feeds off the Rakum. Exclusively. Ferociously. He's a child, but as I said, an awesome power."

Roman's shoulders fell. "What do we do?"

"Leave this place." Damien looked toward the basement door. "And see what God will have us do. We're still alive, so we're still working His purposes." The man didn't move for a moment and Damien prodded him. "Lead on."

Roman grunted and resumed their way upstairs. At the top, he stopped long enough to wrap his handkerchief around Damien's self-inflicted wound.

"We're servants of the Most High. Whom shall we fear?" Whispering to himself as much as to Damien, Roman supported him with one strong arm. "Lean on me, Father."

Damien allowed the youngster to help him, his mind dancing on the future. Storm clouds would inevitably erupt along the way, but the bright promise of seeing Javier again gave him hope. God would let him walk arm-and-arm with Javier soon as they never could before their change.

In the sun.

Under the watchful and loving eye of God.

FiFTY-eiGHT

In the darkened garage, David shielded Chloe with his body. They stood face-to-face and he worked to slow his breathing. He had promised her over the phone that God would take care of them. Now he had to lean on his own advice as the sounds of a raucous fight down the hall, and a noisier one upstairs made him wonder what would happen next. Still, he had Chloe, and she was safe for the moment. That meant a lot.

"We're gonna make it," Chloe whispered, her soft breath like feathers on his cheek.

"We need to get into the yard," David whispered, and absently pushed a strand of her hair behind her ear. "That's where Michael will head when he gets free of that Rakum."

"Thanks for saying 'when'," Chloe smiled, an encouraging confidence in her eye.

David returned her smile and glanced around the dark room. The only light emanated from a weak bulb in the far corner. Three hulking shapes filled the room, obviously cars, but the automatic doors had no windows. The room was painted dark so the Rakum could pass through at all hours of the day. Suddenly struck with paranoia, David faced Chloe and listened for the tell-tale signs of Rakum sneaking up on them in the dark.

Not on the same page, Chloe put her hands on his shoulders and grinned, her face in shadow, but the light glinting off her lips.

"How long were you a Wraith, Dave? How old are you really?"

"What?" Taken aback by the odd question, David stopped listening for the enemy long enough to concentrate on Chloe's new direction.

"The novel said you were born in 1935. Is that right?" Chloe asked and watched his eyes.

David flinched and looked away, he never intended for her to know. Even if they spent the rest of their lives together, his plan had been to forget he'd been born a Rakum.

"I deserve an answer, don't I?" she asked, her tone gentle. David nodded slowly twice and then more resolutely. "You don't look older than twenty. Weird."

"Yeah, weird." David put a finger to her chin and hoped her curiosity was satisfied. It wasn't.

"How old is Javier? And Roman?"

David sighed and leaned back a couple of inches to give them more speaking room. "Javier is over a hundred. Roman over three hundred."

"Goodness," Chloe whispered and gripped his arms. David decided to drive the point home.

"That old man you mentioned was in the basement—Theophilus—he was alive when Jesus walked the earth."

"Unbelievable," Chloe whispered, shaking her head in wonder. Then her expression changed again. "If we'd met back then, when you were a Wraith, would we be friends? You were friendly, right? You were never a monster like some of them."

"Sunshine, shhh," David whispered, shaking his head. "Leave the past in the past."

"But you were sweet, right? You loved your human friends, right? That's what the novel said."

"Chloe," David's heart was too big for his chest as the memories of his former life flooded to the surface. All the friends he'd known, all of them mortal, and of course, the despair at being hated by his own kind from the beginning.

"I think we would have been friends. Even then," Chloe said, smiling.

David bit his tongue, unwilling to say anything that might seem harsh. But she was so naive, he had to say something. He sighed and lowered his eyes.

"Chloe, I used them. All of them. I manipulated them for my own pleasure. My own needs. Only after I read Miss Beth's book did I ever think twice about my lifestyle."

"But you weren't like the others. The novel said that you loved them and were prepared to give your life for them. Is that so wrong?"

"No, that came later." Irritated and uncomfortable speaking on the matter, David raised his voice a fraction. "Is it wrong to be a Rakum? Is that what you're asking me?"

Undaunted, Chloe continued, "Well, yeah. If he's good, then he should be fine."

"Chloe—I thirsted for blood. All the time. I made it a game, to see who'd feed me next and who could give the most blood on any occasion. I planned my life around those donations. If I'd been older, I'd have added debauchery to my list of fleshly needs. Please, don't romanticize something so horrible."

Chloe was quiet a moment and then slowly nodded her head as understanding dawned. "It has to do with drinking blood, then? That's bad, right? God doesn't like that?"

David exhaled. "Drinking blood is part of it, but the Rakum were spawned by a demon, Chloe. Their lives are based on lust and self-gratification—everything God is against. There are no 'good' Rakum in God's eyes."

"But so many of them have become human...they must have been good."

"Okay, now we're into semantics. Chloe, listen," David began, rubbing his face, "the Rakum that hear and obey God will become His children. When that happens, they're no longer Rakum. Get it?"

Chloe opened her mouth, but outside, a car engine roared to life and a horn beeped twice.

"Michael made it to the car. We need to find a way out of here." David stepped back the way they came and a familiar voice trickled in from the hall.

"David?"

"In here, Roman," David whispered and crossed to the door. When he pulled the knob, Roman stood in the darkened hall with a pale Father Damien leaning on his shoulder. David bowed an inch or so to the Father out of respect, then kicked himself inwardly. Sometimes, it was as if he'd never left the fold. He shook his head.

"What's happening?" he whispered, "Is that Michael outside? Where's everybody?"

"In good time. Follow me. Stay close," Roman muttered and stepped away from the garage and down a hallway. "There's a back door right about here," he said as they turned a corner and reached an outer door.

David squeezed Chloe's hand without turning around, and they both followed the Elder and Father into the cold night and toward the waiting truck.

FIFTY-NINE

Rufus was no match for Isaac. Canaan entered the room expecting to charge into the battle, but by all appearances, the boy had vanquished the insane Elder before he arrived. Deflated, Canaan caught Isaac's eye and pointed at Rufus on the carpet, chest heaving, a few feet away.

"What happened to your vision—the one where Rufus and I battle to the death?"

"I got tired of waiting," Isaac answered, his smile to the side. "I left you a little to work with. Go see if you can rouse him."

Canaan was angry at being excluded, but he approached Rufus nonetheless. As he drew near, the vampire shook head-to-toe and clambered to his feet like a dragon coming awake after a long sleep. A dangerous light flickered behind Rufus's eyes and Canaan smiled; he had a little fight left in him after all.

Muscles twitching, Canaan's prepared to attack, but his opponent gathered his strength amazingly fast and made the first strike. The furious vampire-wannabe charged him and as their bodies slapped together, Canaan lost his balance and tumbled back.

"Ouch, Elder Canaan!" Isaac teased from the other side of the room. "Watch it, he's not playing!"

Canaan regained his feet in time to receive another shove from Rufus. This time, he held his ground, and placed a full-powered jab into the Elder's face. Stunned, Rufus growled and moved into a ferocious upper cut that Canaan had waiting for him.

"Boxing, Canaan?" Rufus laughed, spitting black blood. "I don't box."

Rufus lunged again, this time fast enough to pin Canaan's fists. Canaan opened his arms with a powerful shout and broke free, appreciating the surprise in Rufus's face. It was time to change the program.

Grabbing the man by both wrists, he hoped to turn the tables by head-butting Rufus as hard as he could. But it was an Elder trick 700-

year-old Rufus remembered. Screaming with blind rage, the vampire returned with even more power than Canaan projected. By the time Rufus had Canaan by the throat, his head was swimming.

"He's got you now, Elder Canaan! What are you going to do?"

Isaac's voice was playful, but Canaan ignored him, seriously wondering how the Elder maintained such intensity. Rufus was sick with the Dying Buzz, so where was this zeal coming from? Or was Canaan not as powerful as he thought he was?

Pressed nose-to-nose, putrid breath leaking from his lips in exertion, Rufus's long claw-like fingernails dug into Canaan's throat. When the first trickle of blood seeped into his collar, Canaan swatted himself free and rolled away. The physical maneuvers weren't working so Canaan took a crouching stance and prepared to battle the Rakum mentally. Rufus laughed and matched his posture a dozen feet away.

"This is hilarious," he growled opening and closing fists that hung to his knees. "Elder Canaan, you're quite a funny guy."

Canaan did his best to block out the man's insults as he concentrated on Rufus's heart. If he focused with all of his might, he could burst the organ and end the Elder's rule in an instant. Rufus smiled across from him and a searing pain began to travel up Canaan's arm toward his shoulder.

"He siphoned power from Father Theophilus, Elder Canaan. I guess I forgot to tell you that," Isaac said, giggling from his position across the room. Sick at the newsflash, Canaan still didn't look away from Rufus's evil gaze.

"I laugh at you, Canaan," Rufus growled and stepped forward only to stop again, his head tilted to the side. "You feel me, don't you? I'm crawling toward your brain. I need you alive, Canaan. I have big plans for you, but your lobotomy will serve my purposes since we don't see eye-to-eye."

Canaan gasped as fear blossomed deep within. He'd been anxious for Marcy when she was endangered by the twins, but for himself? Never. Fear was an emotion he'd hoped he'd never encounter. The white-hot energy that inched its way into his chest muscle, crawling across his frame like an insect underneath the skin, could possibly reach his head before he could stop it. Canaan's eyes found Isaac's, but the boy displayed no sympathy. Isaac sat in Rufus's throne, legs crossed, watching the show.

He gestured with his fingers. "Go on, Elder Canaan. This is as far as I've seen. Now, do your best. In my vision, it really looks like Rufie wins. But hey—" the boy shrugged, "don't let that get you down."

Canaan gasped as the pulsing fire inched to settle momentarily in the indention between his collarbones. Forced to concentrate his will on stopping Rufus's actions, he dropped all offensive moves. The sound of the insane Elder's laughter only served to remind him that he was being overcome and the reality of it boggled his mind. A poorly-timed plethora of memories paraded past Canaan's consciousness, distracting him from the important work of halting Rufus's efforts. As if from far away, he heard Isaac threaten Rufus in a singsong voice.

"Go ahead and finish him off, Rufie. Then you and I can continue our dance."

Canaan closed his eyes and wished for a friend. Faces emerged in rapid succession; his Elder, Jack Dawn—long since dead. His beloved Marcy, who feared he'd not have what it took to defeat their enemy. Then Javier, with his boyish determination and Roman who fiercely protected all those he loved. Michael Stone and his wife, judging Canaan's every word and deed. The Stone's tiny Rabbit daughter, Grace Louise...

"You're going to make everything right again, Mr. Canaan."

Speaking well beyond her capability, the six year old's promise took hold of his consciousness.

"You have been a wasteland..."

Canaan gasped as simultaneously, Rufus's murderous energy crept to his jaw, its imaginary face set toward his frontal lobes.

"But you will be a place worth saving."

The child's soft voice filled his every fiber and he lost feeling in his body as her recalled prophecy was completed in his mind.

"A place worth treasuring forever..."

Who? Who treasures me? I don't understand. Without realizing it, Canaan's heart cried out questions of its own. Then Mrs. Stone's words filtered in to join her daughter's.

"God loves you, Canaan—and it's not His will that you should perish."

Perish? I don't want to die...

Canaan's knees buckled and he no longer saw out his eyes at all. The bright white light that filled his vision soothed and terrified him at the same time. Rufus's lobotomy was about to take place.

Turn to God.

Canaan didn't understand the advice pressed upon him in an unknown voice, but he did the best he could. With his last ounce of consciousness, he cried out silently to the God of the mortals—whoever He was—and asked to be rescued.

In a blink of an eye, with the sound of a dozen cannons, Canaan fell into the light and lost consciousness.

◆◆◆

Dimple emptied the Glock into his former leader and dropped it only when the slide was back and the magazine was empty. Hit multiple times in the upper torso, side and left thigh, Rufus crumpled to the floor without meeting his attacker's eye. Then a curious thing happened. A cherub of a Rakum youth leapt from Rufus's infamous chair and bit the incapacitated Elder hard in the throat. Dimple's eyes grew wide at the spectacle. The Rakum world had officially spun out of control.

Sighing, he plodded over to the Rakum Elder he'd been inexplicably compelled to aid. From the basement, he overheard the hubbub. Strengthened by the apostate's blood, he headed up to check it out. He had no qualms about shooting Rufus in the back; he'd been disgusted with the incorrigible Elder from the beginning. The Rakum he rescued moaned, but would survive.

"Gotta bigger knife than this?" Holding up a three-inch switchblade, the kid turned to Dimple, his chin dripping with Rufus's blood. Dimple dug around in his deep pockets, withdrew his knife and tossed it over.

"Thanks."

"What's your name?" Dimple asked, instinctively aware of the youth's superiority.

"I'm The Last," he mumbled, his back turned, as he busily sawed off the fallen Elder's head. "For now, call me Isaac."

"Hmph." Dimple nodded once and slumped down next to his sleeping brother. Their world was way off kilter, but maybe this kid could set things right. The Last was real, not just an old Father's tale to share around a group-lair campfire. Finally, a messiah the Rakum could hang their hats on.

Dimple rubbed his healed throat, cursed Meryl in his heart for trying to kill him, and waited to see if The Last would ask for his assistance. He was an excellent servant after all.

sixty

When Michael steered the truck onto the interstate, it was as if a weight had lifted off his shoulders. In the backseat, Chloe gave a subdued cheer and collapsed into David's arms. Squeezed between Chloe and Selene in the wide back seat, Damien sat hunched over, his head in his hands. Selene regarded Michael in the rearview mirror and she offered a half-hearted smile. The woman was still traumatized and Michael asked her if she wanted to call Beth for news about Jesse and Dae Lee. Her eyes brightened and he handed over his phone. Beside him in the front seat, Roman shook his head and sighed.

"Is that it? Is Rufus no longer a threat to us? I'm having a hard time celebrating what I'm not sure of."

Michael had been wondering the same thing. Technically, even if Canaan disabled Rufus, didn't they still have enemies out there? Would they leave Michael and his family alone? How about the remaining Rakum? Would they slink away again as they did seven years back, or would they seek a new leader? Would that be Isaac? The boy had the power to do whatever he chose and that worried Michael more than he'd ever admit aloud.

Selene pushed Michael's ringing phone between the two seats. "It's Canaan," she said, obvious fear in her voice.

Michael read the caller ID and answered. "Canaan?"

"Rufus lost his head." It was Isaac on Canaan's cell. "Thought you'd like to know."

Michael swallowed hard. "And Canaan?"

Isaac paused and then laughed. "Oh, he'll be fine. He can't come to the phone, but don't you worry about him."

"Okay," Michael said, awkwardly. "Thanks."

"I have some instructions for you, Michael."

Noticing the kid had dispensed with his formerly respectful tone, Michael played nice and kept his manner civil. "Okay, I'm listening."

"Send Canaan's woman here immediately. He'll need her here to recover fully, and I need him healthy, got it?"

Michael agreed, confident that Marcy Haddle wouldn't have it any other way. "Is that all?"

"As for you and your, well, posse," Isaac chuckled derisively, "I don't have any plans to molest you. If you steer clear of me, I'll steer clear of you. But—are you listening, Michael?"

"Yes," Michael answered quickly, happy to hear he wasn't currently on the miniature tyrant's hit list.

"Do you remember the Rakum code regarding mortals? I don't owe you anything and you owe me nothing. You've been human long enough to forget, but I won't hesitate to destroy you if you get in my way."

"I understand, Isaac," Michael said, acknowledging a tenet he'd personally lived by for ages. Isaac snickered and disconnected the call.

Roman waited for Michael to repeat all he'd heard and both men sighed with relief and vague trepidation. They had no plans to see Isaac or Canaan again, so maybe they could stick to them. Each man would go back to his life and carry on. Jesse and Selene would return to Birmingham, Roman to L.A.,—Michael turned to his passenger.

"Javier. What about him?"

"I'll pick him up in Memphis at the ER. Canaan said he healed his worst injuries..." Roman said softly.

"And you're confident he'll be okay?" Michael asked and Roman nodded.

"I believe with time. It is likely his back is fractured, but he's not paralyzed. His legs are broken, but Canaan did not feel any of it was life-threatening when we released him to the paramedics. At any rate, I will stay with him until he is completely recovered."

Michael nodded, relieved. Selene's hand appeared and he returned the cell phone. When she was finished, he'd speak to Beth. They'd be home in less than five hours and he'd hold on to her and never let go.

"I will accompany you, Roman, to pick up Javier. Agreed?" Damien's voice filtered to the front seat, although his head was still bowed.

"Of course," Roman answered and fell still.

The car was quiet for a good five minutes before a soft, male voice began to sing in the backseat, off-key but with sincerity.

"Amazing grace, how sweet the sound..." David sang while resting into the seat, eyes closed and facing upward. Within two more phrases, Roman joined in to sing the second stanza. By the time they reached the third, Michael threw in his efforts until the car fairly hummed with praises sent up to God, their true Father who rescued them all. *Again.*

295

EPILOGUE

November 6th

Javier exhaled and watched his breath plume upward and dissipate into the cold night. Slipping out of the hospital had been a cinch and he wondered at the ease at which it had been accomplished. Elder Roman had taught him stealth more than a century ago, and as he maneuvered past the nurses and CNAs that populated the halls of the doctor's tower, he wondered how far the kid Isaac's blood had taken him. Was he back? After one mostly-vomited dose?

An ambulance zoomed past his position and came to a screeching halt in the circle a dozen yards away. Hidden in the shadow of the parking garage building, Javier watched the paramedics yank out their gurney and rush the patient into the waiting arms of the medical staff. Was that a whiff of blood or his imagination? As a Rakum, his sense of smell was extraordinary. Could it be returning? Javier squint his eyes to seek out details a mortal wouldn't be able to see. Was he seeing more clearly now? He tried to pick out the stitching in the attending RN's lab coat. For a split second, didn't he see the individual fibers? Javier stared at the same spot on the woman's lapel another few seconds unblinking and finally sighed and leaned into the wall.

What of Elder Canaan? What of Roman? Javier's watch read 3 a.m. and his compatriots would either have succeeded or failed on their mission to defeat Rufus and regain their friends. What now?

At this hour, it was roughly three hours until sunup. Fear clutched Javier's heart. What if he was allergic to the sun like before? Would he burn to death at dawn? Looking both ways, Javier thought fast. A basement would do the trick. Hospitals had boiler rooms deep in their underbellies. Javier spied a staff-only entrance on his side of the garage and he headed toward it. If it was locked, he was sunk. He tried the knob, it turned, no one was around, and Javier slipped inside.

Five yards in, a stairwell led below ground level. Javier smiled and headed into the gloom. At sundown, he'd venture out and take stock of his situation; see what Isaac's blood accomplished. And when that still, small voice questioned his motives, Javier shut it out.

At least for now.

♦♦♦

Michael, Roman, and David would be home any minute and Beth rubbed her eyes until they watered. She'd only slept about two hours and that was fitfully, sitting beside Marcy on the couch awaiting word. When her husband texted her "mission accomplished" and "we're heading back," a huge weight lifted from her shoulders and she trudged to the stairs. As her fingers touched the banister a horrible nausea washed over her. Beth sucked in a lungful of air and glanced around the darkened foyer.

Marcy was fast asleep on the couch in the next room. She could see her feet dangling over the arm rest. The children should be in Grace's room asleep since the night before.

The nausea struck again and Beth doubled over. A horn honked outside, one short burst and fell silent.

It is for me the bell tolls, she thought miserably, certain that something horrible waited outside. Getting to the foyer as quickly as she could, Beth unbolted the locks and violently pulled open the door, not understanding her sudden panic. Then she saw it—a red car driven by a Rakum she recognized, with two children waving at her from the backseat.

Two little girls that should have been in bed.

She never should have let Isaac into the house, for by so doing, she opened the door for them all. Beth headed for the car, apologizing to God, and planning her next move.

Beth gasped and sat up, the nightmare burned into her soul.

Gracie! She leapt off the couch, inadvertently jostling Marcy awake.

"What? What?" the woman began, but Beth was half-way up the stairs.

Please, please, please let them be okay. Please... Beth reached the girl's bedroom, shoved through, and slapped the light-switch.

Grace and Dae Lee slept on, side-by-side in one bed, two dollies, one brown and one white, standing guard by their heads.

"Thank you! Thank you!" Beth whispered, tears of relief and gratitude on her cheeks. Maybe one day Isaac's vision would come to pass, but not tonight.

Marcy reached the room, her face bloated with sleep, but uneasy just the same.

"What?" she whispered.

"Nothing. Let's sleep in here until the boys get home." Beth whispered back and pointed to the second double on the opposite side of the room. Marcy trudged over and fell onto her side, snoring almost immediately. Beth sent out a blessing to the Lord and thanked Him for being in control. For better or for worse.

When Beryl came to, the sun was kissing the horizon, dyeing the wooded landscape a curious yellow hue. The station wagon, along with Ta'avah and Father Theophilus, was nowhere in sight and Beryl sat up, rubbing his head. How long before the sun erupted over the horizon, it's mere fingers already threatening to blind him where he sat? Rufus's house was around the bend, but still a quarter of a mile away. Should he make a run for it? Beryl got to his feet, discovering he was uninjured. What would he find when he got to the estate? He'd be considered a traitor and if Rufus was still alive, he'd never allow him entry.

Without conscious effort, Beryl's feet began to lead him toward the house. He just might make it if he guarded his eyes and ran like hell. His footfalls increased, a fast walk morphed into a slow jog, which transformed into a full-out run for his life as his sense of self-preservation kicked into overdrive. The gate was open and hanging on one hinge. Beryl sprinted by without giving it a thought.

Half-way across the brown lawn, the sun broke free of the horizon, and a million rays of UV instantaneously stole Beryl's sight. Undaunted, he hurled himself forward by memory, his hand reaching out for the door he'd opened a hundred times in the past. Within moments, he slammed into it full force and his shaking fingers found the brass door handle. Shouting now for help but not hearing his voice, Beryl depressed the latch and shoved the door.

It was locked, and in his weakened state, he made no attempt to open it telekinetically. After a few frantic attempts to crash through the sealed portal, he cried out and sank to the ground. His hand pressed firmly against both eyes, Beryl sat on his knees and faced the door, waiting for the first rays of the hated sun to lash his back like a whip. He'd felt it once before as a child. All Rakum endured the sun at First Ritual. He hated it then and it would be so much worse now. Beryl clenched his jaw and waited while white light crept upon him from the east.

Leave them to their gods, the woman had said.

In his last moments of consciousness, Beryl pondered the phrase again, and wondered if Beth Rider was right. If there was redemption for his kind, and what would happen if he called for help? The God of the mortals, was He real? Beryl couldn't remember His name but he called out, just the same.

What could it hurt?

END BOOK TWO

The Rabbit Trilogy concludes with:

Rabbit Redemption
Released 1/15/18

Rabbit Redemption

SNEAK PEEK

Rabbit Redemption picks up directly after *Rabbit Legacy* ends.

November 7th, 6:30 am (Rufus's Estate, Now Isaac's, Jackson, MS)

Something was not quite right and Canaan blinked his eyes several times to clear his vision. Below him, lying on the carpeted floor, undergoing a violent rejuvenation treatment administered by The Last, Isaac Akaron, was *his* body, pale, limp, and apparently deceased. Yet, Canaan wasn't dead. On the contrary, he watched the scene as if suspended from the ceiling. The last thing he recalled was Elder Rufus invisibly lasering his spine with skill Canaan never expected. If he'd only been more cautious. Yet who would have ever imagined an Elder insane with the Dying Buzz could remain potent enough to incapacitate an Elder as powerful as Canaan?

Standing in a semi-circle around his still form, he recognized his brethren watching the show with keen interest. Dimple, a sturdy Rakum grunt from New Orleans; Boris, six-foot-six and black as night, hailed from Rufus's pack before the Elder went bananas; and Hoss, a muscular grunt known for being slow-witted and obedient. From his insane ethereal position, Canaan counted one more, just outside their group, sitting against the wall and leaning over his knees. No matter how familiar, without his flesh, Canaan had no extrasensory abilities to discern this one's identity.

"YAH-HAH!" Isaac yelped with apparent joy below him, both palms against Canaan's head. "RETURN!" he bellowed and flashed his face toward the ceiling where Canaan hovered. Canaan blinked with surprise and when he reopened his eyes, he was looking into Isaac's face from the floor.

"I am amazing!" the boy said and removed his hands. He rolled onto his rear, crossed his legs Indian-style, and put one hand to Canaan's blond curls. "Hey, there, buddy," the kid said, a victorious smile in place.

"Hey," Canaan said and nodded, trying to appear as unaffected as possible. He was the only Elder present and as such, must maintain superiority—at least among the grunts; Isaac's top-level position remained a brand new revelation.

"How do you feel? Rufus cooked you a little," Isaac said, still awaiting a report. He swirled his fingers a few more times in the wisps of hair on Canaan's forehead and then smoothed his long sideburns with one forefinger.

Canaan did not reject The Last's affections, the previous hours clear in his mind. This blond and perfect, seemingly thirteen-year-old boy was High Father Abroghia's last laugh, the most powerful Rakum ever born. Now, the kid would be in charge of their race, what was left of them. Canaan kept his thoughts positive—the kid was more telepathic than them all.

"I don't mind if you ponder my amazingness, Elder Canaan," Isaac said then, his voice soft.

"Thank you for bringing me back."

"Of course I'd bring you back, silly," Isaac said and hopped to his feet with athletic agility. "I'm not sure it's completely *fair...*" he stressed and turned toward the thick red-headed Rakum nearest him. "Dimple shot Rufus just when it was getting really interesting."

"Shot him?" Canaan said, not really asking. He had heard several explosions before he lost consciousness and now had his explanation.

"Don't get me wrong, Canaan. I want you with me. I *need* you, actually, but..." the kid shrugged, "a gun?" He looked at Dimple again and the guy winced as if he'd been struck. Isaac returned his attention to Canaan, still lying flat on the carpet. "Um, buddy...naptime's over."

"Of course," Canaan agreed and commanded his body to stand. His limbs responded sluggishly, but all-in-all, he probably looked pretty sturdy to those watching on. He had no pain, and only a vague tickle remained along his spine from Elder Rufus's attack to his nervous system. The Last truly was amazing.

An unexpected thought popped into Canaan's mind and he knew Isaac would read it and respond: *Did Roman and the rest get away safely?*

"I let them go, they're gone," Isaac said, ending the discussion. "But that's not all..." Isaac grasped Canaan's hand. "I healed Beryl, too. He had burnt to a crisp running to the house at dawn." Isaac laughed out loud and shook his head.

Canaan was familiar with the twins, Beryl and Meryl, in many ways. Most recently when they served Rufus. A mere week ago, Meryl and Beryl were dispatched by the insane Elder to kidnap Canaan's lover, Marcy, to lure him to Jackson. Meryl had actually buzzed off her before Canaan could intervene. This breach cost the youngster dearly—Canaan broke his neck and left him to die. In addition,

Canaan shot Beryl in the gut before the guy healed from the slug Marcy put in him minutes earlier. So... they had survived. Deep down in a place he wouldn't peek into, Canaan was glad they had.

Isaac caught Canaan's eye and winked. "You can be dangerous, can't you," he giggled, not truly asking a question. "Don't worry, Canaan, Beryl's all fixed up," Isaac said, still giggling at the man's misfortune. "It *was* hilarious, though. He was oozing puss. Completely black and red when *Officer Dimple* yanked him inside." Isaac tugged Canaan to where the Rakum sat with his head over his knees.

Canaan had seen Rakum burnt by the sun, and if they were allowed to crisp up even a few minutes, they would expire. Yet, Beryl had no apparent burns. Canaan looked at The Last in wonder; healing consumed tremendous energy and Isaac had healed two Rakum in one night. Isaac squeezed his hand.

"All of you..." He took a moment to catch the eye of every Rakum standing. "You guys are going to help me set things right."

"*Ta'Avah...*" Beryl whispered from their feet.

"*Pfffft,*" Isaac responded, spitting. He caught Canaan's eye. "Just so you know, while you were passed out..."

His eyes actually shined with humor then, reminding Canaan of their new leader's ruthless nature. Sure, he was the youngest of them all, but there would be no limit to his power or his ambitions.

Reading his run-on thoughts, Isaac smiled as he completed his statement. "...our maker stole Father Theophilus from the basement."

Canaan had questions, but Isaac beat him to it.

"From now on, we will know him as Ta'avah, but he embodied High Father Abroghia in a previous incarnation. All of you," Isaac said to each, "must understand our maker is a spirit, and for the moment, he inhabits this Rakum's dead twin." The kid gestured to the kneeling man.

Canaan sighed; he had his answer regarding Meryl's condition. It was a damn shame. Before he attacked Marcy, Meryl had been his favorite between the two brothers, their personalities more alike. Beryl had always seemed *less than*, and Canaan hadn't been the only Elder that thought so. Without his twin to balance his periodic fragility, Beryl's un-Rakum-like tendencies would only increase.

"Yes, he's a moron, Elder Canaan, we all agree." Isaac interrupted his thoughts. "You're the only one not paying attention. Focus on me. Got it?" Canaan nodded. "I will get Father Theophilus back and he will serve me," Isaac continued easily, "and I will vanquish Ta'avah. It is my birthright to rule our people."

"I'm with you, Boss, one hundred percent," the lumbering black Rakum to Isaac's left said in a low baritone.

"I know you are, Boris," Isaac said touching his arm. "The rest of you—are you with me? Will you stand with me as your Father, against anyone—man or Rakum—who dares challenge me?"

"I will," Hoss said without hesitation, and then Dimple agreed in a low voice. Canaan nodded, which Isaac acknowledged with a wink.

The Rakum on the floor still hadn't moved or looked up. Canaan leaned forward to help him rise, but Isaac booted Beryl with his tennis shoe.

"Beryl, are you with me?" Isaac said and waited. A low "yes" was his response. Isaac paused another second and kicked Beryl in the shoulder harder than before. "We're fresh out of pacifiers, Beryl," Isaac said. "This is no house for babies. Is that what you are?" Isaac looked to Boris and stroked Beryl's soft, brown hair. "You can eat this if it's a baby, Boris. You're my favorite."

"No, Master, I am a Rakum," Beryl said and rolled to his knees, then to his feet. "I will serve you."

The Rakum's gaze remained downcast, but Canaan's eyes grew at the sight. In the history of their race, never had there been born more perfect and beautiful Rakum than the identical twins, Meryl and Beryl. Since their youths, both found it to be child's play to manipulate anyone—man or Rakum—with their looks and charm. Canaan now understood Beryl's depressed demeanor. Isaac had only healed half of the Rakum's face. The other half puckered with red, yellow, and black oozing flesh, trying to heal and being prevented by a consistent and opposing force.

Isaac laughed then and turned away from the circle. *"I do what I want,"* he sent telepathically to Canaan alone. *"Now, come feed me,"* he said silently and crawled into what used to be Rufus's throne. "Come now," he said aloud, although all present understood whom the kid wanted. Canaan crossed the room and rolled up his sleeve.

Please visit our web site at www.ellencmaze and join our Facebook fan group at www.facebook.com, search
Curiously Spiritual Vampire Tales, Ellen C. Maze
Ellen loves to connect with her readers. Please contact her anytime at ellenmaze@aol.com.

Rabbit Redemption Book Three of the Rabbit Trilogy

Whittled down to a few thousand, the decimated Rakum race has been scattered to the wind. Childlike Father Isaac Akaron has the power to return his brethren to their former glory; when the secret that slumbers in his spirit awakens, no flesh on Earth can match him. Ruthless, ambitious, and hungry, young Isaac plans to acquire the blood of the surviving Elders, but he must find them first. Serving under duress, Canaan seeks assistance from a former brother struggling with a bizarre and bloodthirsty secret of his own. **Their ensuing conflict will span dimensions as the fates of thousands hang in the balance.**

Read the Book that Started it All...

**The Judging
The Corescu Chronicles Book One**
Hungary, 1640. With the sharp stab of the demon's fangs, village priest Markus Corescu finds his world turned upside-down, coming to the realization that he has been transformed into an abomination—a vampire. Immediately, the newly-undead clergyman assigns a divine calling to his bloodthirsty nature and satisfies his despicable hunger on the humans around him without remorse. Fast forward to the present, and the priest has suppressed and forgotten his past. With the aid of two mortals, and despite the violent protests of his immortal contemporaries, the old vampire is finally able to see the Truth. As he wrestles with his very soul, he discovers that the thousands of people he has judged were not killed within the will of God, but rather they were exsanguinated to satisfy his lust for blood. Now he must make amends with God, but even if his eyes are opened, his ways are not easily changed.

For more information on other works by
Ellen C. Maze
visit **www.ellencmaze.com**

Little Roni Publishers
Byhalia, MS
www.littleronipublishers.com